A Cause to Kill For

A Cause to Kill For

A Novel

ERIC JACKSON

To order additional copies of this book, contact:
Xlibris Corporation
1-888-795-4274
www.Xlibris.com
Orders@Xlibris.com
25473

Dedication

To my dear family and to my partner for their unconditional love, and to all of my friends for their loving presence in my life.

Acknowledgements

I want to express my deepest and sincere thanks to a number of people and friends who gave me encouragement, support and heartfelt advice in the process of writing and publishing this book: Rachel Koch, Danny Frey, Meera Popkin, Marilyn Rickman, Kurt Sass, Edwin Mirabál, Manuel Peña, Nathaniel Hutner, Stacey Patton, Carol Ayala, Angela Cerio, Marty Cohen, Kevin Maxwell, Liz Castro, Peter Jampel, Susan Friedlander, Hector Rosales, Paul Clahar, Ira Kaminsky, José Cardona, José de Jesús, Dr. Mary Rivera, Dr. Christian Huygen and Dr. René Vázquez. Also, my thanks to Jennie, Felicia, Jackie and Lorraine for their love and friendship. Special thanks to Glen Venezio for his ever-present and unconditional loving support, his computer-savvy skills and his valuable efforts in doing research and finding resources. A special mention to author Susan M. Watkins for her sound "*long distance*" advice on the in-and-outs of the publishing industry, and to artist José Carlos Burgos and his crew, Jackeline Silva Ruiz and Rafael Sotomayor, for his very original artwork for the book cover. And I would like to sincerely thank my friend and business associate Germán González, Esq. for his enthusiasm and his belief in this project from the very first moment when I presented it to him. I am grateful to him for his astute editorial suggestions to make the novel's story more powerful and timely. Germán González has served as lawyer, literary agent, business adviser, editorial consultant, media coordinator, hands-on troubleshooter and many more tasks and efforts that made the publication of this book a reality. To all of you, thank you.

A Note From The Author

When I was a teenager growing up in Puerto Rico, one of my main hobbies – besides writing and making little movies with a super-8 camera – was a "Film Encyclopedia" that I put together myself. I was the ultimate Hollywood movie fan.

I would endlessly scan through newspapers and film and celebrity magazines, looking for photos, promotional materials, excerpts, reviews, etc. on Hollywood movies and Hollywood stars. I would then cut and glue hundreds and hundreds of clippings into the largest school composition notebooks available, until the pages couldn't hold one more single piece of information. I think I gathered twenty-two of these notebooks, or Volumes, as I called them.

As an addition to my Hollywood film clippings collection, I would buy movie soundtracks, and I would get, as much as I could, movie posters and movie still-shots. I was lucky that, at that time, the 1970's, my father worked as a technician for Smith Corona Marchant and several of the offices he serviced were movie distributor's houses. When my father went into these movie houses to fix the secretaries' typewriters, they all knew that he had a son who collected anything that had to do with movies, and movie posters were much-coveted items. After the typewriters were fixed and ready to continue their clerical mission, my father always came home with the goods.

The other part of my movie collection consisted of books. Books of Hollywood movies. These I would buy and daringly attempted to read – with the help of a pocket dictionary – because they were all written in English, which is a foreign language to any kid born and raised on the Spanish-speaking island of Puerto Rico.

When I reached my twenties, my teenage movie collection stayed behind as I moved on to college and to other projects, interests and adventures. Though I graduated college with degrees in advertising and telecommunications, I also took many courses in social sciences, and at one point, I was even majoring in political science. For many years, my reading interests were biographies, and books on history, philosophy, economics and political science.

One day in the late 1990's I happened to accidentally come across a copy of the book *The Pelican Brief* by John Grisham. I curiously glanced at it and began to read it. I cannot describe the powerful way in which that book rocked and shook my emotions and grabbed my immediate interest and attention. I was totally awed and absolutely captivated by the page-turning, non-stop, edge-of-your-seat suspense in that book's story. After finishing *The Pelican Brief* I bought and read each and every one of John Grisham's novels. And by word of mouth, I then discovered Dean Koontz, Mary Higgins Clark, James Paterson, John Sanford and many other suspense-mystery-thriller authors.

Overnight, I became a fan and an avid reader of these unbelievably talented authors. I read so many of their books that, at one time, I had to prepare a list of the titles I'd read to keep track of which ones to read next.

It was in the midst of this reading frenzy that one day I realized that I was doing a lot of reading, but wasn't myself creating anything. I told myself, why don't you try to write something like *that* since I was so enthralled by the genre.

Puerto Rico immediately came to my mind as the place to set the plot. And so I began to write the story that later became *A Cause to Kill For*.

By no means do I compare myself to these super-authors that I became so enthused about. But their different styles and story-lines became a reference point for me to create a thriller set in Puerto Rico with a Puerto Rican theme.

I hope you enjoy this book, which was written with the purpose to entertain the reader and of course, to feature Puerto Rico as a place where *thrills do happen.*

Eric Jackson
Summer 2004

(You can email Eric Jackson at: EricPuertoRico@yahoo.com)

Washington, D.C.
2:30 a.m.

Prologue

Donald M. Clarke, the current U.S. President, had been having nightmares. And he wasn't sharing them with anyone. He was lying on his bed in his bedroom at the White House's private residence. His wife lay by his side, soundly asleep. The room was dark but for the dim moonlight that penetrated a window. The rash of bad sleep started when a friend of his at the Washington Post tipped him off that there was a telephone recording of him calling his son-in-law a "spic," a "welfare-loving whore" and several other more serious epithets disparaging to Latinos.

The President didn't recall making any such remarks. But he couldn't be completely sure that he hadn't. After all, his only daughter had married a Puerto Rican lawyer whose family over there was a potpourri of political contradictions. Some pro-statehood relatives, some commonwealth supporters, some purely and totally apolitical, and some . . . Well. Some were a bunch of very colorful Puerto Rican nationalists who had a history of violence against Americans and American military interests there.

He had privately advised his daughter not to marry the man. She married him anyway. "He was my best friend at Harvard, Daddy," she had said. "It will get you votes from the Latinos."

Okay.

Aníbal Arellanos, Esq., then officially became a member of the American First Family. The day of the wedding, when the President gave his daughter away to the happy groom, the man came close to the

President's ear and whispered, "Are you going to make us the fifty-first state soon?"

The President smiled and without missing a beat told him, "Son, there isn't a political climate to do that."

"Then create it," Arellanos said quickly. "Twist some arms."

President Clarke pulled back and walked away

Almost 3 o'clock in the morning. Can't sleep. Dammit! Can't remember shit. The only time I fought with my son-in-law, the President thought to himself, was when he wasn't yet my son-in-law. And yes, it was over the phone. Three days before the wedding he told me about his nationalist relatives. "Yeah, it's true," he had said proudly. A cousin of a cousin – or something like that – was the grandson of one of the four Puerto Rican nationalists that did that shoot-'em-up in Congress back in the fifties.

President Clarke was raging mad. "You are going to cost me the vote of every single America-loving Latino!" he had shouted. The Cubans will want Florida to secede. The Dominicans will say that they've never shot anybody in Congress so I should stop bedding the Puerto Ricans. The Mexicans will say the same and demand open borders in the south. And the Puerto Ricans? They will demand I take sides in their messy politics.

Did I call him a "spic" then? Clarke asked himself. "A welfare-loving whore?" Maybe even worse things than that?

The President couldn't remember.

What the hell. Nixon said worse things about even more influential people in this country. But then, the voters only found out when tricky Dick was six feet under.

Jesus! The Latinos will fry me like an egg over this thing.

If President Clarke could have seen his face in a mirror at this instant, lying on his bed, his eyes so wide open, it would have scared him. And there was so much sweat on his face and all over his silk pajamas that he looked like a patient waiting for care at an E.R.

When the phone by his bedside began to ring, he graciously welcomed the distraction. An important matter of state would divert his thoughts from his dread of losing reelection over a "Latino thing."

"Hello," he said firmly.

"Mr. President, sorry to disturb you," the man said. "There is a matter that needs your attention."

The man on the other end was Nathaniel Fisher, the President's National Security Advisor.

"What's the matter?" the president asked sitting up straight on the edge of his bed.

"It concerns Puerto Rico."

President Clarke froze. *This is it. There is indeed a tape of me saying those terrible things about my daughter's husband. The closest Puerto Rican to the American President.*

"What is it?" the president asked, expecting the worse.

"Secretary Donahue has just sent me a copy of a classified report from the P.N.S.B."

Lane Donahue was the Secretary of Defense. P.N.S.B. was the Pentagon's National Security Branch. *Perhaps this didn't have anything to do with "spics" and "welfare-loving whores,"* the President quickly calculated.

"What's in it?" the president asked promptly.

"Sir, it confirms that there is indeed a vast reservoir of crude oil off the southern coast of Puerto Rico. Enough to kiss the Arabs and Venezuelans goodbye for the next 87 years."

The President was already on his feet.

"Meet me at the studio in thirty minutes," he said and hung up.

The impact of such news was entertaining to consider. He immediately decided that the knowledge of this had to be kept away from the Puerto Ricans. And especially from the Puerto Rican members of Congress. They were all a bunch of trouble makers. They had incited riots over the Navy's use of the island of Vieques for military practices. "And we were forced to get out of Vieques!" the President shouted to himself, falling back on the bed. *Vieques,* he told himself, *had always been a struggle of the Puerto Rican independentistas (the nationalists). All right. We lost that one. But this one? Oh no, we are going to win this one. And we are going to win big time.*

A pat on his back. The First Lady was now awake.

"Honey, what is it?" she said tiredly. "Gosh, you are sweating."

He kissed her gently on her lips.

"I have to take care of something," the President said softly. "Go back to bed. I won't be long."

President Donald M. Clarke, the most powerful man in the world, walked out of his bedroom thinking that it was about time the United States granted statehood to Puerto Rico. It was time to do justice to the 3.9 million American citizens of that U.S. island. And it was time to show to the 40 million Latinos in the U.S. – the largest minority in the country – that the United States had always been their home. And that he, Donald Matthew Clarke, was their President.

*   *   *

Nathaniel Fisher, Clarke's National Security Advisor, was quick to brief the President on the advanced remote-sensing satellite technology that made it possible to discover oil reservoirs in unexplored territories. The President was fully acquainted with the protocol and was anxious to discuss the political implications. He said, "If the Puerto Ricans find out about this, we can anticipate that support for independence will grow to dangerous levels. They'll think they can survive without us! We can't allow that to happen. That's our oil down there!"

"I fully agree, sir."

"Nobody down there will know about this. Understood?"

"Yes, sir."

"Is Cruz still the governor over there?"

Fisher was amused by the Commander-in-Chief's absence of mind. Elison Cruz, the current governor of Puerto Rico, and a solid supporter of statehood, had gone out of his way to help Clarke become the U.S. president. When Cruz was in the midst of his own election campaign in Puerto Rico, he went to Florida, New York, Connecticut, Illinois, Texas and California to deliver a set of ferocious Spanish-language speeches in favor of Clarke's election. Clarke needed the Latino vote and Cruz was part of Clarke's contingent of Latino leaders to deliver it. And there was also the money issue. Cruz's Statehood Party in Puerto Rico contributed millions of dollars to Clarke's election funds. Presidential candidate Clarke had reportedly said that he favored statehood for

Puerto Rico. The pro-statehood Puerto Ricans put up a serious fight for Clarke's election on the idea that – if elected – President Clarke was to be their most influential friend in Washington.

Nathaniel Fisher, however, knew that once elected, the president had distanced himself from Puerto Rican politics altogether. It seemed as if a "Don't ask, Don't tell" policy had been set in place as far as Puerto Rico was concerned. "Mr. President," Fisher said, "Elison Cruz is already three years into his first term. Puerto Rico holds gubernatorial elections on the same date we hold presidential elections here."

"Of course," Clarke said quickly.

"He was elected the same day you were elected, and he is up for reelection next year, sir."

"Good," Clarke said firmly. "Cruz is our man down there. A proud U.S. citizen. A passionate supporter of statehood. That's exactly what we need. We must make sure he gets reelected."

"I suggest you go down to Puerto Rico and give a push to his campaign."

"I had already thought about that," the President said. "No other sitting President has ever done that for one of our friends down there. This is a matter of justice! I always thought Puerto Rico should join the Union."

Fisher wasn't totally sure about that, but said nothing. He said, "What do you plan to do with Congress about this?"

"I will personally talk to every friend I have. I will be emphatic, forceful and definite. I want Puerto Rico to be our fifty-first state. We'll do our part, but we'll still need a vote on it down there. So, Congress passes a law and I sign it. The 'Puerto Rico Self-Determination Act,' or something like that. We'll give them a plebiscite that will be binding, final. They will have to choose: statehood or independence. And I know they love us over there. Faced with that choice they will side with us. So, statehood wins and statehood we grant."

"It may not be that simple, sir," Fisher said softly.

"No? Why not?"

"Well, the Puerto Rican Commonwealth Party has many friends here in Washington. Especially the corporations that get those huge tax breaks under the commonwealth. They will fight tooth and nail to make sure the commonwealth, or some version of it, be included in any political status plebiscite."

President Clarke gave thought to this.

Fisher said, "The best we can do, I think, is to exclude the commonwealth option from any plebiscite we hold there, and give the voters a very . . . How can I say it? . . . A very 'inedible' version of free association. That should scare many voters into voting for statehood."

"Huh," Clarke said. "How much support for statehood do we have down there on that island?"

Fisher flipped through some of his papers until finding the numbers he needed. "Okay," he said, "there's been three local plebiscites held on the island. The first one was on July 23, 1967. Statehood got 38.9% of the vote versus 60.5% for Commonwealth and 0.5% for independence. The second plebiscite was on November 14, 1993. Statehood got 46.4% of the vote versus 48.6% for Commonwealth and 4.5% for independence. And the last one they held was on December 13, 1998. That plebiscite was a little messy. The Commonwealth Party over there was not pleased with the definition of commonwealth on the ballot so they managed to include a 'None of the Above' column on the ballot and instructed their voters to choose that option. Half of the *independentistas* jumped on that wagon and also voted for 'None of the . . .'"

"What was the final vote?" Clarke asked impatiently.

"Well, statehood got 46.5% of the vote versus 0.01% for commonwealth and 2.5% for independence . . . 'None of the Above' got 50.2% of the total vote."

"Jesus!" the president said. "How much more difficult can those Puerto Ricans be?"

"There seems to be an almost even impasse between support for statehood and support for the status quo. You want to sell statehood to the Puerto Ricans, you will need to make some concessions."

"Like what? What do they want?"

"Governor Cruz wants to keep Spanish as the official language of Puerto Rico," Fisher said softly.

"Big deal! Let them speak whatever they want!" the President said strongly. "Think about all the doors that that opens with the Latinos over here. It will be obscene to vote against me."

"Cruz also wants a ten year moratorium on the implementation of Federal taxes."

"He said that?" the President asked, wide-eyed and incredulously.

"Yes, sir."

Clarke pondered this for a moment. That one hurt.

"Listen," Clarke said, "I may let them get away with that. Let's not lose our focus here. We cannot lose Puerto Rico."

"I fully understand and agree with you, Mr. President."

"What else?"

"They want to keep their Olympic team separate from the U.S. Olympic team."

Clarke sighed, brushing his hand through his thick white hair.

"I'll let Congress deal with that," he said softly and avoiding eye contact with Fisher. "And anyway, the International Olympic Committee has their statutes over that . . . What else?"

"They want to keep their contestant to the Miss Universe pageant . . . and . . ."

"Miss Universe?" the president exclaimed, confused. "What the hell are you talking about?"

"You see, they don't want their '*Miss Puerto Rico*' to have to compete to become 'Miss U.S.A.' in order to participate in the Miss Universe pageant. They want their own contestant – a '*Miss Puerto Rico*' – to compete in the international competition. It's a matter of . . ."

"Stop it!" Clarke ordered. "God damn it! I can't hear all this nonsense about beauty queens and beauty pageants when I'm trying to make history for our nation. We don't fucking control no damn beauty pageant. Donald Trump owns that damn thing! That's his business. Not ours!"

With a smirk on his face Fisher said, "That's true, Mr. President. It's just that some people down there have raised this '*issue*.' As frivolous as it sounds this Miss Universe thing is . . ."

"Fuck that! Enough!" Clarke said furiously. He pointed his finger to one of two telephones available in his studio and said, "Listen, you get on that phone now and call Thompson and Keppler. You tell them I want to see them here. Right now!"

Grant Thompson was the U.S. Senate Majority Leader. Martin Keppler was the Speaker of the U.S. House of Representatives. Both were members of the President's political party, which currently controlled both houses of Congress, and both owed their stature, reputations and political power to President Donald M. Clarke.

Nathaniel Fisher nodded firmly and went to the phone. President Clarke reached for the other telephone and made a few phone calls on his own. When he finished, the President went to his room, took off his robe and pajamas and dressed in khakis, a long-sleeve white shirt and a navy blue jacket. The First Lady did not wake up. And Clarke thought that that was good. His thoughts were racing. There was no time for small talk. On his way to the Oval Office, Donald M. Clarke thought that perhaps he would, after all, be remembered as one of the United States' "greatest" presidents.

An hour later, when Thompson and Keppler arrived to meet with the President in the Oval Office, they found themselves in the company of Greg Harris, head of the C.I.A., Peter Briggs, Director of the F.B.I., Lane Donahue, Secretary of Defense, Nathaniel Fisher, National Security Advisor, Steven Blumenthal, Secretary of State, Jonathan Hawthorne, U.S. Vice-President, and General Kenneth Charles Kendall, Chairman of the Joint Chiefs of Staff.

Each man was greeted with a single sheet of paper:

P.N.S.B.

TOP SECRET – CONFIDENTIAL – FOR PRESIDENT AND HEAD SECURITY AND NATIONAL ADVISORS

(Strictly Need to Know Basis)

ARVIIS III. Overflight 76,000 feet over Central and South Puerto Rico. December 10, 2007. 6:00AM – 2:47PM Clear sky. Low cumulus nimbus clouds. Very High Definition (8,000 x 17,000 pixels) Spectrometry working 98% efficiency. Ground penetration level extremely high. Coastal zone penetration utmost capability. Remote sensing equipment working at full potential. Colors definition being very high and covering complete spectrum – **presence of considerable petroleum deposits discovered running from southern slope of** rainforest (El Yunque) to southern coast platform 7.9 miles insea. (Guayama, Coamo and Ponce Municipalities very rich in deposit). Petroleum upswell being caused by slight movement of Caribbean Sea tectonic plate. Preliminary projections place deposits to be able to cover Nation's needs for next 87.5 years assuming a .8 increase in mainland's consumption over next 50 years and continued availability of OPEC oil. Probability of some amount of natural gas still pending verification.

CONTROL OF THIS DEPOSIT IS URGENT FOR REASONS OF NATIONAL SECURITY

TOP SECRET   TOP SECRET   TOP SECRET

*   *   *

When the sun rose over Washington, D.C., the men were still debating Puerto Rico. At the end of the discussion, President Clarke had secured a pledge that Congress would have the votes to pass the *Puerto Rico Self-Determination Act* to mandate a plebiscite on the political status of the U.S. territory. With the President's party controlling an unprecedented 68% of the Senate and 80% of the House, both congressional leaders present at the meeting assured the Commander-in-Chief that they would deliver the needed votes to pass the legislation.

Though no one made mention of it, it seemed as if over the course of a cold Washington night, Puerto Rico, that small U.S. territory in the Caribbean had suddenly become a major player in American politics. Each man present in this hastily-called meeting knew that, after all, that was what the Puerto Ricans always wanted.

THREE YEARS LATER

Thursday, October 25

Chapter 1

"**O**n November third, cast your vote to make Puerto Rico the fifty-first state of the United States. I challenge you to be a part of history."

He had repeated that line probably two dozen times this morning.

Puerto Rico.

U.S.A.

The marriage of convenience was finally getting to the altar.

Governor Elison Cruz was delivering his speech from the podium on the stage of the main ballroom of the San Juan Hotel & Casino in Isla Verde, a northern coastal city east of San Juan, Puerto Rico. The sniper was waiting for him in a cramped utility room on the fifth floor of the Los Alamos Condominium across the street from the hotel. Through a small window, the killer was scanning the hotel's front entrance, squinting into the telescopic lens of his Dragunov SVD semiautomatic rifle – a high-powered soviet-made weapon with a range of 1,300 meters – acquired through a foreign contact. With thick drops of sweat dripping down over his eyes, his only distractions were the loud chants and shouts of a mob of protesters gathered in the street below, carrying signs and banners to protest the governor's speech. The killer had identified a favorite sign. Held by a woman, it had a red swastika at the top, a bad picture of the governor with a Hitler mustache and the words: CRUZ FASCIST! TRAITOR TO THE NATION! Police barricades kept the protesters pacing in a circle at one end of the street.

After his speech, Elison Cruz would exit through the front entrance of the hotel at close to ten in the morning. From here he was to travel to the Citicorp building in the Hato Rey business district for a meeting at 10:45 with the I.P.R.G. – Invest Puerto Rico Group – to head a panel on foreign investment in Puerto Rico. That was the information the sniper had been given. There would be no changes to the governor's schedule this morning. And despite the protesters outside, the First Executive of Puerto Rico would not exit through a side door. Elison Cruz took pleasure in confronting his opponents face to face, especially if the cameras were rolling.

The killer was up to the challenge. "Cruz's head will explode so badly," he had said, "that the Zapruder film will look like bad science fiction."

Clever.

"Make it happen," had said Rigonaldo Pastrana, the leader of September Twenty-third, the *"patriots"* separatist group to which Oso belonged.

Oso meant "bear". He had chosen the nickname himself for no other reason than the notion of brutal strength. It fit him well. In his mid forties, he was over six feet tall, with strong, muscular arms and legs, a huge, hairy chest, long, messy black hair tied in a pony tail and a thick, unkempt beard. And he was as good with guns as an attacking bear was with its paws and claws. When the idea to kill Governor Cruz in a sniper attack was discussed, Oso was the only choice to do it. This was the morning when it would happen.

"The plan we have crafted is strong in benefits for the people of Puerto Rico," the governor was saying, his deep, penetrating eyes scanning the one thousand-strong, friendly audience of supporters. Each had paid $500-a-plate for the fundraising breakfast; an event organized by Marta and Ricardo Borja, two of the most loyal and biggest contributors to the Statehood Party of Puerto Rico. The Borjas were listening attentively while seated on the stage with other VIPs a few feet behind the governor and on either side of Ana María Cruz, the governor's wife and the popular First Lady of Puerto Rico.

Ana María Cruz.

"Our best First Lady, ever!" the press had declared. She was a strong, charismatic woman who was seriously engaged in the cause of stopping the spread of AIDS on the island – especially within the gay community, a first for a First Lady – and she was equally committed to the prevention of teenage pregnancy, and the promotion of compassionate treatment for the mentally ill.

"We are also witnessing history in the making," Governor Cruz continued, speaking closely into the microphone, sending his sharp, passionate voice echoing through the spacious room. At forty-four, he was one of the youngest governors to have led the country. It wasn't lost on him that many of the votes that had elected and reelected him, came from women – and many men – who considered him a very handsome man with a very handsome woman for a wife. The tabloids had declared him to be "*our hunk in office!*" And his marriage had been described as refreshing and dynamic. "*A role model for the country!*" To the humble populace, they were a perfect and successful Puerto Rican couple. To his enemies, Cruz and his First Lady were nothing but a "*scandalous monument to yuppieism.*" The perfect Puerto Rican "*blanquitos,*" (upper-class, white snobs).

Governor Elison Cruz, nonetheless, was not a man who paid much attention to petty criticism about himself, or about his wife; especially if the offending lines came from his sworn enemies. As he spoke to his audience, Cruz occasionally would turn his head to exchange nods and looks with his wife. "*We are a team,*" was the implicit message.

"This will be the first time in decades that the President of the United States and the Congress of the United States of America will act on the will of the Puerto Rican people," Cruz said, stressing each word for dramatic emphasis and to allow for the notion of history-making to sink into his captive audience. "I am certain that the unequivocal message Puerto Rico will send is a mandate to become the fifty-first state of the great United States of America. That is the message we will send." He raised his voice. "And the President will listen! And the Congress will act! Together we will fulfill our destiny as a people!" he declared with certainty.

The audience stood in a roar of applause. Cruz seized the moment by raising both arms and saluting the crowd with the victory sign.

Instinctively, the First Lady, the Borjas and the rest of the VIPs on the stage also stood, applauding furiously. The chants of the people began, first with a few voices, then as an addictive chorus that enveloped the whole room. "CRUZ, AMIGO, EL PUEBLO ESTA CONTIGO! CRUZ, AMIGO, EL PUEBLO ESTA CONTIGO!" (Cruz, my friend, the people are with you!). This lasted for three whole exciting minutes. They would know because Alan de Jesús, Cruz's young press secretary, was standing backstage and he was an expert at keeping track of those details.

"I can feel your excitement," Cruz said, as the crowd seated and came back to attention. "I am with you, and will be with you until the end of our road. I will be with you on the way to our destiny as a people. God has blessed you with the wisdom to make the right choices."

The audience was now in total silence. Any mention of God was one of the buttons that brought Puerto Ricans to deep thought and attention. Cruz knew it. He had learned it in his six years as governor of Puerto Rico. "Statehood is our best choice . . . it is our best option. It is our passport to continued political stability and assured economic growth. Statehood is an option for the future. It is the only way in which we can have the guarantees and the benefits of United States citizenship for the rest of our lives." He paused. "U.S. citizenship will be lost with independence. And we know that free association cannot guarantee a continuation of U.S. citizenship, as the Commonwealth Party would have you believe. The truth about Puerto Ricans and U.S. citizenship is clear. Only statehood can guarantee it. If you value your U.S. citizenship you must vote for statehood on November third." Cruz said this solemnly. He knew the networks would broadcast the highlights of his speech. And he knew his larger audience.

The issue of U.S. citizenship had been the "kiss of death" for the Commonwealth Party. When the President and the U.S. Congress rejected the continuation of the commonwealth as an option of political status for the island, the Party was left with the option of supporting free association, a political arrangement where the island would have separate sovereignty and separate citizenship under a special pact of association with the United States. The U.S. would grant special residency rights to Puerto Ricans, but U.S. citizenship would not be granted to those Puerto Ricans born after the free association pact went into effect.

This sole issue had caused an avalanche of support for the statehood option from traditional followers of the commonwealth. Puerto Ricans could not conceive of life without US citizenship.

The room was now dead silent. Cruz could feel the people's fears – which he loved to provoke – because he knew how much Puerto Ricans valued their U.S. citizenship, which they'd had since 1917. Statehood would be the sure winner in the plebiscite. He knew it. Fear was one of the best predictors of voting trends.

But there was a man in the audience who was not experiencing any fear. He was indeed enraged. At one instance, his stomach contorted, almost sending a thick rush of vomit over his sharp, black suit. Such was the effect of listening to so much demagoguery coming from the mouth of this "devil," Elison Cruz.

The man in the black suit had been sitting discreetly at a table at the far end of the room. He now had stood and was hurriedly walking to the front-center of the room. He was disappointed that he couldn't smuggle a gun into the hotel. But that didn't matter right now. When he got to within a few feet from the stage – a few feet from Cruz – he began shouting.

"*La única opción es la independencia! Cabrón! Hijo de puta!*" (The only option is independence! Bastard! Son of a bitch!). "*Viva Puerto Rico libre! Libertad o muerte!*" (Long live free Puerto Rico! Freedom or death!). "*Tu eres un traidor y te vamos a matar! Que viva la patria!*" (You are a traitor and we are going to kill you! Long live the motherland!). "*Que viva la patria! Que viva la patria!*"

Although he had encountered hecklers before, Cruz was taken aback by the man's tirade. He wasn't expecting hecklers within this audience. Nevertheless, he stood still and looked defiantly at the screaming man. He then drew a grin on his face and calmly watched as the suit-clad hotel security guards whisked the man out of the ballroom. Cruz's personal security detail stepped onto the stage. He signaled for them to stop and go back to their positions. The heckler kept shouting insults and political statements all the way to the exit.

The audience showed their contempt by booing down the man's shouts. They then broke into furious applause and waited for Cruz to speak again.

"You know," Cruz said mischievously, "by the way he was dressed I can tell he paid the five-hundred dollars to see me."

The audience exploded in laughter and more applause.

"What does that tell you?" Cruz asked grinning. "Even our opponents pay to listen to what we have to say!" He repressed his laughter. "Ironic, no?"

More laughter. More applause from the crowd.

The First Lady stood, wearing a wide smile on her face. She approached the podium, draped her arm around the governor's waist, bent her head to the microphone and said simply, "That's because we are very popular, Mr. Governor."

The audience approved with *bravos* and more thunderous applause. The First Lady then kissed her husband on the cheek and returned triumphantly to her seat. She was a truly beautiful, mature woman of forty-two. Clad in an elegant pink business suit, her slim figure showed prominently. It matched her bright-red, shoulder-length hair. Her hazel eyes, fine facial features and light complexion shone in the spotlight. She was a woman dedicated to worthy causes, to her husband, and to Anthony, their college-age only son.

"Don't you think Ana María is the best First Lady Puerto Rico has ever had?" Cruz asked the audience.

"Yes! Yes!" the audience responded.

"Let us show the First Lady how much we love her," Cruz said, nodding for Ana María to gently get up and receive a standing ovation. She stood and waved to the crowd, which had already forgotten about the crazed man who had yelled nasty things to their leader.

Cruz had not forgotten the man, though.

"Let me tell you something," he began saying as the First Lady and the audience dropped back into their seats. "In many other countries, like in our neighboring Cuba, that man we just met would be put in jail for the things he said here. For the sole reason of expressing his beliefs . . . his opinions." He stopped for dramatic purpose. "But here in Puerto Rico we have a democracy. A strong, solid democracy. We have freedoms which are the envy of many countries, not only in Latin America but all over the world."

Everyone was nodding in agreement.

"And let's not be deceived," Cruz declared. "We owe our freedom and our democracy to our partnership with the United States of America. We have built a solid society of freedom and democracy under the flag of the United States and under the protection of the Constitution of the United States. Nobody," he stressed, "nobody will, or can, take that away from us. Let no one be deceived!" He raised his voice. The audience rose in furious applause. "We are strong! We are united! And we will win! Puerto Rico will be the fifty-first state of the United States!" This is a good moment to finish his speech, he thought. It had been a good speech. "So I pledge with you. On November third, vote for your future . . . vote for economic growth . . . vote for democracy . . . vote for statehood and let us all together welcome a new age of prosperity as the newest state of the United States of America. Thank you and God bless you."

The audience, still on their feet, applauded even more vigorously after those final words of hope from their very own true leader, Elison Cruz. The Governor acknowledged the applause. He stepped aside from the podium, raised his arm and made the victory sign. On cue, the theme from "Rocky" began blasting through the loud speaker system. The First Lady came to Cruz's side and they held hands, wearing their best smiles and occasionally waving to friends and acquaintances in the audience.

This had not been a breakfast of the real "fat cats" of the Statehood Party, though. The ones who pay five or ten grand to wear a tuxedo in the same room with the Governor. But at five-hundred per head, this event had added an approximate half a million dollars to the Statehood Party's account. A healthy sum and not a bad way to start a day.

The breakfast's hosts and organizers, the elegant Marta Borja, and her husband Ricardo Borja, a true "fat cat," approached the Governor and First Lady. They shook hands and exchanged hugs and pleasantries.

The Borjas were an older couple, both in their early sixties. It was said that Marta Borja was to the Cruzes what Betsy Bloomingdale was to the Reagans. She had the same charm and energy and loved the perks of high society. Accordingly, she was a talented host and a skilled fundraiser. So was her husband. Ricardo had retired years earlier from a successful career as a venture capitalist. He had invested wisely and heavily in publishing, eco-tourism, telecommunications and, of course, the stock market. He was a self-made, very wealthy man, a real gentleman and a tested veteran of partisan politics in Puerto Rico. As such, he had served as an official – and unofficial – political consultant to each of the pro-statehood governors of the island. To Cruz, he was also a mentor.

When a thirty-something Elison Cruz entered the halls of partisan politics in Puerto Rico, he soon made it known that his eyes were set on becoming governor. Ricardo Borja was, nevertheless, skeptical of Cruz's potential as a leader and viable candidate for governor, a feeling that was then shared by the old guard of the Statehood Party. Borja and the Party, however, made a three-hundred-sixty-degree turn after seeing Cruz's popularity soar after a brief stint as Attorney General, followed by his landslide election as Mayor of San Juan. He was then only thirty-four years old. The man was decidedly gifted *and* electable. The statehooders kept the party's presidency and grassroots organization in older hands and handed Cruz the leadership he so desperately craved – and deserved. He was elected governor, as he had planned, and was reelected, as he had predicted.

And during his reelection campaign, Elison Cruz had accomplished what no other statehood leader had ever accomplished before. It had been an astonishing and unprecedented feat. Only the brutal shock waves of an earthquake or the fiercest winds of a hurricane could compare with the devastating tremors felt by the political opposition of the island, and with the awe of the public itself. None other than Donald M. Clarke, the sitting President of the United States, had come to Puerto Rico to campaign on Cruz's behalf. No other U.S. President had ever done such a thing. It was evident that the President of the United States himself had obviously recognized in Elison Cruz a true leader, a true American, and more than anything, a visionary. Undoubtedly, Elison Cruz, a man that counted the President of the U.S. as his friend, was the face of the fifty-first state of the United States of America.

As the power breakfast's donors dispersed, Ricardo Borja took a minute to chat with Cruz and with Marcos González, the elder president of the Statehood Party, who had joined them from his privileged seat on the stage. The men talked about the latest polls, which were predicting a victory for statehood in the plebiscite.

Marta Borja smiled broadly and waved her hand. That was a signal for Rosa Vera, a party loyalist, who had dutifully remained backstage during the whole event. It was time to send her two sharply dressed children, one boy and one girl, onto the stage and on their way to the First Couple with huge bouquets of fresh flowers. For this dedicated mother, and her seven and eight-year-old, this opportunity of meeting the governor and his wife would be unforgettable.

The little ones caught the Governor and First Lady's immediate attention. As the children approached, all the First Couple could see were two huge bouquets of fresh flowers with two oddly-looking sets of little human feet coming toward them. Marta Borja held her breath, and attentively observed the moment, which had been endlessly rehearsed by the children at the insistence of their nervous and eager-to-please mother.

Ana María Cruz relieved the boy first, not without some effort to actually get her flowers, since the boy was holding them as if his whole life depended on it. She kissed the boy on his cheek. He mumbled something unintelligible and ran for his life back to his mother's arms before the First Lady could say thank you.

The Governor took his flowers from the little girl who, as Marta directed, said out of breath, "Yeu are en ins . . . pira . . . tion to every . . . one." Marta clapped her hands, pleased.

Marcos González, the powerful and distinguished Party president, was forced to draw a smile on his stone-dead face. Ricardo Borja, the "fat cat," ignored the girl and went up to chat with Carmen Enid Arias, Secretary of State in the governor's cabinet. Cruz bent forward, close to the girl's face and exclaimed, "Oh, that is so sweet of you."

"Thank you," the girl replied.

"What is your name, my little angel?" Cruz asked her.

"My name is . . . Di . . . a . . . na," she shyly replied.

"Oh, just like the Princess of Wales," Cruz said tenderly.

"She's the daughter of Rosa Vera from the first district of the Party in Carolina," Marta Borja pointed out.

"Oh, please send my regards," Cruz said, without the slightest recollection of who Rosa Vera was.

"I will, Mr. Governor," Marta said. "Thank you so much for coming. It was a great speech."

"Thank you for inviting me," he responded.

"Yes, Marta, thank you very much," the First Lady added. "We appreciate all you do."

"It's always my pleasure," Marta replied, proud of herself.

"We should have dinner sometime," Ana María suggested.

Marta's eyes shone.

"Oh! Yes! Yes!" she quickly said. "It's been a while. That will be adorable, simply adorable."

"At your place!" Ana María shot.

"Oh my! Wonderful! Wonderful!" Marta was thrilled. "Honey, I will be calling you soon."

"Great, will do," Ana María concluded.

The Governor and First Lady handed their flowers to Elaine, their very efficient traveling secretary, and went on to greet a few more VIPs on the stage until press secretary Alan de Jesús came to rescue them.

"Mr. Governor," Alan said with insistence. "We have to leave now. We'll just take a few questions from the press on our way out."

Cruz nodded and began walking off the stage followed by Ana María, Alan, Elaine, and a handful of loyal and trusted aides. His four-man security detail walked ahead, suspiciously scanning everyone on their way. At the end of the steps to the stage the press was waiting. And they were yielding their microphones and TV cameras like lightning in an electric storm. There were exactly fourteen of them. Alan de Jesús had counted them.

Cruz's relationship with the press was one full of contradictions. Love-hate. Bitter-sweet. Give-and-take. Depending on the subject and situation, he alternated between voicing ambiguous answers and evasive statements, to stating strong and clear opinions and substantial expositions of policy. He, however, relied greatly on Alan de Jesús to keep the press under control, and to explain to them – with a straight face – the mood swings of the administration with respect to the disclosure of information, explanations of policy positions and any other matter that the press cared for.

However, during an election year or a special vote like the upcoming plebiscite, Cruz was aware of the importance of the press to generate the interest and participation of the people. He was not, nevertheless, a hostage of the media. He kept his distance and protected the little privacy the office of governor allowed him to have. And he had also learned to discern the ideological leanings and political constituencies of the journalists on the island. Based on this, he had come to like some of them, to dislike others, and to be selective with the respect he granted journalists.

Cruz was thinking about that when he saw *her*. She was standing right at the end of the steps, microphone in hand, with Tonio, her very able, young and very "annoying" cameraman by her side. It was Karen Pérez: the influential reporter from the influential Channel Four newscast.

Karen Peréz was one of the few black journalists in the Puerto Rican television news media. This was in and of itself a feat, in a society that still struggled with its African heritage. In the midst of a troop of women journalists with fine facial features and two-piece business suits, Karen stood out with her beautiful and uncommon black skin, and for her trademark attire of sandals, indigenous hand-woven robes, ankle-length, flowered skirts and exotic hand-made jewelry. But it was her fierce, persistent, daring and aggressive tactics as a journalist, her wide connections, and her proven character that made her a face and a voice in the media to which people paid attention. Years earlier, she had managed to broadcast an exclusive and dramatic interview with Rigonaldo Pastrana, a man who was – and still is – the most wanted criminal by the Puerto Rican police and the FBI. Pastrana, who had eluded capture for years, was the leader of September Twenty-third, a separatist, terrorist organization, which had murdered numerous state and municipal police officers, Puerto Rican and American members of the FBI, American military personnel, and even more civilians; Americans and Puerto Ricans alike. Pastrana and his gang of murderers were also responsible for audacious shootings and bombings against federal and state facilities, and for countless bank and armored truck robberies.

And most recently, the terror group was engaged in an aggressive campaign against the plebiscite.

When Karen Pérez's interview with the elusive Rigonaldo Pastrana aired, the whole country embraced the notoriety of the fugitive terrorist, and was in awe of the audacity of the woman journalist who gave him a voice and plastered his face on prime-time TV.

Karen Pérez was also responsible for innumerable television reports and investigations on government corruption, following leads from her contacts in the Puerto Rican Legislature. During Governor Cruz's first term, he saw two members of his cabinet resign, under pressure stemming from accusations made public in her TV reports. One was even indicted and convicted of misappropriation of state and federal public funds. That had been an embarrassment to Cruz's then-young administration, and an unwelcome scandal that required heavy and serious political spin to erase from the public's mind.

And it was true – Cruz's administration had had less corruption scandals than previous administrations. Moreover, to his benefit, by the time he came to power, the Puerto Rican public was so used to and intoxicated by corruption scandals that it was hard to keep track of each one of them. The public's best defense mechanism was to tune out from it all. A short memory came in handy if the public aimed to retain its sanity.

Governor Cruz's memory was of a more lasting nature, though. As he began to walk down the steps and off the stage, he thought of subtle ways to ignore Karen Pérez. She was thirty-nine-years-old, a mere five years younger than he was. She could handle a little attitude, he told himself.

The reporters' questions exploded at him. He purposely looked at Karen Pérez and then turned the other way to answer a question from a male reporter of *El Nuevo Sol*, the largest newspaper on the island. "Mr. Governor," the man began, "in every single status plebiscite held on the island the statehood option has lost. What makes you so certain Puerto Ricans will choose statehood this time? Aren't you worried that the voters will repeat history and defeat statehood once again?"

Microphones and tape recorders shifted toward Cruz's face. Alan de Jesús carefully pushed them away to an acceptable distance. With the blinding lights of television cameras on him, Cruz spoke confidently to the sea of electronic devices in front of him.

"No, I am not in the least worried," he said firmly. "And it is a serious mistake to establish comparisons between past status consultations to the voters and the upcoming plebiscite on November third. I stress, in the strongest of terms, that the U.S. Congress itself defined the political formulas that were acceptable to them. And after a long and arduous political battle, they agreed on the legislation, and the U.S. President signed it into law. Our American friends are legally bound to enforce the results of this plebiscite. This plebiscite is the direct result of the political efforts of the U.S. President and the U.S. Congress. That is the important variable here. This plebiscite is not a beauty contest. And Puerto Ricans will not jeopardize their U.S. citizenship."

The reporter followed up saying, "It has been said that Puerto Ricans are giving away their culture and the Spanish language for the sake of U.S. citizenship, sir."

"That is false!" Cruz shot. "We have been part of the United States for over a hundred years and we still remain a solidly Latin American people, and we still speak our Spanish language. Nobody will take that away from us."

"Wouldn't statehood mean the imposition of the English language on us?" another reporter asked. "The legislation seems somewhat ambiguous on that."

"To impose English as the primary language of Puerto Rico would be a crime," Cruz stated solemnly, knowing he had just given this reporter his big headline. "And that is not the intention of the United States, nor is it the intention of the Puerto Rican people."

"What are our guarantees, Mr. Governor?" another reporter asked.

"The strongest guarantee we have is the strong will of the Puerto Rican people," Cruz said, opting not to get too specific on the hot-water issue of language and culture. "The language of Puerto Rico is the Spanish language. It has been our language for over five hundred years. Statehood will not change that."

Karen Pérez knew the Governor was being evasive. In the same way that the issue of U.S. citizenship had shifted votes to statehood, the issues of language, culture and Olympic sports representation had shifted votes to independence and free association. Neither the President nor Congress had been definite on these issues, leaving what many political analysts called "dangerous loopholes," should Puerto Rico become a U.S. state.

Karen Perez opted to go for the jugular. "Governor," she began firmly, "isn't the issue facing Puerto Ricans one of who is Puerto Rican and who is American? The opposition has said that you have polarized this country like no one before."

"You can be Puerto Rican *and* American!" Cruz barked. "There is no contradiction."

Karen Pérez's turn at asking questions was Alan de Jesús's cue to start getting the Governor out the door. He motioned for the Governor and his entourage to start moving.

"Governor," Karen went on, "there is strong opposition to this plebiscite, which many consider anti-democratic. Why not support the creation of a Constitutional Assembly as was proposed by the Organization of American States and the U.N. Decolonization Committee?"

"We do not need another Constitutional Assembly in Puerto Rico," Cruz said emphatically and with a grin on his face as he began walking in the direction of the exit.

"For the sake of peace," Karen shouted while following her subject, "isn't it wise to compromise with those who have serious reservations about this plebiscite?"

"Puerto Rico is at peace, Ms. Pérez," Cruz said, giving her a last look. "And what is wise to do is to give the people of Puerto Rico the opportunity to choose what is best for them. And that is exactly what we are doing. Thank you all," he finished.

With that, Cruz ignored the rest of the questions fired at him and walked out of the ballroom and toward the main lobby with the rest of his entourage. The press ran ahead of him and toward the front doors to get pictures and video as he exited the hotel and got into his waiting car. They especially wanted footage of the limousine traveling through the crowd of protesters outside. Reporters loved drama.

Press secretary, Alan de Jesús, glanced at his watch to confirm that they were on schedule. It was five minutes after ten. They were on time.

Oso, the sniper, also looked at his watch. Then, once again, he searched the sliding front doors of the San Juan Hotel through the scope of his rifle. This time, he saw a herd of annoying reporters in their fancy power-suits exiting the hotel and positioning themselves around the governor's limo. Elison Cruz would soon surface, Oso knew.

Expectantly, he bit his lower lip and wiped sweat from his forehead. He was sick of the smell of cleaning supplies in the cramped utility room. But there were more pressing matters at hand. The moment had come to rid Puerto Rico of this fascist *piti-yanqui* who wanted to hand the country to the enemy up north. And the cameras were there to get it all on tape, just like he wanted it. A worthless, dead Governor, all caught on tape. An event for the history books, and more. And he was a part of it.

When a second group of men and women in power-suits emerged from the hotel, Oso was not confused. He spotted his target easily. Cruz was not difficult to miss. For Oso, Cruz was the perfect *blanquito* with his trim, tall figure, pale, white complexion, a thin face with fine features, short, golden-blond hair and sky-blue eyes. And accompanied by his wife, who was always by his side, Cruz was an easy target.

The protesters on Isla Verde Avenue also spotted the Governor and, as if hit by lightning, began to shout and chant more aggressively. "CRUZ IS A TRAITOR! FREEDOM FOR THE MOTHERLAND! LONG LIVE FREE PUERTO RICO!"

Cruz was unmoved. He grinned to the cameras and said, "They don't give up, do they?"

"They are the same people, same faces as usual," Alan de Jesús replied with a shrug. "They follow us like the plague."

The entourage approached the limousine.

"So long mother fucker," Oso whispered as he tightened his finger on the trigger of his 9.4 pound rifle, which rested comfortably on his muscled shoulder.

A male reporter, camera in hand, ran into the Governor's path, blocking his way.

"Hey!" Alan yelled running up to him. "Get out of the way!"

Oso pressed the trigger. Three times. Three single shots. The

Dragunov's steel-jacketed bullets flew at a speed of 830 meters per second.

Chaos.

Alan was shot in the head and upper chest. He jerked back violently at the impact, blood spattering on Cruz's face and onto the First Lady's pink suit. The third shot hit a uniformed state police officer in his left shoulder.

"Oh my God!" the First Lady screamed in horror.

"Gunfire! Gunfire!" somebody shouted.

"Get him out! Get him out!"

Frantically, someone yanked open the rear door of the limo and the governor's security aides hurriedly pushed Cruz and the First Lady into the back seat of the vehicle. The driver was in shock.

"Go, dammit! Go!" he was ordered.

The driver stomped on the accelerator, moving away at dangerous speed and passing the screaming protesters that were all totally confused as to what had just happened.

At the hotel's entrance and in the lobby there was chaos, as aides, guards, hotel workers, reporters and police ran for cover, assisted the wounded and tried to determine where the shots had come from. Alan de Jesús was sprawled on the floor bleeding profusely and immobile. The wounded police officer was also on the floor a few feet from him, holding his bleeding shoulder and screaming in pain. "Somebody call an ambulance! Call an ambulance!" someone was yelling. The reporters were in shock but nevertheless kept snapping pictures and video of the horrific scene. Karen Pérez assaulted her cell phone and demanded an interruption of Channel Four's regular programming to give a breaking news live report. This was more drama than they could ever have conceived of.

Oso moved quickly. He knew he had little time. And he knew he had missed. That gravely troubled him. With his gloved hands, he nervously disassembled his weapon into two pieces and hid it inside a black-leather backpack. He knew his drill. He put on dark sunglasses and hid his hair under a red, cotton winter hat. Then, with dead calm so as not to bring attention to himself, he left the utility room, entered a deserted hallway, and quickly disappeared through a door that brought him to the stairs. Nobody saw him then and nobody was looking now. He descended three steps at a time, from the fifth floor to the basement in less than two minutes. Once there, he saw an old security guard with thick spectacles, seated, bored and half asleep on a metal folding chair at one end of the basement. Oso stopped. Then, he walked slowly. The old man paid no particular attention to him. Oso was gone.

He pushed the crashbar of a heavy metal door and was immediately in the exterior parking lot of the building. Teco, his accomplice, was right where he was supposed to be – in the driver's seat of their getaway SUV.

The terrorists exchanged cold looks. Teco started the engine and drove toward his partner. Oso jumped in on the passenger's side, throwing his backpack into the back seat. "Let's go," he ordered flatly.

"Well," Teco said with a grin, "do we have a dead governor?"

"I fucking said let's go!" Oso insisted again, pointing to the road with his finger and pulling an unfiltered Camel out of the pocket of his shirt. His hand trembled when he lit it. He couldn't believe he had missed.

Teco complied with the order and drove away, out of the Los Alamos parking lot and through the Gobernadores Boulevard exit, away from Isla Verde Avenue, where the San Juan Hotel was located. In sixty seconds they were driving down Baldorioty De Castro Highway. The two terrorists quickly disappeared into the sea of morning traffic of the enchanted island of Puerto Rico.

The terrorists were silent, their cold eyes scanning the vehicles ahead and around them, but avoiding the eyes of the people within them.

On the road, it seemed, Oso and Teco had no faces.

They already had no souls.

Chapter 2

A mob of reporters assaulted the governor's motorcade as the black limousine entered the wrought-iron gates of La Fortaleza, the magnificent, colonial Spanish mansion that served as the governor's residence in Old San Juan since the late 1500's. This was huge news: the first assassination attempt against a Puerto Rican governor since the 1950's.

When the last vehicle was safely on the grounds of La Fortaleza, the caretakers of the mansion closed the iron gates. The press was left outside, shouting unintelligible questions, and desperately snapping pictures and video of the Governor and First Lady walking at a fast pace into the white structure.

As Cruz and Ana María advanced through the halls of Fortaleza, concerned members of their staff – maids, butlers, cooks, and other workers in the mansion – appeared from every part of the building, expressing words of support and the occasional blessing.

"We are fine . . . we are fine," Cruz reassured everyone as he walked one step ahead of his wife in the direction of their private residence on the second floor. He had wiped Alan's blood off his face on the way to the mansion. Ana María's suit was still blood-soaked.

When they neared the entrance of Cruz's executive office, Samuel Almeda, Cruz's young scheduling secretary, abruptly came towards them.

"Alan is dead!" he said bluntly and with alarm.

"Oh my God!" Ana María gasped, her hand to her mouth.

Cruz kept his calm. "Sam," he said, "wait for me in the office. I'll come down in a few minutes."

"A police officer was also shot," Almeda went on. "He's alive though."

Cruz nodded. He knew. He had been on the phone with police at the scene of the crime and had purposely kept the news from his wife. He dismissed Almeda with a hand gesture and escorted Ana María up a flight of stairs. They soon reached their private living room. It was an impressively large room surrounded by floor-to-ceiling crystal windows that offered a privileged view of the Atlantic Ocean. There were huge white sofas, heavy oak and glass tables and carefully positioned marble sculptures. A physician was waiting for them.

Ana María ignored the doctor, whom she considered an intruder. Pacing frenziedly, she blurted out in rage. "This is it!" she cried. "You have to resign!"

"Ana María, I . . ." Cruz tried to speak.

"I don't want you dead!" she cut him off. "Those people want to kill you!"

"Ana, we'll find out who they are," he tried to reassure her. "You can bet on that."

"Don't ask me to bet on your life, for Christ's sake!" she snapped.

"Ana María, please calm down!" It was more of an order. "This is exactly what they want."

"I can't calm down! I can't! What are they going to do next? Tell me!" she yelled, her voice quivering.

"Nothing," Cruz said calmly and trying to sound confident. "They are going to do nothing."

Ana María shook her head and collapsed onto a large white sofa. She was now sobbing uncontrollably. The doctor approached her with a tranquilizer and a glass of water. She took it and said nothing. Cruz came close to her and rubbed his hand through her hair. It felt wet and sticky. She had been perspiring as never before.

Cruz dismissed the doctor and knelt in front of his wife. He firmly grabbed her shoulders and let her cry for a moment. Then he said, "Everything will be all right. Nothing is going to happen. To you or to me."

She looked him straight in the eye.

"You have to trust me," he pleaded. "Especially you."

"Oh Elison . . . this is insane," she said with resignation.

"I know . . . I know," he said quietly. "But you have to trust me. We will find out who did this."

She nodded and he held her until the sobs subsided. He then stood and said, "I must be in the office now."

She was silent for a moment, and then shrugged her shoulders as if to dismiss him. "I'll be okay . . . go," she said, wiping tears off her face.

Cruz spoke. "Go and change into something comfortable. Do not take phone calls. Rest." He waited for her to acknowledge him and said, "Also, do something. Call Anthony." Anthony was their nineteen year-old son who was a first-year undergraduate student of Public Affairs at Yale University. "Tell him we are fine. I don't want him to hear this first in the news."

"Of course I'll call him," she said softly.

"Tell him I love him. He can call me later tonight."

Ana María nodded. "Go Elison," she told him sadly.

He began to walk out of the room. He stopped and faced her. They exchanged looks. He then gently raised his fingers to his lips, kissed them and rubbed them slowly against his heart. It meant, "I love you."

Ana María smiled faintly and whispered, "I love you too."

Cruz turned around and went to his office where he expected to find Almeda waiting for him. Near the entrance to his office, he stopped to speak to Damaris, his old and loyal secretary. She was a rounded and plump, short woman of fifty-five, with grayish-white hair, olive skin and a perfectionistic demeanor. She was a Statehood Party veteran. She owed her job to Marcos González, the party's president, who, by placing her there, had intended to have his own set of eyes and ears within Fortaleza.

"Damaris, please hold all my calls. Only Calero," Cruz instructed, referring to Roberto Calero, his veteran Police Superintendent.

"Yes, Mr. Governor," she answered duly.

When Cruz entered his office, Samuel Almeda was dutifully there. He was seated on one of two small, red sofas facing the governor's large oak desk, holding a pen and a yellow legal pad on his lap. Behind the neatly arranged desk, a large floor-to-ceiling crystal window allowed for a view of the ocean, and of the thick and ancient stone city walls which surrounded Old San Juan. The capital of Puerto Rico had been built as a fortress by the Spanish colonizers. The rest of the office was a mixture of wood-paneled and stone walls, adorned with *grabados* (engraved wood-plates) and colorful lithographs of Puerto Rican landscapes. A set of larger sofas for in-person conferences with the governor were positioned at the center of the spacious room.

As Cruz sat behind his desk, Almeda said, "How is the First Lady?"

Cruz shrugged his shoulders and said, "She's obviously shaken." He paused. "Afraid too . . . She wants me to resign," he confessed with a dismissive hand gesture.

The phone rang when Almeda was about to speak again. Infuriated, Cruz stared at the blinking light of his ten-line phone. He ignored the call and instead pushed the intercom button that connected him to Damaris on the speakerphone. "I said no phone calls!" he barked.

"It's the Superintendent, Mr. Governor," Damaris said calmly and matter-of-factly.

"Oh," he said, grabbing the receiver and pressing the blinking line. "Hello," he said with authority and loudly, as was his custom when entertaining power calls.

"Mr. Governor, it's Calero." The Police Superintendent spoke likewise.

"Okay, what do we got?"

"We are gathering a list of the usual suspects. We are looking at September Twenty-third. Of course we'll build up on the intelligence we already have and we'll take it from there."

"You know, they continue to be a real pain in the ass," Cruz said with an edge.

"Their days are numbered, Cruz. The FBI is closing in on them. We are tracking every new lead, too." Superintendent Calero wanted to stress that law enforcement was in control. Cruz was not convinced.

"Anything on this Rigonaldo bastard?" he spat.

"Well . . ." Calero began. "He's elusive, no doubt, but with the plebiscite approaching we believe he'll want more exposure. That will do him in . . . We'll nail him this time." The fugitive leader of September Twenty-third had been on the run for over ten years.

"I hope you are right," Cruz said incredulously. "Keep me posted." That meant goodbye, end of the call.

"One more thing," Calero said quickly. "Give us till three o'clock this afternoon so we can . . ."

Cruz did not hear the Superintendent's full sentence. Instead, he glanced at Almeda and asked him, "Did you send him our schedule?"

"Ten minutes ago," Almeda assured him with a nod. "I faxed it and e-mailed it to him."

"We got you chief," Cruz said to the telephone, scanning a copy of his schedule, placed on his desk in front of him. "We'll do the groundbreaking of the new Ashford Children's Hospital in Condado and then head back here for the day."

"Okay, I'll be there," Calero replied, knowing Cruz had not listened to him before.

"You'll be there?" Cruz asked puzzled.

"Governor, I think it's imperative for me to be around you in the present situation, given the fact that . . ."

"Roberto," Cruz cut him off. "I don't think that is a good idea. You weren't scheduled to be there and the press knows you weren't scheduled to be there." Cruz exchanged looks with Almeda. "They are going to think we are in crisis. I don't think that is the impression I want to give to the public." Cruz spoke categorically as Almeda nodded in agreement.

"Mr. Governor," Calero said with concern. "Those shots were fired at you. You were the target. We have to protect you in the best way we can, and you have to let us do our job." The Superintendent swallowed hard for what he was going to say next. He knew Cruz disliked appearing trapped. "And you should be aware," he said cautiously, "I've decided to increase security around you. At least for the next few weeks, more of us will be travelling with you . . . especially for public activities . . ."

"I don't like that at all!" Cruz snapped.

"Not to worry, sir," Calero tried to reassure him. "I've explained to them how you feel and I've told them to keep a very low profile."

"How low of a profile can they keep?" Cruz asked cynically. "You know damn well the press can spot a contingent of security people from here to Miami. Don't you agree?"

"Governor, I understand your concerns, believe me. But we also know how to handle the press. In fact," Calero said in passing, "Karen Pérez has been calling today and I've all but ignored her."

"Who?" Cruz asked, lost in thoughts about security.

"Karen Pérez, from Channel four."

"Oh yes, her . . . Of course." How could he forget *her*?

"Anyway," Calero hurried to end the conversation on a good note. "I'll keep you posted on any new developments. And I'll see you at the Ashford in the afternoon."

"Okay, you be there, but remember, do not talk to the press!" Cruz ordered.

"That's understood, sir."

Cruz replaced the phone in its cradle. He suddenly found himself with time to think about a painful pressure that had built up behind his head. And the image of Alan de Jesús being killed hit him too. He was lost in thought when he heard Almeda talking to him.

"What did he say?" Almeda asked.

Cruz's scheduling secretary was a young man of twenty-nine. Together with Alan de Jesús, they were known as *los gemelos* (the twins) because of their youth. That is where the similarities ended. Almeda was unmarried, with a tall athletic body, white skin, brown hair cut short, brown eyes, and an impeccable taste for designer clothing. Many wondered how he could afford such a wardrobe on a government salary. Alan de Jesús – now deceased – had recently married his longtime girlfriend and was the father of a baby girl. He was thirty-one, short, chubby and *trigueño* (of mixed race). At his young age, though, he managed to develop fairly good relations with the hard-to-please press corps – unlike Almeda, who was considered to be a spoiled snob.

Cruz remained silent, his hand to his chin. Almeda shifted in his chair and glanced at his Rolex as he waited for an answer to his question.

"Nothing," Cruz finally said. "Calero talked security, as usual. We'll have to work something out, though." He paused. "And, we are looking at September Twenty-third for this morning's incident."

"Again?" Almeda asked incredulously.

"Yes, again."

Just two weeks earlier, the terrorist group had claimed responsibility for a car bombing in front of the gates of the Fort Buchanan Army Base near San Juan. And in a ten-year span they had claimed responsibility for scores of daring and ruthless bank and armored truck robberies, and for bombings and shootings against state and federal personnel and installations on the island. The death toll had reached into the hundreds, with many more injured. September Twenty-third and its leader, Rigonaldo Pastrana, were the most sought-after criminals by the Puerto Rican police and the FBI. The group had declared war on both the Federal and the Puerto Rican governments. They sought independence for the island through the use of force. They felt Puerto Ricans had an inalienable right to it. No matter that only four percent of the electorate favored independence – September Twenty-third wanted to be the voice and leader of the Puerto Rican people. And, as the plebiscite approached and the country moved closer to statehood, the nationalist terrorists feared they were running out of time. Elison Cruz had become the most dangerous threat to the independence of Puerto Rico.

They hate me because I don't share their political ideology, Cruz told himself. He calmly stood up from his seat behind his desk and took a few steps to the immaculately clean crystal window that faced the ocean. And their hatred, he thought, was grossly unfair. He was a statehooder, all right. But he wasn't a right-wing conservative. He never had been. He supported a woman's right to choose, had supported the abolishment of sodomy laws in Puerto Rico even before the U.S. Supreme Court struck them down, had granted domestic partnership benefits to gay and lesbian couples, had vigourously defended the separation of church and state, had allocated a high percentage of the state's budget for social spending programs and subsidies, had created innovative housing programs and out patient services for the mentally ill, had always defended Spanish as the official language of Puerto Rico, and had supported the exit of the U.S. military from the island of Vieques. The list was endless.

"Why do they call themselves September Twenty-third?" Cruz asked loudly, his eyes absently set on the blue ocean facing him.

Almeda was confused. He was uncertain if Cruz was genuinely naïve about the subject or if he was just testing his knowledge of it. He said, "You mean why they . . ." He paused. "Well," he began, "it comes from 1868 . . . An insurrection against Spain in 1868. It was not a big event, though, but it marked the most significant armed uprising against the Spanish forces on the island. It happened in the town of Lares on September 23, 1868 . . . That's why every September Twenty-third the *independentistas* commemorate what they call *El Grito de Lares* (The Battle Cry of Lares)."

Cruz remained still and silent. He said nothing for a few seconds, and then continued to speak calmly as he faced the window. "That's what I thought," he said softly and then remained quiet again.

Almeda straightened himself on the soft sofa-seat searching for words to break the silence. "Actually," he said, "not very many people know about *El Grito de Lares* or what it means . . . You have to be part of the political left . . . mostly . . . to know what September Twenty-three means. If Puerto Rico were a republic . . ." Almeda paused, having second thoughts about what he was about to say.

"Go on," Cruz ordered.

"If Puerto Rico were an independent republic . . . most likely September Twenty-three would be a national holiday."

The Governor gave thought to this, letting it sink in.

Almeda hurried to say, "But of course, Puerto Rico is not and will never be an independent republic."

"I know," Cruz said, glancing at his aide from the corner of his eye. "And," he continued, "Why are they against the plebiscite?"

By now, Almeda knew the Governor was testing his knowledge and reasoning; maybe looking for reassurance. "Well," Almeda said with a shrug, "they believe that as a colony of the United States, a democratic consultation to the voters cannot occur until we have attained full sovereignty and independence . . . According to them we are a country under military occupation."

"Are we?" Cruz asked grinning.

"We certainly aren't, Mr. Governor."

Cruz faced Almeda again. "Of course we aren't," Cruz snapped. "Those stinking bastards!" He walked back to his seat, sat down and spoke rapidly and with newfound enthusiasm. "You know Almeda, we are doing the right thing and we are going to win . . . By a landslide." He clenched his fist and hit his desk. "We are going to be the fifty-first state of the United States and those bastards are going to end up either in jail or in exile . . . I'll send them all to Cuba. Castro will take them." He laughed vociferously at this.

Almeda followed suit and laughed too, nodding his head.

After a moment, Cruz stopped laughing and appeared again to be lost in thought. He said, "Call the Ashford people and confirm that we'll be there for the groundbreaking of the children's hospital."

Almeda nodded and took notes on his yellow legal pad.

"And call the Invest Puerto Rico Group from this morning and reschedule," Cruz went on. "I'm sure they'll understand why we were a no show."

"Certainly."

"Now I have to make a few phone calls of my own. So let's say we meet back here in two hours." Cruz dismissed his aide.

Almeda stood up and turned around to leave. Cruz called him to attention again. "On your way," he ordered, "tell Damaris to call Alan's wife and mother and to transfer the calls to me. They must be devastated."

"Yes, sir."

"And have her keep me posted on the condition of the police officer who took a bullet. If possible, we'll visit him at the hospital."

"Yes, Mr. Governor," Almeda said and left the office.

Alone in his executive office, Cruz thought of his role as the leader of a country he viewed as in transition. He was leading Puerto Rico into a new political era. He was also one of the architects of a new American federated state. A Spanish-American state, as he liked to describe it. Such a task, he believed, would certainly impact the United States, especially the Latino communities there, and Latin America as well. Puerto Rico could become a bridge of understanding between the United States and the nations of Latin America.

In his solitude, Cruz was also tortured with guilt. He had just had a good laugh, but bullets that were meant for him had killed his trusted, young aide. He knew he was responsible for his death. How could he explain that to a mother and to a widow? And Cruz also had his own wife to think about. Ana María had been placed at risk. He would have been destroyed if something had happened to her. How would Anthony, their only son, have felt? Was this political fight that he had chosen worth the serious risks he was facing? He knew the answer to that was in the affirmative. Every single historical political leader had had to overcome great odds and had made great sacrifices to achive their aims.

Cruz grabbed the telephone, punched a line and began dialing. Abruptly, he put it back in its cradle. After a moment, he stood up and walked out of the office. He stopped by his secretary and said, "Damaris, I'll be upstairs for a while. When you get Alan's family on the phone please pass them on to me."

"Very well, Mr. Governor," Damaris said, putting down some papers she was holding.

Cruz turned around to leave.

"Sir," Damaris called him.

Cruz faced her again.

"Are you and the First Lady okay?" she asked, seriously concerned.

"Yes, Damaris," he assured her. "We are fine. A bit shaken, but we are fine. We must thank God."

"I am glad nothing happened to either of you. I know God is with the two of you."

"Thank you, Damaris."

"But poor Alan," she said, her voice trembling. "He was so young and full of life. And he loved his new baby so much. It's just so terrible what happened."

"I know," Cruz said sadly.

Damaris used a tissue to wipe tears off her face. Cruz struggled with a lump in his throat. "I'll be upstairs," he said softly.

With that, the Governor turned around and disappeared down a long corridor adorned with portraits of all the former Puerto Rican governors of the island. Conspicuously absent from this gallery were all the American appointees, except Jesús T. Piñero, who became the first Puerto Rican governor of the island when President Harry S. Truman appointed him to the position in 1946. Every face on the wall represented a piece of history. Cruz stopped for a moment to glance at the men, and one woman, who had inspired and led the country through both good and trying times. One day, his portrait would also be on that wall to speak unsaid words and maybe even to challenge the future leaders of the island.

Cruz bowed his head in silence. He then went up a flight of stairs to join Ana María, his beloved wife, whom he knew now needed him most. His phone calls could wait for later.

Chapter 3

Oso and Teco passed through the third toll, driving south on Highway 52, and soon turned off at the Road 15 exit. They were on their way to their hideout near the town of Cagüey in the heights of the Guarite Forest, some forty miles from San Juan in the south-eastern part of the island. The radio was on, flooded with reports about the shooting. The governor was alive, press secretary Alan de Jesús was dead, and police officer Pedro Santiago had been wounded and was now being treated at the Pavía Hospital in Santurce. The belief that September Twenty-third was behind the sniper attack was in full motion, and the possibility that the shots came from the Los Alamos Condominium was almost certain. A security guard at Los Alamos had seen a man carrying a backpack exiting through the basement, but was unable to give a useful description to the police. The intruder was tall and wore some sort of hat. That was it.

It was impossible to identify Oso as the man at Los Alamos. The terrorists were pleased. At least for that. They were also amused with the radio pundits who were giving "expert" analyses on what all of this meant for the country and how it might affect the plebiscite vote. The pundits warned that if Puerto Ricans believed that statehood would send the country into more violence and chaos, the prospect of independence or free association winning the plebiscite increased by the minute. The terrorists calculated that if such was the case, their actions should indeed become even bloodier. Perhaps a rampage of executions. Mostly civilians. Prominent businessmen and women, and their children.

Some left-wing commentators were directly blaming the U.S. President, Donald M. Clarke, for the current violence and bloodshed in Puerto Rico. Never before, they argued, had a "missing tape" had such serious political repercussions. Years earlier, President Clarke had survived a heated and embarrasing political scandal that could have cost him the Latino vote in the U.S. and probably his reelection. Before the U.S. leader made clear his intention of granting statehood to Puerto Rico, an alleged telephone recording of him making blatantly racist and disparaging remarks about Latinos had mysteriously disappeared from the offices of the Washington Post. The powerful newspaper printed a transcript of the tape anyhow and the President responded with a stern denial of the incendiary comments attributed to him, and with a promise to do "more than what any other president has done for Latinos in the U.S. and Puerto Rico." His support for statehood for Puerto Rico came in the middle of the "missing tape" scandal.

The radio broadcast continued as the car reached the downtown area of Cagüey, a two-hundred-year-old town that had seen a modern revival by hosting a branch campus of the University of Puerto Rico. College students wandered about as if they owned the streets and the town.

A few minutes later, once on the outskirts of Cagüey, the terrorists drove down Road 89, a long, narrow street shaded by trees on either side that took them across an immense sugar cane field that seemed endless. Once the cane field was behind them, the road began to lift into the steep mountains of the Guarite Forest. The air turned cooler and the road became even narrower, and crowded and darkened by trees and heavy foliage on both sides. As they advanced on the road, the terrorists were silent as if conversation would reveal their secret destination. They also kept looking in the rearview mirrors to ensure no suspicious vehicles were behind them. They drove and drove some more, until it was time to get off the paved road. After cautiously looking behind them, they turned right and were instantly on a rocky and narrow dirt road partially hidden by thick brush. It was an arduous and deserted path, crowded by trees and thick foliage on both sides. Besides the vehicles of the terrorist cell, no other vehicles drove through this area. Ever. The only destination was the large, wooden house that the terrorists used as their secret hideout.

The car sped along the rugged trail, sending thick clouds of black, gravelly dust into the air. Within a few minutes that always seemed longer to them, they saw the house, hidden – like a thief – by dense groves of trees and thick brush. It was a large, red-painted wood complex with a rusted tin roof, a small porch and a large garage for several vehicles.

Teco drove into the garage and parked alongside a white and rusted windowless van. He and Oso got out of their SUV and walked straight toward the house, avoiding a flock of ducks and chickens clucking about. A woman drawing on a cigarette stepped onto the porch for a split second as if to confirm that they were friendly visitors. Teco and Oso waved at her and she disappeared back inside.

When Teco and Oso entered the house, the woman was holding a large mug with coffee while seated on an old, dirt-filled couch in front of a TV set which was on at a low volume. Her name was Luna, "moon," and she was the only woman in the tight-knit cell that formed September Twenty-third. She was a *trigueña* (of mixed race) with a tired face that looked older than her forty-one-years of age. Her hair was black and long, and always kept under a kerchief tied around her head. She was of medium height with hands that showed the hardships of working the land and with the animals that were kept in wooden shacks in the backyard of the house.

The living room was small and darkened by thick sets of dark blue curtains that fully covered all the windows. It seemed like a coffin in there, but that was how Rigonaldo, the leader of September Twenty-third, wanted it. Besides the large couch facing the TV set, there were several sofas and wooden chairs scattered throughout the room. The floor had been plastered with colorless linoleum sheets, and the walls were decked with huge yellowish posters of Che Guevara, Mao Tse Tung and Fidel Castro. A small, platinum metal dining table with accompanying chairs was set in a corner of the room just off a crowded, messy kitchen. Two hallways on either side of the room led to the bedrooms where the terrorists slept and kept their weapons.

"Hello, Luna," Oso said calmly.

She glanced at him but said nothing. Her face looked pale, her eyes watery with smeared mascara streaming down her cheeks. Oso knew right away that there had been a brutal argument in the house some time before. And he knew it had to do with him.

Luna's tears, Oso knew, were not tears of weakness. She was not a weak, fragile woman. She had proven herself many times. She had killed in the name of the cause many times. Just like all the men in the cell. Oso decided he would take her aside later and let her vent all her rage on him. He now had to face Rigonaldo.

"Where is he?" Oso asked firmly.

"He's in the back," Luna responded flatly, and emotionless. "Feeding the pigs."

Before he walked away, a news brief on the television caught Oso's attention. It showed the fracas at the lobby of the San Juan Hotel, and ambulances departing with the dead and wounded. That was followed by a wide shot of the Los Alamos Condominium and by an old still photograph of Rigonaldo Pastrana. It was the same portrait that graced the island's FBI Most Wanted gallery.

Luna said nothing. Oso stared at the TV for a few seconds, silent as well. He then walked to his right and through the long corridor that led to the rear yard where the animals – pigs, goats, chickens, ducks, rabbits – were kept. He passed several open doors that exposed poorly kept bedrooms and unmade beds strewn with dirty clothes and weapons. At the end of the corridor he pushed open a screen door and immediately stepped down and sank into a few inches of thick, wet mud. He was not bothered by the putrid smell of animal dung that permeated the air. The animals were kept within rustic wooden shacks a little farther from the house. He could hear the pigs snorting as they struggled for their share of old, spoiled food.

As he approached the shacks, walking through the mud, he saw Rigonaldo. The feared terrorist leader was crouching and jerking his huge strong arms as he threw food from a large tin bucket into the pig's cage. The animals fought and bumped against each other, eating voraciously.

Oso was always intimidated by Rigonaldo Pastrana's presence, as everyone who had ever met him was also. The man was an imposing character. His body frame was large and impressive. He was six-feet-eight with strong firm legs and arms, a broad chest and shoulders and long, messy, grayish-white hair. His wide face bore a thick, long beard, which made him look like a clone of Fidel Castro. And his beard partially disguised a scar on his left cheek and his severe rugged features, signs of long years of bitterness and struggle. He was sixty-two.

Oso came close to him but did not speak. He just watched as Rigonaldo fed the pigs. Rigonaldo saw him but did not acknowledge his presence. He kept at his task, his shirt stuck to his body, drenched with sweat.

Oso knew Rigonaldo had been in a rage earlier and that Luna had had to face it full front. Feeding the animals and walking through the woods was the way he regained his calm. Rigonaldo would not burst into a rage at him now. Although Oso felt he deserved it.

Oso broke the silence. "Rigonaldo," he said calmly. "It didn't work."

Rigonaldo studied him but kept at his task. "I know, son," he said softly and in a patronizing way. "Don't you think I know?"

"Yeah . . . I know," Oso said, avoiding Rigonaldo's penetrating glance. No use to say 'I'm sorry,' he thought. Failure was inexcusable.

For several minutes there was silence. Oso attempted to stare at the sky through the thick foliage of the trees above them. Waiting. Rigonaldo went ahead and finished the feeding, tossing the tin bucket into the mud. He then pulled a Cuban cigar out of the pocket of his shirt. Oso lit it for him and remained silent. Rigonaldo drew deeply on the tobacco, blowing thick clouds of smoke into the clear, fresh mountain air. After a long pause, Rigonaldo spoke slowly, his words poisoned with hatred and contempt. "You know Oso?" he began. "That despicable *worm* . . . Cruz . . . he has no soul." He stopped, glancing directly into Oso's eyes. "Not like our motherland . . . Our country has a very old and ancient soul. It is older than that man realizes."

Oso listened attentively, afraid to even blink.

"He thinks our history began when the Americans first came here," Rigonaldo went on, now talking to the woods. "But he is wrong . . .

Criminally wrong." He spat each word. He clenched his fist. "Somebody in this country has to make him come to terms with our reality." He looked at Oso. "Somebody has to stop him. That is our calling, you know. That is our reason to be."

Oso lowered his head. He had failed. But he was encouraged by his certainty that a man like Rigonaldo would not be permanently stopped by an operation gone wrong. He knew there would be another chance to do something to have an impact. Rigonaldo always used that word.

Of all the recent governors of Puerto Rico, Elison Cruz was the most determined to capitulate to the American occupiers. September Twenty-third believed that. Rigonaldo believed that. The up-coming plebiscite was meant to give Cruz and statehood a victory, which the terrorists believed would be the ultimate and most egregious act of American aggression against the Puerto Rican people. That was the undeniable truth. Rigonaldo was willing to kill and give his life to stop that from happening. Oso and the rest of the cell were also prepared to kill and to fight until death to stop such an abomination. And they were up to the task. Their greatest proof of it was the fact that they had daringly challenged the United States empire and its collaborators in the Puerto Rican colony, and that they were still alive *and* free.

For many years, Rigonaldo and the cell had evaded capture. And September Twenty-third had become a legendary organization with a cult-type following, especially among intellectuals and college students. The success and the resolve of the cell represented for them the ancient struggle of the Puerto Rican people against colonial rule: first by the Spanish empire, then by the United States. If there was ever a need for a clandestine, subversive movement, this was indeed the time, when the President and the Congress of the United States had committed themselves to enforce a vote on statehood. This was indeed a crucial time in the history of Puerto Rico.

"Let's go," Rigonaldo said abruptly. "We have work to do."

He led the way through the mud and into the house. He ordered coffee. Luna got up to make it for all the men. They sat at the small table near the kitchen to plan their next move. Luna would join them soon. Rigonaldo's freedom movement was said to be inclusive of women too. That is why she was there. But the first priority of the liberation now was only one man: Elison Cruz. According to Rigonaldo, in order to stop this governor, Cruz needed to be either killed or badly shaken. That was their manifest destiny. For the sake of the motherland. There was no other way. There was no other option.

Chapter 4

Karen Pérez was at her office in the building of WSTN Channel Four in Santurce, a suburb of metropolitan San Juan. She was seated on a swivel chair behind her messy desk, glancing at a television set on top of a long bookshelf crowded with samples of the many trophies and awards she had collected as a journalist. She had just finished a phone call and could pay more attention now to her own report running on the ten p.m. newscast.

After the footage of the shooting's aftermath, she had taped a segment with supporters of September Twenty-third at the University of Puerto Rico in Rio Piedras. This would be followed by an exclusive interview with Senator Orlando Tonos, an unapologetic leftist who had been elected as an independent candidate on a platform to expose government corruption. Tonos was currently the only senator who did not belong to any of the three major political parties of Puerto Rico: the Statehood Party (SP), the Commonwealth Party (CP) and the Independence Party (IP). Though he was a controversial figure in Puerto Rican politics, he had nevertheless gained the status of a folk hero. He promised to uncover corruption and he delivered.

The students at UPR in the report were fiercely rebellious and hostile. Their faces were hidden under black and red handkerchiefs as they chanted, "Death to the traitors! Life for the motherland!" while jumping excitedly around a burning American flag.

"Every patriot is a member of September Twenty-third!" the student leader said, speaking aggressively into Karen's microphone. "We are with Rigonaldo until death!"

"Aren't you expressing support for a terrorist act?" Karen asked, yelling amidst the shouts of the crowd.

"We are not terrorists! We are patriots!" the young man concluded. As if on cue, the rest of the students joined in to chant, *"Somos patriotas, no terroristas! Que viva el comandante Rigonaldo!"* (We are patriots, not terrorists! Long live commander Rigonaldo!).

The video now showed Karen speaking from the steps of the capitol building in San Juan where she introduced Senator Tonos's segment. She cut to the cramped, small office of the Senator on the basement floor of the capitol building.

"Senator Tonos," she said, "what is the meaning of today's events?"

The Senator was soft spoken and looked directly into the eyes of his interviewer through the top of his silver-framed spectacles. At fifty-five, he held a thin, five-feet tall frame, white skin, and closely cropped black hair which matched his deep, black eyes and thick, black eyebrows. He was neatly dressed in navy blue pants, a starched white long sleeve shirt and his trademark bow tie. Behind him, two framed paintings of Betánces and Albizu, independence icons of Puerto Rico, and a huge Puerto Rican flag on the wall, served as his usual background props.

"Well," Tonos began, "the first thing I should tell you is that what happened today didn't surprise me in the least. This governor has pushed the opposition into a vicious trap . . . to the edge."

Karen nodded for him to go on.

"Just remember our history . . . The 1950's, when former Governor Muñoz was at the peak of his power. Think about it. He made us swallow this U.S. Commonwealth *embeleco* (imbroglio) with the help of his powerful American friends. And we got stuck with the Commonwealth until this very day in the twenty-first century. But, what did the patriots of this country do at that time?" he asked and then answered himself. "They put up a hell of a fight. That's what. They do not teach you that in grade school, of course, but there were violent nationalist uprisings all over the island. And then there was the attempt against Muñoz's life, the attempt against President Truman at Blair House and, of course, the shooting within the U.S. Capitol when armed nationalists attacked the U.S. House of Representatives and wounded five Congressmen. I think history is repeating itself today."

"Why Senator?" Karen asked softly.

"Well," Tonos said waving his hand, feeling he was repeating himself. "As I said, in the 1950's they imposed the Commonwealth amidst a surge of violent opposition. Today, Governor Elison Cruz wants to impose statehood on Puerto Rico and he is facing the same opposition that Governor Muñoz encountered. There are far too many people in this country who favor independence and who will not tolerate the imposition of statehood."

"But Senator," Karen noted, "in every election for the last several decades the independence option has never obtained more than five percent of the popular vote. How do you explain . . . ?"

"Yes we are a minority," Tonos cut her off. "But we are a considerable minority. A minority that cannot be ignored." Tonos emphasized each word. "And that is what this governor is trying to do . . . Just look at the behavior of Governor Cruz today. His arrogance." Contemptuously, he removed his glasses. "One of his aides is killed, an officer of the law is wounded, and what is Cruz doing hours later?" He paused. "He is in Condado with his rich friends, smiling to the cameras as if nothing has happened. And he completely ignores the press who were trying to get a reaction from him about the events of today. He completely ignores the press who are trying to inform the people." Karen knew. She was there. Tonos went on. "But, to be honest with you Karen, I don't think Cruz will be able to continue ignoring the people of this country . . ."

"And the opposition," Karen pointed out.

"Nor the opposition. That is correct."

"Senator," Karen said, "do you think Rigonaldo Pastrana and September Twenty-third are behind today's attempt against the life of Governor Cruz?"

"I don't know," Tonos said carefully. "We don't know that . . . That was information that came from the office of Police Superintendent Calero . . . But he hasn't explained to the public how he reached that conclusion because he hasn't talked to the press either. And they were both together in Condado this afternoon. Cruz and Calero. The dynamic duo. Like Batman and Robin." There was not a trace of a smirk on Tonos's face.

Karen repressed a smile and asked, "Are you, as your detractors like to say, apologizing for Rigonaldo Pastrana and September Twenty-third? Are you trying to sanitize the image of a known terrorist?"

Tonos was annoyed by the question and chose to be sharp in his response. "Rigonaldo Pastrana," he said emphatically, "is a patriot, not a terrorist!" That was the end of the interview.

Karen's phone rang. She reached for a remote control and lowered the volume of the TV set. She picked up the phone. "This is Karen," she said softly.

"Can I see you for a minute?" asked the male voice on the other end. It was Emilio Durcal, the news director of the Channel Four newscast.

"Sure. I'll be right over."

She hung up the phone and stood up. Instinctively, she grabbed her mug from her desk and poured some coffee into it. She kept her coffeepot on a small table underneath a huge, black-and-white official publicity photo of herself on the wall. She had several other pictures with her fellow staff members at the station: Tonio, her young editor and cameraman; Leida Rosado and Vidal Monge, the veteran anchors of the newscast; Emilio Durcal, the news director; Elizabeth Vega, Delia Cordero and Mariano Cintrón, her fellow senior field reporters; and a huge group picture with the whole staff. The Channel Four newscast was a big, happy family.

She sipped some coffee and walked out of her office, immediately stepping into the spacious newsroom. At this hour, most desks were empty, some with their computer terminals left on by staff members who were either careless or too busy to bother shutting them down.

Karen walked a few steps to Durcal's door, which was open. She peeked in and knocked softly on the doorframe. He was behind his desk talking on the phone. He motioned her to come in and said, "Sit down, please," and continued with his phone call. Karen had a feeling that Durcal was up to something. After having worked together for over a decade, they both had a way of knowing each other's intentions.

She entered the office and sat down on a soft chair facing his large, cluttered desk. Nonchalantly, she sipped her coffee and studied him while he spoke almost secretively to whomever it was he was talking to. Emilio Durcal was a veteran, respected newsman on the island of Puerto Rico. That, despite the fact he was an expatriate from Spain. He had lived in Puerto Rico for most of his sixty-eight-years of age, though he received his education in Spain – the Mother Country, as he liked to remind anyone who would listen. Decades in the Caribbean, however, had not erased his peculiar Catalan accent, which he loved to exaggerate when he spoke. He loved being Spanish but he shared a passion for Puerto Rico. It was not lost on him that, at one time, the island had been an important colony of the mighty Spanish Empire. Durcal felt he was himself a metaphor of the Old Glory of Spain. He was balding on top of his head, the white hair that was left was neatly kept and combed, his eyes had required thick glasses since a time he could not remember, and his old, short physique was nevertheless healthy. He could live another hundred years with the help of the eleven-thousand virgins and a few patron saints. The same virgins and saints that had kept Spain a colonial power in Puerto Rico for four-hundred years. Like Spain, which had gone from world power to being an important presence in modern Europe, Durcal saw himself as an old, wise and important presence in modern-day Puerto Rico.

Karen paid no particular attention to Durcal's phone conversation and instead glanced around the office as was usual for her, concentrating on the eight-by-ten color and black and white pictures Durcal kept on his walls. There he was, in various stages of youth and seniority, with every single elected governor of Puerto Rico, including Elison Cruz. And there were other photos with senators and representatives and other influential political figures of the island. And there he was with Fidel Castro of Cuba, Joaquín Balaguer of the Dominican Republic, Violeta Chamorro of Nicaragua, Pedro Salinas de Gortari of Mexico and Alan García of Peru. But Karen's favorite pictures were the ones with Puerto Rican artists and entertainers – singers, actors, painters – most of whom were identified with the political left. Most of them discreet – and not so discreet – *independentistas*, like her.

Durcal said thank you and good night to his caller and put down the telephone. "Quite a day, wasn't it?" he said with his best European smile.

"You're asking me?" Karen exclaimed as both laughed nervously, the day's events playing on their minds.

He asked, "Could you get Rigonaldo Pastrana to speak to us again?" The question was blunt and without a trace of the laughter that they had shared a few seconds earlier.

Karen had stopped laughing too. She sipped some coffee, her thoughts racing. She knew that this moment could come. She was just not expecting it now. It had been five years since her famous interview with the fugitive was taped at an undisclosed location. In the heart of the central mountains of the island, she always suspected. But all in all, it had not been an experience she looked forward to repeating. Back then, she and her cameraman had been blindfolded and transported in a vehicle for several hours before they finally reached Rigonaldo's hideout. Once on Rigonaldo's turf, the other people there wore masks. Spooky. And when they were done taping, they were again blindfolded and forced to endure another arduous and unpleasant car ride until they finally ended up at the surfing town of Rincón on the west coast, some ninety miles from San Juan. She had the station send its helicopter to "rescue" her from the most exhausting day of her life. But, there were other obstacles to Durcal's request.

"Well," she began calmly, "I don't know." She waited for a reaction from Durcal. When he said nothing, she said, "Basically, the way it works is that I don't contact them . . . they contact me."

For a few seconds there was silence. Karen was glad she brought coffee with her to appear occupied. She just sipped it and said nothing.

"Can't Tonos arrange something?" Durcal said, grinning and serious at the same time. "I mean, he talks as if they were buddies." He paused. "Just kidding."

"I don't think so . . . No," Karen said, nervously. "If Tonos knows how to contact Rigonaldo, he will not say it. Especially not to me. I'm still press, you know."

Durcal nodded. He knew that, of course. But he also loved Puerto Rican political intrigue. He knew a contact to the fugitive would have had to have been made at that time. He, however, knew better not to have ever asked Karen about it. And she certainly never talked about it. To anybody. Tonight Durcal had planted a seed. That is how he saw it.

That is all he needed to do to get his best field reporter interested in a story.

"Okay," he said softly. "I just had an idea and thought about sharing it with you."

"I understand," Karen said. "Maybe I'll try to put the word out that I want the interview." She paused. "But, as I said, the way it works is that I don't contact them, they contact me."

"I know Karen. I just thought to ask."

With that, Karen nodded and left his office and walked back to hers. This was definitely the end of her working day. A day which had started with a horrendous shooting against the governor of Puerto Rico, and ended with the future possibility of her facing the man who gave the order to do it. She was definitely done for the day.

She took a minute to grab her shoulder bag and a few documents to take home, and then turned off the light in her office and walked out. She crossed the newsroom saying the occasional goodnight to any staffer working late. After walking through a series of dimly lit corridors and down a set of stairs, she finally reached the lobby and exited the building into the parking lot. It was a terribly hot, humid night. She immediately missed her air-conditioned office. She rummaged through her bag and found the keys to her green, late-model Saab. She got into her car, started the engine and rushed to turn the air conditioner on to high. She sighed in pleasure as the cool air hit her body. When she glanced at her face in the rearview mirror, she felt amusedly ashamed of herself. It struck her as ironic that she was a Puerto Rican *independentista* who could not stand the hot Puerto Rican weather. Was that why so many *independentistas* ended up in New York City? she asked herself. Of course not. Anyway, she knew her critics on the left already thought she was a proud member of the *bourgeoise*. But, you know what? She did not give a damn about what her critics said. She was Karen Pérez. The one and only.

Empowered by her self-awareness, she sped out of the station's parking lot waving goodbye to Pablo, the nightwatch at the security guard's post. She was so immersed in thought that she did not see the black vehicle with two men in dark suits that began to follow her as soon as she got out of the station. The vehicle kept a discreet distance all through the twenty-minute ride from Santurce to Karen's house in the exclusive sector of Miramar, also in metropolitan San Juan. The men watched her get out of her car and disappear through the front door of her elegant, white-stucco house. They watched the house for a few hours until it was their time to go. Tomorrow, as planned, they would follow her everywhere she went.

Friday, October 26

Chapter 5

As usual, Cruz awoke early in the morning and after a light breakfast with Ana María, he went downstairs to his office. Damaris was there waiting for him with a fresh cup of coffee and the day's newspapers neatly placed on his desk. The headline of *El Nuevo Sol* caught his immediate attention: "SHOTS FIRED AT CRUZ. ONE DEAD. ONE WOUNDED. 'YOU HAVE TO RESIGN' SAYS THE FIRST LADY."

"Great!" he said disgustedly as he opened the paper to read the story. He scanned through the article and immediately grabbed the telephone and punched the three numbers to Ana María's office. She answered on the first ring.

"Hi honey," Cruz said softly. "Have you seen *El Nuevo Sol*?"

"I saw it Elison," she quickly said. "It's horrible."

"I know," he agreed.

"How did they get that there?" she asked puzzled.

"I have no idea, hon', but you'll have to deny it. This is exactly what our enemies want."

"Of course."

"We'll do it together," Cruz said, reaching for his leather-bound calendar for official activities. He opened the page for today. "I'll tell Almeda to call a press conference for ten this morning and we'll be there together. How is your schedule?"

"Ten is fine."

"Good. Bye hon.'"

They both hung up. Cruz was also puzzled by the audacity of the press and wondered about leaks. This sort of news headline was evidence to him that the office of the governor had the least amount of privacy than that of any other public figure in the country.

Ana María was also furious about the report and tried to figure out how it was possible that *El Nuevo Sol* had gotten the story. It was now clear to her why, at a little after eight in the morning, every media outlet on the island seemed to be calling her office. She brusquely instructed Virginia, her middle-aged secretary, to say she was unavailable for comment at the moment but that there would be a press conference at ten in the morning.

Then, Marta Borja called. They had spoken yesterday after the shooting. Marta was extremely concerned for the Cruzes. She had also confessed she felt somewhat responsible for the incident, given the fact that she had been the organizer of the event. Ana María had reassured her that something like that could have happened anywhere, at anytime.

Ana María spoke to her friend with kindness and interest. "Hi, Marta," she said. "What's up?"

"I was thinking of you dear," Marta said. "Ricardo and I just got back from our morning walk on the beach and . . ."

"Oh, a walk on the beach," Ana María said daydreaming. "I think that's exactly what Elison and I need. I envy you sometimes, you know. We cannot do that without being followed by a troop of security and a pack of reporters. It kills the intimacy of the moment."

"Well, I think I know what you mean, which is why I'm calling. I read the papers today. I feel for the two of you. You two must be exhausted, and I just thought I should take you up on that dinner invitation we spoke about yesterday at the hotel."

"Oh, that's so nice of you, Marta," Ana María said sincerely.

"I knew you'd be pleased. Let's make it for lunch. Tomorrow is Saturday and the weather will be nice so I thought about having a luncheon by the pool. Nothing big, of course. Just the four of us, very relaxed. We'll have time to talk and maybe sort things out a little."

"I think it will be good for us to relax a bit," Ana María said as an understatement. "I'm sure Elison will like the idea."

"Then let's do it honey. You two deserve a rest."

"Okay, Marta. Count on us, we'll be there. I'll talk to Elison right away and I'm sure he'll be thrilled."

"Great, dear. I'll see you tomorrow around noon."

"See you tomorrow."

Ana María hung up and walked a few doors down to Cruz's office. On her way, she ran into Almeda who was just arriving to work that morning. "Good morning Sam," she said casually. "Have you talked to Elison?"

"No, I'm just getting here."

"Come on," she told him, signaling with her hand for him to follow her.

They both entered Cruz's office and found him seated behind his desk.

"Oh, hi Sam," Cruz addressed his aide. "Did you see this?" He showed him the front page of *El Nuevo Sol.*

"I sure did," Almeda said seriously. "What are you going to do?"

"Well," Cruz said, "we will call a press conference for ten a.m. today and both the First Lady and I will stand together and tell the country that this is nonsense. No one," he said angrily, "absolutely no one in this house has talked or will talk about resignation. The story is absolutely false. That's what we are going to do."

"That seems like the right thing to do, sir," Almeda agreed firmly.

"Good," Cruz said, tossing the paper back on his desk.

"Sam," Ana María said, "what do we know about Alan's funeral arrangements?"

"Monday. Nine in the morning," Almeda informed her. "I have confirmed the attendance of both of you."

"We'll be there, of course," Cruz said.

For a second, guilt came to the mind of the Cruzes. Alan de Jesús was not supposed to die. Almeda lowered his head, understanding the Governor and First Lady's silence, and glanced at his Rolex. He quickly requested to be excused, left the room, and walked down the hall to his office.

"Marta Borja called," Ana María said softly.

"How is she doing?" Cruz asked.

"She's fine. I think she still feels guilty about yesterday since she organized the whole thing."

"She has nothing to feel guilty about," Cruz said, dismissing the idea and thinking about his own sense of guilt.

"I told her. She'll be okay. She wants to have us for lunch tomorrow around noon. Just her, Ricardo, and us. I told her we'd be there."

"Fine, that's fine with me."

"Good. I knew you'd like the idea."

"Let me write that down," Cruz said, reaching for his calendar for private activities.

Ana María blew him a kiss and said, "I'll see you at ten." She returned to her office.

As Cruz was writing in his calendar book, Damaris's voice came over the intercom.

"Mr. Governor," she said in her most official tone. "I have Marcos González on line five."

The president of the Statehood Party did not usually call so early in the morning. But the call did not surprise Cruz. He knew the resignation story in *El Nuevo Sol* would cause a stir within the party's ranks.

"Put him on," Cruz ordered, and at once, the phone rang, line five blinking. Cruz punched the line on the first ring and spoke with a strong, loud voice.

"The story is absolutely false, Marcos," Cruz said quickly. "Ana María never said such a thing. She is one-hundred percent behind me."

"It's good to know that, Elison," González said softly.

"Was that what you wanted to talk to me about?"

"Well, yes. We can't have that sort of thing. Not at this time. Not at any time."

"I agree, Marcos," Cruz assured him. "We are taking care of it. Press conference at ten this morning. You are invited."

"No, no. It's okay," González said. "As long as you effectively kill these resignation rumors, I don't think I need to be there."

"Good enough."

"Elison," González said dramatically, "we are probably at the most critical time in the history of Puerto Rico. We can't allow anything to get in our way."

"Marcos, have I ever let you or the party down?"

"No."

"Good. So don't worry. We are almost there. We are going to win this plebiscite. That's my only focus at this moment."

By the time the governor ended the call with González, the Statehood Party's president was reassured that Elison Cruz was solidly in charge. That is what he was elected for. The opposition would be defeated. And the terrorists would be caught. Puerto Rico would remain at peace with the statehooders at the helm. Anyone who believed otherwise was a fool.

Chapter 6

At six in the afternoon, Rigonaldo, Luna, Oso and Teco were in front of the television watching the evening news. They were amused by the report on Cruz's ten a.m. press conference where he and the First Lady denied any talk of resignation. But more amusing still was Cruz's warning to the "terrorists" that their days of acting with impunity were numbered.

The wall-phone in the kitchen rang and Luna got up to answer it. "Hello," she said, still trying to glance at the TV set in the living room.

The male voice on the other end of the line spoke rapidly and almost in a whisper. "He'll be at 365 Italia Street in Condado . . . Tomorrow at noon."

Luna's eyes widened and she immediately ignored the television. "Hold on," she said, hurriedly reaching for a pen and paper.

"It's a private residence," the informant continued. "Marta Borja's home."

"What else can you tell . . . ?" Luna began asking.

"That's all," the man cut her off.

"That's all?"

"Yes, that's all," the man said rudely and hung up.

The dial tone sounded in Luna's ear. She drew a conspiratorial smirk on her face, put the receiver in its cradle and came back to the living room. "Well," she said grinning, "it seems the chicken is home to roost."

She got everyone's attention.

"What is it?" Rigonaldo asked expectantly.

"Tomorrow at noon, our dear friend the Governor, will be at 365 Italia Street, the private residence of Marta Borja in Condado," Luna reported.

"Oh, I know about that rich bitch," Oso said to the group.

"Good," Rigonaldo said, getting up from the couch and turning off the TV set. "Let's get to work then. Oso and Teco, go to Condado now and find out what it takes to assault the residence, and which is the best getaway."

Oso and Teco jumped to their feet. Teco went into the kitchen and got the keys to their red Montero.

"And get Tino," Rigonaldo ordered.

Tino was a young "troubleshooter" for September Twenty-third. That's how Rigonaldo liked to describe the many idealistic university students who worked with the cell upon request.

"Will do," Oso said, following Teco out the door.

From the top of the mountains in the Guarite Forest, the sky looked clear and illuminated by millions of stars. Oso and Teco walked to the garage, jumped into the Montero – Teco driving – and lit the first of many cigarettes they would smoke during the hour and a half drive to the affluent Condado neighborhood in metropolitan San Juan.

This new operation sounded exciting. Bloodshed in the snobbish, rich neighborhood of Condado. The cell's informant knew how to justify all the money he was being paid to snitch for.

Chapter 7

Karen Pérez was already at her house. It was a little after seven p.m. She had gone home earlier than usual after a day spent reporting on the governor's activities. The ten a.m. press conference had been tedious and long. According to the governor, the resignation story was false, and he was decidedly in charge. The First Lady stressed her support for the Governor and found time to give an update on her new "second chance" campaign affecting people with mental illness who are first-time criminal offenders. Even Police Superintendent Calero showed up to talk about the investigation of the shooting incident. He confirmed that September Twenty-third had claimed responsibility for the assassination attempt. In the group's usual fashion, a faxed message had been sent to police headquarters from an office supply shop in Mayagüez, a coastal town on the western end of the island. Calero also launched an attack on Senator Orlando Tonos for calling Rigonaldo a "patriot." He dramatically produced a picture of the Senator and the fugitive together. "A disgrace," he called it, but refused to say if the picture had been taken before or after Rigonaldo became a fugitive. Cruz accused Tonos of "abusing the democratic process."

The longer part of the press conference was dedicated to the plebiscite of November third. "You cannot stop history from happening," Cruz had stated. He was also eager to point out that the *independentista* opposition to the plebiscite had no credibility whatsoever, given the fact that the Independence Party was participating in the historic vote. He would not bow down to the capricious wishes of a handful of "radicals" and "anarchists" who represented less than "zero percent" of the people of Puerto Rico. Cruz was not too convincing, however, when he said that the "terrorists' days of impunity were numbered."

After showering, Karen stood in front of her bathroom mirror to comb her recently relaxed and brown-dyed hair. She used to keep her hair untouched with her natural curls, but after much pondering on the idea, she decided she wanted a change. White women with straight hair got perms and turned curly. No racial questions asked. So, she did it on the same note. A little feminine vanity. She was amused, however, by the gossip columnists who wrote about her new "image," making sure that anyone who had not noticed her new hairdo would notice it. "KAREN WENT STRAIGHT!" quipped a gossip headline. "I didn't know I was a lesbian," Karen had said to that one, thinking about her many lesbian friends.

She finished with her hair, got into a thick white bathrobe and went into the kitchen to prepare a sandwich and fresh coffee. When she finished preparing her light dinner, she took it to the living room. She sat on a yellow couch facing a large glass and mahogany round table with her cordless phone on top of it. She was surrounded by fine locally handcrafted furniture and by Puerto Rican art hanging on the tall, white walls. She seemed to have a piece of artwork by each important native painter. And each piece was personal since she was a friend of each of the artists whose works adorned her walls.

She was a single woman with many, many friends, especially among the power elite of the island. She claimed, nevertheless, not to have much time for romance. Her power and celebrity threatened most men she had dated. But she loved her job, her profession and what she had accomplished so far. She knew that when the right person came along, she'd be ready.

She also had enemies. Most of them were disgraced public servants who had been caught in dubious and criminal endeavors committed during their public duties. And she had every single broadcast journalism award given on the island to prove it. One award for each enemy she had made, she liked to point out.

Tonight she was set on interviewing Rigonaldo Pastrana once again. Durcal's interest had awakened her own interest in the story, even though she was aware that it sounded wicked to give airtime to a man who had been named the country's number one criminal. But to her, those were the perils of the Puerto Rican political dilemma and of the political left. Something she was fully acquainted with.

In her days as a student of journalism at the University of Puerto Rico, she had been a member of several leftist organizations and had edited a radical, socialist-*independentista* student newspaper. That is who she had been when she was younger. Today, like many others before her, she had become a centrist *independentista* intellectual who also happened to be a respected journalist. Yes, she favored independence for the island, but she believed in the electoral process. Her memories of college, however, allowed her to comprehend those who, like Rigonaldo Pastrana, did not believe in elections. She still harbored certain respect for those *independentistas* who had declared war on the United States. She was, if anything, ambivalent about the American nation.

She had lived in the United States during a one-year internship at the University of Connecticut, had taken a train ride to Washington, D.C. to see the White House, and had dated, several years ago, an African-American businessman from California. That was it. In the meantime, she managed to learn fluent English and had subscriptions to the *Christian Science Monitor*, the *New York Times*, the *Miami Herald*, *Time*, *Newsweek*, *U.S. News & World Report* and to many more U.S. publications. She knew she was a little "colonized." And, like almost every single journalist on the island, she subscribed to the U.S. cable system. She loved CNN, the History Channel and A&E. In her mind, she entertained the possibility of a Puerto Rican independent republic with friendly relations with the United States. This was attainable, if not desirable.

She finished her sandwich, got more coffee from the kitchen and sat back on the couch. This time she grabbed her cordless phone and sat there debating what to do and how to do it. "I don't contact them, they contact me," she had said. But was that the whole truth? Five years ago, it had taken her a long while to figure out how the first interview with Rigonaldo had come about. Yes, they contacted her. But, had it been out of the blue? She thought not. It happened after she had mentioned to a "friend" that she wanted to meet Rigonaldo. That is what she always thought had happened. And now, she wanted to touch base with that friend whom she had not spoken to in maybe two years. In total silence, she tightly held the phone in her hand, thinking whether she should make the phone call.

*　　*　　*

The old Domingo Montalvo, the illustrious intellectual who was a tenured professor of Puerto Rican history at the University of Puerto Rico, was at his small apartment in the Santa Rita *urbanización* (residential community) right off the UPR campus. That's where most students and professors lived. He sat by a little table with a decorative lamp in his cramped study, a small room surrounded by crowded, floor-to-ceiling bookshelves. At this very moment he was finishing up the final pages of the lecture he would give on Monday morning to his students in his course, "*Non-Spanish European Presence in Puerto Rico: Sixteenth to Eighteenth Centuries.*"

Through his thick reading glasses, his eyes were set on his paper, which he wrote in longhand; a defiant sign of his personal aversion to computers, which he never used, because he considered them a "decadent vice" of the capitalist world. He was an old man set in his own ways of doing things. Having the weekends free to read for pleasure was one of them. That is why finishing his lecture this Friday night was important to him. And that is why, when his telephone rang in the other room, he cursed like an old bull. He was disturbed by the distraction and decided to ignore it. To no avail.

The telephone kept ringing. His hope that the caller give up was shattered. And he could not let "the machine pick up" because he did not have a telephone answering machine either. He was against those too.

Furious and annoyed, he put his pen, writing pad and his glasses down on the table. He got up with some effort, sign of old age, and walked towards his modest living room thinking that whoever it is that was calling would have to be damn quick. And if it was a student, he or she would not hear the end of it.

"Hello!" he said with an edge.

"Good evening, Domingo?" It was not a student. "This is Karen."

"Karen!" he exclaimed, collapsing onto a sofa seat and forgetting his thoughts about a quick call. "I'll be darned! How are you, superstar?"

Karen laughed loudly and said, "I'm fine, just fine. How are you? I should ask."

"Fairly well. Fairly well. My God, it seems like an eternity since we last spoke."

"I know. I'm terrible at keeping in touch. I'm ashamed of myself," she said apologetically.

"Well," he dismissed the apology, "don't be ashamed. I guess I do not keep in touch with old friends as I should either. How have you been lately?"

"To be honest Domingo, dead tired and dead busy."

"I believe you, certainly. With everything that is going on, that is probably an understatement."

"Oh well," she sighed. "This is the life that I chose so I shouldn't complain."

"Are they treating you well at the station? I hear those television types can be a pain sometimes."

"Well, I can't complain. I'm still covering Fortaleza for the most part. And I have Tonio, who is an excellent cameraman and editor. We make a good team. Long hours, though. I'm out of here by eight in the morning and usually don't come back until ten-thirty at night."

"My dear," he said grinning, "you should have chosen the academia. You are home by four p.m., you get the summers off and, once you are tenured, they cannot fire you. In the classroom you are a God."

"I know." She paused. "Well, it's not that bad for me." How can I ask him about Rigonaldo, she thought. "Tell me Domingo, how are things going for you? Are you keeping yourself abreast with what is happening?"

"You mean that that *snake*, Cruz, is still alive?" he asked bluntly.

She repressed a smile. "Jesus Christ, Domingo, that was very close for him. I was there, you know," she said with sincere concern.

"I know. I saw you on the news."

"What do you think is going to happen?"

"What do I think?" he asked rhetorically. "Well, let me tell you this. In eight days we are going to have that damn plebiscite, and statehood is going to win – because this country is moving to the right with every passing day – and when statehood wins, all hell is going to break loose. The Americans will not know what hit them. That mess in Iraq is going to look like a picnic, and the *yanquis* will pull their hair out until they go bald. I'm not sure that they know what they are getting into here. And I can't stop asking myself, what in God's name do they see in Puerto Rico? Why do they want us? This just doesn't make any sense."

"Are you voting in the plebiscite?"

"Hell no!"

She laughed.

"Boycotting that thing," he said, "is a stronger statement than being a part of it. You know me."

She felt she had reached her moment and asked, "Have you known anything about Rigonaldo?"

Domingo lost his breath for a second. "Me?" he said nervously. "No . . . nothing . . . nobody knows anything about him . . . He's like a ghost."

"The station wants him on again," she finally revealed.

Silence. Then, "I see," Domingo said simply.

"My boss talked to me yesterday."

"Well," he said matter-of-factly, "your boss is a very audacious man."

Karen said nothing.

"And you too," Domingo continued. "A very audacious woman, that is."

"I guess I am. But believe me, I don't know how we are going to do this."

Domingo pondered her frustration for a moment. "Okay, Karen," he finally said. "Let me tell you this. I do not want to sound paranoid, but every time that Rigonaldo sneezes, the FBI goes ballistic and begins to wiretap the telephones of every single decent individual who roams about in this country. It's a joke, for Christ's sake!" He laughed. "Do you understand? Do you follow what I'm saying?"

"Yes, I definitely understand," she said, knowing she needed to decode his words.

"As for me," he went on, "I don't care anymore. I honestly do not give a shit. I am too old to be concerned about people listening to my phone conversations. After all, my life is very boring nowadays. After you pass sixty there seems to be no more fun."

Karen laughed and said, "Oh, don't say that, Domingo. You are making me afraid to grow old."

"Don't listen to me, young woman. Actually, I'm not serious. There is life after sixty. Believe me."

"That sounds more like you."

"Hey, who knows if I'll find me an old lady who'll marry me. But she has to love books. That's my only demand."

"I'll keep my eyes open."

"Thank you, my dear."

"Okay, listen, I won't keep you any longer. It was nice talking to you."

"It was nice to hear from you too," he reciprocated. "And listen, don't be discouraged. We will keep in touch with you. Do you follow me?"

"Yes, of course," Karen said simply.

"Okay, bye my dear," he said in conclusion.

"Bye Domingo," she said, ending the call.

That was fast, Karen thought as she found herself free of the pressure she had felt before making the call. She pondered Domingo's concerns about the FBI bugging phones. Of course, she told herself. Five years ago, she'd had her very own showdown with the FBI when she was bullied and harassed in their attempt to get her to reveal information about how she had gained access to Rigonaldo. She adamantly refused to give them any information about her sources and got the support of the station when they took her to court to make her talk. The FBI lost the case, and Karen became a heroine of a free press on the island. So today, she perfectly understood Domingo's caution when speaking on the phone.

"Okay," she said aloud. "Done." She reached for the remote control of her thirty-inch TV and pushed the on button. The TV came on. Ednita Nazario was performing. She recognized the song, *Lloviendo Flores*. I love Ednita, she thought.

Tomorrow, Saturday, Karen planned to sleep all day. For now, she stared at the TV trying to concentrate and not think about work. She needed a rest.

Chapter 8

Teco drove by 365 Italia Street, in the exclusive neighborhood of Condado, for the third time. The street was dimly lit. Scattered palm trees and flower beds stood in front of the manicured lawns of the Art Deco beachfront mansions. There was a huge residence right across from the home of Marta and Ricardo Borja. Teco thought it was likely that the people in that house would notice any unusual activity at the Borja's home. But this was in no way a deterrent to their plan to assault the house tomorrow. Only a concern.

"We'll need two vehicles to do this," Teco said, a cigarette dangling from his lips.

"I agree," Oso responded. "We'll take this car and the white van."

"I think we'll have it easy," Teco said confidently.

Oso said nothing. Killing a public figure was never easy. But that is how Teco was. Despite being in his forties, like Oso and Luna, Teco was not the brightest man available and he sometimes lacked insight into what it took to do the work of September Twenty-third. He was a good accessory, though, and he had good relations with foreign communists, one of the sources of financing for the operations of the cell, besides the loot from bank and armored car robberies.

"Let's check Rosales Street again," Oso ordered.

They had chosen Rosales Street a few blocks away, because it was a partially deserted street that housed several abandoned homes. They had identified the spot where they would park their getaway vehicle. Once they assaulted the Borja home and the governor was dead, they would change vehicles. They would drive away in the van, and the red

Montero would be equipped with a time-set explosive that would fully destroy it. Tomorrow, Condado would be known for more than just tourists, rich homes and glittering hotels and casinos.

After driving down Rosales Street again and rehearsing their escape route for the third time, the terrorists were confident that they had a good plan. Now the adrenaline was beginning to rush with expectations. They simply could not wait till tomorrow.

"Let's get Tino," Oso said, as he lit one of his unfiltered Camels.

"Let's get Tino," Teco repeated in a sing-song voice. "He's gonna love this one, that kid." He was always amused by the youthful idealism of the college kid they were about to recruit.

Oso said nothing. He personally did not like when college kids got involved in the hands-on work of September Twenty-third. But that is how Rigonaldo wanted it. And Oso realized they sometimes needed the extra help. The cell could not do everything alone. That was just the way it was.

Oso's silence prompted a smirk on Teco's face. They did not speak another word all the way to Santa Rita, the college neighborhood off the campus of the University of Puerto Rico, where Tino lived.

Let's get Tino.

Saturday, October 27

Chapter 9

Marta and Ricardo Borja woke up early as usual to their morning ritual of walking barefoot on the stretch of beach behind their house in Condado. It was a perfect day for a quiet barbecue on their patio by the pool. The sky was clear, the sun was out, and a cool breeze competed with the warm day's temperature.

A long, six-foot tall concrete wall served as a divider between the beachfront and the Borjas' manicured back patio. After their morning stroll along the beach, the Borjas returned to their residence by pushing open a thick, heavy wooden door that connected the beach to their back patio. Marta and Ricardo inspected the area. Everything was where it was supposed to be: the barbecue grill, the charcoal bags, the Rattan furniture, the wrought-iron tables, the checkered table cloths. The pool was clean. The many flowers and plants had been watered. They would only need minor preparations to get the patio ready for the Governor and the First Lady.

In Fortaleza, a relaxed Governor Cruz, wearing long khaki pants and a white *guayabera* shirt, was at his desk in the executive office reviewing some documents. Almeda had been asked to come to work for a few hours and he arrived at nine-thirty.

For several hours, Cruz and Almeda reviewed official documents and went over the scheduled activities for the coming week. A high priority on the list was a late morning meeting on Monday with Grant Thompson, the U.S. Senate majority leader, who was also the author of the Puerto Rico Self-Determination Act mandating the status plebiscite on the island. Cruz was somewhat disappointed that Thompson's trip to the island was expected to be short. And the Senator had also scheduled meetings between himself and the presidents of the Commonwealth and Independence parties, thus limiting further the time Cruz could spend with him.

"We'll have to find a way to meet with Thompson for more than just forty-five minutes," Cruz said.

"I'll let them know we want more time," Almeda said, making a note on a yellow legal pad.

Cruz was about to speak when suddenly, Ana María, wearing a simple yellow skirt and white blouse, entered the office. "Surprise!" she said, as a cute little girl in a flowered dress came in behind her. It was Alejandra Colón, the eight-year-old daughter of Aida Colón, Ana María's older sister.

"Hi Uncle Elison," the girl said in a childish voice.

"Hi! Look at her!" Cruz exclaimed as Alejandra approached him to give him a bear hug. He kissed her on the cheek, took her in his arms and sat her on his lap. "Sam," he proudly said to Almeda, "meet Alejandra, our little princess."

"Hi, sweetie," Almeda said, smiling.

"Alejandra," Cruz said to the girl, "this is Samuel, a friend of mine and of Aunt Ana."

The girl bowed her head shyly and said, "Hi Samuel."

"Hi, Alejandra," Almeda replied.

"Well," Ana María announced, "the little princess is going to spend the afternoon with us."

"Oh, I'm happy to hear that," Cruz exclaimed.

"Mommy told me to behave good," Alejandra revealed.

"Well, how about that?" Cruz said, smiling and caressing the girl's hair.

"Well," Ana María said, "are you ready, honey?"

"Already?" Cruz looked genuinely surprised. "What time is it?"

"Time to go," Ana María said bossily. "It's quarter to twelve."

"Wow, time flies around here," Cruz said.

"Especially if it's Saturday, hon'," Ana María said matter-of-factly.

"Okay," Cruz said, glancing at Almeda who looked bored holding a batch of documents on his lap. "Sam, do you want to accompany us to the Borja's?"

"Oh, no, no," Almeda said quickly. "I have to catch up on some things."

Cruz got up, holding the girl in his arms, and told him politely, "Well, allow yourself to take a break."

"No, honestly." Almeda was equally polite. "I have a few things to take care of."

"Okay, it's your choice," Cruz said finally.

"Thank you for the invitation anyway. Enjoy yourselves."

"Thank you," Cruz said, and quickly began walking out of the office with Alejandra in tow, and Ana María just behind him.

"Bye now Sam," Ana María said as she went out the door.

Chapter 10

The Governor and First Lady left Fortaleza in a black limousine and a caravan of three unmarked vehicles. There were two security agents in each vehicle. Two state police officers on motorcycles led the way. That is what Cruz considered to be enough for a private outing. Police Superintendent Calero had grudgingly agreed.

It was a fifteen to twenty minute ride from La Fortaleza in Old San Juan to the Borja mansion in Condado. Alejandra spent the entire trip jumping from the laps of her uncle and aunt to the carpeted floor of the vehicle.

"Mommy bought me a new bathing suit," the girl said proudly.

"I know, sweetie," Ana María said, stroking her hair. "And you can play in the pool all day."

"Mommy doesn't have a pool," Alejandra complained.

Cruz and Ana María laughed at this.

"Well, honey," Ana María said, "I'm sure that when your mommy and daddy get a new house they will have a pool for you to play in. You just have to be a little bit patient."

"Patient?" Alejandra wondered, taking a second for a few thoughts. "Are you patient, Uncle Elison?"

Cruz smiled. "Yes sweetie, and so is Aunt Ana."

"Hmmm," Alejandra said, this time crawling to peek at the passing cars through the vehicle's black-tinted windows. "I wanna be patient too."

Cruz and Ana María stared at each other and smiled silently. Alejandra reminded them of when Anthony, their only son, was also that age. He was now a grownup nineteen-year-old. They had last spoken to him on Thursday when Ana María called him at his dorm at Yale University. And later that night, Anthony had called his father. The young man could not stop worrying about the safety of his dear parents.

Cruz observed Alejandra looking out the window and thought about lowering it down to let the girl enjoy the fresh tropical air. He promptly gave up on the idea, reminding himself that to do so would be a breach of security. He sighed. He did not want to push the issue of security any more than he had. And anyway, in a few minutes they would be out in the open air, enjoying the sun and the fresh ocean breeze. He was truly glad that Marta Borja had invited them to an afternoon by the pool in her home. Good. Good.

Chapter 11

The terrorists had gone through their last toll on Highway 52 about half an hour ago. They were now driving within the metropolitan area and would reach the Condado neighborhood within thirty-five minutes. Teco, Luna, and Tino, their young recruit for the operation, were driving in the red Montero. Oso was behind them in the white van. They communicated from vehicle to vehicle through cell phones.

As they came closer to their destination, the adrenaline and anxiety were apparent in their tense conversations. Repeatedly, they reviewed their plan to assault the Borja mansion. First, Luna would distract the agents likely to be outside, and kill them. They would shoot the door down, storm into the house, kill anyone who got in their way, find Cruz, and kill him. Then, they would speed to Rosales Street, abandon the Montero with the time-set bomb and escape in the van. They knew they couldn't spend more than a few minutes on the entire operation since they had all agreed that the neighbors would call the police once the first shots were fired. And, to their disadvantage, there was a police precinct nearby on Loiza Street which may or may not have been alerted about the presence of the Governor at the Borja residence.

"We have to make Rigonaldo happy," Luna said over the phone once they were finished reviewing their plan.

"He'll be happy," Oso replied, before ending the call and tossing the phone onto the passenger seat. We cannot screw up again, he told himself. With his eyes on the road and on his accomplices driving ahead of him, he lit a cigarette and once again played out the assault on the

Borja home in his mind. He was one of those people who believed that by thinking the right thoughts and using visualization, he would *create* the reality he wanted. That was a very appropriate technique for a man like him, he felt. Someone so dedicated to the business of making history.

Rigonaldo was certain that Cruz's assassination would stop the government from going ahead with the plebiscite. The *Puerto Rico Self-Determination Act*, approved by the Congress of the United States in a solid majority vote, included a clause allowing the cancellation of the plebiscite in the occurrence of *"Emergency or extraordinary circumstances, which hinder, deter, impede, interfere, obstruct, offset, preclude or thwart the fairness of the plebiscite. Such action to be exercised by the President of the United States or the Governor of Puerto Rico."* With Cruz suffering a violent death, Rigonaldo believed that the U.S. President would have no other option than to declare that the fairness of the election had been compromised. Not that Rigonaldo thought that this plebiscite was fair in any way whatsoever.

Oso kept driving and smoking furiously. He almost couldn't withstand the deep emotions that ran through him every time he realized that he was a part of a courageous pack of *patriotas* (patriots) that were about to change the course of history.

Chapter 12

The governor's motorcade had arrived at the Borja mansion. The two motorcycle cops and four security agents had positioned themselves in front of the house. The other two agents had done a quick search of the patio and inside premises. They settled at the beach side of the wooden door that led to the patio where the Cruzes and the Borjas had gathered. Through tiny wireless microphones attached to their suits' lapels, the agents on the beachfront communicated with their colleagues in front of the mansion.

Cruz could not have felt more relaxed on this extraordinarily clear and sunny day. He was animatedly talking with Ricardo Borja, who was wearing Bermuda shorts and a short sleeve, yellow cotton shirt. As he talked with the governor, Ricardo tended to several thick and tempting *churrasco* steaks on the barbecue grill.

Ana María was helping Alejandra change into her flowered bathing suit. Marta Borja and Lorena, her fifty-year-old live-in maid, were busy making trips between the kitchen and the patio bringing food and utensils to the tables by the pool. Soon, Ana María joined Marta and Lorena in the task.

"You know, honey," Marta was saying, "I strongly think I could use another live-in maid in this house."

"I hear you," Ana María said, smiling.

"Which makes me think," Marta went on, "of what we were talking about yesterday and I find myself dead with envy for you and your life in Fortaleza."

"Oh, believe me, after a few years you begin missing doing things yourself," Ana María said, a sense of nostalgia in her voice.

"I guess you're right. However, to tell you the truth, I had to fight with Ricardo to get us Lorena. He just didn't seem to realize what it took to care for a house like this."

"Well," Ana María said with a smirk on her face, "I have to tell you a secret."

"Which is?" Marta asked, filled with curiosity.

"Before Foraleza, we never had a live-in maid," Ana María revealed.

"You said what?" Marta stopped cold.

"I'm serious," Ana María said, smiling. "Before Elison became governor we never had a live-in maid."

"You never had a live-in maid in that big house of yours?" Marta asked, incredulous.

"Nope," Ana María said with a laugh. "I had some help, of course, but mostly I was just a regular housewife," she said proudly.

"You know, honey, appearances are deceiving," Marta said, as she remembered several parties she'd attended at the Cruzes' home in the affluent *urbanización* Torrimar in Guaynabo. She had mistakenly thought that the caterers were part of the Cruzes' house staff. "How come that fact never came out during the campaign?" she asked. "My dear, the housewives of this country would have given your husband a bigger landslide win."

Ana María laughed harder as the two reached the patio for the last time and sat down comfortably on a pair of Rattan chairs by the pool near Cruz and Ricardo.

"Well," Marta said secretively, "don't tell that to Ricardo."

Ricardo had been eavesdropping. "Uh-oh, I heard that," he exclaimed as he turned a thick steak on the grill. "Okay, what are the two of you conspiring about?"

Cruz laughed.

"Oh, nothing, dear," Marta said with a smile. "I just found out that the new fragrance by Jean Luc Renoir that I'm buying next is a little more expensive than what I thought." She winked at Ana María, who repressed her laughter.

"Hmmm," Ricardo said, raising his eyebrows as the two women stared at each other. "Are you sure that Jean Luc Renoir is involved in any of this?"

The two women laughed mischievously. Cruz was enjoying the exchange.

"Marta needs another maid," Ana María said flatly but in a polite tone.

"Oh, now we are talking," Ricardo said, smiling and feeling trapped as everyone remained silent waiting for his next words. "Well, Mr. Governor," he said seriously, "what would you do in my position?"

"You can always negotiate," Cruz said quickly, grinning. "And if you negotiate aggressively, the odds are you will win."

"Did you hear that, honey?" Ricardo said to his wife.

Marta said nothing.

"Okay," Ana María snapped, smiling and hoping to end the exchange, "you can always take the matter to arbitration."

They all laughed.

"We'll see what we can do, Marta," Ricardo said finally.

"Good," Marta said. The seed of understanding had been planted. Pleased, she gave Ana María a reassuring look.

"Aunt Ana! Aunt Ana!" Alejandra yelled from the edge of the pool, positioning herself to jump. "Look! Look!"

They all stared as the little girl jumped into the water. The group clapped in approval and encouraged her to do it again. She did. Then, the ringing of a telephone distracted the adults. It was Cruz's cell phone, which he kept in the pocket of his khakis. He moved away from the pool, fumbled with the phone and answered the call.

"Hello," he said.

"Mr. Governor, it's Almeda."

"Hello, Sam, what is it?"

"Well, uh . . ." Almeda was hesitant. "I'm sorry to disturb you, but we just got a call from Senator Thompson's people . . . They've informed us that he'll be arriving at the airport . . . today, within a half hour . . . and . . . well, they said that due to security concerns they changed his schedule . . . So instead of Monday, he is arriving today and they are requesting us to grant him living arrangements here at Fortaleza."

"That is just great!" Cruz said, pleased.

"All of this on a half hour's notice, sir," Almeda complained.

"Absolutely no problem," Cruz said, knowing that this was his opportunity to spend a longer amount of time with the U.S. Senator. "I'll tell you what. I will meet the Senator at the airport myself and will bring him here to the Borja's house for the afternoon. I am sure he will enjoy that. Did his wife come with him?"

"No, sir. He is traveling alone. American Airlines, flight 407, from Kennedy Airport."

"This is good news," Cruz said excitedly. "Very good, Sam. You get the staff ready for him at Fortaleza."

"Yes, sir."

Pleased, Cruz ended the call and replaced the phone in his pocket. Then, he said, "Hey Marta, can you make room at the table for a United States Senator?"

Marta was surprised by the request, but was immediately enthusiastic. "Oh, Governor," she said, her eyes shinning, "we'll be more than honored. Certainly, certainly."

"Good. I have to go now," Cruz announced. "Senator Thompson is arriving in thirty minutes. He will be staying with us in Fortaleza. I'm going to get him at the airport now and bring him over here."

"Did Marianne come too?" Ana María asked.

"No, he's by himself. Anyway, I think he'll enjoy an impromptu day sitting outside in the sun."

"Absolutely," Marta enthused. "We'll be thrilled to have him. Isn't it so, honey?" she asked Ricardo.

"Sure," Ricardo said, "but it's a shame we didn't know he was coming. We could have prepared a more traditional menu. You know, like a good *arroz con pollo.*"

"Oh, don't worry about that," Cruz reassured him. "We ourselves didn't know he was arriving today. We expected him Monday." He thought for a moment about the impact that Thursday's events were having on the image of the island.

Security.

"No problem, I guess," Ricardo said. "Anyway, it's a good thing Thompson is spending a few days here. I don't know what you think,

Elison, but some of these U.S. politicians always come to Puerto Rico and leave in a rush."

Cruz nodded. "I agree with you," he said, "but don't quote me on that."

"I know," Ricardo said.

Cruz kissed Ana María, then walked across the patio and pushed open the back wooden gate. He told his security people of his unexpected trip to the airport. The agents immediately began an exchange with the others. One agent stayed at the wooden gate, and the other one followed Cruz out of the house and positioned himself at the front door. The Governor got into his limousine and left in a caravan led by one motorcycle police officer and two more vehicles with four agents in tow. The other police officer remained seated on his motorcycle just off the driveway and used his radio to request that a police contingent meet the governor's caravan on its way to the airport. At this moment, everything was uneventful and under control at the Borja residence. The real security concern, the Governor, was on his way to Luis Muñoz Marín International Airport in Isla Verde, to pick up a United States Senator.

Chapter 13

None of the "pack," as the terrorists called themselves when acting in a group, saw the governor's caravan speeding away out of Condado. They were a few blocks away on Rosales Street. Oso parked the white van in the driveway of an abandoned house and climbed into the Montero carrying a heavy duffel bag with their weapons: a powerful Smith & Wesson magnum .357 for Luna and a Walther P-38 for Tino – both equipped with silencers – a .45 caliber Glock semi-automatic handgun with hollow-nose bullets for Teco, and an HK91 assault rifle for himself. The pack quickly grabbed their weapons along with hand gloves and ski masks to wear during the assault.

Teco drove off of Rosales Street. One street away from Italia Street, where the Borjas lived, Luna got out of the vehicle. She was wearing a red wig, a hat, dark sunglasses, a pair of jeans and a white, baggy blouse. She opened the back door of the Montero, took out a baby stroller and placed her ski mask and gun inside of it. "All right, I'll walk the baby now," she said to the pack and closed the door. She began pushing the stroller along the sidewalk, walking towards Italia Street. Teco went ahead and drove down the street, parked the Montero a few houses from the Borja home, and waited. Oso and Tino had already placed their masks half way on, pulled down to their foreheads.

Luna was now walking down the sidewalk on Italia Street. When she passed by the Montero, she nodded to her accomplices. Then, she advanced toward house number 365, where she had already spotted the motorcycle cop in front of the house's driveway and a plainclothes security agent guarding the front door. She knew she had to be fast and precise. She needed to incapacitate both men with a single shot each.

As Luna neared the house, Teco began to drive slowly towards it. Oso and Tino put their masks on and firmly held their weapons. Teco had placed his on his lap. He was to stay outside during the operation, ready to drive the pack to their getaway van.

Inside the Borja home, Alejandra played by the pool, Ana María and Marta chatted animatedly and Ricardo kept at his task at the grill.

Both the policeman and the agent outside saw the woman pushing the stroller approaching, but did not suspect anything out of the ordinary. She was only a few feet away when she decided to act. In a split second, she grabbed her gun and aimed at the plainclothes agent by the door, hitting him with a single shot in the chest. The man cried out in pain and fell to the ground. The policeman watched in horror, quickly reaching for his gun. He fired twice at Luna who ducked behind the stroller. She aimed at him and fired two shots, hitting him in the face and stomach. The officer fell to the ground moaning in pain.

Teco stopped the Montero in front of the house and Oso and Tino stormed out, running toward the front door. Luna was fast to dispose of her disguise and put her mask on. The front door was unlocked.

Inside, Ana María had asked, "What was that?" as they all heard noises that sounded like gunshots. The agent at the beach was now on the patio trying to communicate with his partner in front of the house. When he got no response, he pulled out his gun, ordered everyone to stay on the patio, and began running towards the front door. He thought he had heard gunshots too. When he reached the living room, he came face to face with three armed, masked intruders.

"Stop!" he yelled, aiming his gun toward the group.

Luna and Oso fired at him.

The agent let out a shrill scream and fell to the ground, blood splattering onto the white furniture and carpet. Wounded, he tried to lift his arm to fire his weapon. Tino walked steadily toward him and shot two bullets into his head, killing him instantly.

The terrorists stumbled through the spacious and luxurious living room, not knowing exactly where to run to. Luna cursed, remembering that their informant had hung up the phone on her when she had asked for more information. Now they were literally clueless about where to run to within this huge house.

"Where the fuck do we go?" Tino asked.

Before anyone could answer, they spotted the old maid, who stood terrified in an adjacent hallway.

"Where's the governor?" Oso yelled, pointing the gun at her.

Frightened, Lorena tried to speak but no words came out of her mouth.

"I asked you a question!" Oso shouted, firing a single shot at the wall, six inches away from the maid's head.

"They are on the patio!" Lorena screamed, crying. "Please don't kill me!" Lorena pleaded as she pointed the way with her finger. "The patio! Please don't kill me!"

"Take us there, God damn it!" Luna ordered, pushing the woman with her gun.

In a matter of seconds, the killers reached the patio and confronted Ana María, the girl, and the Borjas, who stood stunned and motionless. Alejandra was shaking in terror at the sight of three masked figures pointing guns at them. Ana María held her, trying not to scream.

"Get out of my house!" Ricardo yelled, defiantly.

"Where is he?" Oso yelled back.

Silence.

"I said, where is he?" Oso asked threateningly.

"Where is who? Damn it!" Ricardo responded furiously.

Oso pointed his rifle at him and pressed the trigger, shooting him in the stomach. Ricardo screamed and fell to the ground, moaning in pain.

"Oh my God! Oh my God!" Marta cried in horror as she ran to her husband. "What are you doing? In God's name, what are you doing?"

Oso moved a few steps closer and pulled Alejandra out of Ana María's arms. The girl was crying hysterically. Oso pressed his weapon against her head. Ana María was speechless.

"You tell me where Cruz is or I'm going to blow her head off!" Oso threatened.

"Are you out of your mind?" Tino yelled nervously. He did not have the stomach for such a thing. Not a little girl.

"Shut the fuck up!" Oso ordered angrily. He looked at Ana María. "Okay, bitch, where is he?"

"He's not here for God's sake!" Ana María cried, tears streaming down her face. "He's not here! Please, don't hurt the girl!" she pleaded.

Oso exchanged looks with Luna and Tino. He was making a fool of himself, he thought. "Search the fucking house," he ordered.

"We don't have much time!" Tino worried.

Jesus H. Christ! What is wrong with this kid? This time Oso yelled, "I said search the fucking house!"

Luna and Tino complied with the order and stormed into the house, vandalizing the premises as they searched for Cruz. Oso remained on the patio holding his weapon to Alejandra's head, while Ana María kept begging him not to hurt her.

Two minutes that seemed like an eternity passed, and Tino and Luna returned to the patio. They knew there were rooms in the house they did not search. There was no time. The police would be here any second.

"He's not here!" Luna yelled.

"Fuck! Fuck! Fuck!" Oso cursed.

"We are not lying to you," Ana María said between sobs. "He is not here. He left for the airport a few minutes ago . . . Now, please, let the girl go . . . please."

Oso kept cursing. Second attempt. Second fiasco.

"He's not here, let's go!" Tino said, frantically.

"Let the girl go, please," Ana María pleaded one more time.

Oso stared at Luna, then at Tino and then pointed his rifle at Ana María. He let go of the girl, who immediately ran to her aunt crying uncontrollably.

"You are coming with us," Oso told a stunned Ana María.

"Oh, no! Please, no!" she cried.

Oso aimed his rifle and fired a shot at the ground, inches away from Ana María's feet.

"Oh, God almighty!" she cried in horror.

"Let's go, bitch," Oso said, grabbing her by the arm and pushing her into the house on the way to the front door. Alejandra tried to stop him. Luna pushed Alejandra to the ground, and, along with Tino, followed Oso to the front door.

Teco saw them coming. Why are they bringing that woman with them? he thought. "Let's go! Let's go!" he yelled. The pack and the First Lady made it into the Montero. Teco attacked the accelerator with his foot and sped away.

Everyone was yelling and cursing. The terrorists unmasked themselves. Ana María was terrified, crying.

"What took you so long? Damn!" Teco yelled. "And why is she here?" He eyed Ana María in the rearview mirror.

"He wasn't there!" Oso barked. "The son of a bitch wasn't there!"

"We searched the house and we couldn't . . ." Tino began to explain.

"You shut up, you fucking little prick!" Oso cut him off in a violent tirade. "What was wrong with you in there? Don't you ever, EVER, question what I do, or what I tell you to do! I was ready to shoot YOU!" Oso could have killed him with his glance.

Tino. Young kid. A mere twenty-two-year-old. Even nerdy-looking with his short missionary haircut and prescription eyeglasses.

"I'm in fucking charge here!" Oso went on.

"Okay, okay!" Luna snapped. "Don't be so hard on him!"

The wailing siren of an approaching police car shut everyone up. The vehicle passed by the Montero at high speed going in the opposite direction, but soon made a dangerous U-turn and began pursuit of the terrorists. Evidently the police had a description of the vehicle.

"Go faster, damn it, faster!" Oso yelled as the police car came near, almost bumper to bumper.

"That mother fucker!" Luna cursed, pulling a hand grenade out of the duffel bag.

"Do it! Do it!" Oso yelled.

Luna extended her hand out the window and threw the grenade at the police car. It exploded on its hood, stopping it cold. Teco kept speeding, finally reaching Rosales Street. In a flash, the pack stormed out of the Montero, pushing Ana María along with them. Luna carried the bag with the weapons, Oso took a second to set the time bomb in the Montero and Teco took hold of the steering wheel of the van. They could now hear police sirens shrieking in the distance and coming closer. But soon, they were all aboard the white van. Teco and Oso in the front seats, the rest in the back, with the First Lady sprawled on the floorboard.

Teco drove off of Rosales Street in the opposite direction. He drove slowly to avoid bringing attention to their getaway vehicle. A little further down the road, two police cars stormed past them and Teco saw them screech to a stop and block the entrance to Rosales Street. Teco kept driving. Slowly. Then faster, faster.

There were now four police vehicles surrounding the red Montero abandoned in the middle of the road on Rosales Street. A troop of six policemen came to inspect the car and soon realized that it was empty. All they saw were discarded ski masks strewn on the seats and old newspapers on the floorboard. They glanced at the abandoned houses on either side of the street and decided to do a quick search. One police officer stayed behind, walking to his car to answer a call on his CB radio.

"Rivera here," he said.

The dispatcher spoke flatly. "License plate on red Montero, R-T-M-3-2-1, belongs to a 2005 Grand Mercury, reported stolen on May 13 in Mayagüez. Owner is a Mr. Juan Alicea."

"Ten-four, out," Officer Rivera said, placing the receiver down. The license plate of a stolen car placed on a Montero that I bet is also stolen, he thought. He decided to inspect the vehicle. He walked a few steps ahead and was immediately thrown to the ground by a violent explosion from inside the Montero. The car was torn to pieces; huge flames were rising up and shooting out sideways from it.

The rest of the officers ran out of the abandoned houses and were stunned by the huge explosion so close to their patrol cars.

Rivera crawled on all fours, away from the flames. "I could have been killed!" he said, shocked.

That was it. Whoever it was that had escaped from the home of Marta and Ricardo Borja in that red Montero was now gone. This was their way of proving it.

Chapter 14

"Welcome to Puerto Rico again," Cruz said to U.S. Senator Grant Thompson, firmly shaking his hand.

"It's always a pleasure to be here," the Senator said in a deep, strong voice.

Grant Thompson had an impressive, commanding presence. He was seven feet tall and well built, with broad shoulders, pink-white skin, snow-white hair and shinning blue eyes underneath silver-framed glasses.

"Did you have a good trip?" Cruz asked, as both men walked out of the airport's VIP reception area followed by a heavy security detail.

"Yes, very pleasant indeed. I apologize for arriving on such short notice."

"It is not an inconvenience at all," Cruz quickly said. "My wife and I have taken the liberty to make some arrangements for today. We are spending a lovely afternoon at the home of Ricardo and Marta Borja. We'd like you to join us."

"Certainly. I remember the Borjas very well. A fine couple. It will be nice to see them again. How is the First Lady?"

"She is fine," Cruz said proudly. "As usual, very involved in our local campaigns."

"Marianne sends her regards," Thompson said politely.

"We appreciate that."

The two men exited the main entrance of the Luis Muñoz Marín International Airport and boarded their waiting vehicle. The black limousine drove away, flanked by an escort of three unmarked vehicles and six motorcycles.

"I must tell you that we were very concerned with what happened on Thursday," the senator said somberly.

"I appreciate your concern," Cruz said sincerely. "We did lose a fine young man."

"That is a tragedy, absolutely. Unfortunately, sometimes that is the price to pay when you are writing history."

"I'm aware of that. He was only thirty-one-years-old with a young wife and a little baby girl. His death is a shame."

"I'm sorry to hear that."

"However, Senator, nothing is going to stop us. This island has a right to decide its future. I have a strong commitment to make that happen."

"I want to tell you," Thompson said, looking straight into Cruz's eyes, "the President thinks very highly of you. He is impressed by the passion you have brought into this process."

"That means a lot to me. And to Puerto Rico. Have you two spoken recently?" Cruz asked with more than a passing interest. It had been months since his last personal conversation with the U.S. President.

"Yes, indeed. I met with him recently in preparation for this visit. He is personally committed to the success of our policy in this region, and the American citizens of Puerto Rico are at the top of his list. He will do all he can to facilitate the process of Puerto Rico joining the Union."

"I am sure of that. However, I must say that within the last months we haven't heard any statements coming from the White House with respect to statehood for Puerto Rico."

"His support for statehood is unbreakable."

"I know that. He has told me so. I just feel that it would indeed help our cause if the President takes a more proactive role."

Thompson thought for a moment, then he said, "Mr. Governor, the President has been advised against making any more statements in favor of statehood before the actual consultation occurs. Our advisors think that at this stage, it would prejudice the process and could alienate some of the parties involved in this. As you know, it was a quixotic accomplishment to have the Commonwealth and Independence parties agree on this consultation. Should the President continue to speak in favor of any of the formulas, we jeopardize the very process we put in motion here and in Congress. And the President's objectivity and openness in this process is important in the eyes of the international community, which, as you know, has been somewhat skeptical of our intentions for Puerto Rico . . . The President, as you well know, is on record as a strong supporter of statehood. At these crucial moments however, he will speak in general terms in favor of self-determination for Puerto Rico. It is incumbent that he shows to the world that whatever political status the Puerto Ricans choose will have his unconditional support."

"Then I must be confident that that explains the President's silence about Puerto Rico for the past months."

"I can assure you that it's so."

"But privately," Cruz said carefully, "nothing has changed."

"Nothing has changed, Mr. Governor," Thompson said quickly. "The President and I have spoken at length about this subject. I don't think there's ever been a U.S. President who has taken Puerto Rico so seriously."

"I'm pleased," Cruz said calmly, "and relieved to know that."

"Puerto Ricans are an important constituency, Mr. Governor. And this also has tremendous implications for all Latino constituencies on the mainland. Many interesting things are happening."

"Good," Cruz said pleased. "This was something long overdue."

"We agree."

The ringing of the car phone interrupted the conversation. Cruz excused himself and answered it. "This is Cruz," he said softly.

"Mr. Governor, this is Calero," the Police Superintendent said with a weary voice.

"Calero, what is it?"

"Governor, there's been a shooting at the Borja home," he said bluntly.

"Oh, God! What happened?" Cruz tried not to sound shocked.

"The residence was assaulted by three masked men and a woman. We have two agents and a police officer dead. Ricardo Borja was shot in the stomach and has been taken to Ashford Presbyterian Hospital. Marta Borja and your niece were both unharmed. Mrs. Borja is at the hospital. Right now I'm on my way there to talk to her."

"Calero," Cruz said, "how is the First Lady?"

Silence.

"Calero, how is Ana María?"

"Governor, I am sorry to inform you that your wife is missing."

"Missing? What do you mean 'missing'?"

"She's been taken, sir. She's been kidnapped."

"You are not serious, are you?"

"Governor, we are moving fast on this. We've inundated the streets with our people, especially the highways. And I've put every single chopper we have in the sky. We believe the kidnappers are still on the road. I have ordered over one-hundred-fifty agents on this operation."

"It's September Twenty-third, isn't it?"

"We haven't confirmed that officially, sir. But I am convinced they are behind this."

"I'm going to the hospital," Cruz said, controlling his rage. "I want to talk to Marta Borja myself."

"Cruz," Calero said with authority, "we advise you to return to Fortaleza immediately. The FBI wants to meet with you there. I just spoke to Bill Montana. He's on his way to Fortaleza."

Cruz said nothing.

"Let *me* talk to Marta Borja," Calero continued. "I will immediately meet you at Fortaleza."

More silence.

"Mr. Governor?"

Cruz was dead. He had met death right at this very moment.

"Calero," Cruz said, repressing his grief, "I'll meet you at Fortaleza." He hung up.

As sweat poured down his forehead, Cruz looked at Senator Thompson, stunned.

"Is everything all right, Mr. Governor?" Thompson asked, fearing the response.

"My wife has been kidnapped," Cruz said flatly.

The U.S. Senator, speechless, turned his head and looked out the window at the city landscape around him. "Good Lord," he said, as if reciting a desperate prayer.

Puerto Rico, the island of enchantment, was now a dangerous place in which to be an American or an American sympathizer. That much the Senator knew.

Chapter 15

The First Lady of Puerto Rico was sprawled out over the filthy floorboard of a white van surrounded by a pack of ruthless criminals. She had been blindfolded with a dirty rag that was now soaked with her own sweat. She had not yet uttered a word. She was racked with terror. And her horror increased two-fold when a man who called himself "Oso" spoke on the phone.

"Rigonaldo," Oso said loud enough to send chills through Ana María's body.

God almighty, Ana María gasped silently at the mention of the name of the man she feared. Please, my Lord, she prayed, have mercy on me.

"Talk to me," Rigonaldo said calmly.

"Cruz wasn't there."

"That's not good news, Oso."

"We searched the whole house. There is no way he could have escaped from us. He was not in the house. His wife said he had left a short time before we arrived."

"His wife," Rigonaldo said simply. "I see."

Oso looked at the scared woman behind him. Luna had her foot on top of her. "We brought her with us," Oso said, grinning.

"You have Ana María Cruz with you?" Rigonaldo asked, eerily calmed.

"Yes, sir," Oso said, proudly.

"Good," Rigonaldo said. "Very good."

"We'll be there soon," Oso was glad to report.

"Well done, Oso, well done."

Oso pushed the end button on the phone and handed it to Luna.

"What did he say?" Teco asked.

"Well done."

The terrorists high-fived each other. Now they felt they were major players in the sphere of events that were sweeping Puerto Rico. An otherwise uneventful afternoon had turned them into heroes of the motherland. From now on, their voice would be heard. Loudly. Just as it always should have been. Their powerful enemy in the north and its lackeys in Puerto Rico would now be forced to listen. No. They would be brought to their knees.

Chapter 16

The Associated Press was the first news outlet to report the shooting at the Borja home and the unconfirmed news that First Lady Ana María Cruz was missing. Emilio Durcal got Karen Pérez on her feet and into the field at once. Her hopes for a quiet, relaxing Saturday had vanished.

After a quick visit to the Borja mansion to tape exterior visuals, Karen and Tonio, her young editor and cameraman, drove in the station's van to Ashford Presbyterian Hospital on Ashford Avenue, the lifeline of the affluent Condado neighborhood. They had learned that Ricardo Borja was being treated there and that Police Superintendent Roberto Calero was in the building with Marta Borja and Alejandra Colón, the niece of the First Lady. The whereabouts of Governor Elison Cruz were unknown. For the moment, Fortaleza was refusing to inform the press where the governor or his wife were.

For obvious reasons, the hospital's administrators refused to let any of the reporters into the building. Almost two dozen of them were forced to wait outside in front of the main entrance. They frantically used their cell phones to call anyone they felt could give them information about what was happening. But, at this time, Police Superintendent Calero seemed to be the man to talk to. And he was here.

On the fifth floor, Marta Borja, with Alejandra seated quietly by her side, waited in a visitors' lounge some thirty feet from a nurses' station for word on the condition of her husband. Calero and two agents were a few feet away from them. The Superintendent had a cell phone to his ear, talking endlessly. He rushed to finish the call when he saw a team of physicians in white lab coats approach Marta and the girl.

"Mrs. Borja," the doctor called. His nametag read, J. Vilella, M.D.

Marta Borja jumped to her feet. Tears swelled in her eyes.

"Your husband will be fine," Vilella said in a somber low voice, but with a streak of confidence. "He is a very strong man."

"I want to see him," Marta replied.

"He is heavily sedated now. You'll be able to see him after we operate."

"What kind of operation?"

"It's not as serious as it could have been," Vilella said quickly and gesturing with his hands. "The bullet rested in his abdomen but it didn't pierce any vital organs. We'll keep him in intensive care for some time, but we expect him to survive."

"And you say he'll be fine?" she asked for reassurance.

"Yes, yes," Vilella assured her. "It was very close, but he'll be fine."

Marta Borja sat down again and used a handkerchief to wipe away tears. She believed the doctor, but still, the whole incident had shaken her very soul.

Calero spoke briefly to the doctors before they disappeared down a long corridor. He then came close to Marta. "Marta," he told her, "I know you are very upset right now, but I need to ask you a few questions."

She hesitated and looked at him, then said, "Go ahead."

"Okay, did the terrorists mention any names?"

"No. Nothing."

"You told the agents there was a woman. What about the woman? Any name for her?"

Marta struggled to focus on his questions. The woman? "No, no," she said. "They didn't call each other by name. This man, the tallest one, he seemed to be the leader. He kept asking, 'Where is he?' 'Where is he?'"

"They were looking for the governor," Calero interjected.

"Yes. Yes. That's all he kept asking, 'Where is he?' And when he realized Elison wasn't there he shot Ricardo and took Ana María with him." She sobbed. "Oh, it was so horrible, horrible. Everything happened so fast."

"Now, I want you to tell me something," Calero went on. "It's very important."

"What?"

"Who knew that the Governor and the First Lady were going to be at your house today?"

Marta was puzzled by the question. "Who?" she said. "Nobody, nobody knew, as far as I know."

"When did you make plans to have them at your house?"

"Yesterday, Friday morning."

"Who did you talk to? Was it by phone? Did you make the arrangements by phone?"

"Well . . . yes . . . yes. We talked on the phone early Friday morning. Ana María and I. And she said she would talk to Elison."

"And besides you and Ricardo," Calero pressed on, "who else knew they were coming?"

"No one. Absolutely no one."

"Are you completely sure? What about your maid? Is it possible she overheard your conversation?"

"No. No. I was alone in my room when I spoke to Ana María."

"When did the maid find out they were coming?"

"When they arrived. I mean, a little after eleven I told her we were expecting guests, but she didn't even know who was coming until they actually arrived."

"What about Ricardo? Did he talk to anyone about the Governor and the First Lady coming?"

"No, I don't think so. I did not see him on the telephone between Friday and today. And we didn't have any guests either."

"So you think it is very unlikely he told anyone?"

"Yes, I'm almost certain. He's very discreet about his personal relationship with Elison."

Calero tried to process the little information he had been given when, abruptly, a woman stormed into the visitors' lounge. Alejandra jumped to her feet yelling, "Mommy! Mommy!" and ran to embrace her mother, Aida Colón, Ana María's sister.

Unlike her glamorous and very public sister, Aida Colón was a simple-looking woman who liked and enjoyed her privacy. In her mid-forties, she was darker than her sister with black hair, black eyes, a prominent jaw and nose, and full lips. She usually dressed in casual baggy pants and blouse with little make-up and few pieces of jewelry. And she was a committed *independentista*, unlike her sister, who was a staunch supporter of statehood for Puerto Rico and was married to the fiercest pro-statehood governor the island had ever had. Furthermore, Aida's husband was Miguel Colón, Esq., a former vice president of the Independence Party, now working as an international consultant on maritime law.

Despite their prominence in Puerto Rican society, both of the Colóns kept a low profile in Puerto Rican politics. Miguel Colón had had a falling out with the leadership of the Independence Party and was fed up with the politics of politics; and Aida did not like her face plastered across newspapers and television. However, they had strong opinions about Puerto Rico and carried much weight within their intimate social circle of elite friends. That is where they made a difference. And in those circles, they were known to be strong critics of the Cruz administration. Especially Aida who, nevertheless, in deference to her sister, kept her contempt for the pro-statehood Cruz out of public knowledge. She had never talked to the press about how much she disliked her brother-in-law governor, whom she considered an ideological fanatic and a demagogue. But she did love her sister and that was why, now, she was extremely concerned, troubled and angry.

Aida Colón raised her daughter into her arms. The girl wrapped her arms and legs around her mother. "Oh my baby, my baby," Aida said as she stroked her daughter's hair. "Are you all right?"

"I'm scared mommy."

"It's all right, mommy is here. We'll go home now."

"A bad man took Aunt Ana away."

"I know sweetheart. But don't worry, Aunt Ana will be home soon."

Calero nodded to Aida. They had met only once before, but he knew about her, of course, by reputation.

Aida studied the Police Superintendent. He was a short, heavy man in his fifties who, she thought, could probably not even pass a physical to be a police officer. But, politics *and* connections had given him the job of police chief. Those were all that mattered in Puerto Rico, she believed. Politics and good connections.

"Hello, Mrs. Colón," Calero said.

"Hello," she said, an edge to her voice.

"I'm relieved the girl was not harmed," Calero said sincerely, ignoring her tone.

"How could this have happened?" she asked sharply. "How is it possible something like this could have happened?"

Calero tried to be as calm and diplomatic as he had learned to be. He knew he was being indirectly accused of incompetence. "Aida, we are dealing with a pack of ruthless criminals here," he said matter-of-factly.

"Did Rigonaldo do this?" she asked, her question like a threat.

Rigonaldo Pastrana.

Like many in the political left on the island, Aida Colón was truly annoyed and fed up with the tactics and political ramblings of the elusive fugitive, whom she thought she knew only too well. Every *independentista* – left, right or center – felt he or she had to learn to understand Rigonaldo's motivations even if they personally disagreed with his tactics – which most *independentistas* did. And for Aida Colón, Rigonaldo Pastrana had now crossed a forbidden line. He had hit home.

"We haven't confirmed that yet. But I don't have any doubt he is behind this." Calero actually felt incompetent for a moment.

"Do you have any idea where he's taken Ana María?" she said, repressing her rage.

Calero shook his head. "Not yet. But, don't worry, we will find her. I have over a hundred agents working on the case right now and the FBI is already involved."

"And where is Cruz?" Her tone felt like a sword. Her question was an accusation. Her sister had definitely married the wrong man.

"The Governor," Calero said, intentionally calling Cruz by his title, "is on his way to Fortaleza." He had to protect his boss, even from angry in-laws. And he had heard enough. "I wanted to ask you," he said quickly. "Did you talk to anyone about your daughter going to the Borjas with the Governor and the First Lady?"

"No."

"When did you make the plans?"

"I didn't."

"What do you mean?"

"I didn't make plans. Ana María called me this morning. A last minute thing, and I walked Alejandra up to Fortaleza. That's it. I mean, other people live in Old San Juan too, you know."

He ignored her sarcasm. "And you didn't tell anyone about it?"

"I told you, no. Miguel is on a business trip in Maracaibo. An oil spill."

"Okay, Mrs. Colón, you've been very kind to speak to me." He lied.

"Okay," she said simply. That was her greatest attempt at politeness to a member of Cruz's cabinet.

With her daughter in her arms, Aida Colón ignored Marta Borja and left. The only thing that mattered to her right now was to see her sister again.

Calero took a deep breath and used a handkerchief to wipe his face, which felt warm and sweaty. After making note of Marta's phone number, he excused himself and nodded to his agents to follow him to the elevator. Once inside, the privacy of the elevator cabin hit him and forced him to realize how troubled he was about this crisis. The country held him responsible for the security of the First Family. And the terrorists had struck twice in less than five days. He did not need confirmation. He knew that only someone as ruthless and desperate as Rigonaldo Pastrana and his gang were capable of doing something like this.

When Calero got out of the elevator and walked into the lobby, he immediately saw the mob of reporters waiting for him on the other side of the sliding glass doors. He wanted to shout at them and tell them that he had wanted to increase security around the governor and that he had faced opposition to his plan from the governor himself. He, Calero, could have prevented today's events with more security around the First Family. I wash my hands like Pontius Pilate, he wanted to say. Blame Cruz.

Facing the press, Calero could hardly discern the questions being shouted at him. He waved his hands for silence and said, "Today in the early afternoon, two men, a woman and a third subject in a getaway car, assaulted the residence of Ricardo and Marta Borja here in Condado. One police officer and two security agents were killed. Mr. Borja was wounded but is expected to live. Mrs. Borja and Alejandra Colón, the First Lady's niece, were both unharmed. Governor Cruz was not at the residence at the time of the assault."

"What about the First Lady?" someone shouted.

Calero breathed deeply.

"The First Lady is missing," he said somberly.

"You mean she's been kidnapped," Karen Pérez said as a statement. "You confirm that?"

"We are treating this as a kidnapping. That is correct." Calero's eyes met Karen's.

"By whom?" Karen asked next.

"At this moment we cannot confirm it, but we fear this is another act by Rigonaldo Pastrana and September Twenty-third."

"Do you have any leads as to where the First Lady has been taken?" Karen was as stunned by this news as the rest of her colleagues.

Headline: Terrorists kidnap First Lady of Puerto Rico.

"I cannot share any information about that with you," Calero said, attempting to hide his emotions. For a second he had a vision of himself as a buffoon. "At this moment, however, we are urging that any citizen with information as to the whereabouts of First Lady Ana María Cruz contact our office or the FBI. All informants will remain anonymous."

With that, Calero excused himself and walked away, ignoring the rest of the questions shouted at him. He jumped into his waiting car and rudely ordered his driver to speed away to the governor's mansion. He could have prevented this, he said out loud. He then repeated the thought to himself, over and over again.

Chapter 17

M r. Governor, who was aware of your schedule for today?" asked William Montana, the Assistant Director in Charge (ADIC) of the FBI in Puerto Rico.

A year earlier, the Puerto Rico field office of the FBI had undergone a major internal restructuring, and the number of Special Agents assigned to it had tripled. The Puerto Rico office was now as large as the FBI offices in New York City and Washington, D.C. And all international investigations pertaining to Central and South America were now monitored by the Puerto Rico office with the approval of the host countries and in coordination with the U.S. Department of State and any other involved agency through the FBI's Legal Attaché Program. As the ADIC in Puerto Rico, William Montana was a man of great responsibility.

Montana was an imposing black man with huge hands, black hair cut short, piercing green eyes, a well-built torso and a tall figure, always clothed in expensive Italian suits. He enjoyed the challenges and the power that came with his office. And, as a black man of power in Puerto Rico – a society he considered to be infected with pervasive racism – he took shit from no one. He had a pragmatic, no nonsense demeanor. Moreover, ever since his appointment as head of the FBI on the island, eyebrows had been raised within the white Puerto Rican power-elite. He was forced to be a man on the offensive.

He had just ended a call on his cell phone with Police Superintendent Calero, who reported on his conversations with Marta Borja and Aida

Colón. For reasons he didn't explain, Elison Cruz was not interested in knowing what Aida Colón had to say.

Governor Cruz, U.S. Senator Grant Thompson and Montana were in the living room of the private residence of Fortaleza. Cruz was pacing frantically from side to side, talking to himself. Thompson was seated on a sofa talking on his cell phone, his mean-looking bodyguard standing nearby. Montana was smoking his umpteenth cigarette, eager to get to the bottom of the crisis they now faced. He knew September Twenty-third was behind the kidnapping of Ana María Cruz. And he was determined to make this the very last operation of the terrorist group.

"Who knew about the visit to the Borjas today?" he asked again, smoke blowing out of his mouth and nostrils.

Cruz stopped pacing. "My assistant, Almeda," he said. "And probably Damaris, my secretary, and Virginia, my wife's secretary."

"You told them you were going to the Borjas?" Montana pressed on.

"That wouldn't be unusual . . . but no . . . I only told Almeda."

"When did you tell him?"

Cruz was forcing himself to concentrate. "Oh, I don't know . . . It must have been yesterday, mid afternoon, before he left. He left earlier than normal yesterday and I asked him to come today for a few hours in the morning. He must have been here until just a short while ago."

"And what about the secretaries? How would they find out?"

"Damaris has access to both my official and private calendars. She may have looked into it, she may not have. And Virginia may have known from Ana María herself or she might have looked into her calendar." He paused, then said, "Elaine found out late in the morning today."

"And who is she?" Montana asked.

"She's my traveling and weekend secretary. I mean, someone has to know where the governor is at all times."

Montana said nothing. Cruz pondered the implications of Montana's questions and now his silence.

"Listen," Cruz said quickly, "these are public servants, and these secretaries have been with us ever since we arrived here. There is nothing suspicious about them. Trust me."

"Did the First Lady make a note in her calendar about the Borjas?"

"I don't know."

"Can I take a look at her calendar?"

"Sure," Cruz said, reaching for a telephone on a small oak table by a large white sofa. He pressed zero and got Elaine, the weekend secretary who also handled the switchboard. He gave her instructions and hung up only after Elaine informed him that the phones were ringing off the hook.

A maid entered the room and offered to bring coffee. Cruz and Montana declined. Senator Thompson accepted. Then, a butler named Eduardo came into the room followed by four men whom Cruz knew immediately were federal agents. In their dark suits and ties, short haircuts and dark sunglasses, they looked like clones of each other. Two of the men were carrying two heavy platinum suitcases which Cruz soon learned carried telephone monitoring equipment.

Montana introduced the foursome as Special Agents Pratt, García, Walker and Morales. "They'll be staying with you here," he announced. "We need to install the tracing equipment here and in your office." Pratt and García took that as their cue to start setting up.

Cruz felt more vulnerable than ever before in his life. He waved his hand, sat down on the sofa and said, "Do what you have to do."

"Governor, where do you keep the phone records?" Montana asked.

"In the computer room in the basement," Cruz answered.

"Okay, I want to go through Ana María's phone records for yesterday and today. And I want to take a look at the calls that Elaine handled this morning."

Cruz felt truly invaded, but of course said nothing. "I'll have Eduardo take you there," he said, waving to his butler.

Montana gave instructions to Agent Walker and ordered him to take care of the phone records. Walker followed the butler to the basement. As they left, Elaine came in with Ana María's calendar. She also handed Cruz a batch of phone messages before leaving the room. Cruz glanced at a few of the messages. It seemed the whole world was trying to reach him. He tossed the slips on a table and looked in Ana María's calendar on the page for Saturday, October 27. She did not make an entry for the Borjas. He showed it to Montana.

"Okay," the FBI Assistant Director said. "Governor, would it be possible to have Almeda, Damaris and Virginia come here today? I just want to ask them a few questions . . . It's routine."

Cruz considered this for a second. "Yes, of course," he said softly. "None of them live far from here. I'll get their private numbers from my office. I'll be right back."

Cruz excused himself and walked out of the living room, realizing that if he could, he would break down and cry. But, he thought it would not be proper for the Governor of Puerto Rico to fall into despair. He had to be stronger than he had ever been. He needed to send Ana María, wherever she was, his strength and his energy. Sometimes they had said to each other they were psychic. The few times they were separated, they said they knew when one was thinking about the other. A silly romantic thought. But now, more than ever, he wished it was true.

In his executive office, the governor searched for the phone numbers he needed. As he closed the top drawer of his desk, he glanced at a picture of his wife on top of it. It was from a long ago trip they'd taken to Costa Rica. He fought back tears. She looked so beautiful, so full of life. He stared at her face. Her smile. And he soon found himself struggling between deep sadness and intense rage. What should he feel right now? he asked himself. What? . . . Rage? . . . Sadness? Rage, he decided. "Nothing is going to happen to you, Ana María," he said firmly. "Nothing."

He touched the picture with the tip of his fingers and left. He was ready to fight for the woman he loved most in the world.

Chapter 18

Luna forced Ana María into the house. In the living room, the men stood nearby as Rigonaldo came close to the two women, puffing on a thick cigar. Ana María was at once hit by the heavy smell.

Abruptly, Luna pulled the blindfold off of Ana María's eyes and the First Lady of Puerto Rico came face to face with the man she knew as the Devil. She gasped, and a tortured "No!" blurted out of her mouth. Her legs almost faltered, but she stood there, terror stricken, facing her fiercest and most hated enemy. Rigonaldo enjoyed the moment and laughed as hard and as loud as he could.

"My God," Rigonaldo told her. "You look like you've seen a ghost." He paused. "Actually, some people say that I *am* like a ghost." He laughed. "And the Devil too."

Ana María said nothing. She couldn't.

"Put her in the back!" Rigonaldo barked, his face hardened.

Luna took the captive through the corridor that led to the backyard, stopping at the last door on the right of the hallway, just before the back exit. She kicked it open. The room was extremely small and dark, lit only by the dim light that came from the corridor. It could have been a storage room. Before the pack arrived, in a rush of creativity and expectations, Rigonaldo had sealed the only window of the small room with nails and plywood sheets, and had stripped it of all furniture, except for a wooden chair.

Luna pushed Ana María inside and forced her to sit on the chair that stood alone in the center of the small room. The heat, the humidity and the dust-filled air of the dark room immediately struck Ana María.

Then, suddenly, everything went from dark to pitch-black nothingness. Ana María had been blindfolded again and she was being firmly tied – wrists, feet, torso – to the chair's arms, body and legs.

Done.

"You are ours now!" Luna said ominously. "I hope you enjoy our five-star accommodations. Just pretend that you are at the presidential suite in *El Conquistador.*"

Luna laughed; her laughter as deep as the howling of a rabid dog.

"Why are you doing this?" Ana María said weakly.

"Are you stupid enough not to know?" Luna said sarcastically.

"I want to talk to my husband."

"No, no, no, no. '*I want to talk to my husband,*'" Luna mimicked the First Lady. "You ask me, I don't think your husband gives a shit about you. You must be some kind of dumb bitch."

Ana María said nothing.

"I mean, when you hop into bed with him, isn't it a little crowded? We hear he goes to bed with the *gringo* president every night."

"My husband is a Puerto Rican like you," Ana María dared to say.

"Fuck your husband!" Luna yelled. "And fuck you too!"

Utterly annoyed, Luna left the room and slammed the door behind her. She quickly returned to the living room, leaving the First Lady of Puerto Rico alone, in complete silence and total darkness.

Captured.

The men were now seated facing each other. All of them smoking furiously.

"Guess what the bitch just told me," Luna said, reaching for a cigarette herself.

"What?" Rigonaldo asked.

"*My husband is a Puerto Rican like you.*" She spat. "Some nerve. I should have slapped her."

"Why didn't you?" Oso asked, grinning.

"I just did my nails!" Luna said and laughed furiously.

"*You* do your nails?" Oso joked.

"Fuck you, Oso!" Luna said exasperatedly.

The men laughed. Luna told them off. She was proud to be the cell's only woman, though. Perhaps, when the revolution would triumph, she could be the president of the *Federación de Mujeres Puertorriqueñas*, Puerto Rico's version of the *Federación de Mujeres Cubanas* (Cuban Women's Federation). The thing she most admired about the Cuban Revolution was that it gave women there a prominent position in society. That was quite an achievement despite the evident *machismo* of the Cubans, and it was something she wished would happen in Puerto Rico despite the silly *machismo* of Puerto Rican men. As far as she was concerned, there would come a day when throngs of Puerto Rican revolutionaries would march into San Juan. And when that day would come, *machista* men could go fuck themselves. Women would finally have real power and equality in the new, free Puerto Rico.

"Go on, Oso," Rigonaldo said, as Luna sat at the table with the men.

"So, once there, we moved fast," Oso said. "They were all on an outside patio. Cruz wasn't there. We searched the whole house and couldn't find him."

Rigonaldo listened intensely.

"There's no way he was in that house," Oso assured him.

Teco was pensive. Tino, after his earlier scolding, dared not speak.

"Where was he?" Rigonaldo asked, smoke blowing out his mouth and nostrils.

"Well, the bitch said," Oso said, mimicking Ana María, "*He left for the airport a few minutes ago . . . Please let the girl go.*" He laughed, almost choking.

"At the airport," Rigonaldo said, pausing to draw on his cigar. "I see . . ." He considered a thought. The governor was at the airport when he should have been at the Borja home. Something was wrong here.

Rigonaldo's face hardened. He took a last drag on his cigar and stubbed it out in an ashtray.

The terrorists waited in silence for their leader's next words.

Rigonaldo said, "Oso . . . get on the phone . . . call Almeda again."

Chapter 19

Samuel Almeda, scheduling secretary to the Governor of Puerto Rico, pushed open the front door of his house in Ocean Park, an affluent suburb next to Condado in metropolitan San Juan. In his car on the way from the supermarket he had been listening to radio reports about the kidnapping of Ana María Cruz. Almeda's mind was both blank and racing at once. When he walked through his living room carrying two plastic grocery bags, he noticed a blinking light on his answering machine. He had one message and he was afraid to think who could have called.

Nervously, he tossed the grocery bags on his kitchen counter and walked back to the machine. When he stretched his hand to push the play button, he realized that he was shaking. He played the message.

"Almeda, this is Cruz calling," the Governor's voice reverberated through the room. "We have a situation here. I'm sure by now you have heard about my wife. Please come to Fortaleza as soon as you can. The FBI is here and they would like to ask you a few questions. It shouldn't take long. So please, as soon as you hear this, I'd appreciate it if you'd come over. We'll be upstairs. Thank you."

A high-pitched beep indicated the message was over. The shrill sound was like a gunshot fired at his chest. His heart sank. He didn't know if it was the mention of the FBI wanting to talk to him or if it was the weight of what he had done. The sound of the Governor's voice gave away nothing, though. The man didn't know. He couldn't know.

The phone began ringing. Almeda jumped. He was sweating now. Calm, he told himself, I need to be calm. He picked up the receiver.

"Hello," he said out of breath.

"He wasn't there!" Oso said testily.

"Who is this?"

"Almeda, you know exactly who this is." Oso's bullshit detector went on high mode.

Almeda collapsed on his sofa seat. "I . . . I . . . didn't recognize your voice," he said, shaking.

"Cut the bullshit!" Oso yelled.

"I . . . I didn't expect you to call me today."

"Fuck that! Cruz wasn't there! We deserve to know what happened," Oso demanded.

"I don't know what happened . . . I'm sorry."

"Listen, Almeda, 'Mr. Big-shot wannabe' . . . Don't sorry me, okay? You cost us a lot of money and we expect you to deliver. He wasn't there; now you tell me what happened." It was an order.

Almeda cursed the day he had gotten involved with these people. "Something came up in his schedule," he said elusively.

"Something like what?" Oso asked angrily.

"Senator Thompson arrived from New York. Cruz went to meet him at the airport. It was unplanned."

"And you didn't know about it," Oso said incredulously.

"No!" Almeda snapped. "I didn't know about it. And from now on, I don't know anything. Nothing! Nada! I want out of this bullshit! Do you understand?"

"You know what pal? You are a real rotten rat!"

"Fuck you!"

"No, fuck you, snake! I expect you will return our money."

That stopped Almeda in his tracks. The money, of course. "Listen," he said, "you can have your money back. I don't want it. The FBI wants to talk to me."

"Oh . . . I see. Now we are talking," Oso said with dead calm. "And what are you going to tell them?"

"I don't know! I don't know what they want. But this I know: do not ever call me again! From now on, I don't know you people. Goodbye!"

Almeda slammed down the phone. He was breathing heavily and sweating uncontrollably. He remained motionless for a minute. What the fuck am I going to do? he kept asking himself. What does the FBI want with me? He took a deep breath, counted to ten, grabbed the receiver and dialed the number of the Governor's residence. Cruz answered on the first ring.

"Governor, this is Almeda," he said calmly. "I'm sorry about what happened."

"I know," Cruz said. "Can you come over?"

"Yes. I'll be right over." He paused. "How can I be of help?"

"Just come over, son," Cruz said softly. "They need you here."

"Okay."

Both men hung up. Almeda stood up and walked to his bathroom. He looked at himself in the mirror. He was pale. He bent over the sink, turned on the faucet and watched the water run. For a few seconds he just stood there resting his arms over the sink; then he cupped his hands under the water's flow and splashed his face a couple of times. He used a towel to dry his face and shortly after, walked out of the house. He got into his black late model BMW and sped away. Cruz can't know, he kept telling himself. *I need to be calm.*

Chapter 20

FBI Assistant Director, William Montana, was in a large, windowless conference room near the governor's office reviewing Ana María Cruz's phone records. There weren't too many calls recorded. Montana knew that the system did not log phone calls that had been blocked by the caller. And all of the few calls that were on record seemed to be of an official nature: Mental Health and Addiction Services Administration, Family Department, Women's Affairs Commission, Socioeconomic Development Administration, Youth Affairs Office, and so forth.

The governor had assured Montana that he didn't think Ana María would have discussed the outing with the Borjas with officials at those agencies.

Montana pushed the phone records aside, lit another cigarette and studied the notes he had taken on a yellow legal pad of his earlier meetings with Cruz's secretary, Damaris, and with Virginia, secretary to the First Lady. Actually, he thought there was nothing there. Both women assured him that they didn't know the Cruzes would be at the Borja home today. Both women had a long, working experience with the Cruzes and at the Statehood Party headquarters, and both seemed genuinely concerned about the welfare of the Governor and First Lady.

His short meeting with Elaine, the weekend secretary, did not produce any information of substance either.

The director took a bold, black pen and wrote, SAMUEL ALMEDA, on a clean sheet of paper at the top of the page. Almeda was next and he was waiting in the hall to be invited into the conference room. Montana finished his cigarette, got up and opened the door.

"Mr. Almeda," he called.

Almeda stood up from his seat and went into the room.

"I'm sorry to have kept you waiting," Montana said as he shook Almeda's hand.

"Not to worry," Almeda said confidently.

"Sit down, please," Montana invited, pointing at a chair at one end of the large conference table.

Almeda sat down. Montana lit another cigarette and sat a few feet from the man. He offered a cigarette to Almeda who accepted it. A cloud of smoke filled the room.

"Almeda," Montana began, "the situation we have here is very serious and sad." He waited for a reaction to this.

Almeda took his cue. "I'm terribly sorry for what is happening. Cruz must be heartbroken."

"How long have you worked for the governor?" Montana asked.

"Me? . . . Oh . . . Six months . . . close to six months."

"And what is your position?"

"Scheduling secretary."

"You handle the governor's schedule."

"Yes. That is correct."

"For a private outing like the visit to the Borjas today, who is aware of the governor's schedule?"

"Obviously, the First Lady. And the secretaries, Virginia, Damaris, Elaine. Me. I mean, somebody has to know where the governor is at all times."

"What about the governor's security detail? Aren't they aware of the schedule beforehand?"

"For a private visit . . . sometimes. If there is a need to scout the area in advance, then they would know in advance."

"But today," Montana pointed out, "they weren't told where Cruz was going until the last minute. Is that correct?"

"Yes, that is correct as far as I know."

Montana said nothing for a second, then went on. "You've only worked for the governor for six months. That's not too long. What did you do before working here in Fortaleza?"

"I worked at the headquarters of the Statehood Party in Guaynabo. I was an executive assistant in the office of Marcos González, the party's president."

"How long were you with him?"

Almeda thought for a moment. "Nine months . . . I worked for him for nine months."

"Nine months," Montana repeated. "That's not too long either. Can you explain that?"

"Sure. I'll be very honest with you. Before working for the party, I was working at the Senate as a legal assistant, and believe me, the pay was poor, very poor. So I took the job with González because it paid better. And . . . and . . . when I learned about the job with Cruz I took it because it was even a higher salary."

"So it was money," Montana stated.

"Yes, sir, you can put it like that."

"Do you have money problems?"

"Well," Almeda said, pausing, "I have a late model BMW and I live in Ocean Park. Believe me, that costs money."

"I know. I understand," Montana said with a polite smile. "Okay, let me ask you, when did you find out that Cruz and the First Lady were going to spend the afternoon with the Borjas?"

"Yesterday . . . in the afternoon."

"And, tell me, did you by any chance tell anyone about it?"

"No . . . I didn't tell anyone."

"Not family? Friends? Co-workers?"

"No one. Absolutely no one. And I usually don't think about work when I'm at home. I mean, this job is already too demanding here . . . So, at home, I try to rest and take a break."

"Do you live alone?"

"Yes, I live alone."

Montana tried to process what he'd heard. Unlike the secretaries, Almeda had known about the governor's visit to the Borjas a full day in advance, he had money problems, and he'd only been on the job for six months. This man could have a motive to sell information. Money? Perhaps.

"Where did you go to college?" Montana asked.

"The University of Puerto Rico. The Rio Piedras campus."

"There are a lot of radicals there," Montana said quickly. "Don't you agree? Communists, Socialists, Marxists, Nationalists, *Independentistas*! A whole bunch of them." He spat each word.

Almeda considered this for a moment. Then: "Well, I would say that there are a lot of politically active people on the campus. A lot of political activity. It's a colorful place to be a student."

"Have you kept in touch with any radicals you met there?"

"I . . . I was never . . . I never met any radicals there," Almeda said nervously.

Montana didn't believe his answer but said nothing. "Okay," he said after a short pause. "I'm finished. Thank you for your time, Mr. Almeda. And again, I apologize for making you wait."

"I understand."

Both men stood up and shook hands. Almeda was glad the meeting was brief. He left the room and walked towards the staircase to the private residence. At one time he looked over his shoulders and realized Montana was following behind.

"I'm going that way too," Montana said, smiling briefly.

When the two men reached the residence, they found Cruz, Calero and Thompson conversing privately in a corner of the living room. Thompson's bodyguard looked bored by the window talking to Agent Walker, while Agents Pratt and Garcia sat near a table they had placed by the phone. They were both wearing earphones attached to the phone monitoring system. Their colleague, Agent Morales, was in Cruz's office doing the same task. Montana expected the terrorists to try to reach the governor at some point.

Almeda shook hands with Cruz, Calero and Thompson.

"You don't have to stay, Sam," Cruz told him.

"I want to help in any way I can, Governor," Almeda offered.

"Thank you."

Montana joined them. "Maybe we'll call you if we need you again," he told Almeda.

"Sure," Almeda said. He didn't like the tone of the FBI Assistant

Director's voice but thought better of saying anything. "I'll stay for a while," he said, and sat down at a small couch farther from the men.

Montana studied him for a moment, and then sat down with Cruz, Thompson and Calero. "Governor," he began, "I'm confident that with the resources of the Bureau and with the full cooperation of the Puerto Rican police, we will break this case. We will rescue your wife and we will arrest Rigonaldo Pastrana and his people. This week we'll be moving on some people for questioning. Especially some students at the University of Puerto Rico at the Rio Piedras and Mayagüez campuses. We've had them under surveillance for some time." He paused to light a cigarette. "Also, you should know that since Thursday's attempt, we've increased our surveillance of several people whom we believe have had contact with Rigonaldo Pastrana in the past, or whom we have reason to believe may have access to him. I'm talking about artists, intellectuals, journalists, college professors, and at least one member of the Puerto Rican Senate."

"Good," Thompson said approvingly.

"Pastrana wants to be a part of what is happening in Puerto Rico today," Montana said, smoke blowing out of his mouth. "In his own way he wants to participate in the process . . ."

"The plebiscite is killing him," Calero said. "He knows we'll win. That's my theory."

Cruz remained silent.

"He is desperate," Montana went on. "He hates being in hiding. He wants exposure. He wants people to know what he thinks, what he wants and so forth. He will pop up somewhere."

Calero said, "A few years from now, expect to take some heat once it becomes known that we put surveillance on all those people."

"I'm not worried about that," Montana responded firmly. "We are not breaking any laws."

"Oh, I agree with you," Calero affirmed.

"The laws in the states and in Puerto Rico are very clear," Senator Thompson added. "We are going against terrorists, not against people with *ideas*."

"That's right," Montana said. "Here we are not going after anyone merely for their ideas. We have targeted these people for their possible association and collaboration with September Twenty-third, which is clearly a very organized criminal operation."

"That is all perfectly true," Calero said. "Still, you'll have people denying their association with the terrorists and claiming they were targeted because of their ideas. It's happened before."

"I can live with that," Montana said.

"I'm just playing devil's advocate, I guess," Calero said. "I mean, we blew it in the *Cerro Maravilla* case and we got kicked in the ass with the *Carpetas* (secret dossiers) issue. I'm just saying we need to be careful and go by the book."

Cerro Maravilla. July 25, 1978. The police of Puerto Rico murdered in cold blood two young *independentistas* during an undercover operation orchestrated by the Puerto Rican police and the FBI. Heads rolled.

Las Carpetas – Las Listas de Subversivos (the subversives' dossiers). Late 1980's: The Puerto Rico Supreme Court declares unconstitutional the practice of opening police files on the U.S. citizens of Puerto Rico who are adherents of the *independentista* option. Tons and tons of dossiers were made public, over 150,000 people were targeted, and hundreds of public figures were affected. The law enforcement agencies on the island were exposed as extremist, out of control operations, orchestrated from top to bottom by the most wicked and fascist minds in the country. Gross violations of civil rights were committed. A public relations disaster for the Puerto Rican police and the FBI.

"We've learned from our mistakes, I think," Calero continued. "And at least my department has gained a wider perspective on the problem of terrorism here. We've had our share of right-wing terrorism, and I am a witness that Governor Cruz has done more than any other governor to attack it from up front. Even when the terror came from the right, Cruz was there to condemn it and to impart justice for all. That's why I think that what September Twenty-third is doing is grossly and absolutely unfair."

Cruz heard the mention of his name and that brought him back from deep thought. He had not shared in the men's conversation. He heard their exchange but was not particularly listening. His mind was set on only one thing: Ana María.

Ana María.

Ana María.

Ana María.

The phone began ringing. Cruz excused himself and walked to the table to answer it. He looked at the ten-line phone panel. Line one was blinking, which meant the call hadn't come through the switchboard. It was a direct call to the private residence.

He picked up the receiver and said, "Hello."

"Governor Cruz, please," an unfamiliar male voice said.

"This is Cruz."

"Governor," the devil said. "This is Rigonaldo Pastrana."

Chapter 21

The man's mention of the terrorist's name sent a subtle chill through the governor's body. And the voice sounded as if coming from afar. Cruz furrowed his brows, puzzled, even incredulous. This was either a tasteless joke or the real thing.

"Rigonaldo Pastrana?" Cruz said loudly enough to be heard by the FBI men and signaling with his hands for the agents to start recording and tracing the call.

Everyone's eyes were now on Cruz. Almeda kept calm.

"And how can I be sure that you are who you say you are?" Cruz asked, afraid of the answer.

Rigonaldo nodded to Luna who was holding a blindfolded Ana María near the phone. He placed the receiver against her lips. "Talk to him," he ordered.

Ana María was in pain as Luna was roughly twisting her arm against her back. "Elison! Elison!" she yelled. "It's me! I love you!"

Luna twisted harder.

"Ahh! You are hurting me!" Ana María screamed.

Rigonaldo came back to the phone as Luna took Ana María back to her holding room.

"Governor?" he said calmly.

"You let my wife go, you son of a bitch!" Cruz yelled at the top of his lungs.

"Governor," Rigonaldo said with dead calm and a measured voice, "we don't have much time."

"You hurt her and I'll kill you with my own hands!"

"She won't be hurt if you do what is asked of you."

"What the fuck do you want? You stinking bastard!"

"It's very simple . . . You cancel the plebiscite and I'll let her go . . . You don't cancel the plebiscite and you'll never see her again."

"I don't have the authority to do that."

"Wrong, wrong, wrong," Rigonaldo said. "It seems to me these are some very serious '*emergency and extraordinary circumstances*.' You go ahead with this plebiscite, Cruz, and your wife dies. The illustrious authors of the plebiscite law were right to provide you – and the U.S. President – with such a clever emergency *lifeline* . . . literally."

"You have no idea about any law of this country."

"Oh, but I do, Cruz . . . Read the law. So long." Rigonaldo hung up.

The dial tone came on. "Hello! Hello!" Cruz kept saying while he pressed the disconnect lever. Silence. He slammed down the phone.

"We got nothing," Agent Pratt said, taking off his earphones. "Not enough time."

"He hung up on me!" Cruz complained, shaking.

Montana said, "He'll call back. Not today and maybe not tomorrow, but he'll call back."

Cruz just glanced at him. "How the fuck does he have this private number?" he said, frustrated.

Almeda froze.

"We'll figure that out," Montana assured Cruz, glancing discreetly at Samuel Almeda. "But believe me, by talking to you that man's ego is stretching from here to the moon. Trust me, he'll want to talk to you again."

"He wants me to cancel the plebiscite!" Cruz said, his arms jerking in front of him.

"Okay, we know what he wants," Montana said. "That gives us at least seven days to find them. If his demand is to stop the plebiscite, I have a gut feeling that he won't do anything desperate before the plebiscite is held."

Cruz snapped, "He has my wife already. How much more desperate can he get?"

"We will have to be careful and patient. I believe that he will make mistakes," Montana assured him.

"He's been on the loose for ten years now!" Cruz said furiously and dismissing Montana's optimism. "Ten years! And it seems clear to me that he hasn't made any mistakes along the way. Don't you think?"

"I'm aware of that," Montana said firmly. "But this is the first time he seems to be sunk up to his neck in one of his own operations. Believe me, either he or one of his people will make a mistake. We have a lot of people on this case right now. This time I think we'll catch him."

Cruz collapsed on the sofa. "I don't think I have many choices here," he said. He glanced at Senator Thompson and told him, "We can't stop the plebiscite because of this terrorist!" His voice was heavy with contempt.

"That's not going to happen, Governor," Thompson said, leaning toward him. "I do think that within the next few days you should keep a very low profile, so as not to challenge him into doing something crazy. The rest of us, on the other hand, must present ourselves as if this matter hasn't reached us."

"What do you suggest?"

"To begin with, me and President Navas of the Commonwealth Party and President Ramos of the Independence Party will hold our press conference on Monday afternoon as planned. I strongly advise you not to be present. Send someone else to represent the Statehood Party."

Cruz considered this.

Thompson went on. "We will make it evident that the process for the consultation is still in motion. We have to stress that the majority of the Puerto Rican people, the President, the Congress and the local political parties are in favor of this plebiscite. I believe that is the message we must send."

Cruz was mute. He imagined his wife at that moment. She must be so scared, terrified.

"I also believe," Thompson continued, "that you should refrain from making any public pronouncements for the statehood option until we can rescue your wife."

"I agree with you for the most part," Cruz said finally. "But my silence will certainly hurt statehood in the actual vote." A shade of guilt crossed his mind at having expressed such a statement knowing that his wife's life was also at stake.

"I don't think so, Cruz," Thompson said quickly. "I'm told that right now there are several hundred people gathered at the front gates of Fortaleza showing their support for you and their repudiation of the terrorists. I believe that that will be the trend until this matter is resolved. People will spontaneously continue to support you out of a thirst for justice. The people of Puerto Rico are committed to democracy. We all know that. They don't want to see their values and their institutions defecated on by a group of ruthless criminals. People from all sides of the political spectrum will be on your side. I strongly believe that."

Cruz placed his hands over his lips and sighed in frustration. How is Ana María? Where have they taken her? This can't be happening! Should he have resigned like she said?

He had the absurd thought that her captors would see in her the good, compassionate woman that she was. But Rigonaldo Pastrana was a murderer. Cruz knew that he would kill Ana María if it would achieve some sinister political goal. And that knowledge scared him despite Senator Thompson's confident talk and despite the assurances from Montana and his FBI.

Cruz said, "I can't stop thinking of my wife surrounded by these evil strangers who hate me, and who hate everything I represent. Do you have any idea how she must be feeling right now?"

"Governor," Thompson said, "you have my deepest thoughts, from all of us. The conscience of the American and Puerto Rican people is with you and your wife. Everyone is on your side at this moment."

A maid entered the room and offered coffee. As a distraction, everyone accepted, except Almeda who had not dared utter a word. He got up and said, "I must be going. Governor, would you like me to stay?"

Cruz shook his head. "No Sam, it's all right. Go home and rest."

Almeda excused himself and left. Quietly, he walked out into the front garden of the mansion and took a look at the several hundred people gathered outside the wrought-iron gates on Fortaleza Street. He also saw a horde of reporters taking his picture with their telephoto lenses. Behind them, a man held a white sign with black bold letters: "DEATH PENALTY FOR TERRORISTS." Almeda considered this for a second, then got into his BMW and exited the mansion through the gate on Recinto del Oeste Street away from the crowd and reporters.

Karen Pérez reported live to her viewers that a top aide to Governor Cruz, Samuel Almeda, had just left Fortaleza. The reporters were now waiting for Police Superintendent Calero to come out and brief the press on the latest developments.

Within the mansion, William Montana approached Cruz and Calero. He lit a cigarette and considered the best way to express some thoughts about his interview with Samuel Almeda. He was distrustful of the man. Almeda's not-very-stable job history and his money-hungry track record had raised serious doubts in the Assistant Director's skeptical mind.

It was late afternoon in Puerto Rico. The sun would soon fall, bringing the night into Old San Juan. Governor Elison Cruz could have never imagined he would have to endure a day like this. Not even in his worst nightmare.

Chapter 22

Late into the night, Luna was driving to Santa Rita, the university town, to bring Tino back. The young man was pleased with his work today and was glad he had been useful to the higher cause. Luna tried to appease Tino's differences with Oso by assuring him that all the men of the cell were controlling, perfectionistic and *machistas*.

Tino said he understood and that, perhaps, he shouldn't question an order during an operation. He had things to learn.

Tino felt at ease with Luna. Though he was much younger, this forty-something woman seemed like the perfect lover to have. But Luna didn't particularly act like a lover to him. At least most of the time. She was what she was – a revolutionary comrade. Someone who could pull the trigger and follow orders when she had to. The latter was where Luna thought Tino needed training. She had told him so.

"Nothing happened today Tino, you understand?" Luna said.

"I know."

"Don't talk about today's operation with anyone. Not even the campus cell."

"Don't worry, Luna. I know how to keep my mouth shut."

"I know you do."

"So, why mention it?"

"This is one of the cell's most important hits. It's nothing personal with you."

"Okay."

"Good." Luna smiled. "So, what are you up to for the rest of the night?"

Tino knew that that was not an invitation to get laid.

"Gotta read some books," Tino said. "A fucking test on Monday."

"Hmmm . . . pretty impressive," Luna said while grinning. "No Saturday night sex orgy. No drunken escapade."

"Oh, I love orgies. I just don't have one planned for tonight."

Both of them laughed.

"Tell me a little about the UPR's sex scene nowadays," Luna asked seriously.

Tino was not shy to answer, but the question made him reconsider Luna's intentions.

"Are you hitting on me, Luna?"

"Maybe."

"Oso will really kill me if he hears us taking about this, you know."

"Fuck Oso. We haven't had sex in months. Besides, what I have with Oso is just sex."

"Is that all you want to have with me?"

"Maybe."

Tino was quiet for a second. Then, "I can handle that."

"Good. I know you can."

Tino knew this promising sex invitation was not to be done on this night, let alone in his place in Santa Rita. No one from Rigonaldo's cell was ever allowed to visit any of the cell's troubleshooters at their places of residence. Especially no one from the cell of the University of Puerto Rico, a place very closely watched by the island's security agencies.

Both of them knew this. Both of them knew the rules. This was probably what caused both their silence during the rest of the car ride.

Once in Santa Rita, Tino got out of the car at the edge of an open field on the grounds of the University of Puerto Rico. None of the cell members had ever driven him to his apartment, and tonight wouldn't be any different. Besides, perhaps Luna was just playing games with his head.

It was close to eleven p.m. when Luna made it back to the cell's hideout in the Guarite Forest. She found the men smoking and cleaning their weapons in the living room.

"Any news?" she asked.

"They said on TV that we want the plebiscite canceled," Oso

answered her. "They didn't mention that Rigonaldo spoke to Cruz, though."

"Which hurts my feelings," Rigonaldo said, laughing sarcastically.

"I think this time they'll take us seriously," Oso said, putting down a Winchester 300 rifle and reaching for a Smith & Wesson .357 Magnum.

"This time Cruz is the one who is trapped," Rigonaldo said bitterly. "And he thought this island was his private farm. Not anymore! He'll be finished after this."

"He's a fucking lackey of the *yanquis*. That's what he is," Oso said. "This will teach him that there's a high price to pay for treason."

"He hasn't seen the end of this," Rigonaldo declared. "From now on everyone in this country will know what I am all about. People will listen."

Oso exchanged looks with Teco. Earlier in the night, they had talked secretively about why Rigonaldo was set on killing Cruz instead of kidnapping him. Doing such a thing would have, even more strongly, pressured the political establishment into the goals of September Twenty-third. Just like they were doing now with the country's First Lady. And Oso – privately – took credit for it. In matters of strategy, they sometimes never fully understood Rigonaldo, but they knew better than to question or contradict him.

"Let me check on our guest," Luna said.

"She should be fine," Oso told her.

"Learning a little history," Rigonaldo said, grinning.

Luna went to the back room and found they had placed an old, thirteen-inch, black and white TV set hooked to a VCR in front of their prisoner. Luna recognized the footage on the TV screen: *La Larga Lucha* (The Long Struggle), a rustically-made documentary about the history of the armed struggle against American colonialism in Puerto Rico.

The blindfold had been taken off the eyes of the First Lady. Her body, still firmly tied to the chair, was brightened by the glow from the TV screen.

Luna was about to close the door of the room when a bad odor hit her nostrils. What the fuck? she thought. She looked around carefully and saw the "fluid" under the woman's chair.

"Shit," Luna said and then yelled in the direction of the living room. "Hey! This one pissed on the floor!" She closed the door and walked to the living room. "I ain't cleaning that shit!"

The men laughed at this.

"Didn't you take her to the bathroom when I was gone?" Luna asked as she lit up a cigarette.

"No," Oso said.

Rigonaldo had a smirk on his face. "I thought I heard her yell for us," he said.

"I heard her yell too," Oso said.

"Me too," Teco added.

They laughed.

"Well, I ain't cleaning it," Luna complained and went into the kitchen.

"Are you making coffee, Luna?" Rigonaldo asked.

"Yes," she answered, annoyed.

"Good, I'll take a cup," he said.

"Sure."

Rigonaldo said, "Don't worry about the mess in there. It will help her to acclimatize to her room."

Sunday, October 28

Chapter 23

Karen Pérez had a ten a.m. appointment with Senator Orlando Tonos at his home on Barkley Street in the *urbanización* Baldrich, an upscale neighborhood in Hato Rey, the business district of metropolitan San Juan. Tonio, her cameraman, was at the steering wheel of the station's van driving at the speed limit and distracted by music blasting from the radio.

Karen was reading clips from the newswire services that she had collected early in the morning. A report from Reuters had caught her attention. The P.R.R.A., Puerto Rican Revolutionary Army, another clandestine organization committed to violence against U.S. military personnel and installations in Puerto Rico, was severely criticizing September Twenty-third and Senator Tonos. She used a yellow marker to highlight the parts she needed and made a note on a writing pad to get a reaction from Senator Tonos during her interview with him.

Neither Karen or Tonio were aware they were being followed by a black car with two men in suits and dark sunglasses. They were the same men who had followed Karen since Thursday. They kept a discreet distance during the trip from Karen's home in Miramar to the TV station in Santurce, and now to Baldrich in Hato Rey.

When Tonio parked the van in front of Senator Tonos's house, the men parked a few houses down and watched.

Tonio unloaded his tripod and camera and followed Karen up a red-brick path to the front door. When Karen was about to ring the doorbell, the door suddenly opened and Karen came face to face with

Senator Tonos and a young man who was about to exit the house. The young man was Tino.

Tino. Rigonaldo's troubleshooter.

"Oh!" Karen exclaimed. "Good morning."

"Good morning, good morning," Tonos said smiling. "I call this good timing."

"It must be a sign of good fortune," Karen said.

"It must be," Tonos said, looking at Tino, then at Karen. "Karen, have you met Tino?"

"No, I don't think we've met."

"Tino," Tonos said, "this is Karen Pérez from Channel Four. One of the best journalists in town."

"Thank you for the compliment," Karen said as she shook hands with the young man.

"How do you do?" Tino said.

"Tino has just recently joined my staff," Tonos informed. "He troubleshoots at my office and occasionally serves as my chauffeur."

"Very good," Karen said politely. "Nice to meet you, Tino."

"Nice to meet you too," Tino replied.

"He's also a night student at the UPR," Tonos said. "Political Science."

Karen liked that. She said, "Oh, so you are a regular at the Social Sciences building, where all the action occurs."

Tino laughed approvingly. "You're surely right about that, Ms. Pérez," he said.

"I know that building like the palm of my hand," Karen said with a sense of irony; her years as a student activist flashed through her mind.

"Okay," Tonos said abruptly and addressing his young aide. "Thank you for stopping by, Tino. I'll see you in the morning, the usual time."

Tino nodded, excused himself and left. He was thrilled to have met the legendary Karen Pérez.

"Well," Tonos said to his guests, "come on in, please."

Karen and Tonio walked into the house and the Senator closed the door behind them.

The house's living room was spacious with fine Puerto Rican art hanging on all the walls. Immediately, Karen was greeted by Barbara Tonos, the senator's wife. She was a tall woman – a few very notable inches taller than her husband – and at forty-five, ten years younger than him. She had short black hair, smooth white skin, dark brown eyes, and a prominent nose and chin. She was an attorney, well known in Puerto Rican art circles and, at the present time, she served as a senior staff consultant at the Office of Historic Sites Preservation of the Institute of Puerto Rican Culture; a coveted position among Puerto Rican intellectuals.

"Karen Pérez!" Barbara said, embracing the TV reporter. "It's so nice to see you again."

"Nice to see you too," Karen responded.

"Would you like some coffee?" Barbara asked.

"Oh no, that's fine," Karen said politely while glancing at Tonio. "We've both had breakfast."

"Oh, please," Barbara dismissed her. "What's a little coffee going to do? I know you and Orlando have a lot to talk about, so let's start with coffee at the table."

Karen smiled. "Okay. Milk, no sugar," she said.

"That's better," Barbara approved. "And for the gentleman?" she asked Tonio.

"Milk and sugar is fine with me," Tonio said.

"Good. Now, make yourselves at home. I'll be right with you."

As Barbara left to the kitchen, Tonos said, "Dear, we'll be on the patio."

On Barkley Street, the men in suits – Mark Sulsona at the wheel and José Canseco in the passenger's seat – drove past Tonos's house for the second time. They stopped farther down when they spotted another dark vehicle with two more federal agents inside. These two – Melvin López at the steering wheel and Esteban Allende in the passenger's seat – had been assigned to watch Senator Tonos.

Sulsona came close to their colleague's vehicle and pushed the automatic button to lower the car's window. "Working overtime?" he said to Agent López.

"I'll be darned," López said. "Big Mark is in the neighborhood." He patted Allende's leg to wake him up. Allende straightened himself up in the seat and said hi.

"How's it going?" Sulsona asked.

"Boring, for the most part," López said. "Your lady is here, you know."

"I know, that's why we are here," Sulsona said, glancing for a second at Tonos's house in his rearview mirror. "What's Tonos doing?"

"Not much, actually," López said with a shrug. "Once he is home, he's home."

"Who was that kid that just left?"

"His driver. We have to check him out." He paused. "That's basically it here. Not much happening. I tell you, it's boring."

"Well, try to follow a TV reporter around. It's like a carousel. It can make you dizzy," Sulsona said seriously.

"Do you want to trade subjects? A Senator for a TV type?"

"Naaah," Sulsona said. "We get to do a lot of sightseeing."

"Okay, that's fair."

The agents stopped talking for a moment as a car drove past them.

"I wonder what those two are up to," Sulsona said.

"Well, with Pérez you can catch it on the news half of the time. That's what she does for a living: talk, ask questions and show face."

"Yeah," Sulsona said, "but I bet the best part is what we don't see on the news."

"Oh, I'll have to agree on that."

Another car was approaching.

"I'll catch you later," Sulsona said.

"Adios."

The agents nodded to each other. Sulsona drove to the end of the street, made a u-turn and drove past Tonos's house, parking a little further down the street with a clear view of the house in his rearview mirror. Next, they chain-smoked cigarettes and waited for Karen Pérez to come out of the house again.

The patio of Senator Tonos's home was a refreshing place full of tropical plants and flowers of all sorts. It was a forest of *Claveles, Margaritas, Girasoles, Alelies, Lirios, Violetas, Amapolas, Orquideas,* and so forth. The coffee had arrived, Tonio had set his camera on the tripod, and Karen was ready to begin her interview.

Senator Tonos was now finished reading the Reuters report with the press release of the clandestine Puerto Rican Revolutionary Army. He sighed, straightened his glasses, handed the report to Karen and said, "That definitely sounds like something they would write."

"I'm going to ask you to comment on it," Karen told him.

"Sure."

Karen addressed Tonio. "Are we ready?"

"Rolling," Tonio said as he scanned his shot through the camera's lens.

"All right," she said. She smiled, then: "Good morning, Senator Tonos."

"Good morning."

"Today we received a press release from the Puerto Rican Revolutionary Army. This is what they have stated, and I quote." She began reading. "*We want to express our position with regard to recent events in Puerto Rico. We are concerned that our comrades in September Twenty-third are not working for the best interests of our struggle for freedom and independence. Our common enemy is the government of the United States and its armed forces. We do not consider the Governor of Puerto Rico or much less his wife as worthy targets of our military actions. To divide Puerto Ricans against other fellow Puerto Ricans is the goal of the evil American enemy. Military actions must be directed toward the American government and its installations on our island. The Governor of Puerto Rico and his wife are not the problem we face. It is the system they support and represent, against which we must direct all of our operations.*

We also repudiate the comparisons that the Honorable Senator Orlando Tonos has made between the nationalist uprising of the 1950's and the actions of September Twenty-third today. They are in no way similar in nature.

We nevertheless agree with the Senator that the boycott of the upcoming plebiscite on the political status of Puerto Rico is the best way to advance the cause of independence for our nation. This plebiscite has been orchestrated by the United States and is designed to grant a victory to statehood. This is not, in any way, a democratic consultation. The participation of the Independence Party in this plebiscite is a mistake and a historical aberration.

We unequivocally propose to all patriotic organizations in Puerto Rico to join us in our declaration of war against the real enemy of the Puerto

Rican people – the U.S. government. Against the American oppressor we direct all of our military operations. Viva Puerto Rico Libre!'"

Karen placed the report on her lap and said softly, "Senator, what is your reaction to what the P.R.R.A. has stated?"

Tonos spoke with a soft demeanor. "I said to you earlier that this is expected from them. They have always strictly concentrated their activities against American targets. Whereas September Twenty-third has always included Puerto Rican collaborators as targets.

"If anything, the statement from the P.R.R.A. exposes the deep divisions amidst the independence forces of this country. I am going to ignore the criticism they've made of my assessment of the history of the independence movement in Puerto Rico, and I will concentrate on the things which we agree upon; and that is the boycott of the plebiscite of November Third."

"How do you explain the decision of the Independence Party to participate in the plebiscite?"

"The Independence party is out of focus on this issue. Their leadership is delusional if they think that they will bring independence to Puerto Rico through a plebiscite which was designed by the Americans, or if they, for that matter, participate in any electoral process in Puerto Rico."

"What is your solution then?"

"Independence will come through our efforts in international forums and through the creation of a Constitutional Assembly."

"Governor Cruz has said that Puerto Rico does not need another Constitutional Assembly," Karen stated.

"Oh, really?" Tonos said cynically. "If all of the political problems of Puerto Rico were solved in the Constitutional Assembly of the 1950's, then why is Cruz so obsessively trying to destroy our current constitutional status? Why does he want to abolish the constitution of the Commonwealth and make Puerto Rico a state of the United States? What he says makes no sense and he is clearly contradicting himself. This country needs a new Constitutional Assembly, no argument about it."

"Senator," Karen went on, "as we all know, Governor Cruz is going through a very difficult time personally, as we have learned that

September Twenty-third has kidnapped First Lady Ana María Cruz and has demanded the cancellation of the plebiscite of November Third as a condition for her release. Do you think that . . . ?"

"What this governor is facing," Tonos said sharply and cutting her off, "is not a personal problem. It is a political problem and he can solve it in a political way by canceling the plebiscite. It is as simple as that and . . ."

"Yes, I understand your point," Karen interrupted, "but, don't you think that September Twenty-third has gone too far this time? Isn't kidnapping an extreme act?"

"To attempt to make Puerto Rico a state of the United States is not only extreme but criminally explosive. In this case Elison Cruz is the extremist. That is why I have said that the actions of September Twenty-third do not surprise me in the least. They are the only logical consequences of the actions of this governor."

"Are you condoning the actions of September Twenty-third?"

"I am saying that I *understand* the actions of September twenty-third. That is what I'm saying."

"But," Karen pressed on, "do you condemn the kidnapping of Ana María Cruz?"

"I condemn the attempts of Governor Cruz to advance his agenda of statehood for Puerto Rico. That is a crime against the people of Puerto Rico."

"Nevertheless, Senator, the people of Puerto Rico seem to be very content with their relationship with the United States. That is what is implied by the electoral behavior of the people, as in election after election, nearly ninety-six percent of the voters cast their ballots in favor of the Statehood Party or the Commonwealth Party, both of which support the continuation of our relationship with the United States."

"Your numbers are not necessarily correct," Tonos said, dismissing Karen's statement. "You are not taking into consideration those of us who at one time or another have boycotted elections in this country." He leaned forward. "Let me tell you something about elections in Puerto Rico. And I want you to listen very carefully." He took off his glasses for dramatic emphasis. "There are no free elections in Puerto Rico. We do not have democratic elections in Puerto Rico. That is an illusion. A people who have been subjected to five-hundred-years of colonialism – as we have – cannot consciously and freely vote in any election. In order for us to have free elections you have to decolonize *first*. When we are free, that is when you can call a Puerto Rican election a free and democratic election."

"Aren't you underestimating the wisdom of the Puerto Rican people?"

"Absolutely not," Tonos said emphatically. "I am exposing the realities of colonialism and the predicament of the colonized. This predicament repeats itself everywhere in the world where colonialism has been a reality."

"But, when you criticize the electoral process of Puerto Rico, aren't you criticizing the very process that got you elected? Are you saying that the very process that has granted you the opportunity to become a senator in our legislature is mortally flawed?"

"I think that's different," Tonos said quickly. "The people who vote for me are voting against government waste and against government and police corruption. During my three terms in the senate, I have been able to expose corruption in practically every single government agency, including the mighty police department. I am very aware of what my calling is and what the voters expect from me. I am an independent thinker and an independent doer with an independent platform that the voters approve of and . . ."

"Aren't those same voters capable enough of making informed, conscious decisions when they vote with respect to our relationship with the United States?"

"I strongly believe, as I said, that colonialism plays a major role in the electoral behavior of the Puerto Rican voters when it relates to expressing choices or preferences of political status."

"Okay," Karen said, deciding not to press the issue any longer, "one more question, and it will be my last. What would be your prediction concerning what actions September Twenty-third might take within the next few days?"

Tonos was fast in his answer. "I am not a member of September Twenty-third, therefore I don't know the answer to that question."

"Based on your political experience and your knowledge of this group what . . ." Karen pressed on.

"I said I don't know the answer to that question," Tonos said firmly. "You are going to have to ask *them* that question. They themselves should know what they will do next. They should know."

Karen nodded. "Thank you for your time, Senator Tonos."

"Thank you," he said seriously.

It had been a good interview, Karen thought.

Tonio shut off his camera and immediately lit up a cigarette, which he held awkwardly as he began to dismantle his equipment. Barbara Tonos came back onto the patio. "Well," she said to Karen, "that was fast."

"Believe me," Karen said, "in televison minutes, this is as long as the *Titanic* movie."

Barbara laughed at this.

"It will run tonight on the six and ten o'clock editions," Karen reported.

"Good," Barbara said, "Eugenia will be able to catch it. After all these years of her father being a public figure, she still likes to see him on TV. She videotapes everything he's on. I say she is permanently starstruck."

Karen laughed politely. Eugenia was the Tonoses' nineteen-year old daughter.

"Don't mind her," Karen said. "I would probably do the same with my father. Where is she now?"

"Old San Juan," Barbara said. "Her best friend is putting together an exhibition at Café Berlin, so she's helping out."

"Oh, yes, I know the place. Very cozy. Did she get to go to Havana?"

"Yes, yes," Barbara said excitedly. "Actually, we went together."

"That's nice. How did you like it?"

"Eugenia was thrilled, of course. She wants to go to school there. To study film at the New School of Latin American Cinema . . . As for me . . ." she sighed. "To be honest with you I almost wanted to cry. Old Havana is a jewel of a city, but it breaks your heart to see the deterioration of the buildings, and they have almost no resources for restoration projects."

"I know," Karen agreed. "I noticed that too when I visited there."

"When was that?"

"Nineteen-ninety, just when the biggest crisis was starting."

"It is so sad what the U.S. embargo has done to Cuba," Barbara said softly.

Senator Tonos spoke this time. "What is sad," he said, "is to see every single American president being held hostage by that Cuban mafia in Miami. And those Cubans? They come here to Puerto Rico and all of them – every single one of them – votes for statehood. Talk about why statehood support has grown in this country and look at the statistics of Cuban immigration into Puerto Rico. *There* is your answer. It's a scandal! If I were governor I would ban Cuban immigration into Puerto Rico!"

Karen laughed but said nothing.

"Oh dear," Barbara said mischievously, "if you ever hold higher office in Puerto Rico, I hope it will be as President of the Republic. Nothing less than that."

"Are you that ambitious?" Karen asked seriously.

"Hell no!" Tonos exclaimed. "The first president of the Republic of Puerto Rico has yet to be born."

"Do you think so?" Karen asked, seriously interested. "Will it take that long?"

"I try to be optimistic," Tonos said. "But it wouldn't surprise me if we drag out the status issue for another forty to fifty years."

Barbara said, "Orlando thinks that the status debate in Puerto Rico is the bread and butter of the people."

Karen smiled. That's what journalists think too, she thought to herself. "You'd be amazed how many people feel that way," she said, glancing at her wrist watch. "Well, we should be going now." She got up and shook Tonos's hand. "Thank you very much, senator."

"Always my pleasure," Tonos said.

"And one of these days," Karen said, "we can talk about Cuba . . . on tape."

"Good. Just let me know."

Karen and Barbara kissed on the cheek. "Bye, Barbara. It was nice to see you again," Karen said. "And send my regards to Eugenia."

"She'll appreciate that," Barbara said sincerely.

The Tonoses led the way to the front door, and with a hand wave, bid farewell to Karen and Tonio.

The reporter and her cameraman jumped into the station's van and sped away.

Federal Agents Sulsona and Canseco followed them in their black vehicle at a discreet distance.

"I don't care who he is," Tonio said as he lit up a cigarette while waiting for a green light at Domenech Avenue, "but sometimes I really don't know how Tonos can get away with some of the things he says."

"What do you mean?" Karen asked while looking at her notes on a yellow writing pad.

The light turned green and Tonio stepped on the accelerator. "Didn't you see how he totally avoided censoring September Twenty-third?"

"Yeah?"

Tonio mimicked the senator and said, "'Colonialism is a crime' or 'statehood is a crime against the people of Puerto Rico' or whatever it was he said." He frowned. "Yeah, right. What about kidnapping? Now, *that* is a serious crime."

Karen looked up from her notes. Discussing her personal views about an interviewee with a young cameraman was something she didn't normally do. She said, "The people are fed up with corruption. That's why they keep electing him and he knows that."

"I guess," Tonio said, knowing that that was as much as Karen would say. He turned on the radio and said, "Okay, where to now?"

"Back to the station."

"Okay, boss."

Karen leaned her head back against the seat and let her thoughts drift about the interview she'd just finished and about the interview she wanted to do next: Elison Cruz. A face to face meeting with the governor. I'll talk to Emilio about it, she said to herself. I definitely want a talk with Cruz.

Chapter 24

"He's not talking," Emilio Durcal said from behind his crowded desk. "The man is completely mute! And check this out, we got CBS, NBC, ABC *and* CNN in town and he's still not talking. Can you believe that?"

"No," Karen said matter-of-factly.

"Go figure," Durcal said, lighting a cigar. "Though, I do have an idea of what they're doing."

"Is he talking to Telemundo or Univisión?"

"Nope! With them even less. You know how colonized he is," Durcal said seriously.

"So," Karen said, frustrated, "who's talking then?"

"Arias," Durcal said, referring to Carmen Enid Arias, the flamboyant Secretary of State in Cruz's cabinet. "And she should like the exposure. She wants to be governor some day."

"I see," Karen said simply.

"Don't be discouraged now. Very soon Cruz will have to break his silence, and I promise you I'll do all I can to hook you up with him one on one. Actually," he said, pausing to reach for a white sheet of paper from his desk, "we have good news for him."

"What is it?"

"In our latest poll he came up with a seventy-five percent approval rating. His highest ever. And," Durcal continued, "Twenty-five percent of that is cross-partisan support."

"Wow, that should make them happy."

"I know," Durcal said, pushing the paper aside. "Okay, how did it go with Tonos?"

"Fine," Karen said with a shrug. "The usual Tonos we know."

"I bet he's not shedding any tears nowadays," Durcal pointed out with a grin.

"At least he explains himself very well," Karen said with a bit of irony.

"Okay, we'll run that at six and ten. In the meantime, go and talk to Arias. We gave her our poll numbers and she is completely elated. She'll be happy to see you."

"Is she at State?"

"No. She's at Fortaleza. And, by the way, she'll be there tomorrow with Navas, Ramos and Thompson."

"Thompson," Karen said thoughtfully. "What do we do with him?"

"Press conference tomorrow. He's not giving one on ones. I tried to get him for today but he declined."

"Oh, he's here already?"

"Yeah. He's been here since yesterday but," he paused, "he's leaving tomorrow. No personal interviews. I gather he's trying not to outstage the others. And I also think he's going through a security scare."

"I don't blame him," Karen said, getting up. "I'm ready to go. Anything else?"

"Hmmm . . . Tomorrow morning, I want you to cover Alan de Jesús's funeral."

"I know. I have that on my calendar already. Is Cruz going to be there?"

"No. He canceled that too. Arias will be there instead."

"Interesting."

"I'm telling you, the man is out of the picture. Apparently for now."

"Apparently something finally got to him. You know, personally."

Durcal nodded.

"Okay," Karen said, "I'll see you tomorrow. After I see Arias I'll come back to edit and go home. I need some rest."

"Sounds fair to me."

Karen walked out of Durcal's office, found Tonio in an editing room and in a few minutes both left for Fortaleza. On her way there,

Karen thought of Durcal's words, "Arias will be happy to see you." Oh well, she told herself. She drafted a few questions for the Secretary of State and then tried to take a nap the rest of the way. She couldn't wait to go home and rest.

Chapter 25

At around seven-thirty p.m., Cruz was at the residence working on some documents. A temporary desk had been brought into the private residence where Cruz had transferred most activities from his office in order to remain near the phone line the terrorist had used. Agents Prat and García sat boringly on a couch close to their phone interception equipment. FBI Assistant Director Montana, Police Superintendent Calero and Secretary of State Arias had left half an hour earlier. They all watched Channel Four's newscast with the good news about the approval poll for Cruz, and the "disturbing" interview with Senator Orlando Tonos. "That bastard," Cruz said of the Senator. "We've had him under surveillance since Thursday night," Montana had said. "And Pérez too." Cruz was pleased.

In the afternoon, Cruz spoke by phone with his son in Connecticut. He then discussed, once again with Montana, the Assistant Director's concerns about Almeda. "I trust him," Cruz assured him.

And then, during the whole day, there was the anxious wait for Rigonaldo to call again. It was nerve-wracking. They waited and waited. But the call never came.

Chapter 26

The sound of the *coquíes* (the native tiny tree frogs of Puerto Rico) and a cooler temperature were the only indications to Ana María Cruz that night had fallen. She had been kept blindfolded all the time and by now it was evident to her that the terrorists would not remove her from the chair she was tied to and into a bed.

Her back and buttocks were in horrendous pain, but at least the night had allowed for cool air to overcome the intense heat she had felt most of the day. And she was hungry. They had only fed her once. Bread and water. Why, God? Why? Please bring some compassion into the hearts of these people, she prayed.

She didn't know what time it was, she didn't know where she was and she didn't know how long it would take before she'd be rescued. Because she did have that hope. To be rescued. To go back home. She knew that if Elison could, he himself would break down the door of this hell house and rescue her.

She prayed for hours and cried at the same time. Her blindfold was drowned in tears. Eventually, exhaustion overcame her and she fell asleep.

When she awoke again, the *coquíes* had stopped singing.

Monday, October 29

Chapter 27

Alan de Jesús was buried at the Buxeda Cemetery in Baldrich. Secretary of State Carmen Enid Arias delivered a moving eulogy in which she praised the virtues of the young public servant. She was back in Fortaleza by eleven in the morning, in time for an impromptu lunch at the private residence with Cruz, Senator Thompson and with President Arturo Navas of the Commonwealth Party and Andrés Ramos of the Independence Party. U.S. Senator Thompson had pressed for the gathering.

Navas was a tall man in his fifties with gray hair, dark brown eyes, light skin, and a long nose that held gold-framed spectacles. He was wearing a sharp black suit.

Ramos was the shortest of the group, nearing his sixtieth birthday, with white hair, pale white skin, blue eyes and a fine nose and lips. He wore a navy-blue suit.

Carmen Enid Arias was a woman of forty-nine with perfectly styled brown hair held still by lots of L'oreal hair spray. She wore lots of makeup to enhance her otherwise simple features. Her heavy mascara brought to mind Tammy Faye Baker to those who knew who the hell Tammy Faye Baker was. Arias was slightly overweight despite all of her attempts at dieting. Today she was wearing a dark-brown, two-piece business suit.

Senator Thompson was pleased that the staunch political rivals had agreed to meet socially. This was their second meeting together. The first one had been months earlier at the Oval Office in the White House in Washington with the President of the United States. That meeting had been the culmination of an arduous and long process of negotiations that produced the almost miraculous agreement to hold a plebiscite to finally settle a permanent political status for Puerto Rico. After much mud-throwing, name-calling, back and forth accusations, threats of boycott and brutally heavy lobbying in Congress, the U.S. President invited the warring parties to his office to use his charm and his insight to convince them that this was indeed a historical opportunity, where all roads had led to the same destination: a final solution to the Puerto Rican political dilemma. No other U.S. President had become so directly and personally involved in Puerto Rican politics as this President. And he confided to the Puerto Rican visitors that after Puerto Rico, his next big effort in the Caribbean would be aimed at solving the impasse between the United States and Cuba.

At Fortaleza, the political rivals conversed amicably, putting the most controversial political issues aside. Navas and Ramos reassured Governor Cruz that they were indeed extremely concerned about the situation with the First Lady, and that they hoped for a favorable resolution to the crisis.

By quarter after twelve the lunch was over and all the parties had agreed that U.S. Senator Thompson would open the press conference by reading a joint statement signed by Cruz, Navas and Ramos.

Cruz shook hands with his political rivals and retired to the living room to watch the press conference on live TV. Secretary of State Arias and the rest of the group walked to the press room of Fortaleza where their respective aides joined them. Samuel Almeda was with her.

The press room was packed to full capacity and the presence of the U.S. networks added a major significance to the event. Three oak podiums with microphones had been positioned at the front of the room facing the press corps. Thompson and Arias stood behind the center podium with Navas and Ramos at the podiums on either side.

As agreed, Thompson spoke first in a deep and firm voice. "Good afternoon ladies and gentlemen. I am honored to have been chosen by Presidents Ramos and Navas and by Governor Cruz to open this press conference today. I have here a joint statement which I will kindly read for your benefit." He put on his reading spectacles and read from a sheet that had been typed earlier by Damaris, Cruz's secretary, in a frantic rush. *"As representatives of the people of Puerto Rico we have come together at this historic time to begin the process that will solve, once and for all, the debate over the political status of Puerto Rico.*

'The plebiscite to take place this Saturday, November 3rd is the starting point of that process. It is our duty, as representatives of the people, to encourage all eligible voters to cast their votes for that political formula which best represents their goals and highest aspirations. We believe this to be at the core of our democracy.

'We stand united with the support of the people of Puerto Rico and the people of the United States to make history. There is nothing that will distract us from this great responsibility that the people have bestowed upon us.

'On November 3rd come to the polls, cast your ballots and let your voice be heard. We owe it to ourselves and to future generations of Puerto Ricans.

'May God help us as we embark on this historic task," he paused. *"'Signed today, Monday, October 29. Arturo Navas, Andres Ramos and Elison Cruz.'"*

Thompson paused briefly to nod deferentially to the leaders standing beside him. "I would like to add," he said, "that this consultation to be held in Puerto Rico has created enormous interest among the American public. The President of the United States is closely following the course of events here. He has expressed publicly and privately his commitment to the self-determination of Puerto Rico. In no uncertain terms, he wants this done and he wants this plebiscite to be validated with the highest ever voter turnout Puerto Rico has ever seen.

"We in congress as well, look forward to the final results of the vote. We have a mandate to work together with the Puerto Rican people in their democratic aspirations." He paused. "In my name, in the name of the U.S. Congress and in the name of the President of the United States, thank you very much." He stepped back from the podium, allowing Arias to move forward to the microphone.

"Okay," she said, "we are ready for your questions now."

An avalanche of voices battled to be heard at the same time. All of them had questions about First Lady Ana María Cruz. Not a single question about the plebiscite.

"Wait. Wait. Wait," Arias chuckled nervously. "We are going to answer your questions. But I want to remind you that President Navas, Ramos and myself are here to inform the public about the plebiscite on Saturday and . . ."

Another avalanche of questions. This time more brutal than the first.

"Wait. Wait," Arias tried again. "We, as well as Senator Thompson, are committed to the success of the plebiscite. It is a matter of . . ."

"Aren't you concerned," a reporter shouted, "that to go on with this plebiscite will endanger the life of Ana María Cruz?" It was Berk Waters, the correspondent of CNN.

Karen Pérez cursed. That was her exact question.

"Listen," Arias said, failing to fake calmness, "this will be the most that I will say about that subject because we have to go on with the business of this country." She paused. "We are all concerned with the welfare of First Lady Ana María Cruz. All of us. But you must understand that this is a very delicate situation, and I mustn't comment any further about it."

Karen Pérez shouted, "Do you have any leads as to where she is being held?"

"That is part of an ongoing investigation by the Police Department and the FBI," Arias said carefully. "I don't think I should comment on it."

"Have you had any contact with Rigonaldo Pastrana or any member of September Twenty-third?" another reporter shouted.

"I have no comment," Arias said flatly.

"Have they set a deadline for their demands to be met?"

"I don't have a comment on that," Arias stood her guard.

"We have just learned that the FBI has detained several students in Mayagüez and Rio Piedras for questioning in relation to Ana María Cruz. Have you actually linked those students to the kidnapping of the First Lady?"

"I'm not aware of what the FBI is doing," Arias said with an edge, and beginning to lose her patience.

"Oh, come on!" some reporters said in unison.

Arias said, "As I said, I am not going to comment on an ongoing investigation."

"Senator Thompson," Linda Smith of CBS asked, "have President Clarke and Governor Cruz spoken about the possibility of cancelling the plebiscite?"

There was a short silence in the room.

Thompson approached his microphone and said, "I am not aware of any recent conversation between the President and Governor Cruz."

"Secretary Arias," Karen said, "where is Governor Cruz? Why isn't he here?"

Arias stepped aside from the podium visibly frustrated. She ignored the questions for a moment, whispered something to Thompson, and then said, "Governor Cruz is not here because he does not want to distract you from the purpose of this meeting which is to discuss the plebiscite. And I ask you to please focus on that issue in deference to all of us here on this stage."

There were whispers all across the room. Then the room became quiet as the press gave thought to this. Alina Casiano, a reporter from *El Nuevo sol*, was the first to pose a question.

"Senator Thompson," she began, "what is your reaction to the argument that this plebiscite is designed to give a victory to statehood?"

Thompson leaned towards the microphone. "I don't think that question should be addressed to me," he said softly. "But I think that the participation of the Commonwealth and Independence parties in this plebiscite is evidence that this is an open process, the outcome of which is subject to the actual preferences of the voters."

"At the beginning of this process, the U.S. President openly supported statehood. Doesn't that prejudice the outcome of this plebiscite?" asked Bill Moore from ABC.

"The President supports self determination," Thompson said flatly.

President Navas of the Commonwealth Party spoke into his microphone. "We believe that we are facing a very fair election here. All of the status options have been clearly defined, both by us and by the U.S. Congress. We all know what we have to lose and what we have to gain. If we had thought that there was any unfair advantage for any of the choices, we would not be participating as aggressively as we are . . ."

President Ramos of the Independence Party cleared his throat and said, "The Independence party is participating because we see it as an excellent opportunity to educate the people about the benefits of independence. We do not think that this plebiscite is moving Puerto Rico any closer to statehood. Whichever option wins will be weakened by what we believe will be a strong showing of the independence forces."

"You should know," Navas said, "that we are confident the people will choose free association over the other two options. It represents the middle ground that Puerto Ricans have always opted for."

"President Ramos," Carol Andino from Associated Press said, "what do you have to say to those groups within the independence movement who criticize your participation in this plebiscite?"

"We do not have any contact or influence over fringe groups that operate in Puerto Rico in the name of independence," Ramos said flatly. "I do not have anything to say to them."

"What do you say to the argument," Karen Pérez asked, "that there are no democratic elections in Puerto Rico, given our condition as a colony of the United States?"

Thompson shifted uncomfortably on his feet.

President Ramos said, "The Puerto Rican electorate is very mature, well-informed and sophisticated. Nobody disagrees that we are a colony. That's why the public is so interested in the outcome of this plebiscite."

"Let me say something," Navas interjected. "To say that Puerto Ricans are incapable of making conscious choices in a voting booth is insulting and absolutely preposterous. We have been exercising our right to select our government for over six decades. To say that there are no democratic elections in Puerto Rico is a flat-out lie."

The next question came from Anne Simons of NBC. "Secretary Arias," she said, "are you disappointed that President Clarke has not vigourously spoken in favor of statehood during these crucial months and that his position now is to support self-determination?"

"The way I see it," Arias said, "President Clarke expressed his support for statehood, but at the same time set the stage to consult the Puerto Rican people about it. His support for self-determination is what is expected of the United States. To my understanding, the U.S. presidents who publicly supported statehood before him, Gerald Ford, Ronald Reagan and George Bush Sr., always knew that a plebiscite was needed to legitimize the process. This is a democratic process and the people of

Puerto Rico will make a final determination. The importance of American support for statehood is that it shows that the idea of Puerto Rico being a state is not something that comes unilaterally from us. We have many friends on the mainland who see our goal of statehood as an issue of human rights and equality for the U.S. citizens of this island. So no, we are not disappointed. We strongly believe that statehood will win this plebiscite . . ."

Then there was a shout coming from the microphone next to her.

"Puerto Rico will never be a state of the United States!" Navas exclaimed bluntly.

Arias was taken aback by the solidly direct statement.

The President of the Independence Party took his turn to be blunt. He said, "We will be an independent republic when the dust settles. You'll see."

Arias said, "Well, that's why we are going to the polls. The people will decide that."

The press was amused by the exchange. After a second of silently observing and listening to the three rivals taking shots at each other, the room burst into laughter. Then Thompson, Arias, Navas and Ramos laughed along with the crowd. Nervous laughter, but laughter nonetheless.

Chapter 28

But Rigonaldo Pastrana, watching the exchange on live television, was not laughing. He was indeed enraged. He abruptly got up from the couch and repressed his impulse to break the television set into a million pieces. "They think this is entertaining!" he said, pacing frenetically. "They think this is a joke? They think Puerto Rico is a joke?"

He stared at his pack of accomplices expecting no reply. "They think I'm playing," he barked. "I'll fucking teach them how I play." His face was now as red as blood, the veins on his throat protruding noticeably. Heavy drops of sweat fell into his eyes. He walked hurriedly to the kitchen and brought a butcher's knife back with him to the living room. He wielded the weapon in Luna and Oso's faces as Teco watched from a corner. Nobody dared to make a move.

"I will teach them how I play," Rigonaldo said furiously as he disappeared towards the back room. He kicked open the door to Ana María's holding room while mumbling obscenities. Ana María shook violently at the sound of the door opening and the monster's voice. Her face was pure terror when Rigonaldo abruptly took off her blindfold and wielded the knife in her face.

"Your bastard friends think this is a game," Rigonaldo told his captive in a menacing voice.

Right at that moment Ana María knew that this man was capable of anything; capable of unspeakable horrors.

"What do you want?" Ana María asked weakly while repressing tears.

Rigonaldo pressed the knife against her face. It felt cold on her skin. He then flicked her ears with it. He kept flicking her ears with it.

"Did you ever hear about what they did to that Getty boy?" Rigonaldo asked her.

Ana María said nothing. Of course she knew what kidnappers did in 1973 to John Paul Getty III, grandson of oil billionaire J. Paul Getty: they cut off his ear and sent it to the billionaire when he refused to pay the $17 million ransom.

"I want to talk to my husband," Ana María was able to say.

Rigonaldo ignored her and kept flicking her ears with the knife. Ana María was now so filled with dread that her thoughts seemed to have stopped.

The knife was now wet with Ana María's own sweat.

"This won't hurt too much," Rigonaldo said simply.

Chapter 29

Several hours later, Luna was walking hurriedly through the crowded streets of Old San Juan. She wore dark sunglasses, a pink hat, a blond wig, white gloves and a beige, two-piece business suit. In one hand she held a cigarette; in the other she carried a large, black glossy shopping bag with the *"Vanities"* logo, a fine crystal and jewelry store.

It was a beautiful, sunny afternoon in the old capital city. There were four cruise ships docked in the piers. Tourists, mostly Americans, with their tanned red skins and bright colored clothing crowded the streets, along with government workers on their obligatory coffee break. And the ever-present afternoon shoppers, always attracted by the enchantment of the old city, struggled to walk along the narrow streets. Luna the terrorist mingled with the crowd as if she were one more passerby.

She maneuvered her way through the crowd until reaching her first destination: the public payphone in front of the main entrance of the building that housed the offices of the State Electoral Commission on *Recinto Sur* Street. She entered the phone booth and placed her bag on the floor. She grabbed the receiver and pretended to be placing a phone call, looking around in every direction. There were no cops in sight. That was good. Not that it would make a difference.

After several office workers smoking in front of the targeted building disappeared back inside through the glass sliding doors, Luna felt safe. She discreetly rummaged in her *Vanities* bag and pulled out a smaller paper bag. The shoe box inside of it was heavy, as it should be. She quickly peered inside of it and then looked at her wrist watch. Everything was in order.

She placed the bag with the heavy shoe box on the floor of the phone booth and cautiously pushed it into a corner with her foot. Then, she took chewing gum from her mouth, and, from her bra, she produced a small paper note inscribed "out of order" and stuck it firmly over the coin slot. Now she just needed the assholes to stay away from this phone.

"Excuse me, are you going to be long?" a woman asked from behind the glass door of the booth.

Luna was annoyed. She faced the woman and said casually, "It's not working. It just ate all my money. I'm trying to get it back."

"But it was working this morning," the woman insisted.

"Well, it's not working now," Luna said calmly. Get out of my face you fucking idiot, Luna thought.

"*Coño*," the woman exclaimed. "Nothing works in this country!" She left in a hurry, furiously cursing about the phone company.

Luna grabbed her *Vanities* bag, placed a second "out of order" note on the glass door of the phone booth and walked away. She didn't look back. She just walked to the corner of *Recinto Sur* and *Tanca* Streets and waited.

An American family, a blond, slender woman and a young-looking man pushing an infant in a baby stroller, were now standing a few feet from the phone booth in front of the State Electoral Commission. The woman was looking over a map of Old San Juan. They were lost and asking for directions from the pedestrians walking past them. They finally settled for a young man in a sharp black suit and tie.

"Yes," the young man had answered, "I do speak English."

"Oh, thank God," the woman tourist said, relieved. "I think we are lost. We are trying to find *El Morro* Fortress. Can you help us?"

"Yes," he said. "That's not too far from here."

The young man began to give directions.

Luna began to count the seconds. Three . . . Two . . . One . . . Boom!

The explosion was fierce and destructive. It was heard over several blocks in the old city. In the spot where the young man and the American family had been standing there was now only concrete rubble and debris. Their broken bodies had been violently slammed into the glass sliding doors of the building. The glass had been shattered by the impact. There was no trace of the phone booth and a fire had started. Screams could be heard from inside the building as workers of the Electoral Commission began exiting onto the street, their clothes and faces blackened by heavy smoke. Startled onlookers began to gather around the site. Some offered help to the injured. "Call an ambulance!" "Where are the firemen?" "Call the police!" "Help! Help! Help!" What the hell happened here? the people asked.

Chaos in Old San Juan.

Luna was now walking north on *Tanca* Street. Some things are so easy, she thought. She thought the Puerto Rican Police and the American FBI were so, so stupid and incompetent. It worked to her advantage, she thought. She turned west on Fortaleza Street and walked for four short blocks in the direction of the governor's mansion. She stopped and went into another phone booth, this one in front of the *Caravaggio* Café. She could see the governor's residence one block away at the very end of the street. Cautiously, she repeated her act. She produced a second paper bag out or her *Vanities* shopping bag, and placed it on the floor in the corner of the booth. The bag was slightly stained with blood. Then, she placed two "out of order" notes on the coin slot of the phone and on the glass sliding door of the booth. That done, she quickly left the phone booth, grabbed a cell phone from a pocket in her expensive business suit and called Rigonaldo. He answered on the first ring.

"It's me," Luna said. "The package is at the *Caravaggio*. Call them."

"What about the Commission?" Rigonaldo asked calmly.

"We hit them good."

"Well done, Luna."

"Top notch!" Luna said grinning. "I'll call you when they pick it up."

She ended the connection and walked to the *Emerald*, a fine jewelry store right across from the *Caravaggio* Café. She went into the store and browsed around undisturbed while keeping an eye on the phone booth at the *Caravaggio*. She was pleased her "out of order" notes were indeed keeping pedestrians away from it. She went to a clerk behind a glass counter and said, "Hi dear, I'd like to take a look at your Rolexes in the front display case."

"Yes, madam," the clerk said to this most well-dressed and sophisticated client.

Chapter 30

In Fortaleza, the phone rang in the private residence as Cruz was conversing with Calero and Montana. Agents Pratt and García were seated by their phone intercept equipment, while agents Walker and Morales stood in a corner.

"Hello," Cruz said into the receiver.

"Elison?" Rigonaldo inquired.

"This is Governor Cruz."

"Mr. Governor, Rigonaldo Pastrana here."

The agents were already taping and tracing.

"How do I know you are who you say you are?" Cruz asked calmly.

"But, Elison, we spoke on Saturday, have you forgotten already?"

"Let me talk to my wife," Cruz said rudely.

"Your wife is a little indisposed and can't come to the phone right now but . . ."

"I want to talk to her!" Cruz demanded.

"She is unavailable, as I said," Rigonaldo said calmly. "But, you can find a piece of her in the phone booth in front of the *Caravaggio* Café right there in your backyard on Fortaleza Street."

"What the fuck do you mean? What have you done?" Cruz asked impatiently.

"There is a paper bag on the floor of the phone booth in front of the *Caravaggio* Café. Pick it up. We will talk again."

Rigonaldo hung up.

Cruz kept barking "hello" to the dial tone.

"They must have some sort of device that blocks our trace," Agent Pratt said. "We can never get anything."

"What did Pastrana say?" Montana asked Cruz.

Pacing back and forth, Cruz was afraid to say what he feared was something very, very bad. "He wouldn't let me talk to my wife," Cruz said. "I demanded it."

"Governor, what did he say to you?" Montana repeated.

Cruz spoke fast now. "The son of a bitch said 'you can find a piece of her in the phone booth in front of the Caravaggio Café.'"

"I know the place," Montana said quickly.

Cruz said, "He said to pick up a fucking paper bag on the floor of the phone booth."

Montana said nothing. A bomb? he thought. He looked at Calero and said, "Would the crazy bastard have sent us a bomb?"

Calero went to reach for his cell phone. Montana told him to wait.

"Walker, Morales," Montana told his agents, "go and check that out. Scan it for metals or wires. If it's safe, bring it in. Be extremely, extremely careful."

The agents rushed outside.

"What could he have possibly meant by 'a piece of her'?" Cruz asked nervously. "Do you think he's hurt her?"

"Let's not . . . let's hope not," Montana said

A few minutes later, Luna was enjoying the moment. Two unmistakable federal agents, wearing surgical gloves, were now carefully inspecting her little bloody package. She was still at the Emerald jewelry store. It was amusing to see federal agents, wide-eyed, and nervously scanning her present with hand-held metal detectors.

"Oh," she said to the store clerk who was holding an impeccable Rolex wrist-watch in front of her. "Are those real diamonds?"

"Yes ma'am," the clerk said excitedly.

"There is no metal in this," Walker told his partner. "I think we are safe. I see blood, though. Lots of it."

"Open it up," Morales said.

Walker lifted up the bag. It immediately struck him that it was extremely light. He wondered whether there was anything in it. He peered inside. All he could see was a batch of blood-soaked rags.

"Let's go inside," he suggested.

The agents glanced about at the faces of the people passing by, the people sitting comfortably in the café, and the people browsing at the display windows of the many stores close by. They knew that whoever had placed this package there was still around. Probably looking at them right at this very moment. Both agents felt like fools.

They began walking back to Fortaleza.

Luna thanked the clerk for his patience and left the store buying nothing. The clerk was annoyed. She called Rigonaldo and told him the agents had picked up the package. Rigonaldo was pleased. Luna too. She lit up a cigarette and walked south in the direction of the piers. The ferry to *Cataño*, a town just across the San Juan Bay where she had parked her red Toyota Solara, would depart soon. She couldn't wait to get out of Old San Juan. Too crowded for her taste. When their revolution would triumph, she knew that Old San Juan would become the home of members of the Communist Party. It wouldn't be a place infected by capitalists' commercialism. And La Fortaleza, that symbol of the old colonial governments, would be bulldozed to pieces of dust. Just like the Taliban had done with those Buddha statues in Afghanistan.

Chapter 31

In Fortaleza, Calero's cell phone rang.

"This is the Superintendent," he said into the phone.

"Chief," the caller said, "there's been an explosion in Old San Juan at the Electoral Commission."

"I'm in Fortaleza. What happened?"

"Witnesses say the blast came from a phone booth in front of the building."

"Is there a gas line underneath there?"

"I don't think so, sir. No. This was no gas line. We think it was a bomb. A powerful one."

"Was anybody injured?"

"We have three adults and an infant. Dead on the spot. We believe they were pedestrians. Inside the building we have six people injured, so far. We are still assessing the situation."

Calero was silent for a moment.

"Sir?"

"I'll be there in a few minutes," Calero said finally and ended the call.

"What happened?" Cruz asked.

"Explosion – at a phone booth – in front of the Electoral Commission," Calero reported. "Possibly a bomb blast."

"Was anybody hurt?" Cruz asked, concerned.

"I'm afraid so. I'm going there now."

Cruz and Montana glanced at each other. Calero waited. All three men were thinking about the same thing: the package in the phone booth at the *Caravaggio* Café.

At that moment, Walker and Morales walked in, grabbing everyone's attention. They all looked at the bloody paper bag in Walker's hand.

"Did you check that thoroughly?" Montana demanded.

"Yes, sir," Walker said, "it's safe." He placed the bag on a black marble table.

"What's in it?" Montana and Cruz asked in unison.

Walker ripped the bag open little by little, exposing the bloody rags. Cruz took a step back and covered his mouth with his hand. Calero swallowed hard and stared. Montana lit up a cigarette. Everyone's heart beat faster. Walker dug into the bloody rags. He dug inside . . .

First, he felt them, then, he saw them. Blood! Blood! Flesh! Flesh!

Pigs!

Pigs!

"These are pig's ears!" Walker said, stepping back.

"Jesus Christ!" Calero said, somewhat relieved.

"That son of a bitch!" Cruz barked furiously.

"Okay," Montana said. "At least we know Pastrana didn't hurt Ana María."

Cruz exploded at him. "You say 'at least'!" he yelled. "Look at this! That bastard is laughing at us. And that bomb today came from him. I know it." Cruz was in a rage. "Do you realize what he's doing? Do you see how close he's come to us? This terrorist is operating with impunity, and we are doing nothing to stop him! Absolutely nothing!"

"Governor," Montana said, frustrated, "we are doing what we can."

"What you can?" Cruz screamed at him. "Don't do what you can! Do *all* you can! Everything! Anything!"

"We are doing it," Montana said calmly.

"That man has been hiding in this country for ten years," Cruz complained bitterly. "Ten years! And you haven't a clue as to where he is. Now he has my wife. Am I to think that now all of a sudden you are going to find him in a matter of days?" He gestured to the bloody bag with the pig's ears. "Can you believe that that . . . *thing* in that bag could have been hers? Jesus Christ! What is next? What is he going to do next?"

"Whatever we do," Montana said firmly, "we must remain calm, Mr. Governor. We must not allow him to shake us."

"Listen to me, God dammit!" Cruz shot back. "Don't tell me to be calm when we are here sitting on our asses while my wife is being held by a maniac who will kill her if we don't find her. Do you have any idea who we are dealing with here?"

"Mr. Governor, we have a good profile of this terrorist and we do not underestimate his intentions but . . ."

"If you know what that bastard is capable of," Cruz cut him off, "then do something for Christ sake! You are the FBI! I don't care what you do to get her back. But whatever you have to do, do it. And I mean whatever, anything!"

The ringing of the phone shut the two men up. All eyes stared at the phone. Cruz wiped sweat off his face using his bare hand. Agents Pratt and García activated the tracing equipment.

"Mr. Governor," Montana said, "if it's him, try to remain calm. Don't let him know you are upset."

Cruz ignored him and glanced at Calero.

"Do what you can," Calero told him.

Cruz sat on the sofa by the phone, took a deep breath and answered the phone.

"This is Cruz."

"Governor," Rigonaldo said, "I am so pleased to talk to you again."

"Let me talk to my wife," Cruz demanded.

"No!" Rigonaldo barked firmly.

"I want to know that she is all right," Cruz said, raising his voice.

Montana came close to him, realizing that Cruz was about to lose his calm.

"You are running out of time, Cruz," Rigonaldo declared.

"You do anything to her," Cruz threatened, "and I will kill you, you son of a bitch!"

"I'll take that as a challenge," Rigonaldo said with a grin.

Montana reached for the phone. "Let me talk to him," he told Cruz.

Grudgingly, Cruz handed him the phone.

"Mr. Pastrana," Montana said loudly and firmly, "this is William Montana, I'm the Assistant Director in Charge of the FBI."

"I know who you are," Rigonaldo said, annoyed.

"We got your package and we were also informed of an explosion at the Electoral Commission . . ."

"Oh, news travels fast down there," the terrorist said. "I am very much impressed."

Okay, he did it, Montana thought. "Mr. Pastrana, we must establish a better system of communication. We are working on the request you made to the Governor on Saturday. You must believe us when we say we are working on it. What we need is time."

"Listen," Rigonaldo said furiously, "don't bullshit me with this 'we need time' crap. Listen to me very carefully. Tell Cruz he has until noon Friday to make an announcement that there will be no plebiscite. And it is this simple: no announcement and the bitch is dead. Believe me, the next thing you will pick up won't be pig's ears, it will be her head in a plastic bag!"

"We'll need more time than that and an assurance that there will be no more bombings . . ."

"You are truly an idiot."

"I would like to speak to Mrs. Cruz to ensure that she is unharmed." Montana knew the terrorist held all the cards now.

"You will get no more time," Rigonaldo told him, ignoring his request. "Friday at noon. It will be your loss, Mr. FBI. Goodbye."

Montana had chills through his body at the sound of the dial tone in his ear. Pratt and García took off their headphones, frustrated at the sight of consecutive zeros and ones on their digital screen. They got nothing. The terrorists were blocking the intercept, they explained.

"He gave a deadline," Montana said, lighting a cigarette. He spoke to Cruz. "By Friday at noon he wants you to make an announcement that there will be no plebiscite."

"That's four days from today," Cruz said dumbfounded. "Are you trying to tell me that in four days you will find a man who has eluded you for ten years?"

Montana tried to sound reassuring and said, "Governor, let us do our job. Now we have a deadline and I've got a couple of ideas. Trust me, we are going to break this case."

"What are you planning to do?" Cruz asked.

"I have to get on the phone. I'll keep you abreast." Montana picked up his suit jacket. "The bomb at the Commission," he said. "It was him."

Calero nodded. Cruz shook his head.

Montana excused himself and left in a hurry. No handshakes were exchanged. On his way out, he ran into Senator Thompson. The two men greeted each other and went into an empty conference room.

Quickly, Montana briefed the U.S. Senator on the latest developments, and explained the extraordinary measures that the FBI and the Puerto Rican police were taking to ensure that Thompson got safely back to the airport. The Senator was to catch a flight to Washington, D.C. in a short while.

When Montana left, Senator Thompson stayed in the conference room. He carefully locked the door, pulled out a cell phone from his jacket and dialed a number.

"Yeah?" a man answered.

"Donald? It's Grant."

It felt good to be on a first-name basis with the President of the United States, Thompson thought.

"What the hell is happening over there?" the President asked, annoyed.

"Don't worry," Thompson said. "Everything is on course. The situation with the woman is a distraction. This kidnapping won't affect anything."

"I don't give a fuck about that woman!" Clarke barked.

"I know, I know," Thompson said quickly. "Don't worry."

"Well, for your information," the President said, stressing each word, "Harris from the CIA and Briggs from the FBI both say that statehood may lose this plebiscite. You heard what I said? We may lose this thing. I won't allow that to happen. You know how damn important this is for us, and that is an understatement."

"Donald, listen to me," Thompson said firmly. "When has the FBI or the CIA been right about anything? We succeeded in keeping the 'black issue' out of all of this." (The "black issue" was the code for the Puerto Rican oil deposits). "We will also succeed in the plebiscite vote. Trust me."

"That's not what I'm hearing from Harris and Briggs," Clarke said bitterly. "They are seriously advising me that I take advantage of this kidnapping shit and call off the vote by invoking the emergency clause. Or better yet, they want me to call up Cruz over there and order him to cancel the damn thing. Do you hear me?"

"That would be a terrible, terrible mistake," Thompson said ominously. "I strongly disagree. You do that and you'll both come out as being soft on terrorism, especially you. I can see the headlines: 'Clarke Defeated by a Gang of Puerto Rican Thugs.' I don't think you'd like that. I think that you must . . ."

"The bottom line is . . ." Clarke brusquely interrupted, "is statehood going to win this plebiscite, yes or no? That's all I fucking care about. Am I making myself clear?"

"Yes, that has always been the . . ."

"Shut up, Grant," the President ordered. He was exasperated. "We should have never included free association in that plebiscite. That gave the Puerto Ricans an escape route. The question should have been: Are you American or Puerto Rican? That's it. Statehood or independence. No middle ground . . ."

"Donald," Thompson began saying, "you know we did what we could to . . ."

"I know exactly what we did," Clarke cut him off. "We shot ourselves in the foot. Have you forgotten what is at stake here?"

"Of course not," Thompson said quickly. "I think that . . ."

"Listen to me," Clarke interrupted again. "I am going to listen to you, and I will allow that plebiscite to go forward. I don't want to hear anything about kidnappings or about Puerto Rican thugs, or . . ."

"No one here has even remotely implied that you get involved in the situation with Cruz's wife."

"Good, because I wouldn't anyhow," the President said firmly.

"My best assessment of the situation here is that statehood will indeed win the plebiscite. It will probably be a close vote, but it will be a victory, regardless. And that's all we need to move ahead with what we want."

"It better be that way, Grant!" President Clarke warned.

"Don't you lose any sleep over this, Donald," Thompson said, knowing about Clarke's legendary bouts of insomnia when things weren't in his favor. "I have things under control here. I'm flying to Washington in a few hours and I will see you as soon as . . ."

The President hung up.

Thompson cursed to himself. He put his phone back in his jacket pocket, unlocked the door of the conference room, and went out. He walked in the direction of the private residence to bid goodbye to the governor. The U.S. Senate's Majority Leader was anxious to get the hell out of Puerto Rico. He feared that at any time, a sniper would shoot a bullet through his head, or that riding in his limo on the way to the airport, some terrorist freak would shoot a hand-held missile launcher and blow him to pieces. He was correct, he assured himself, to have categorically told his wife, "No! You are not going to Puerto Rico with me on this trip. Go to the beach in Key West or somewhere. You tan very easily. No need to go to Puerto Rico for *that*." His wife had put up a bitter argument, and accused him of neglecting her. He stood firm and came to Puerto Rico alone. He knew that for his wife's own sake, he did the right thing.

Near the entrance to Cruz's private residence, Thompson faced Police Superintendent Calero who was on his way out.

Calero shook hands with the Senator and went his way. To Thompson, Calero seemed extremely depressed.

As he walked out of Fortaleza to the site of the explosion in Old San Juan, Roberto Calero was engulfed by a deeply rooted sense of powerlessness and frustration. All of these tragic events were happening on his watch as Police Superintendent. The same feelings of incompetence that he felt when talking to the cynical Aida Colón, the First Lady's sister, were coming back to him now. He had tried to dismiss these emotions by committing himself to frantically working the phones, and to thoroughly searching the Police Department's intelligence files for any leads to the terrorist cell of Rigonaldo Pastrana. Anything he might have missed before. There had to be something, somewhere. He was sure of it.

Flanked by half-a-dozen bodyguards, Calero reached the bombing site in a matter of minutes. The explosion had carved a huge crater in front of the State Electoral Commission building. And the scene was chaotic with every single emergency agency present there. He repressed tears when he saw the remains of a baby stroller amidst the wreckage. The blast had dismembered the poor infant, he was told. He bit his lip. I could put a bullet in Rigonaldo Pastrana's head at this very moment, he told himself.

Now *that* would be justice.

Chapter 32

Montana's chauffeured car had been caught up in the heavy traffic that tortured the old city. The usual congestion was now even heavier as some streets had been closed to allow the emergency assistance vehicles to operate at the site of the bombing.

The cobblestone streets of Old San Juan were extremely narrow, allowing only one straight line of vehicles moving in a single direction. On either side of the street, the buildings were Spanish colonial structures with their peculiar balconies and the occasional resident trying to catch a breath of fresh air. The whole city was surrounded by the thick, centuries-old stone walls. Montana always felt trapped when visiting Old San Juan. Today, even more, he worried that it would be a while before they could get out of the old city.

"Brian," he told his driver, "I'm going to walk to Café Berlin on *San Francisco* Street to grab something to eat. Try to get out of this mess as soon as you can, and pick me up on Columbus Square in front of the *Tapia* Theater."

"Yes, sir," Brian answered.

Montana got out of the car and the intense afternoon heat struck him like a sword. He thought of taking his jacket off but instead kept walking. When he reached *San Francisco* Street he grabbed his cell phone and dialed a number. A woman answered.

"Good afternoon," she said.

"Yes, please," Montana said as he walked along the narrow sidewalk, "may I speak with Brenton."

"Mr. Matos is not in right now."

"Where can I find him?"

"Who is this?" the woman asked protectively.

"My name is William Montana. I'm an old friend of his."

"Hold on, let me make a note."

This is urgent lady, Montana thought, there is no time for notes. "Ma'am, it is very important that I speak to him. Urgently." He knew he was probably talking to a maid or a cleaning lady.

"Well, Mr. Matos is not in right now and he didn't say he was expecting any calls."

"I know he wasn't expecting this call," Montana tried again, "but if he knows I'm calling he'll want to talk to me. Where can I find him?"

"He's at the shooting . . ." the lady began saying but stopped in mid-sentence.

"He's at the shooting club?" Montana followed up. "Which one? What's the number there?"

"Mr. Matos does not like to be disturbed when he's practicing," the lady said nervously, knowing she probably had made a mistake by telling something about Brenton Matos's whereabouts to a stranger.

"Let me have the number. I promise this won't get you into any trouble."

The lady said nothing.

"Hello!" Montana said impatiently.

"Okay," she finally said, "give me your number. I'll try to contact him and have him call you."

That was better. "I'm on a cell phone." He recited his number. "Did you get that?" Montana wondered whether he sounded a little desperate. He was.

"Yes, yes. I got the number. And you said your name was?"

"Montana. William Montana. He calls me Bill."

"Okay, sir. I'll see what I can do." She hung up.

There were three shooting clubs in the metropolitan area: the Silver Bullet in *Guaynabo*, the Point Blank in *Hato Rey* and the Idaho in *Miramar*. Montana considered calling each one of them but dismissed the idea. He would give his friend Brenton fifteen minutes to call. If he didn't call, then he would place calls to the three clubs. He hoped Brenton was at the Idaho because it was in *Miramar* which was closer to the *Condado* Lagoon where Montana expected to meet with him.

Montana arrived at Café Berlin and took a seat at one of the tables on the sidewalk under a huge, bright-yellow umbrella. He placed his cell phone on the table, lit up a cigarette and waited to be served. He looked at his watch, then directly across from him at the statue of Christopher Columbus in the middle of the square. He could see the *Tapia* Theater farther down the street. Brian and his vehicle weren't there yet.

A male waiter brought him a menu. Montana put it aside and ordered a cappuccino for now and the vegetarian lasagna to take out.

Five minutes. How long could it take to contact Brenton? he thought impatiently. Maybe I should try the shooting clubs myself.

The waiter brought the cappuccino and went up to serve a couple at the next table. Montana put two spoonfuls of brown sugar in his coffee. He looked at his wrist watch again, and then looked at the statue of Christopher Columbus staring at the old city.

Brenton, Montana told himself, *I need you to kidnap someone for me.* He repeated the thought several times. The idea sent chills up his spine. He pondered this, his face hardened by the thought. Yes, it needs to be done, he had decided. Fighting terrorism nowadays takes some bold moves. Besides, he didn't have much to bargain with. If Governor Cruz doesn't make an announcement on Friday that the plebiscite has been cancelled, Rigonaldo Pastrana will kill Ana María Cruz. Montana was sure of it. Brenton Matos was the right man to do what he had in mind. He had retired from the Bureau two years earlier. He was discreet. And he was ruthless.

Another tortuous five minutes passed. Montana was about to call Brenton's house again, when the phone rang.

"Hello," Montana said, answering on the first ring.

"Bill? It's Brent."

"Brenton, I'm glad you called me back. Where are you?"

"I'm at the Idaho. Where are *you*?"

"I'm in Old San Juan waiting for my car to get out of a traffic jam."

"You sound preoccupied. What is it?"

"I need your help. We have a very delicate situation. I need you to do something for me."

"I'm listening."

"No, it's better if we talk in person. Can you meet me in *Condado*? Half an hour?"

"This sounds serious."

"I'm afraid it is. Do you still have that house in *Luquillo*?" Montana asked. The house was at the foot of *El Yunque* rain forest.

"Yes, I do. You need my house?"

"Sort of," Montana said simply. "So, can we meet in *Condado* in thirty minutes?"

"Yes, of course. I'm worried about you." Former special agent Brenton Matos knew that William Montana, Assistant Director in Charge of the FBI in Puerto Rico, needed his house in *Luquillo* for something more serious than a clandestine romantic fling.

"I'll wait for you by the first light pole on the bridge at the entrance to the lagoon," Montana instructed.

"I'll be there."

Montana ended the call. He again looked across Columbus Square, impatiently hoping to see his chauffeured vehicle. He was lost in thought when the waiter brought his take out food in a fancy paper bag. He paid, gave a generous tip, and to his relief, he spotted his car, now waiting for him in front of the *Tapia* Theater. He walked across Columbus Square and quickly got into the car realizing that the line of vehicles on Fortaleza Street was still barely moving.

"How the hell did you make it out of there?" he asked his driver.

"I drove with two wheels over the sidewalk," Brian said with a grin.

Montana smirked, lit up another cigarette and gave instructions on where to go now. They were soon driving on Ponce de León Avenue. They passed the Puerto Rican Capitol, the home of the Puerto Rican Legislature, a building modeled after the U.S. Capitol in Washington, D.C. Montana glanced at the white, marble structure.

Tonos, Montana whispered.

Ultra-radical-leftist Senator, Orlando Tonos.

He must be there now, Montana thought. We'll see if he persists in denying that he has access to Rigonaldo Pastrana.

With a hardened face, wrinkled by anxiety, the FBI Assistant Director turned his head, leaving the Capitol building behind him, with Orlando Tonos in it.

Chapter 33

"**D**oes this have to do with the Cruz case?" Brenton Matos asked his friend of fifteen years.

Brenton was a tall and robust *trigueño* in his early fifties, with hazel eyes, prominent cheekbones, a wide nose and full lips. He was dressed casually in white sneakers, worn-out blue jeans and a dark blue t-shirt.

Montana nodded yes to the question as he calmly drew on his umpteenth cigarette. They were on the bridge over the Condado Lagoon, with hotels and luxurious condos not too far away. Brian waited in the car a little farther down.

"That looks pretty ugly," Brenton said, almost as an understatement.

"It is," Montana said softly. "And it will get uglier if we don't do something about it."

"Okay," Brenton said, pausing to ponder this. "What do you want to do?"

Montana was blunt. "I want you to kidnap the wife of a state senator whom we believe can lead us to Rigonaldo Pastrana."

Boom!

"Uh . . . huh," Brenton said simply.

"This must be done fast and clean," Montana continued. "The woman must *not* get hurt in the process. She must be well treated. Obviously she will be scared, but we can't avoid that. I can't predict what the reaction to this will be, but this is probably the only shot we have to get Ana María Cruz free and alive before Friday. The terrorist's deadline is noon, Friday. I'm sure you can understand our predicament. Pastrana has been in hiding for ten years and we haven't a clue as to where he is.

Now we have four days to find him. I am one-hundred-percent sure that he is holding this victim himself. So, we find him, we find her."

Silence.

The water caressed the rocks underneath the bridge.

It was so peaceful here.

"Who's the woman?" Brenton asked quietly.

"Barbara Tonos. The wife of the Senator."

"Sure," Brenton said. "It makes sense."

"Tonos has been under surveillance since Thursday, but my agents are not around when he's out of the house. So you won't run into them while the job is being done. His wife usually stays behind in the mornings. And they have a nineteen-year-old daughter, Eugenia, who might also be in the house when you get there. If she's there, lock her in a closet they have in the living room. We've been in the house, you know. You'll have pictures of the inside. I want you to do the job tomorrow morning. You'll get some help. His name is Burke. He will contact you with whatever information you need, and will provide whatever vehicle you'll need. He's good. You'll like him."

For some reason, Brenton took all of this matter-of-factly.

"And you want me to keep her in my house in *Luquillo* for as long as necessary," Brenton pointed out.

"Right," Montana said, knowing his friend understood the task at hand. "Burke will fill you in on how you will approach the Senator, and who will take responsibility for the kidnapping. Do you have any questions?"

Brenton said nothing. He gave thought to this: a kidnapping plot orchestrated by the Assistant Director of the FBI in Puerto Rico, in a less-than-two-minute conversation. He was going to make a joke that this made John Gotti look like Mother Teresa, but decided to keep his mouth shut. This was something very serious. And this was something that a friend *had* to do for a friend, maybe even for the country. "No, no. I'm clear," he said. "I suppose that after we get the First Lady out alive we'll both get the Presidential Medal of Freedom." He had to sneak in a joke. "Or maybe Director Briggs will make you his deputy, you know, a Washington honcho."

Montana attempted a smile. Was he going too far?

"We'll play golf at *El Cerromar*," Montana told his friend. Then, his face hardened.

Brenton lit up a Winston. "You should be easier on yourself, Bill," he said with concern.

"I'm all right," Montana said softly. "It's a long shot, but I think it will work. And right now this is all we have."

"Is Briggs in on this?" Brenton asked seriously. Peter Briggs was the Director of the FBI in Washington, D.C.

Montana didn't answer immediately. He just stared at the soft and peaceful flow of the lagoon's water.

"Briggs," Montana said quietly, "knows that we are in a desperate situation down here."

Brenton knew better than to ask another question about Director Briggs's knowledge of this operation. Montana's penetrating glance gave away nothing. But something in Montana's words told Brenton that the higher-ups in Washington were ready to fight terrorists and terrorism by all necessary means.

The voice of a young boy was heard in the distance as he called to his friends to watch him jump from the concrete fence of the bridge into the calm waters of the lagoon. The children caught Montana's attention for a second, as the boy jumped, and quickly another one climbed the fence to imitate the act.

"This is a good, peaceful country, Brenton," Montana said thoughtfully. "We need to protect it at any cost."

Brenton watched the children play in the water.

"I agree," he said simply.

Tuesday, October 30

Chapter 34

On this morning, Karen Pérez was in her office reviewing a video tape that had been sent overnight to Channel Four from a TV station in Miami, Florida. It contained interviews with both sets of parents of the American tourists who had been killed yesterday by the bomb blast in front of the State Electoral Commission. The American family had come to Puerto Rico on the *MV Felicity*, a Caribbean cruise ship. The other man killed was Julio Echegaray, a young Puerto Rican who worked as a legal clerk at Montijo, López & Garcey, a large law firm in Old San Juan.

Karen was also awaiting word from Emilio Durcal, who was aggressively attempting to get her an interview with Governor Cruz. After yesterday's bombing, all the media had exerted pressure on Cruz to break his silence. Since yesterday, there had not been any comment from Fortaleza about the bombing, though in a flat press release, Police Superintendent Calero had confirmed that September Twenty-third was behind it.

Karen kept studying the footage of the grieving families to see what she would use. A picture of the baby who had been killed in the bombing appeared on the screen. That was pretty sinister, Karen thought. What kind of political goal could justify the senseless killing of innocent people who had only traveled to Puerto Rico to enjoy our sun, our food, our beaches and our people? None, she concluded. Absolutely none. This was plain, cold-blooded murder. This was nothing like the occasional attack on U.S. military installations on the island, which she somehow seemed to digest a little easier. This was a cold criminal act. And the kidnapping of the First Lady? That was plain vicious.

Karen looked at her wrist watch. In about half-an-hour she was scheduled to travel to Carolina to interview Carmina Echegaray, the mother of the murdered law clerk who lived in a modest home in Country Club, not too far from Luis Muñoz Marín International Airport. From what Karen had learned, Julio Echegaray was a young man who wasn't even registered to vote. He wasn't interested in politics at all. He was just a plain young man who had put himself through college with the help of loans and a Pell Grant, and who was proud to be working for attorneys in the capital. And one day, his mother had said to her on the phone, he hoped to fulfill his dream of becoming an attorney himself. But now, all of those dreams had been shattered by the acts of September Twenty-third. This is senseless, Karen kept telling herself.

When the telephone rang in her office, she expected it to be Emilio Durcal with the news that he had landed her the interview with Cruz, or probably that, once again, Secretary of State Arias would be serving as spokesperson for Fortaleza. She grabbed the receiver and answered casually.

"Karen," she said softly.

"Karen Pérez?" asked the unfamiliar voice on the other end of the line.

"Yes? This is Karen Pérez."

What she heard next stopped her cold.

"Do you want to see the First Lady?" Luna asked with no emotion in her voice.

"Who is this?" Karen asked as she straightened herself on her swivel chair.

"We heard that we could talk to you," Luna said. "We know you want to meet with Rigonaldo."

For a split second, Karen's mind was blank. Then it hit her and she remembered her phone call to Professor Domingo Montalvo. "Yes, yes, of course," she said nervously, eyes wide open.

"We will let you see the First Lady and you will talk to Rigonaldo."

"Okay, okay," Karen said, feeling a current of cold air hit her body.

"What do you want me to do?" She managed to reach for a pen and a writing pad.

"Same drill as before," Luna said. "We will be there in an hour. Watch for a white van with no windows on the sides. We will honk the horn three times."

'Same drill as before,' Karen thought. Déjà vu. That meant to wait at the Matisse Café on Ashford Avenue in Condado. "I have a different cameraman now," Karen said. "I mean it's been five years since . . ."

"We know," Luna interrupted. "One hour. At the Matisse. Don't talk to anybody." She hung up.

They know? How could they possibly know what goes on in the station? Karen thought. She now sat straight and still on her chair, but her thoughts were racing. Do I really want to do this? she asked herself. I can't back down now, she decided. She got up from her chair and walked hurriedly across the newsroom where every desk was now occupied by thrill-seeking and adventure-loving journalists, commentators and news writers. She reached the hall of the video editing rooms and went into the one labeled 2-G. Tonio, her cameraman, was inside editing footage of yesterday's bombing. He was smoking while working and the small room looked like the top of Mount Everest enveloped by heavy clouds.

"Hi, Tonio," Karen said, faking a grin. "Can I have one of your cigarettes?"

Tonio turned his attention away from the video screen and studied her. "*You* want a cigarette?" he said incredulously. "But, you don't smoke."

"I just feel like having a cigarette," Karen said nervously.

"Okay," Tonio said in a sing-song voice. "What's up?" He handed her one of his Marlboro Lights.

Karen put it to her lips as Tonio lit it for her. She took a quick drag, as an inexperienced smoker would do. She could count with her fingers the times she had ever smoked. Today was one of those days when she felt she needed it.

"Thank you, Tonio," Karen said. "Listen, don't go anywhere. We are going on a trip."

"Where are we going?" he asked, curiously.

"I'll let you know in a little while. Thank you for the cigarette." She left the smoke-filled room before he could ask any more questions. When she closed the door behind her she took a deep breath, holding the cigarette awkwardly between her fingers. She walked out of the video editors' hallway and crossed the newsroom in the direction of Durcal's office. When she reached his office, she went in without knocking and found him seated behind his desk as usual.

"Hi," she said, smoke blowing out of her mouth.

"Well, hi," Durcal said, immediately knowing she was up to something. "My goodness, I didn't know you smoked."

"I don't," Karen said, taking a last drag before killing the half-finished cigarette in an ashtray filled with cigar butts on top of Durcal's desk.

"I see," Durcal said, studying her body language. He waited for her to say something. When she didn't speak he said, "I'm still working on Cruz's people to get you that interview, but so far it seems we'll have to deal with Arias."

"That's all right," Karen said. "That's not what is on my mind right now."

"Oh, no? Then, what's on your mind?"

"Can you arrange for Elizabeth to take over for me this morning?"

Elizabeth Vega was a fellow senior field reporter at the station.

"Elizabeth?" Durcal said, somewhat puzzled. "Well, I guess I could, but why? Where are you going?"

"I have to go on a trip and I don't know how long it will take me."

"A trip?"

"Yes, and I'm taking Tonio with me. So you'll have to cover for him too."

"I see," Durcal said softly and pondering this. "You are going on a trip, and you are taking Tonio with you. What's this all about? I'm listening."

Karen realized she was about to say she needed another cigarette. She restrained herself. "Let's say that something important will come out of this. I can't say right away what it's all about, but you'll have to trust me. It's important that I go."

Durcal now had a puzzled look on his face as he tried to guess what Karen was up to. He was also thinking of all the schedule changes he would need to make.

"Okay," Karen said, understanding his silence. "Let's say that this is about what we spoke of on Thursday."

"Thursday? We spoke on Thursday?" Durcal couldn't recall a specific topic of conversation between him and Karen. So many things had happened since then.

"If anything goes wrong," Karen said reassuringly, "I'll call you right away."

"Now you are worrying me," Durcal said, reaching for a cigar in his desk's drawer.

"There's nothing to worry about," Karen said quickly. "We'll be taking my car so you don't have to worry about Elizabeth using the unit."

Durcal lit up his cigar, taking a long drag and puffing the smoke into the air. He waited for Karen to say more, anything that would give him a clue. But he also knew that Karen was his best field reporter and he trusted her judgment. If she said this was important, then it truly was.

"Okay," he said finally. "Go. Do what you have to do. I'll have Elizabeth cover for you. Just fill her in on whatever she needs to know to follow up on your story. Remember Karen, you are the face of this story. I want you up to your neck in it."

"Emilio, I am indeed up to my very neck in this story," Karen said with a bit of irony. "Thanks a lot for your help."

She left his office before he could say anything else. She looked at her watch. She had less than fifty minutes to be at the Matisse. She hurried into her office, grabbed a pen and a writing pad and scribbled some instructions on a sheet. She grabbed her shoulder bag and the pad and rushed out of her office. She took a glance around the newsroom trying to spot her co-worker. When she didn't see her, she walked to the desk of one of the newsroom's secretaries. The woman, an anxious look on her face, looked totally overwhelmed with work as was evident from the hundreds of papers, news clips and video tapes on her desk.

"Where's Elizabeth?" Karen asked her.

"I don't know," the secretary said, turning her face to her computer screen as if trying to avoid being given another task. "She is around."

Karen ripped her notes off the writing pad and handed them to her. "Give this to Elizabeth ASAP. Don't forget." She turned around to leave.

"What's this?" the secretary asked, annoyed by the rush.

"She's covering for me, don't forget," Karen said, walking rapidly to the video editors' hallway. She reached 2-G in a matter of seconds and pushed the door open.

Tonio jumped.

"Let's go, Tonio, now!"

"Whoa!" Tonio said with a grin. "What's this, early morning syndrome?"

"Don't joke, Tonio. We don't have time. Get the camera and let's go."

Tonio was immediately infected by the rush-adventure-bug and quickly got up, grabbed his camera and tripod and followed Karen out of the room. They caught everyone's attention as they literally ran out of the newsroom. Emilio Durcal watched them through the glass window that separated his office from the newsroom.

In the parking lot, Karen and Tonio got into her Saab. Tonio threw his equipment on the back seat and asked, "Where the hell are we going?" He had been asking since they left the newsroom.

"Okay," Karen said finally, as she drove to the parking lot's gate, "right now we are going to the Matisse Café on Ashford Avenue in Condado. That's where we are going."

"I know the place. I've been there many times with my ex."

"Good," Karen said, hoping the matter settled. No more questions.

"And what is happening there?" Tonio asked as he pulled out a cigarette from the pocket of his shirt.

Karen didn't answer.

"Hello! Avon calling," Tonio joked. "What in the world is going on?"

Karen turned on the air conditioning. "Tonio," she said calmly, "I will let you know what is happening once we are there. That's a promise."

She looked him straight in the eye. She truly wanted a car ride free of questions.

Tonio got the message. "Okay, I guess." Tonio lit his cigarette. "Do you care for one?" he offered.

"No," Karen said, "I'm fine now."

Mood swings, Tonio thought. All reporters are bipolar, he told himself.

Karen waved at the security guard at the gate and sped away.

It was Agent Sulsona who spotted her first. Agent Canseco was also watching and expecting her to drive out of the station in the news van.

"Here we go again," Sulsona said, annoyed about the idea of following a very public figure – and a reporter at that – during her official and public activities. He thought that if you are going to tag behind a reporter with questionable friends and activities, the best time was when she wasn't doing her job.

Following Karen Pérez.

As usual, the agents kept a discreet distance, driving through the congested streets of Metropolitan San Juan.

Chapter 35

Senator Orlando Tonos had left his home in Baldrich a short while earlier. As usual, Tino served as his chauffeur. The senator's wife and daughter, Barbara and Eugenia, had stayed behind and they were in the kitchen finishing up their breakfast and scanning the morning's newspapers.

As soon as the senator was out of sight, Montana's "fixer," Brenton, and his accomplice, former special agent Burke Rosado, drove by the house several times. After agreeing they were in the clear, they finally parked their "Richie's Pizza" van in the Tonoses' driveway, blocking the way of a green Volvo parked there. That was Barbara's car.

Brenton and Burke were both severely disguised with fake mustaches and beards, baseball caps, dark sunglasses and leather gloves, and white "Richie's Pizza" uniforms that made them look more like caretakers in a 1950's insane asylum.

While Burke stayed behind the steering wheel with the van in neutral, Brenton got out of the vehicle and walked to the front door carrying a large box of pizza, which actually did contain a large pizza pie.

When the doorbell rang at the Tonoses' home, Barbara Tonos expected it to be either the Mormons or the Jehovah's Witnesses doing the rounds in the neighborhood. She slowly looked up from a story on Ana María Cruz she was reading in *El Nuevo Sol* and said, "Gina, hon', would you answer that please?"

Eugenia drank a sip of her coffee and got up without complaint. She looked out the window before opening the door and was more amused than puzzled at the sight of a pizza man at the door. She was one-hundred-percent sure that the man had the wrong house. And she wondered which of her sophisticated neighbors had ordered a pizza this early in the morning. She opened the door.

"Good morning, may I help you?" she said politely.

"Yes," Brenton said, looking briefly at a receipt glued to the pizza box, "I have a delivery for Mrs. Barbara Tonos."

"That's my mother," Eugenia said with a smile on her face, "but I can assure you we didn't order any pizza." She glanced at the van blocking their driveway.

Brenton was fast and ruthless. "You did now!" he said kicking the door wide open and pushing himself into the house. Before Eugenia could speak he pulled out a gun and pointed it at the scared girl. The pizza dropped to the floor.

"Mom!" Eugenia cried out in terror, taking a step back.

Brenton closed the door behind him. "Now, tell me where your mother is. Hurry, I don't want to hurt you!"

Barbara came rushing into the living room at the sound of her daughter's scream. "What is this?" she yelled.

"Mom, he's got a gun," Eugenia warned, shaking and rushing to her mother's side.

Brenton pointed the gun at both of them. "You do what I say and nobody will get hurt," he said firmly.

"You can take anything you want," Barbara said, shaking with fear. "We have money, jewelry. Tell me what you want."

"Be quiet," Brenton ordered. "You," he told Eugenia, "go in there." He pointed to the closet in the living room.

"Mom?" she cried.

"Move it, move it!" Brenton yelled.

"Go, Gina, go," Barbara told her daughter, not taking her eyes off of the gun pointed at them.

Crying and trembling, Eugenia went into the closet and held back a croaking scream when she heard the outside lock secured after she went inside. She was now in total darkness as she struggled to hear the voices outside.

"Now," Brenton said to Barbara, "we are going to walk out that door as naturally as you walk, and you will get in the van outside. Do you understand?"

"What are you doing?" Barbara managed to say. "Where are you taking me?

"That's not your problem, lady," Brenton said. "Now, move before I start shooting bullets through that door." He pointed the gun at the closet's door. "I don't think you'd like that."

Barbara moved. She walked to the front door with Brenton behind her. She felt the gun at her back. They quickly exited the house. Barbara glanced at the house right across from theirs, hoping the neighbors would see them. But she knew that nobody was home there at this hour. The Martinezes were already at the bookstore they owned in *Guaynabo*. Nobody was looking, she knew. Nobody knew what was happening to her.

When they reached the van, Burke opened the sliding door and let them in. Brenton instructed Barbara to lie down on the floorboard, and he immediately placed handcuffs on her wrists and tied a blindfold over her eyes. Burke now drove slowly away from the house, glancing carefully in all directions. He felt safe. It had been a clean job.

They drove onto Domenech Avenue and soon turned onto the highway. It would take them at least forty-five minutes to an hour to reach Brenton's house in *Luquillo*, at the foot of *El Yunque* rain forest.

Brenton was now thinking of all the pressing matters that needed to be done once they got to *Luquillo*. But the first one was rather simple. He was hungry. He told Burke, "How about if we order a pizza? The first one was DOA."

Both men laughed.

Chapter 36

Karen parked her car a few stores down from the Matisse Café on Ashford Avenue in Condado. Tonio got his equipment and they both walked to the café and sat at one of the tables outside along the sidewalk.

Agents Sulsona and Canseco parked their car across the street a few stores ahead of the Matisse with a clear view of Karen and her cameraman. "Why didn't they go inside?" Canseco asked. "Do you think she's seen us and is posing just to fuck with us?"

"She didn't see us," Sulsona answered confidently.

"So," Tonio said after the waitress had placed two cups of Colombian coffee on their table, "tell me now, where the hell are we going?"

Karen paid the bill and tipped the waitress. "We are going on a trip," she said, glancing at her watch for the hundredth time.

"I know that, but where? What's going on?"

Karen took a small sip of coffee and said, "Well, there's nothing to be afraid of . . . but we are going to see the First Lady and to talk to Rigonaldo Pastrana."

Tonio almost choked on his coffee. "You've got to be kidding," he said, clearing his throat.

"No, no," Karen said, speaking calmly and in a low voice. "I am dead serious. In about fifteen minutes a white van will pick us up, and they will take us to wherever it is they are keeping her. And Rigonaldo Pastrana will be there."

Tonio was speechless.

"And you should know," Karen went on, "most surely they will blindfold us for the ride and most likely once we are there whoever we meet will be wearing masks or hoods. We won't see their faces."

Tonio's mouth was wide open, his skin as pale as if he'd seen a ghost. He forgot about his coffee. "Jesus Christ! Karen, why didn't you tell me earlier about this?"

"Why? You don't want to go?"

"Oh no, it's not that," Tonio said, lighting a cigarette at the speed of light. "It's just that I would have liked to have prepared myself for something like this. You know, mentally."

"I'm sorry, Tonio, but there was no time to prepare. I myself didn't know about this until less than an hour ago. That's the way they operate."

Tonio shook his head in disbelief. He liked adventure, like going surfing in *Rincón* or hiking in *El Yunque*. But mingling with a bunch of terrorists-on-the-run had never been on his list. Until now.

"Listen, Tonio," Karen said, not knowing his true feelings, "if you don't want to go I will understand. That will be fine. I will take care of the camera myself. I'll set a shot on the tripod and tape the thing all by myself . . ."

"Hell no! I'm going. This is massive, Karen, bigger than huge!"

"Yes, I know this has great significance. Now, you have to believe me that nothing bad is going to happen to us there. And keep in mind, once we are there, try not to engage them in much conversation. The less we talk about non-related subjects the better. We are there to get Pastrana and the First Lady on tape and . . ."

"What happened the first time you went to see Rigonaldo?" Tonio asked, offering a cigarette to Karen. She refused it.

"Nothing. Nothing happened. As I said, they blindfolded us for the ride, and once there all of them had masks or hoods. The only face I saw was Rigonaldo's. We set the camera, taped the interview and that's it. They brought us back."

"Where were they hiding?"

"I never knew."

"Who went with you?"

Karen allowed the questions to make him feel comfortable. In reality she needed and wanted Tonio with her for this project. "Alex Perreira went with me," she said. "You never met him. He left the station before you started."

"I don't blame him."

Karen smiled. "He's with Telemundo in Miami."

Tonio tried to organize his thoughts. He kept smoking silently, glancing at every passing vehicle driving along Ashford Avenue, trying to spot a white van. A white van.

"Any more questions?" Karen asked him, finishing her coffee.

Tonio took in a long drag of smoke. In a way he felt he didn't have time to sort through his real emotions right now. "No," he said slowly. "Karen, this is deep shit, you know."

"Something like that," Karen said.

A few minutes that seemed like forever passed. Then, a dust-filled white van, no windows on the sides, one single small window in the rear, stopped in front of the Matisse and honked the horn three times.

"Let's go," Karen said quickly, getting up.

"Oh shit," Tonio said, grabbing his equipment and following Karen to the van.

The rear door of the van flew open. A woman, Luna, in a blond wig, a hat and dark sunglasses greeted them saying, "Get in."

Karen and Tonio followed the order. Luna hurried to shut the door. In less than a minute the reporter and her cameraman were both sitting on the floorboard and blindfolded. Teco, wearing a hat, dark sunglasses and a fake beard and mustache, was at the wheel.

Agents Sulsona and Canseco watched the scene with interest.

"That surely doesn't look like a news van to me," Sulsona said, beginning to discreetly follow the vehicle.

"You got that right," Canseco agreed.

The van quickly left traffic-congested Ashford Avenue and turned onto a side street where most of the affluent homes were. Luna looked out the dirty, dust-filled rear window and made an inventory of all the cars that were behind them. A black Lexus with tinted windows was among them. So far nothing looked suspicious.

Teco stopped at an intersection. Sulsona pulled the Lexus to the side of the street. Moments later, Teco drove down *José de Diego* Avenue and after a little struggle with traffic, they turned onto the highway. Sulsona followed at a safe distance.

Once on the highway, Sulsona instructed Canseco to call a number on his cell phone and ask for Vicky. When Vicky came to the phone, Sulsona picked it up as he drove.

"Hello, Vicky? Marky here," Sulsona said.

"Hello special agent," a flirty woman's voice said.

"I need you to run a plate for me," Sulsona said quickly, "and call me immediately."

"No problem. What's the number?"

"R-N-U-3-7-4. Did you get that?"

"Yes. I'll call you in a sec'. Are you on your cell?" Vicky asked.

"Yes."

"Okay," she said and hung up.

The vehicles on the highway were not moving yet at the normal speed. Probably an accident farther up was slowing down the three lanes. Luna kept at her task of taking inventory of every suspicious-looking car behind them. Karen was mute. Tonio was smoking. Both of them sitting on the dirty floorboard.

Sulsona got his call.

"Marky?" Vicky said with some excitement in her voice.

"Shoot."

"The license plate belongs to a 2007 Ford Taurus reported stolen June fifteen of this year. It is registered to a Mrs. Mildred Carrión on *Serralles* Street in Ponce."

"Lovely," Sulsona said with a smirk. "Thanks a lot, Vicky."

"Any time. Hey, are we still on for Friday?"

"I'll be there," Sulsona said, confirming his hot-sex date with Vicky. He pushed end on the phone before she could keep talking.

"What's the story?" Canseco asked.

"License plate belongs to a stolen Ford," Sulsona said excitedly. "And I bet you that that van is also stolen."

"Well," Canseco said, "we always knew that that woman journalist was shady. I smell a rat! What can she be doing in a dirty, run-down stolen vehicle?"

"We'll find out soon."

"Should we call the chief?" Canseco asked, reaching for the cell phone.

Sulsona stopped him. "Put that down," he said quickly. "We'll call when we have something more to report, like for example, where she's going."

"But don't you think we should call to let him know that 'shady' Pérez is riding in a 'shady' vehicle?" Canseco asked.

He was dumb. Special Agent Mark Enrique Sulsona had always thought that his partner, Special Agent José Canseco, was as dumb as a dumb blonde. He didn't have any ambitions besides being called "Special Agent José Canseco." Not like Sulsona. He wanted to someday become Assistant Director in Charge of the FBI in Puerto Rico or in any other location that needed bilingual staff. If by some stroke of destiny, it fell into his hands to make a breakthrough in the First Lady's case, with all the media attention that this case had brought to this tiny island, Special Agent Mark Enrique Sulsona would be known all over the continental United States and maybe even all over the world. That is what was at stake here. And Canseco was dumb enough not to have a clue that this case was a career-making case. There would be no phone calls to the Assistant Director or to any of his deputies until Sulsona had information that could make a breakthrough in this extremely important case. For now the chase was on. Karen Pérez was going somewhere and he, Mark Enrique Sulsona, was behind her tail like a dog following the smell of a rotten corpse.

"We'll phone Montana when Pérez reaches a destination," Sulsona said firmly.

"Sounds okay to me, I guess," Canseco said simply.

They were now driving south on Highway 52. When they reached the first tollbooth, Teco threw a handful of coins into the coin basket, waited one second for the green light and went on driving. Luna was still at her spot by the window scanning the vehicles behind her. She thought she recognized a black vehicle trailing a few cars behind but couldn't be sure. What was it? A Volvo? A BMW? A Lexus? She couldn't tell. She kept looking out the small window and said nothing.

Karen was sweating and the floorboard was extremely hot and uncomfortable. And she couldn't stand the blindfold. It made her feel claustrophobic, as if she was in a closed, pitch-black room. This was definitely the last time she would do something like this. Next time some obscure terrorist wants to be on TV, she thought, he'll have to come to the Marriott for the encounter. Speaking of which, she thought that after this adventure she had just earned a month-long vacation to Australia or New Zealand. Somewhere very far from the Caribbean. Very far away from Puerto Rican politics.

Within the hour, the vehicles passed through the second and third tollbooths. Exiting eastbound on Road 15 they reached downtown Cagüey in a matter of minutes. Once in the town they were forced to slow down due to heavy traffic on the streets surrounding the *Plaza Pública* (Central Square), which housed City Hall and the ubiquitous Catholic Church. Luna scanned the vehicles behind them and this time she was worried about what she thought she saw.

Teco drove out of the congested downtown area and got on Road 89 where traffic was considerably lighter even though there were only two lanes for vehicles going in opposite directions. When they were crossing through the large sugar cane field Luna felt a cold shiver envelop her body when she got a definite look at the dark vehicle only three cars behind them.

"We've been followed!" she yelled hysterically.

"What?" Teco asked as he instinctively attempted to look at the cars behind them in his side mirror.

"We've been followed!" Luna repeated.

"Are you sure?" Teco asked nervously.

"Yes! I'm sure," Luna said, crawling over Tonio to get a Magnum .357 out of a duffel bag. "That black Lexus behind us was in Condado when we left." She positioned herself by the rear window again. "I'm gonna blow the mother fuckers off," she said to Teco. "Do what I say!"

"Don't fuck us off," Teco warned her.

"Just do what I say!" she repeated frantically.

"I don't like this." Teco was sweating now. "This is bad, bad, bad."

"God damn it!" Luna cursed. "Just fucking listen to me."

"What do I do?" Teco asked, scared.

"Slow down!" Luna ordered. "Just fucking slow down. Let all the other cars pass you until that black Lexus is directly behind us."

Teco looked in his side mirror. "Okay, I see them." He began to slow down almost as if they were going to stop right there in the middle of the road. He extended his arm out the window and began signaling for the vehicles to pass them by crossing into the lane for cars coming in the opposite direction.

"What are they doing?" Canseco asked.

"It looks as if they are going to stop," Sulsona said, fearing they may lose their cover.

The third vehicle passed the terrorists' van. Now the black Lexus with the two federal agents was the only car behind the white van. Teco came almost to a stop, forcing Sulsona to approach their van.

"Shit!" Canseco said. "You are going to have to pass them."

There was no time. In a violent jerk, Teco drove furiously in reverse crashing the rear of the van into the agents' vehicle.

"Fucking shit!" Sulsona screamed, his hands firmly grasping the steering wheel.

Canseco jerked forward, almost hitting the dash board with his forehead.

Luna pushed open the rear door of the van, pointed the gun at the agents and began shooting. The Lexus' windshield shattered. Sulsona stomped on the accelerator and sped quickly in reverse, hitting a red Suzuki Jeep behind them.

Teco attacked the van's pedal and drove dangerously into the oncoming traffic lane to pass the vehicles that blocked his way.

"Did you hit them?" Teco yelled to Luna. "Are we clear?"

"God damn you!" Luna spat. "You gave me no time!"

"Did we lose them? Did we lose them?" Teco kept asking.

"No, asshole," Luna told him as she struggled to keep her balance at the open rear door.

The van's rear glass window shattered. Three gunshots missed Luna's head by inches.

"Son of a bitch!" Luna yelled, crouching for cover.

Sulsona was closely behind them, his car's siren wailing. Canseco was shooting at the van. Other vehicles on Road 89 were plowing into the side of the road, trying to avoid the speeding cars.

"What's happening?" Karen asked, sweating profusely. "Oh, God, what's happening?"

"Stay down!" Luna ordered as she fired a few rounds at the Lexus.

"I want fucking out!" Tonio yelled, reaching for his blindfold.

Luna kicked him. "Don't even try it, boy," she warned him.

Three more shots perforated the van's rear doors.

"We need back up!" Canseco blurted out, firing his gun again . "We gotta call the chief." He reached for the cell phone.

Sulsona slammed the cell phone out of Canseco's hand. "Don't you fucking dare!" Sulsona roared. "This is our show!"

"Are you crazy?" Canseco said, wide-eyed.

"Just keep shooting . . ." Sulsona ordered, glancing at him. "Keep shoot . . ."

"Watch out!" Canseco screamed. "Watch out!"

Bang!

Once again, Teco's van went furiously in reverse, crashing brutally against the Lexus. Luna aimed her gun and fired. She hit the driver first. A clean shot to his throat, then a few more to his chest. The man in the passenger seat, the shooter, tried to duck but Luna was sure she hit him also.

"Let's fucking go," Luna ordered. "Go, go, now!" She shut the van's bullet-ridden door.

Teco stomped on the accelerator and sped away.

In the Lexus, Canseco tried to use one hand to stop blood from pouring out of Sulsona's throat, and he used his other hand to frenziedly look for the phone. He didn't have a chance to touch his own body to find where he had been shot.

"Mark!" he called. "Marky, talk to me . . . Mark . . . talk to me . . ."

Special Agent Mark Enrique Sulsona did not talk to him. He was very much dead, along with his dream of becoming Assistant Director in Charge of the FBI.

As for Canseco, he noticed he was bleeding profusely from his chest. He gasped. He couldn't breathe. He was dizzy. He was losing his sight. In less than three seconds, he passed out.

Farther down on Road 89, Teco was now driving at the speed limit.

"I want to know what the fuck is going on," Tonio said, his voice quivering.

"Is everything all right?" Karen asked, trembling.

"Everything's fine," Luna answered. "Stay on the floor. Both of you."

Karen said okay and went back to a silent prayer she had started when the shooting began. This was definitely the last time she did this sort of story.

"I want a fucking cigarette," Tonio said.

"Go ahead, boy" Luna told him. "You've been smoking all through the trip." She didn't look away from the rear window. The road was now clear.

"Well, what do you see?" Teco asked his accomplice. "Are we clear now?"

"Yes," Luna said confidently.

"Fucking shit," Teco cursed.

Luna was worried. Very worried. This had been a mistake. She should have known much earlier that they were being followed. She should have known. This was too close to their hideout. She knew that. She didn't need to be told. Rigonaldo Pastrana will be extremely pissed off when he finds out about this; she knew it.

Chapter 37

"Welcome!" Rigonaldo Pastrana said enthusiastically when he made his grand entrance into the living room where Karen and Tonio had been told to wait. The pack, Luna, Oso and Teco, were sitting on folding chairs with their backs to the wall. All of them were wearing hoods over their heads. All you could see of them were their eyes. Those scary, cold-blooded eyes, Tonio thought.

"Hello again," Karen said, shaking hands with the most feared and most wanted criminal in Puerto Rico. She glanced around the room and immediately concluded that this was not the same place she had been in five years ago. This was a new hideout. She acknowledged Tonio. "This is Tonio," she said, "my new cameraman."

"How do you do, young man?" Rigonaldo said politely.

"Oh, hi," Tonio said flatly. He studied the room very carefully and especially the three hooded figures by the wall behind him. This was scarier than the most sinister movie he had ever seen. All the drapes were drawn shut. In this darkness, he thought, with these three silent corpses with snake eyes sitting behind him, and this devilish, Fidel Castro look-alike with a grin on his face, all we need now are candles and a coffin to make it cozy.

"Well," Rigonaldo said, "make yourselves comfortable. Estrella will make coffee for us."

Luna waved and rushed to the kitchen. Karen and Tonio sat down.

"I hope you had a smooth trip here," Rigonaldo said. "Sorry about the blindfolds, but I'm sure you'll understand the circumstances."

Impulsively, Tonio began saying, "There was a shoot . . ."

"Tonio!" Karen stopped him, swallowing hard. "I think you should get the camera ready."

Tonio shut up quickly and, taking his cue, got up to set up his equipment.

Karen smiled.

Rigonaldo smiled in return.

"He's new," Karen said.

Rigonaldo nodded. Hadn't she already said that? he thought for a moment.

Karen tried to read Rigonaldo's puzzled look. She studied him. He looked thinner than the last time. "You've lost some weight," she told him.

"Have I? Well, I may have. You look the same yourself," Rigonaldo replied. "Maybe it's because I see you all the time on television."

Karen was about to say something when the woman in the kitchen called on Rigonaldo. He excused himself and went into the kitchen.

"What is it?" he asked.

"Something happened on the way here," Luna said, disguising her worry.

"What happened?"

Luna told him about the shooting.

"You shot them on Road 89?" Rigonaldo said, containing his fury.

"I had no choice," Luna said as she took care of the coffee.

"Why the hell did you wait until they were so close to us to take care of them?" He was perplexed.

Luna knew that Rigonaldo would not explode into a rage with Karen Pérez in the house. "I wasn't sure they were really following us."

"Get the fucking coffee," Rigonaldo snapped. "We'll talk later about this."

He came back to the living room and said, "Sorry about the interruption."

"I think we should get started," Karen said quickly, nodding to Tonio to get ready.

"I'm ready when you are," Tonio said, a cigarette dangling from his lips.

A second later Luna came in with the coffee and placed the tray on a small table. Tonio grabbed his coffee and drank it in two big gulps. Karen took longer, pondering how to break the ice. She wanted to see the First Lady before the interview.

"Do you think," she asked Rigonaldo, "that the governor will comply with your demands?

Rigonaldo drew a smirk on his face and leaned back against the couch he had chosen to sit on. It felt like a king's throne. At this very moment, Rigonaldo Pastrana thought he was the most important man in the world.

This guy, Tonio thought, is really very pathetic.

"He has to comply with what I've demanded," Rigonaldo said. "If he wants to see his wife again, he has to comply. He doesn't have a choice."

"Where is she?" Karen asked, looking him straight in the eye.

Rigonaldo pulled a Cuban cigar out of the pocket of his shirt. "The woman is in the back room. We are taking good care of her." He lit up his cigar and the heavy smoke quickly traveled through the air.

"I need to see Mrs. Cruz," Karen said firmly. "I need to take some video of her with me."

Rigonaldo said nothing. He just smoked. He had planned to let Karen see Ana María Cruz only after they had taped his interview. And he hadn't really planned to allow any videotape of his captive. He felt Karen was pointing a gun at him with her eyes. He liked that. Such resilience and determination in a woman.

"You want to videotape her?" he asked.

"Yes, it will complement our interview."

Rigonaldo took a long drag on his cigar and glanced at the pack, all of them waiting for his response.

After a long silence, Rigonaldo said, "All right, you can do that."

"Thank you," Karen said softly.

Rigonaldo said nothing. Karen was expecting to be led to the First Lady now, before the interview. Rigonaldo got the message when Karen kept silent.

"You want to see her now?" Rigonaldo asked, somewhat disarmed.

"Yes," Karen said, exchanging glances with Tonio. "You are ready, aren't you?"

"Surely," Tonio said.

The air had become subtly tense.

"Okay," Rigonaldo said finally, "go and take your video. Estrella, take Ms. Pérez to see Mrs. Cruz."

Luna quickly got up. "Come with me," she said.

Karen got up, leaving her purse and writing pad on the dirty sofa. Tonio grabbed the camera already screwed to the tripod and they both followed "Estrella" down a hallway. They passed several rooms until they reached a closed door right before a screen door through which the sun's light came in. Tonio took a quick glance out the screen door and saw a deep grove of trees and what looked like a wooden shack like the ones used to house domestic animals.

Luna opened the door to the room where Ana María Cruz had spent the last three days in captivity.

The first thing that hit Karen was the severe stench. What was it? Sweat? Urine? Feces? She couldn't tell. And the room was pitch-black, scarcely brightened by the light that came through the screen door. But she was able to see the First Lady of Puerto Rico blindfolded and tightly tied to a chair in the middle of the small room.

"I need some light in here," Tonio said, visibly disturbed by what he had seen so far.

Luna flipped a switch on the wall and a single light bulb dangling from the ceiling came on. "Here," Luna said, nervous and annoyed, "hurry up."

The sound of voices seemed to have awakened the First Lady as she began to jerk her head to all sides trying to identify who had come into the room. Karen took a deep breath. Ana María's wrists, tied behind her back to the chair's arms, were swollen and red with irritation. She was drenched in sweat. What was exposed of her face was dark, dirty and swollen. Her hair was wet and unkempt. Her clothes were dirty.

Karen held back tears. Here was a woman of such grace, Karen thought, that even if you didn't agree with her politics, she didn't deserve this brutal treatment. God almighty! Have they beaten her? Have they raped her? Does she sleep in this chair? There is no bed in this room. This room was almost as small as a walk-in closet.

Tonio held his deep contempt and remained silent. He positioned the camera a few feet from the First Lady and waited for his cue to start taping.

"Could you please uncover her eyes?" Karen asked "Estrella."

Luna hesitated. She wasn't sure that Rigonaldo would approve.

"It's fine," Karen told her, reading her silence. "We'll tape her with the blindfold, but I just want her to see me and exchange a few words."

Then the First Lady spoke.

"Who's there? Who's there?" she asked in a tired voice.

"Mrs. Cruz," Karen responded firmly, "this is Karen Pérez, from Channel Four. I came to see you."

"Oh, God! Oh, God!" Ana María cried. "Please help me, help me. These people are monsters."

"Take the blindfold off, I said!" Karen ordered, almost yelling at Luna.

Luna did it.

Ana María was blinded by the light. She opened and closed her eyes trying to get used to it. Tears were streaming down her cheeks from her black and swollen eyes.

Karen could not believe what she was seeing.

"Have you talked to my husband?" Ana María asked.

"I'm afraid not. He's not talking to reporters."

"Where are we?"

"I don't know," Karen answered, frustration in her voice.

Luna tried to blindfold the First Lady again but Karen stopped her.

"What do these people want?" Ana María asked, crying.

"You mean, you don't know?" Karen asked, somewhat surprised, but inferring that the First Lady had been kept in total and absolute isolation.

"That's enough!" Luna yelled, this time tightening the blindfold around Ana María's eyes.

Unable to stop her, Karen said, "They want the Governor to cancel the plebiscite."

"Elison can't do that!" Ana María said angrily.

"Okay!" Luna snapped. "I said that's enough. You," she addressed Tonio, "take your pictures. Do it now or you can forget about it."

Tonio stared at Karen who nodded for him to go ahead. The First Lady tried to speak again but Luna ordered her to be silent. Ana María sobbed.

After what seemed like an interminable thirty seconds, Luna yelled, "That's enough! Shut that camera off." She quickly turned off the room's light. And they were all in darkness again. Tonio grabbed his equipment, walked out of the room and stood by the screen door, taking a good glance at the rear yard as he waited for Karen to come out.

"Please!" Ana María pleaded. "Don't leave me here with these people! Do something, please!"

As Luna pushed Karen out of the room, Karen said, "I'll try to talk to the Governor when I get back. I promise you . . ."

Luna slammed the door shut.

Ana María Cruz was alone in the dark, cramped room again.

"Hey, you!" Luna said to Tonio, who was still by the screen door. "Get over here."

Luna walked behind them to the living room again. To Karen she said, "Talk to Rigonaldo now, that's why you are here!"

Chapter 38

Karen sat on a couch across from Rigonaldo who was still puffing on his cigar. She looked at him saying nothing. She was shaken, angry and depressed. She nodded to Tonio to begin taping. He did.

"Mr. Pastrana, the First Lady does not seem to be in good condition . . ."

"She is fine," Rigonaldo said quickly. "In any case it is her husband's fault."

"What do you want to accomplish with this? And, why hasn't the First Lady been well treated?"

"I am not going to discuss the woman we are holding," Rigonaldo said, dismissing the question. "But my goal is very simple, and the country already knows it: I want Governor Cruz to cancel the plebiscite of November third."

"Isn't this kidnapping a cruel, extreme action to take?"

"When we have a man in Fortaleza who is so obsessively trying to make Puerto Rico a state of the United States, I consider that not only extreme, but a crime against the Puerto Rican people."

Karen said, "The Governor might not have the authority to interrupt the plebiscite at this stage of the process."

"I have spoken to Cruz on two occasions already and . . ."

"You mean you have spoken with the Governor personally?"

"Yes, yes, I have spoken with him twice," Rigonaldo said, grinning. "I have made it clear that I expect him to do whatever he needs to do to cancel this plebiscite. This is not going to come down to a question of who has the authority. I will not be fooled. Along with the President of the United States, Elison Cruz is mainly responsible for having initiated the plebiscite process. He, Cruz, used all of his influence and the power of his office to bring this plebiscite about. So, therefore, I hold him accountable to end it. And he *does* have the authority, Karen. The plebiscite law provides for the cancellation of the plebiscite should, and I quote, *'emergency or extraordinary circumstances occur.'"*

"What is going to happen if Cruz cannot stop the process and the plebiscite goes forward?"

"As I said Karen, Cruz *can* indeed stop the plebiscite," Rigonaldo said without blinking. "If he doesn't he will not see his wife again."

"You are going to hold her indefinitely?"

"He will not see his wife again," Rigonaldo repeated.

"Are you planning to kill the First Lady?"

Rigonaldo said nothing, then, "Go and ask Cruz what our plan is."

"I am asking you," Karen pressed.

"Listen, Ana María Cruz is here with us. If the governor wants to see his wife alive again, he must comply with my demand which I don't think is too hard to meet."

"How is the First Lady passing her days?"

"I am not going to comment on that," Rigonaldo said bluntly.

"Is she being fed?"

Silence.

"Has she been allowed to stand up from that chair to which she is tied?"

Silence.

"From what I saw, I gather she hasn't received the best treatment here. Why?"

Silence. Silence. Silence. Rigonaldo was speaking through his deep, dark eyes. He wanted his enemies to know that he was capable of anything.

"Will the First Lady be released promptly?"

"If the governor cancels the plebiscite, yes, she will be released," Rigonaldo said without much conviction.

"Has she been allowed to speak to the governor?"

"Karen," Rigonaldo said calmly and in a patronizing way, "I want the focus of our conversation to be the plebiscite and the immense damage that Governor Cruz is doing to our country. I don't want to . . ."

Karen cut him off saying, "Why have you decided to take such a dramatically personal action against the First Family of our country?"

"Listen," Rigonaldo said, hardening his face, "the United States government cannot operate in this country in the way it is doing without the cooperation of the likes of Governor Cruz. This is the same as with the Nazi collaborators in World War Two."

"Are you comparing Nazi Germany to the United States?"

"Yes," Rigonaldo said firmly. "The government of the United States is a racist, fascist regime, just like the Nazis were."

"Why kidnap Ana María Cruz? How does she fit into this?"

"She is the wife of the fascist governor of this island," Rigonaldo said, raising his voice. "She is not an innocent bystander."

"You have been criticized for this even by the Puerto Rican Revolutionary Army."

"I am not concerned with them. We are comrades in arms but we operate at different levels."

"The P.R.R.A. has said and I quote . . ."

"I know what the P.R.R.A. has said. They don't target Puerto Rican collaborators."

"They don't think they should be a target."

"I disagree," Rigonaldo said, annoyed. "For me anyone who collaborates with the U.S. government in Puerto Rico is an enemy of the people. I think I've made that clear."

"But don't you think that the P.R.R.A. and your organization September Twenty-third are commonly . . ."

Rigonaldo cut her off. "Karen," he said aggressively, "you are pushing me on this, and I don't like it. I am not going to engage in a public debate about the tactics that September Twenty-third uses and how those differ from those of other patriotic organizations, the P.R.R.A. included."

Karen heard the three hooded figures behind her murmuring to each other. She asked a few questions quoting the press release from the P.R.R.A. she had read to Senator Tonos, but got no response from Rigonaldo.

"Tell me, Mr. Pastrana," she went on, "why is this plebiscite such a threat to you?"

"This plebiscite is a threat to all of us Puerto Ricans who love our language, our culture, our traditions," Rigonaldo stated, stressing each word. "This plebiscite violates the right of Puerto Rico to independence. A right which is inalienable, you cannot renounce it. This is a trap to impose statehood on us."

"In what way is this plebiscite a 'trap,' as you say, to impose statehood on Puerto Rico?"

"Because that is exactly what it is. This is not a democratic election where people choose freely one formula over the other. If you closely study the U.S. Congressmen who are involved with this, and if you pay close attention to the actions of the current U.S. President, you will realize that this is a trap to bring statehood to Puerto Rico. The Americans would have never committed themselves to act on a process like this if they didn't know the outcome of it in advance. That's the way they do everything."

"The American President has said he will support whatever status the Puerto Ricans choose."

"Oh, come on, Karen. You know better than that. We have dealt with American presidents for a long time to know how to discern their motivations. The fate of this plebiscite was already decided by the American President and by the Pentagon."

"How do you explain the participation of the Commonwealth Party and the Independence Party in this plebiscite? I mean, if it is a trap as you say, why are they participating?"

"Listen," Rigonaldo said angrily and leaning forward, "I am not going to even acknowledge those devils at the Commonwealth Party and their motivations. And as far as the Independence Party is concerned, I am aware that someone recently described them as being 'delusional' if I am not mistaken. I think that explains their participation."

"That was a description used by Senator Orlando Tonos," Karen pointed out.

"Yes, I think that is correct."

"Many of your political positions are similar to those of the senator."

"I think Senator Orlando Tonos is the only truly honest and

independent voice that the people of Puerto Rico have in their Legislature. The rest of them are a bunch of lackeys."

"Do you keep in contact with Senator Tonos?"

Rigonaldo raised his eyebrows and said, "My circumstances do not allow me to answer any questions about what type of contacts I have with people."

"How does it feel to be so isolated from the people?"

"I am a man who is free because I am fighting our war of independence. A man who is in the trenches, fighting for his country, is not in isolation. Our enemies have not been able to isolate us. September Twenty-third is an extremely active group, and we are proud of our record and of the many supporters we have."

"Rigonaldo," Karen said, "Have you had any contact with your family in the last few years? I know you have a wife, Idalia, and three grown children and a number of grandchildren. Have you spoken with them? Have you seen them?"

"Listen," Rigonaldo said carefully, "I am not going to comment on that. My family is September Twenty-third and its supporters."

"Do your wife and children support you?"

"I am not going to talk about that. What I will say is that I know that the FBI and the Puerto Rican police are constantly and incessantly harassing my family. That is the most vicious thing, what they are doing to my family. They listen to their phone conversations, they follow them everywhere they go, they go to their homes to interrogate them for no reason at all, they harass my wife's friends, the friends of my children, they go after my other relatives, even after my mother who is ninety-years-old . . ."

"Why don't you quit this life you have chosen for yourself?"

"Never!" he said strongly. "I am willing to die for the independence of Puerto Rico!"

"If you are ever offered exile to Cuba in exchange for stopping the activities of September Twenty-third, would you accept it?"

"They will never offer that to me. They want to see me dead. And anyway, where did that idea come from?"

"Some Senators have privately discussed that as a way of dealing with you."

"Those fools don't know me. I will always remain the leader of September Twenty-third. I take pride, especially, in the support we get from the younger generations of independence fighters. And I can assure you that we will continue to be an inspiration to them for as long as we live. That is part of our calling: to lead, and to fight for the independence of this country 'til death."

"In every status consultation ever held in Puerto Rico, the people have rejected independence," Karen said calmly. "And in every election held here every four years the parties that advocate statehood or commonwealth always win by a landslide. The independence column has never gotten more than six percent of the vote, why?"

"You are a political reporter, you should know this," Rigonaldo said, looking her straight in the eye. "Every country that is under the boot of colonialism, and I am repeating myself, has an inalienable right to independence. That means that the right to independence cannot be renounced. That is the natural right of every country that at one point or another has been subjected to the horrors of colonialism. Puerto Rico is no different. We are one of the last remaining colonies in the world. Our time is long overdue."

"Why do Puerto Ricans seem so content with their association with the United States?"

"That is a lie. That is an illusion. This is a situation where you have the most powerful empire in the world occupying our country. We are a country under military occupation. Do not forget that, ever! No thinking individual can be content with such a situation. The United States is the oppressive, military-occupying force of our country. Nobody can be content with their oppressor."

"What options do you give to the Puerto Rican people? How can we solve the question of colonialism in Puerto Rico?"

"A Constitutional Assembly has been suggested. That is a good start. And if that comes to pass, we will want to participate in that. But we will never renounce our right to independence."

"Some have argued that you want the political destiny of Puerto Rico to be given to a Puerto Rican Constitutional Assembly because it would be easier for you and your supporters to stage a coup d'etat if the Americans stay out."

Rigonaldo laughed. "I am honored every time I hear that I am feared."

"How can you participate in a Constitutional Assembly in the so-called 'civil society' after your organization has engaged in so many obviously violent and criminal activities for so many years now?"

"There are precedents of clandestine organizations making a leap into 'civil society.' But before I go on, let me correct you." Rigonaldo pointed a finger at Karen's face. "We are *not* a criminal organization. We are a *patriotic* organization. All we do is within the framework of our war against the government of the United States. That is a legitimate war. Look, for example, at what happened with the PLO in Palestine and with the IRA in Ireland. These were organizations that were deemed to be 'terrorist' and 'criminal' in nature and that operated clandestinely for many, many years. And today, those organizations are at the forefront of the mainstream political scenario in those countries. I think we can honestly establish comparisons here. Ours is not a unique situation. The perils of colonialism repeat themselves everywhere around the world. What is unique to us is that our enemy and our colonizer is the United States. A terrorist empire like no other in history."

"Mr. Pastrana, can there ever be peace and reconciliation between you, September Twenty-third and the United States?"

"If the Americans remove their military forces from our country, if they respect our right to independence and stop interfering in our affairs, yes, there can be reconciliation. Otherwise, no. We will fight them for as long as they are here and by whatever means it takes to get them out of here. This is our land; they don't seem to understand something so simple."

Karen pondered for a moment looking at her notes. She was ready to end the interview.

"Let me tell you one thing," Rigonaldo went on. "I sympathize with the people of the United States. They went through their own struggle of independence against the British. That was the right thing to do. But it seems they suffer from a short memory and that's why they cannot understand the quest for independence of the Puerto Rican people. But, if you ask me, I think the situation is about the same."

"Yes," Karen said, furrowing her eyebrows, "but wasn't there a general feeling of discontentment with the British that led in part to the American Revolution? That feeling is totally nonexistent in Puerto Rico."

"We cannot say that the relationship between the Americans and Puerto Rico has been benign. It has been tragic. There are reasons why there aren't many more independence advocates and fighters in Puerto Rico. You very well know that over the course of all these years the independence movement has been violently crushed and brutally repressed by both the U.S. government and the puppet colonial regime here. If events in history had been allowed to run their natural course, Puerto Rico would have become an independent republic a long time ago. I know that for a fact."

Karen looked over at Tonio who looked bored to death smoking his umpteenth cigarette. His face pleaded, "please end this NOW!"

"Okay, Mr. Pastrana," Karen said, "thank you for allowing me to come here. Is there one last thing you would like to say to our viewers?"

Rigonaldo looked at the camera and said, "Long live a free Puerto Rico! We will not be defeated!"

Faster than a bullet, Karen got up and Tonio shut his camera off. Though they wouldn't communicate it to each other, both of them thought that this had been the "interview with the devil."

Chapter 39

Karen and Tonio declined an offer by Rigonaldo to stay a while for "lunch." Karen wanted to get back to the station as soon as possible in order to put together her video report. She wanted to air the whole interview as a special report during the six and ten o'clock newscasts. And she didn't really want to spend any more time in Rigonaldo Pastrana's hideout. Not after what she had seen.

Oso and Luna disguised themselves and blindfolded the reporter and her cameraman. Karen and Tonio were led to the rear of a Toyota station wagon and were told to sprawl out on the dirty floorboard. They were covered head to toe with two checkered quilts.

As the car sped away, Rigonaldo watched them from the porch while smoking another of his Cuban cigars. He was pleased with the interview. All of Puerto Rico would be getting his message today. And the Governor, and that annoying man from the FBI, would know that he is serious. If there is no announcement on Friday that the plebiscite has been canceled, he will send them the head of Ana María Cruz in an ice cooler.

Oso maneuvered the vehicle over the dirt road that connected the hideout to Road 89. Once there on the paved road he drove slowly, constantly looking in the rearview mirror for any suspicious-looking vehicle behind them. And Luna had told him about the earlier incident. They couldn't afford another mistake. The shootout by the cane field had been extremely risky.

"So," Oso said to Luna, "did Rigonaldo get mad when you told him that you shot them by the cane field?" He was speaking in a low voice trying to not be overheard by the reporter in the back.

"I could tell he was fuming," Luna said. "But he contained himself."

"Of course. He didn't want to make a scene in front of them," Oso said, pointing to their "cargo" in the back.

"But, what was I supposed to do?" Luna asked rhetorically. "I wasn't sure we were being followed until I told Teco about it."

"Rigonaldo has a bad temper."

"I hate his bullshit!" Luna snapped, lighting a cigarette. "And every time he explodes I happen to be the one who is around. There are many things that you and Teco don't see."

"Oh no, I know what's going on. And most likely Teco is getting an earful now."

"Sometimes," Luna said pensively, "I feel like fucking quitting, you know. Leaving! Moving out! Quitting the fight!"

"You don't want to do that. He'll have a lot of people looking for you wherever you go."

"I know, I guess," Luna said, dismissing the idea. "I'm just talking crazy. I wouldn't quit. I believe in this struggle. It has nothing to do with that. But sometimes it pisses me off, you know. The contradictions. You want to build a better society and yet, he behaves like an ogre in the house. And the machismo. I can't stand it! That's what I hate the most. He says that once we are 'free,' women are going to be equal to men. But, how does he treat me? Like a maid. Like his fucking maid."

Oso laughed.

"Don't laugh," Luna told him. "It's not funny. I'm speaking the truth. Small things like that make a difference and tell you how serious you are about what you preach. If you are preaching justice and equality for all, you have to start in your own house. That's what Marxism is all about: radical change in human relations at all levels."

"I hear you," Oso said, giving thought to this. "Have you tried to talk to him about it? About how you feel?"

"Yes, I have. I have even quoted fucking Marx!"

"And, what has he said about it?"

"He says," Luna mimicked Rigonaldo, "*'as long as we live in a capitalist regime there cannot be equality between men and women.'* Bullshit! He just wants to get away with being a fucking male chauvinist."

Oso was about to speak but his attention shifted to the road. Traffic was becoming heavier and slower with the vehicles almost coming to a stop. They were approaching the site of the shooting.

"Watch out," Luna said, looking at the road. "We are almost there."

A state police officer was directing traffic. The agent's car had been removed from the road and was now parked at the edge of the embankment. Each vehicle passing by would slow down to take a look at the now empty vehicle with bullet holes and a shattered windshield.

Oso also drove slower as he passed the cop and the agents' car. He avoided eye contact with several police officers that were posted in the area. After the spot of the shooting, traffic became normal again. Luna looked behind them. They were fine.

"Do you think you killed them?" Oso asked her.

"I don't know," Luna said. "I'm sure I hit both of them."

"Feds?"

"Most likely."

"We'll have to get rid of that van now."

"Sure, we'll burn it."

"I think we'll be okay," Oso said, trying to sound unconcerned, though he was truly worried.

During the whole trip, Karen and Tonio didn't speak to each other. They kept their attention on whatever they could pick up of the conversation between the man and the woman who were driving them to who knows where.

When Oso drove through the second tollbooth going north on Highway 52, he exited the highway. In a matter of minutes he reached their chosen destination. They drove into the parking lot of a strip mall and stopped the car far away from the stores.

"Ms. Pérez!" Luna said.

"Yes?" Karen said, hoping this was their final stop.

"You may uncover your eyes, both of you. And get out of the blankets," Luna instructed.

Karen and Tonio did as told.

The rear door opened and the blond woman with the hat hurried them out of the vehicle. Without saying a word, Luna walked hurriedly to her seat on the passenger's side of the station wagon.

Karen was a little disoriented. "Where are we?" she asked the woman in the station wagon that was now speeding away.

"You are in Caguas!" Luna yelled from the moving car. "Do some shopping! Bye!"

Chapter 40

"What time is it?" Tonio asked as the station wagon sped away.

"It's almost two o'clock," Karen said as she began walking to the stores.

"I memorized their license plate," Tonio said proudly.

Karen told him, "It probably belongs to a stolen vehicle, Tonio. So don't get any ideas. They are not going to put us through what we went through to be given away by a license plate."

He wrote it on a piece of paper anyway.

After a mild argument, Karen gave in to Tonio's choice of a place to eat: McDonald's. They went into the fast food restaurant. Karen ordered a salad and a diet Coke and went straight to the ladies' room to wash her face and touch up her makeup. When she came back from the restroom, her salad and Coke were on the table. Tonio was gulping down two Big Mac's with fries and soda as if he had never eaten anything before in his life.

They ate for a few minutes without saying a word. Karen was trying to hurry, in order to make a phone call to the station. Tonio finished his first burger and said, "I hope they catch them."

"I'm sorry?" Karen said, lost in thought.

"I said," Tonio repeated, "I hope they catch them."

Karen said nothing.

"What do you think?" Tonio asked her.

"I don't think," Karen said with a smile.

"Now what does that mean?"

"It means that I am not going to voice my opinion about it, Tonio," Karen said softly.

"Why?"

Karen was not going to discuss something so delicate with a cameraman. She said, "It's nothing personal, Tonio, but I just think it's better that way."

"Well," Tonio said, a French fry dangling from his lips, "I don't know how you can contain yourself."

"I'm a journalist. My job is to discover what other people think and do and report to the public about it."

"But," Tonio insisted, "after what you saw today, how do you feel about this Rigonaldo freak?"

Karen repressed a smile. She said, "I'd rather not talk about it." She kept eating her salad and endured Tonio staring at her. He stared and stared, waiting for a reaction from her. She gave in. "No," she said softly. "I don't like what they are doing, Tonio. I don't like it."

"Did you see the First Lady?" Tonio went on. "How terrible she looked? How absolutely scared and terrified?"

Karen thought for a moment about what to say. "I think it's tragic what is happening to her." She paused. "Now, let's change subject."

Tonio lit up a cigarette.

Karen said, "I just wanted to tell you, I know you are entitled to your feelings and opinions, but with this interview we did today, try to be a little discreet . . . Please."

"Sure."

"Good."

Karen finished her salad, rummaged in her purse and grabbed her cell phone. "I'll be outside. I have to call Emilio." She went down her list of contacts and pressed "talk" on Emilio's direct number. By the time she went through the exit of the restaurant, Emilio Durcal was on the other end of the phone.

"Karen!" he exclaimed as if he'd been sitting in his office just waiting for this call. "Where are you?"

"I'm in Caguas."

"The FBI wants to talk to you," Emilio informed her. "Some agent named John Walker, an assistant to William Montana, called here asking for you."

"What do they want to talk about?"

"He mentioned something about you being a witness to the murder of a federal agent in Cagüey this morning. Tell me what's going on. Were you in Cagüey today? What's happening?"

"Emilio," Karen said, "I had no idea that we were in Cagüey, and I didn't see anything of what the FBI is talking about. That's the truth."

"So, what happened in Cagüey then?"

Karen took a deep breath, then said, "I have Rigonaldo and the First Lady on tape."

Silence. Then Emilio said calmly, "I was hoping you'd say that. I sort of figured it out. How did it go?"

"Rigonaldo's people picked us up, you know. And, it went fine for the most part. Except that on our way there, there was a shootout. Now that you've told me about Cagüey, I guess that's where we were; and I guess they must have shot at the FBI. They were apparently following us. But I didn't see anything because we were blindfolded, and whoever it was who shot at the agent was disguised. We didn't see anything. I have nothing to say to the FBI. I'm innocent of all charges!"

"You know, this sounds a little messy," Durcal said, pausing to light a cigar. "But anyhow, did you speak to Ana María Cruz?"

"Only for a minute and not on tape. They really didn't want us there with her. She looks awful; eyes swollen, wrists red and swollen. She is tied to a chair in a pitch-black room and it seems she hasn't been allowed to move ever since they took her. Believe me, it wasn't a pretty sight at all. We shot like half a minute of video of her in the room where they are keeping her. I'll fill you in on everything when I get back. You'll have to send the chopper to get us because my car is in Condado."

"Of course," Durcal said immediately. "Where exactly are you?"

"We'll be right in the parking lot outside the McDonald's in the Santa Iglesias Shopping Center."

"I'll send the chopper right away."

"Thanks," Karen said.

"There's something else happening," Durcal said with concern. "I wanted to tell you."

"What is it?"

"Eugenia Tonos called you."

"Eugenia? What did she want?"

"Well, she said that an armed man broke into their house this morning and took her mother with him."

"Oh, God."

"She was forced at gunpoint into a closet. It took her hours to get out."

"Did she call her father?"

"At first she couldn't locate him. That's why she called you. But, I'm sure that by now Tonos knows about it."

"What do the police say?"

"We don't have any information yet on what the police are doing. And we haven't heard anything about Barbara Tonos's whereabouts either. We are blank on this one. Elizabeth is working on it."

"Oh, God," Karen said again. "I hope Barbara is all right."

"I hope so too . . . Okay, let me go now. I need to work the phones. We'll talk when you come in."

Karen ended the call. Something told her that Barbara's incident was not happening in a vacuum. She went back into the fast food restaurant and grabbed her purse. "Tonio," she said quickly, "let's wait outside. Emilio is sending the chopper for us."

"A chopper ride!" Tonio exclaimed. "Hell, that sure compensates for all our troubles."

"Come on."

Chapter 41

It was close to six p.m. Channel Four would air Rigonaldo's interview in its entirety, preceded by the footage of Ana María Cruz in captivity. Emilio Durcal had notified Fortaleza.

In the newswire services room, a report from the Associated Press caught a young news writer's attention. He read it in full and quickly ran out to find Karen. She wasn't in her office or in the editing rooms. He finally found her in the control room cabin. There, she stood side by side with Emilio Durcal facing the glass partition to the studio where anchors Leida Rosado and Vidal Monge waited for their cue to begin the broadcast.

"Ms. Pérez," the young man said, handing her the report, "we just got this."

Karen thanked the young man, who left quickly back to his post at the newswire machines, and began reading the AP report. She read it twice. "How much uglier will this get?" she said when finished and handed it to Durcal.

Durcal read out loud but in a whisper. "*We are July 4th, the Warriors and Keepers of Democracy. Today we have captured Barbara Tonos, the wife of Senator Orlando Tonos, in retaliation for the kidnapping of First Lady Ana María Cruz . . . To Rigonaldo Pastrana and his communists' September Twenty-third we send a clear message: release our First Lady and we will release Barbara Tonos. As keepers of democracy in Puerto Rico we will not remain idle as communist terrorists attempt to violate our people and destroy our institutions . . . We are July 4th, the warriors, keepers of democracy."* He finished, sighed and handed the report back to Karen. "I've never heard of these people."

"Neither have I," Karen said.

Seated behind the control desk, Arturo Ramírez, the director of the six o'clock news, gave the cue to the anchors in the studio. The newscast started with the usual music and video introduction, but an obvious streak of alarm showed in the anchors' faces when they talked to the audience. A still picture of Ana María Cruz blindfolded and tied to a chair was their background as they explained Karen Pérez's audacious and daring trip to "somewhere in Puerto Rico" to bring this report to Puerto Rican households.

Durcal said to Karen, "Elizabeth found good footage of Barbara Tonos. Get it and use your own footage of Senator Tonos. Make a tape with this 'July 4th' shit and we'll run it in this broadcast as soon as it's ready." To the Director: "Get ready for a hectic broadcast. And we'll run overtime."

The director looked at him annoyed.

"Karen," Durcal said, "can you reach the Police Superintendent now?"

"I can try."

Durcal gave instructions at a fast pace. "Get the tape ready first. Then, try to find out what Calero knows about this group 'July 4th'. If you get him we'll air the information tonight too. I'll try to reach someone at the FBI to see if they've got anything on them . . . And try to locate Tonos. See if he wants to talk to us. We'll patch his phone call live to the studio. You'll have to draft some questions for Vidal and Leida."

Karen rushed out of the control room. Late tapes, unscheduled segments, live calls into the studio. The director of the newscast was furious. "Where is the tape with Barbara Tonos?" he barked. "It is late already!"

Durcal pressed the man's shoulder. "Relax," he told him.

Karen found senior reporter, Elizabeth Vega, talking on the phone at a desk in the newsroom. "I need your tape of Barbara Tonos," Karen told her. Elizabeth pointed to a pile of tapes on another desk. "There, the one with the blue label," Elizabeth said and kept on with her phone conversation. Karen found the tape with no difficulty, went into her office for her own tape of Senator Tonos, and quickly walked to the editing rooms to look for Tonio.

She found him walking out of his editing room, carrying a backpack and calling it quits for the night. Karen stopped him.

"Tonio," she told him quickly, "I need you for a minute."

"Oh, no! Not again. What is it? I'm out of here." There was no way Tonio would go out again to tape scary, obscure terrorists on the run.

"This will only take a minute."

"We are not going anywhere, are we?"

"No, no," Karen assured him. "I just need you to edit this for me and then we'll do a voice over."

Tonio sighed with relief. "Okay, let's do it fast. Rápido!"

They went into the editing room and finished the tape within ten minutes. Karen rushed to the control room and handed it to the director who complained he didn't like to receive tapes that were not entered on his broadcast log. Karen shot back telling him, "Well, change jobs and go direct a *novela* instead of a newscast." That was the end of the argument. The director refrained from commenting when Karen told him that if she located Senator Tonos and Police Superintendent Calero, there would certainly be more changes coming his way. After this little incident with the director, Karen returned to her office to use the phone.

"Oh, Christ!" she exclaimed, collapsing onto her swivel chair. "I need a vacation!"

As she picked up the phone, Tonio peeked his head into her office. "Knock, knock," he said jokingly. "I'm out of here, Karen. How are you getting back to your car? Do you want a ride?"

"No, thank you, Tonio," she said in a tired voice. "I still have to make a few phone calls. I'll take a cab. Thanks anyway."

"Okay, see you tomorrow," he said and left.

In three seconds his head was back in sight at the door. "Karen," he said.

"Yeah?"

"You look like you need a vacation."

"Shit if I don't know it," Karen said. "Phone calls, Tonio."

"I'm out of here," Tonio said, and this time he finally left.

Karen dialed Calero's office but got a recording. She tried other numbers and after getting a few recordings, a woman finally picked up the call and told her he was in Fortaleza. She made the call.

"Governor's office," Damaris said.

"Yes, good evening, this is Karen Pérez with Channel Four. I'm trying to reach Police Superintendent Calero."

"Ms. Pérez?"

"Yes, from Channel Four."

"One moment, please."

Soft music played while she was on hold. The thought came to Karen that if Calero was in Fortaleza with the Governor, most likely they were still watching the broadcast with Rigonaldo Pastrana getting his prime-time exposure. Two minutes went by and Damaris came back on line.

"Ms. Pérez?" Damaris said.

"Yes, I'm still here."

"The Superintendent is in a meeting with the Governor and the Assistant Director of the FBI. What is this in relation to?"

Karen told her briefly about the AP report. "Would the Superintendent have any information on this group 'July 4th, The Warriors, Keepers of Democracy?'"

Cruz's secretary wrote down the information. "Okay, Ms. Pérez," Damaris said, "I'll give your message to the Superintendent. May I help you with anything else?"

Karen found the politeness rather unusual. "That will be it for now," she said. "I'll be expecting his call."

"Thank you for calling, Ms. Pérez." Damaris hung up.

Karen took a second to turn on her TV set. The broadcast was now in the middle of her interview with Rigonaldo Pastrana. She turned the volume low and got up to pour herself a cup of coffee. As she sat back in her chair behind her desk she found herself craving a cigarette again. "What is happening to me?" she thought. She grabbed the phone and dialed Senator Tonos's office and got an answering machine. She hung up without leaving a message. She then dialed his home number. Eugenia answered.

"Hello!" the young woman said, sounding frantic.

"Eugenia?"

"Yes?"

"It's Karen."

"Oh, God, I'm so glad you called!"

"Sorry I couldn't call you earlier but I was away from the office and . . ."

"I couldn't find Dad."

"I know. Is he home?"

"Hold on."

Karen could hear Eugenia calling her father and the Senator asking who was calling. In a few seconds the Senator was on the line.

"Karen," he said.

"Hello Senator. I'm really sorry about . . ."

"They just called!" he cut her off with alarm in his voice. "About an hour ago."

"Who called?"

"Whoever it is that has Barbara."

"What did they say?"

"You want me to tell you exactly what he said?"

"Please."

"A man calls here, I come to the phone and he says, 'Listen mother fucker, you give us Ana María Cruz and we'll give you your wife back'. That's all he said and hung up."

"What do the police say?"

"They aren't being cooperative at all," Tonos said furiously. "They were here early this afternoon, two of them, and they said they would be back. I'm still waiting for them. I take that as payback time. Trying to get even with me." He was referring to the numerous police corruption investigations he had initiated.

"Are you watching Channel Four?"

"The TV is on. Tino is here and he's watching it. Eugenia and I are just too frantic to watch TV now. She's taping it, though."

Karen said, "We are running a story on Barbara. Associated Press sent a wire with a press release from the alleged kidnappers. Let me read it to you. Hold on." Karen searched for the report among the scattered papers on top of her desk. She couldn't find it immediately and thought that she may have left it in the editing room. As she was ready to run there, she found it. "Here it is," she said. "Listen." Slowly, and stressing each word, Karen read the report from July 4th – The Warriors, Keepers of Democracy. Tonos listened carefully.

"July 4th?" he said when she finished. "I've never heard of such a group."

"Neither have I."

"It sounds bogus."

"I'm trying to reach the Police Superintendent to see what he has on them."

"I called that bastard myself a few times today and he hasn't returned any of my calls."

"So, what do you plan to do?"

"Oh, I'm calling the police until they get tired of me. I want them here. I want my phone traced and intercepted."

"We want to have you on the broadcast tonight. A live talk via the telephone. Do you want to . . . ?"

"No," Tonos was quick to answer. "I don't think I should do that now. This whole thing looks very suspicious to me, and I don't have much information yet on what is truly going on."

"You can blast the police department," Karen instigated. "Tear them to shreds. The audience will love that."

"Let me wait until I have more information. Then I'll give you the best show your audience has ever seen. Calero will shit his pants with what's coming his way."

"Okay."

"Can you do me a favor?"

"What is it?"

"Could you fax me a copy of that AP report?"

"To your Senate office?"

"No, no. I have a fax here at home. Here is the number." He gave her the fax number.

"Okay," Karen said quickly, "I'll fax it right away."

"Thanks a lot, Karen. Let me go now. I want to get the pigs in here."

"Who?"

"The pigs, I mean, the police."

"We'll talk again, Senator," Karen said and hung up.

Karen put down the receiver and tried to stretch her body. She was exhausted. She got up and poured herself another cup of coffee. The TV broadcast was now on a commercial break. She grabbed the AP brief and walked a few steps to her fax machine. She dialed Tonos's number and pressed the send key. She gave thought to what Tonos said about the whole thing being "bogus" and "suspicious."

There was a knock on her door and Emilio Durcal came in. "What are you doing?" he asked her softly, aware of her tired face.

"I just faxed the AP report to Tonos. He didn't know about it."

"What else did he say?"

"Well," Karen said sitting down on her swivel chair, "he got a call from some freak who told him, 'Listen mother fucker, you give us Ana María Cruz and we give you your wife back.' That's all the man said and hung up."

"Hmmm."

"Yes, hmmm."

"Well," Durcal said calmly, "he's up to his neck in this now."

"I think that's clear to him."

"What do the police say?"

"He says they are not cooperating in retaliation for his investigations on police corruption. He will have Calero 'shit his pants' – his words – when he realizes what's coming his way."

"Did you ask him to go on the broadcast tonight?"

"He won't do it until he has more information."

"What about Calero? Did you speak to him?"

"I left a message for him with Cruz's secretary. They are all in Fortaleza. Cruz, Calero, Montana. Did you get through to the FBI?"

"No, nothing yet."

For a moment they both went silent. Then, Durcal said, "Listen Karen, I know you've had a long, difficult day . . ."

"Tell me about it."

"So, go home now and get some rest. I don't want you to burn out."

"That sounds nice. I don't think Calero will call, anyway."

"I'll have someone take care of that."

"Thank you."

Durcal said, "Expect a very busy day tomorrow. After this coup with the First Lady, everyone will want to talk to you."

"I won't talk to anybody until this thing is over."

"Good thinking," Durcal said. "I'll see you tomorrow."

"I'm taking a long vacation. Soon."

Durcal smiled, nodded and left her office.

Before the phone would dare ring on her, Karen grabbed her purse and quickly left her office. Whatever might come up tonight would have to wait until tomorrow. She went to a secretary in the newsroom and asked her to call a cab for her. The secretary did it in a flash.

"Congratulations on that interview, Karen," the secretary told her.

Karen smiled but avoided small talk. She walked to the parking lot and waited for her cab to arrive.

This night in Puerto Rico was like many others. A clear sky with the immensity of the universe crowded with stars. And then there was the cool breeze that caressed her skin. It was ironic that so many terrible things were happening amidst this quiet scene. She felt the pain of the events that were occurring in Puerto Rico. *Her* Puerto Rico. It was ironic too, that for a moment she wished she had the power to do what many Puerto Ricans were doing during this time of crisis: turning off their TV sets to avoid the ugliness of the stories that the news shows were bringing into the sanctity of their homes. No. Karen Pérez couldn't do that. She couldn't just be like any other man or woman on the street.

Karen Pérez was one of the ones responsible for those stories coming into people's homes. For her, the stories went with her everywhere she went. She was fully aware of that.

Chapter 42

The cab ride was uneventful but for the thoughts running through her mind. So, Rigonaldo Pastrana is hiding in Cagüey, she thought. I would have never figured that out, she told herself. In her broadcast there was no mention of that fact. Neither Karen or Emilio Durcal felt comfortable with the way they had gotten that piece of information. And then there was the fact that, curiously enough, no news agency had reported anything about a "shooting of federal agents" happening on the outskirts of the town of Cagüey this morning. Durcal wanted to wait for more information to see how that affected Karen.

Ashford Avenue in Condado at night is a pleasant sight. There are the hotels and the casinos and the restaurants and the tourists; dozens of them strolling down the street looking at the scenery and taking pictures. And there were also of course, the natives from all across the island that always came to Ashford Avenue to see and enjoy their dosage of luxury. There was always a mild traffic jam but it wasn't a nuisance. Even though it was a Tuesday night, Condado was bursting with activity. Lots of people and lots of things going on.

Karen's cab pulled over right in front of the Matisse Café. She got out and paid and tipped the driver. A generous tip despite the fact that the driver had unsuccessfully attempted to engage Karen in small talk that she wanted none of.

As Karen was walking to her car she realized that she was hungry. Had she had time to eat dinner yet? She couldn't remember. By the time she approached her car she had decided to go eat something. She would treat herself good tonight. In fact, she would indulge. She walked in the direction of the Marriott Hotel. Not long ago, a colleague had recommended their Italian restaurant, Venezio.

For a few seconds, lost amongst a crowd of strangers, most of them not knowing who she was, Karen felt free and anonymous. Good feeling.

But all too short-lived.

"Ms. Pérez!" a man's voice called from behind.

Karen slowly turned her head and saw them. Two men approaching her, dressed in expensive suits and one of them holding some sort of leather accessory in his hand. What was it? His wallet? She soon found out it wasn't a wallet. And she immediately found out the hard way that no, she wasn't an anonymous face in this Ashford Avenue crowd.

"Good evening, Ms. Pérez," the man said flashing, his FBI identification in her face. "We are with the FBI. I am Special Agent John Walker and this is my partner Special Agent Steven Morales. We would like to have a word with you. This won't take long."

Karen Pérez felt as if, at this very moment, she was trapped in an animal's cage, right here in the middle of Ashford Avenue. She smiled politely to the FBI but kept walking at a slower pace.

"How can I help you?" she told Walker.

Walker was annoyed. "We'd appreciate it if you'd stop walking, Ms. Pérez, and speak with us."

"I am speaking with you." She stopped.

"Can you tell us a little bit about what happened today in Cagüey?" Walker asked in his most official and serious tone.

Karen was silent for a moment, thinking of what to say. "I'm on my way to the Marriott," she said casually. "Would you like to walk with me?"

"No, ma'am," Walker said, exchanging looks with his partner. "You damn well know this is a busy night for us."

Morales said, "Are you aware that a Federal agent was killed today and a second one was badly wounded by shots fired from a vehicle in which you and your cameraman were passengers?"

"My boss, Emilio Durcal, informed me there had been a shooting of that sort," Karen said flatly. Shit!

"Well," Walker said, "can you tell us what happened? Are you denying that you were in that vehicle?"

Silence.

Karen said, "There isn't much that I can say. Both my cameraman and I were blindfolded when the shooting occurred."

"Really? Why was that Ms. Pérez?" Walker pressed on.

"I was on my way to conduct an interview."

"Really? Is that something that you normally do, Ms. Pérez? To go blindfolded to an interview in a stolen vehicle?" The cynicism was like a cutting knife.

Karen was struck but she held her ground. "The nature of the interview required that we went blindfolded. And I certainly didn't know that they had picked us up in a stolen vehicle, as you claim."

Walker said, "We know you were on your way to interview a fugitive. Rigonaldo Pastrana, to be exact. Did Mr. Pastrana shoot our agents?"

"No, he did not."

"Really? How can you be so sure? Weren't you blindfolded?"

Karen knew they were trying to upset her. "Rigonaldo Pastrana was not in the van with us," she snapped.

"Okay," Walker went on, "so who was the shooter? Could it have been Antonio Vargas, your cameraman?"

"Of course not!" Karen said angrily. "For Christ's sake!" She now took a step back as if to leave.

"We are not finished, Ms. Pérez," Walker said as an order.

"Listen," she said furiously, "I am being very polite with both of you, and I am answering all of your questions. You don't have to be nasty to me. I don't have to answer your questions if I don't want to."

"It's not that easy, Ms. Pérez," Walker said calmly. "One of our agents was murdered today, and you were in the vehicle where the shots came from. You could be lying to us. For all we know you could have been the shooter . . ."

"Don't insult me!" Karen said sharply. "You know better than that."

"We don't know what happened and we want to find out," Walker pressed on.

"I am not lying to you," Karen said firmly.

"We are giving you the benefit of the doubt here. We hope you appreciate that. Do you understand?"

Karen said nothing.

Morales said, "We could haul your ass to federal detention as an accessory to murder if we want to."

Karen's eyes and mouth were wide open. She wanted to curse at these two motherfuckers, but thought better of it.

"No," Walker said to Morales, "we really don't want to do that." Good cop-bad cop routine. "We just want a few answers, Ms. Pérez."

Karen pulverized him with her eyes.

"So, tell us, Ms. Pérez," Walker asked, "who shot at our agents?"

"It was a woman!" Karen snapped. "That's all I know."

"She was in the van with you?"

"Yes."

"What's the name of this woman?"

"I don't know."

"A woman with no name. That's not much help, Ms. Pérez. What did she look like, anyway?"

"She was disguised in a hat, sunglasses and a blond wig," Karen said flatly.

"Sounds like Lana Turner to me," Morales said, annoyed. "Or like one of those other platinum blondes of Hollywood of the thirties."

"Oh, wait!" Karen said, suddenly remembering how Rigonaldo referred to the woman. "Her name was Estrella! They called her Estrella."

"Estrella?" Morales asked incredulously. "That's it?"

"Yes, sir," Karen said. "That's all I know."

Walker and Morales glanced at each other. No, both agents thought, you know a lot more than that, bitch.

"Tell me," Walker said, "from the site of the shooting until you arrived at the place where Mr. Pastrana was staying, how much time elapsed?"

Karen knew where this conversation was headed and she didn't like it. She had beaten the FBI in court once and she thought she could do it again if she had to.

"I don't have any idea," she said calmly.

Morales said, "I know you are being a wiseass. Try us. This time that *I have to protect my sources'* shit will get you nowhere. We'll make sure to get a Reagan appointee in Federal Court to hear our case."

"That's it, gentlemen," Karen said with an edge. "If you have more questions, I'll have to tell you to contact my attorney. Call my boss, Emilio Durcal, and he will refer you to the station's counsel and . . ."

Walker cut her off. "It's okay, Ms. Pérez. We don't have more questions at this time."

Karen turned and began to walk in the direction of the Marriott Hotel.

"Have a good night, Ms. Pérez," Morales told her.

Karen turned and said, "Good night, gentlemen."

With that both agents smiled at her and walked to their car, parked a few doors down from the Matisse Café. "Let's go and see the kid," Walker told Morales.

Karen saw them speed away. Bastards. She was shaken, no doubt. For a second she stood there on the sidewalk but she nevertheless decided to go on with her plans. She walked hurriedly to the Marriott and disappeared through the lobby. She went into the Venezio and took a table in the darkest corner of the restaurant. The patrons were mostly American tourists. She really wanted to be incognito tonight. At least for a few hours. And especially after that run-in with the Feds.

Karen thought of the issues that the FBI could raise against her this time. But, she was ready to put up a good fight. Again.

Chapter 43

Agents Walker and Morales were now driving north on Sacred Heart Street after passing by the front gates of Sacred Heart University in Santurce, a suburb of San Juan. Antonio Vargas, aka Tonio, had studied telecommunications at Sacred Heart and had kept the same apartment he lived in while he was an undergraduate there.

The agents parked a few doors down from house number 257, where Tonio lived.

"Let's go easy on him," Walker told Morales. "See how he does."

Morales nodded and followed Walker to the front door of the house. They could hear extremely loud music blasting from somewhere in the back of the house. It was Bon Jovi's *Blaze of Glory*. They knocked a few times on the front door, unsure if they were being heard. A minute later, the door opened and a short, white-haired, elderly woman with thick glasses greeted them.

"Good evening, ma'am," Walker said loudly enough to be heard above the blasting music. "We're looking for Antonio Vargas."

"You mean Tonio?"

"Yes, yes, Tonio." They were both yelling.

"He's in the rear apartment," the old lady said, pointing with her wrinkled fingers. "Follow the noise. You won't miss it."

"Thank you, ma'am."

As the agents turned, the lady yelled, "And please, tell that boy to turn down that noise!"

"We'll do ma'am," Morales yelled back.

They went around the house, opened the gate of a metal fence and walked through, following the music, which became louder as they neared a back door. There was a glass window by the door, which seemed to be vibrating with every beat of music, but the drapes were drawn and they couldn't see inside.

Walker drew his fist and hit the door hard a few times but got no response. He hit harder a few more times until his fist hurt. Then he hit the window, afraid it would break into pieces.

Then, the door opened. The agents were struck full-force by the volume of the music, and there he was, Tonio, barefoot, wearing a white T-shirt, green Bermuda shorts and smoking a cigarette.

Walker was glad he wasn't smoking a marijuana joint.

"Hey," Walker yelled, "the lady up front wants you to lower the music!" How clever for an introduction, Walker thought.

"What?" Tonio yelled back.

"The music, lower the volume!"

"Hold on!" Tonio said and rushed to lower the volume on his stereo. He came back to the door. "I'm sorry, but she never complains when I play Ednita or Yolandita Monge."

"I like Ednita myself," Walker said.

"Yolandita is better," Morales told them.

"You don't like Bon Jovi?" Tonio asked.

"We both like Bon Jovi, don't get us wrong," Walker said as he and his partner tried to scan the tiny apartment.

"You are not with the landlady, are you?"

"Not really," Walker said, searching for his ID. He flashed it in Tonio's face. "We are actually with the FBI. I'm Special Agent John Walker and this is my partner Steven Morales. We'd like to speak with you for a minute."

"Oh, God!" Tonio said, glancing at the FBI ID in front of him. He had never seen a real one. Only on the X-Files. "Are you for real?"

"Yes," Walker said, "we are the real enchilada. This should only take a minute."

"Am I in any shit?" Tonio asked nervously.

"Antonio . . . ," Walker began.

"Tonio," he corrected.

"Okay, Tonio, why don't we just talk for a minute?" Walker was calm and pleasant.

Tonio shrugged his shoulders. "Come on in," he said softly. "Please don't look at the mess."

"Not to worry, son," Morales said.

Both agents entered the tiny living room. There was a dining table and a small refrigerator in the corner close to a cramped kitchen with piles of dirty dishes in a platinum sink. A small futon couch sat in front of a bookshelf. There was not a single book on the bookshelf. It held instead a huge TV set, and a DVD/VCR with dozens and dozens of DVD's and videotapes scattered around it. Amazingly, there was room somewhere for a medium size aquarium with tiny goldfish swimming in the water. The walls were bare except for two old posters of the movies Chinatown and Network.

Walker and Morales sat on the couch. Tonio brought one of only two wooden chairs from the dining table and sat facing them.

"Sorry about the mess," Tonio said. "I wasn't expecting any visitors."

"Do you know why we are here, Tonio?" Walker asked softly.

Tonio took a long, last drag on his cigarette and quickly lit up another one. He said, "Shit, I don't know. I guess I have an idea." His hands were trembling.

Morales said, "You don't have to be nervous, Tonio. You've done nothing wrong."

"You have a lot of tapes," Walker said.

"Yeah," Tonio said softly. "I tape everything. Movies, documentaries, concerts, variety shows, comedy shows."

"I do the same," Walker said.

"Me too," Morales added.

Tonio nodded. "Would you like anything to drink?"

The agents glanced at each other. "Yes," they said in unison.

"I only have a couple of Cokes."

"Coke will be fine," both men said.

Tonio got up, went to the sink and rinsed two crystal glasses. He rummaged in his fridge, got ice and quickly poured the sodas for his unexpected guests. He came back to his seat after handing the agents their sodas and turning off the stereo.

"I bet you never get bored with all those tapes," Walker said.

"Yeah," Tonio said shyly. "I always have something going on."

"You can say that about our job too, you know," Walker said, nodding to his partner. "Isn't that right, Steven?"

"Yes, yes," Morales said quickly. "Absolutely. We always have something going on."

"It's really a good job," Walker went on. "Only that sometimes we have to deal with some unsavory characters."

"I would imagine so," Tonio said, feeling more at ease.

"But, once in a while," Walker said softly, "we get to meet some very nice people . . . Like you, for example . . ."

"Thank you," Tonio said sincerely.

"So tell me, Tonio," Walker began, "what did you do today? What happened today that was somewhat unusual for you?"

Tonio took a long drag on his cigarette and blew the smoke into the air. He remembered Karen's words, 'try to be a little discreet about this interview we did today.' He thought for a long moment and then said, "I'm really not supposed to say."

"You have to talk to us," Morales blurted.

"Hey!" Walker told Morales. "Let me talk to Tonio, okay?" He looked Tonio straight in the eye. "Steven here gets a little impatient. Don't mind him."

Tonio nodded.

"Listen, Tonio," Walker went on, "this conversation is between you and me. Nobody will know we talked. You've got to believe me. And I also think that you *do* want to talk to somebody about what happened to you today. Am I right?"

"I guess, yeah."

"Okay, so tell me, I do know what you did today, but I want you to tell me. I want you to trust me."

"We interviewed Rigonaldo Pastrana," Tonio said bluntly, "and we saw the First Lady."

"She's alive?"

"Yeah, she's alive. In bad shape, but alive."

"And where was this?"

"I don't know."

"You don't know?"

"I don't. Sorry," Tonio said apologetically. "The people who picked us up blindfolded us for the ride to their hideout and for the ride coming back. That way we wouldn't know where we were."

"What about Ms. Pérez, did she tell you where you were?"

"No. Karen doesn't know where we were either. She was also blindfolded."

"Okay."

Both agents glanced at each other. They were pleased that the cameraman didn't know anything about the likelihood that Rigonaldo's hideout was in Cagüey.

"Now, tell me," Walker continued, "tell me a little about the ride up there."

Tonio was pensive. "Well," he said slowly, "the trip was rather long. Two hours, maybe, maybe a little less than that. We left from Ashford Avenue in Condado but I didn't check the time." He paused. "What I do know is that for a good part of the ride we were on a highway road."

"How do you know that?"

"I was able to count three toll booths on the way there. I know it because of the sound that the coins make when you throw them in the coin basket. And the machine makes a sound too before it allows your car to pass through."

Pretty clever, Walker thought. "Now, what happened after the third toll booth? After you were no longer on the highway? Tell me whatever you remember."

"Oh, I don't know," Tonio said, pausing to gather his thoughts. "I guess we drove some more, we slowed down, drove some more, slowed down, came to a stop, drove some more . . ."

"What else?"

"Well, at one point the woman who was in the van with us, she yelled 'we've been followed' and next thing I know it's bang! bang! bang! The crazy bitch started shooting at somebody."

"How exactly did that happen?"

"She told the driver to slow down to let other cars pass by. I can't fully remember, but I think she said it was a Lexus that was following us. All I know is that the other crazy bastard, the driver, he went in reverse, hit whatever and then shots were fired."

"How do you know it was the woman who did the shooting?"

"Well, she was the only one in the van with us besides the driver."

"Tell me something," Walker said, "when you got into the van in Condado, did you get to see the face of this woman or of the driver?"

"Only for a second. The woman, not the driver."

"What did she look like?"

"Karen Black in Family Plot."

"What?" Walker asked, somewhat puzzled.

Morales repressed a smile.

"It's a Hitchcock movie," Tonio told Walker.

"His last movie," Morales said.

"Yes," Tonio said, excited.

"Okay," Walker said, "why did she look like . . . like . . . ?"

"Karen Black," Tonio added.

"Yes, her."

"Her first scene in the movie," Tonio began, "she is wearing a hat, dark sunglasses and a blond wig. That's what the woman in the van looked like."

"How do you know she was wearing a wig?"

"She looked odd. Her hair just didn't match her skin."

"Was she white? Black? *Trigueña*?"

"She looked *trigueña* to me."

"Did you notice any birthmarks or tattoos on her?"

"Not really," Tonio said dissapointedly. "You have to remember that the inside of the van was very dark. There were no windows on either side, only a small window in the rear."

"It's all right, Tonio," Walker said with a smile. "We know you are talking about Estrella." He glanced at Morales.

"That's right!" Tonio said excitedly. "That's what Pastrana called her when we were in the house!"

"Did Estrella wear her wig when you arrived at your destination?"

"No," Tonio said firmly. "Everyone was wearing hoods in that house. Except Rigonaldo."

"Okay," Walker said, "but before we get to that, tell me, how much time elapsed between the site where the shooting occurred and when you arrived at the house? Try to remember that."

"Oh, I don't know for sure," Tonio said pausing. "Twenty minutes, I guess. Half an hour."

"Twenty minutes to half an hour," Walker repeated.

"Yeah . . . no more than that, I think."

"Good," Walker said, glancing at his partner. "Okay, now tell me about the ride between the site of the shooting and the house. Whatever you remember."

Tonio lit another cigarette. He said, "Well, at first the driver sped away really fast after the shooting . . ."

"Do you have a name for him?"

"The driver?"

"Yes."

"No, nobody ever called him by name."

"Okay, go on."

"Well, like I said, he drove away really fast," Tonio went on. "That's when I heard a police siren behind us. More shots were fired. He came to a stop and went back in reverse. He hit another car, I'm certain. I was rolling all over the floorboard. The woman shot another round and then yelled at him to keep driving. Soon after, he slowed down again. Then we drove for a while until we began going up, like up a hill or a mountain or something."

"How do you know that?"

"Because of the sound of the van's engine. You can tell when the road is hard on the engine. The shifts sort of change. Even though the van had an automatic transmission you could still feel it trying to pick up speed when going uphill. That happens in all automatic vehicles. Have you ever gone to the rain forest? *El Yunque?* You can tell when you are going up a mountain."

"Yes, I absolutely know what you mean," Walker said, pleased. "I'm curious, how do you remember all those details?"

"Because once I got into that van in Condado and they pulled this blindfold shit I was suspicious and . . . and . . . a little scared, I guess. I admit it. I immediately wanted to know where the hell we were going. That's why I paid attention to every move and sound around me."

"Good," Walker said approvingly.

"That's very good, Tonio," Morales added. "I would have done the same thing."

"Okay," Walker said, "go on, what happened next?"

"Well, we kept going uphill for a while and at some point we got onto a dirt road . . ."

"A dirt road? How do you . . . ?"

"I could tell by the sounds of the tires as they drove over gravel and rocks. It was definitely a dirt road, absolutely not a paved road like before."

Walker and Morales exchanged nods and glances.

"How long were you on this dirt road?" Walker asked.

"A few minutes, I can't remember, maybe five to ten minutes."

"What happened next?"

"That's when we came to a stop. They took us out of the van, still blindfolded. I heard a flock of chickens roaming about. We walked through mud, then we went up some wood steps onto what I assume was a wooden porch, and then we were inside the house. That's when they took the blindfold off."

"What happened inside the house?"

"They made us wait in the living room until Rigonaldo showed up."

"How many people were in the house? Besides Pastrana."

"Three more. One, whom I supposed was our driver, the woman, Estrella and one more man."

"Tell me about the house, you said there was a wooden porch . . ."

"It sounded like wood when we walked on it . . ."

"Okay, but the inside, was it wood or concrete?"

"Wood. Definitely wood panels."

"Describe to me what you saw. Tell me what I would see if I went inside."

"Well," Tonio said, pausing to light yet another cigarette, "once you step in, if you stand facing the living room, to the right you have the kitchen with a dining table; to your left there is a hallway that I guess leads to bedrooms, I don't know, I didn't walk that way . . ." He blew some smoke into the air and then described every detail of the living room right up to the posters of Fidel Castro, Mao Tse Tung and Che Guevarra on the walls.

"Where are they keeping the First Lady?" Walker asked impatiently.

"I was getting there . . ." Tonio said with a smile on his face. "To the right of the living room there is another hallway. That one I did walk through. There are a few doors on the right of this hallway when you walk from the living room . . ."

"How many doors?"

"Three, four, I really don't remember . . ."

"Go on."

"What I do know is that the room where they have the First Lady is the very last door in that hallway. It would be the first room in the hallway if you were coming in through a screen door from the back. I could see out through the door into the yard, and there was a barn, like the ones used for domestic animals."

"Okay, wait," Walker said. He wanted to get this information correct down to the last detail. "There is a screen door at the end of that hallway. That's where you saw their rear yard with possibly a barn or something to keep animals, correct?"

"Yes, correct. There were also trees and bushes in the back. Thick underbrush and foliage."

"I need to get this right," Walker went on. "The room with the First Lady is the first door to our left if we come through that screen door, is that correct?"

"Yes, yes. If you come through the back screen door, her room will be the first to your left."

"Okay, tell me about her and the room."

"We were in there for less than two minutes. Estrella was very rude and rushed us out."

"It doesn't matter, whatever you remember of those two minutes."

"Well, it was a very tiny room, almost like a walk-in closet, and it was pitch-dark when the light was off. I couldn't tell if it was that there were no windows or if the windows had been sealed like when a hurricane is coming. I don't know."

"Go on."

"I think I saw a very small, old TV set . . . The First Lady was tied up to a chair with her hands against her back. And it struck me that when we entered the room she was blindfolded even though the room was already pitch-black . . ."

"What about her legs? Were her legs tied up to the chair too?"

"I think so . . . I think that may show on the video I made of her. But I think all I got was a medium shot. I mean, that Estrella woman really rushed us out of there fast. Have you seen the video?"

"We saw parts of it," Walker said. "Did the First Lady say anything to you?"

"She spoke to Karen."

"What about?"

"She asked about her husband . . . the governor."

"What else?"

"She asked about where we were, and about what they wanted from her, you know, what were the demands of the terrorists."

"What did Karen Pérez tell her?"

"She told her that they wanted the governor to cancel the plebiscite."

"What did Mrs. Cruz say?"

"She said that her husband couldn't do that. She sounded pissed off about that."

"You said that the First Lady was alive but in bad shape, what do you mean?"

"Well, she is all swollen, dirty, unkempt . . . it looks like . . ." Tonio paused.

"Like what?"

"It looks like they haven't allowed her to go to the bathroom . . . If you know what I mean."

"Okay, what else?"

"That's about it. The whole thing lasted less than two minutes. I got out of the room and went to the screen door to look at the rear of the house. It looks like the house is in a forest or something."

"What happened next?"

"Nothing. Estrella shut the door and left the First Lady there. We went back to the living room and there he was, this freak, Rigonaldo, with a look on his face as if he was some big shot. It was pretty pathetic to me."

"Okay, so you went to the living room and interviewed Pastrana. Tell me, what we saw on your station's broadcast, was it edited or was that the whole thing?"

"It was the full interview," Tonio said quickly. "Just as we taped it."

"Are you completely sure of that?"

"Yes, I'm the one who prepared the tape."

"And after you prepared that tape, nobody else touched it or edited it?"

"No. I am sure of that."

"Okay," Walker went on, "so you did the interview and tell me, what were the others doing all that time? Where were they?"

"They were all wearing hoods and seated behind us against the wall. None of them spoke a word."

"Did the phone ring while you were at the house?"

"No."

"Okay, now tell me, what happened after the interview was over?"

"The freak offered us lunch, which we of course declined. They blindfolded us again and took us into another car. This time they used a brown station wagon, I saw it after we arrived in Caguas."

"Caguas," Walker repeated.

"Yes, that's where they dropped us off. I actually got their license plate number. Here . . ." Tonio got up, went into his room and came back holding a small piece of paper. He gave it to Walker.

"It's probably of no help," Tonio said quickly. "Karen said it probably belonged to a stolen vehicle."

Walker and Morales exchanged looks. There it goes, both men thought, Karen Pérez saying that she didn't know they were riding in stolen vehicles.

"Did anything happen on the way back?" Walker asked.

"No. We just sat there under a blanket while the woman and the man talked."

"What did they talk about?"

"I couldn't make out what they were talking about. Sorry."

"That's all right. Where did they drop you off?"

"At the parking lot of the Santa Iglesias Shopping Center."

"Ms. Pérez's car was in Condado. How did you two get back into the city?"

"By chopper. The station sent a chopper for us."

"I see," Walker said. He thought he had covered everything he wanted to cover. He glanced at Morales. "Do you want to ask anything else?"

"No," Morales said. "I think you pretty much covered everything we need for now." He looked at Tonio and said, "You've been a great help, Tonio."

"Thank you. I wish I knew more."

"You did fine," Walker said. "What I would really like is if you could possibly keep this conversation between us. Don't tell anyone we spoke."

"Sure."

"Don't tell anyone, friends, no one. Especially don't talk to any member of the press about this. That includes Karen and anyone at your station. We wouldn't like this information printed or broadcast anywhere. We have some very specific reasons for that. The First Lady's life may depend on it. Can we trust you on this?"

"Sure, sure," Tonio said seriously. "I myself wouldn't like Karen or Durcal to know that I spoke to you."

"It's all right, you don't need to worry about this conversation being known," Walker said reassuringly.

"Okay."

Walker and Morales stood up. Walker said, "Thank you for talking to us, Tonio."

"Yes," Morales said. "Thank you very much."

Tonio stood up and shook hands with both men. The agents quickly walked to the door. Tonio opened it for them and let them out. Walker turned and pulled out one of his business cards. "Keep this," he said, handing it to Tonio. "If you ever get in any trouble, give me a call."

Tonio watched the agents leave. He closed the door as he scanned Walker's FBI business card.

He was now totally alone and in silence in his apartment. So many things had happened to him today. He tried to dissect his day in silence. In the morning you meet the devil in his hellhole. The most sought-after criminal on the island. In the afternoon you prepare a video of him to show on prime time TV. And in the night, you spill your guts to the FBI hoping they will catch the son of a bitch.

Tonio grabbed a remote control and pushed several buttons on it. His stereo came on. This time at a lower volume than before. In five seconds, Yolandita Monge was singing *Laberinto Sin Salida* (Labyrinth Without an Exit).

Tonio lit a cigarette, sat on the couch and kept looking at Walker's FBI card. Tomorrow, he decided, he would not show up for work.

Chapter 44

Once in their vehicle, Walker quickly rummaged through his jacket. He pulled out a tiny microphone attached by a thin wire to a small tape recorder in his underpocket. He rewound the tape a little and pressed play. Tonio's voice clearly came up: "By chopper. The station sent a chopper for us."

"Good," Walker said and pressed stop. He looked at Morales. "Do you want to hear Pérez?"

"No," Morales said quickly. "That bitch didn't give us anything."

"We pissed her off, didn't we?" Walker said, grinning and starting the engine.

"She's a fucking bitch!"

Walker sped away. "Let's call the boss," he said, grabbing his cell phone and dialing Montana's number.

Montana answered on his cell phone while still at Fortaleza with the Governor and the Police Superintendent.

"Montana."

"Boss, Walker here."

"What do we got?" Montana asked quickly.

"Pérez didn't give us much, as expected, but her camera guy talked like a parrot. We got a good description of the house where Pastrana is hiding the First Lady, and pretty good information in terms of time frame and road description between the site of the shooting and their actual hideout."

"Good."

"Canseco was right," Walker went on. "It was the woman who did the shooting. Estrella is her alias. No description, though. Two more men with Pastrana. No descriptions either."

"Everything is on tape?"

"Yes sir."

"Did the boy know about Cagüey?"

"No, sir," Walker reported. "It seems that Pérez and company are keeping mute on that."

"Good," Montana said, pleased. "I'm calling Emilio Durcal now. Come back here now. Drive fast."

With that, Montana ended the call.

Governor Cruz and Calero waited for Montana to talk to them. Montana said, "My boys are coming back with some tapes for you to listen to. Excuse me for a second, I have to call Channel Four."

Cruz nodded. Montana dialed a number on his cell phone.

"Good evening, WSTN," the switchboard operator at Channel Four said pleasantly.

"Emilio Durcal, please," Montana said.

"Who's calling, please?"

"This is William Montana, Assistant Director in Charge of the FBI in Puerto Rico, ma'am."

"Hold on, sir."

Soft music came on. Two minutes passed before the woman returned to the line. Montana was annoyed, but said nothing.

"Mr. Montana?" the operator said.

"Yes?"

"Hold on for Mr. Durcal."

Five seconds.

"Emilio Durcal here."

"Mr. Durcal? William Montana."

"Good evening, how can I help you?" Durcal said carefully. He didn't know if Montana was calling about Karen, or about July 4th and Barbara Tonos.

"Mr. Durcal, the Governor, the Police Superintendent and myself watched your broadcast tonight with more than a passing interest."

"I fully understand," Durcal said. He was listening intensely.

"We were pleased that there was no mention of the shooting of our agents in Cagüey this morning and that you didn't report that Rigonaldo Pastrana may be hiding and holding Mrs. Cruz in or near Cagüey."

"I see," Durcal said.

Montana said nothing.

Durcal said, "Well, we weren't comfortable with the way that that information became known to us. That's why we didn't report on it. You see, Karen Pérez had no idea that she was in Cagüey, so . . ."

Montana interrupted, saying, "I have to rush off the phone, Mr. Durcal. I just wanted you to know that this has worked out better for us for two reasons. The first is that we were able to conceal our agents from the local police there, and we are portraying the shooting as drug related. We don't want anyone to know at this stage why our agents were there, or that they were there at all. Our second reason is that if, as it seems, Pastrana is hiding the First Lady in Cagüey, we don't want him to know that we know that. We don't want him to get nervous and move her to another site. At this moment that would be disastrous to our investigation."

"I understand," Durcal said. "So, what is your concern?"

"I would appreciate it if you'd refrain from reporting about anything to do with Cagüey."

Durcal said, "I don't see a problem with that. We weren't planning on it anyhow."

"Good. Thank you, Mr. Durcal."

"Before you go, Mr. Montana," Durcal said quickly. "I'd like to ask you a question."

"What is that?"

"I suppose that you are aware of the kidnapping of Barbara Tonos?"

"Yes, I saw your report."

"Nobody seems to know anything about that group, July 4th-the Warriors, Keepers of Democracy. Do you have . . . ?"

"Never heard of them," Montana said flatly.

"No information on them?"

"I'm afraid not."

"Do you have any idea who may be behind this?"

"Mr. Durcal," Montana said firmly, "the kidnapping of Ana María Cruz has touched a nerve with a lot of people here on this island. I am sure you are well aware that we also have right wing extremists operating in this country."

"I know."

"That's a place to start, Mr. Durcal. I promise you that as we gather information on the situation with Barbara Tonos you will be the first one I will call. I know you are very thorough in your reporting."

"Thank you, Mr. Montana."

"My pleasure," Montana said, and ended the call.

Emilio Durcal took three seconds and dialed Karen's cell phone. She answered after a few rings.

"Karen," she said softly.

"Karen? Emilio. Where are you?"

"At the Venezio in the Marriott."

"Good," Durcal said, "nice relaxing place."

"I needed this."

"Sorry to bother you, but I just got off the phone with William Montana."

"What did he have to say? He sent me two of his thugs." Karen briefly told Durcal about her conversation with Walker and Morales.

Durcal said, "His main concern now is that we don't report the shooting in Cagüey or about the possibility that that is where Rigonaldo and his gang are keeping the First Lady."

"Good, we weren't reporting on that anyhow – yet."

"I told him."

"Okay."

"Good, now let me let you enjoy your dinner."

"Did Calero call?"

"No. And I heard from Montana's own mouth that they have nothing on whoever it is that kidnapped Barbara Tonos."

"I think I'm going back to my Veal Marsala."

"See you tomorrow Karen."

Wednesday, October 31

Chapter 45

PUERTO RICO IS SHATTERED! screamed the headline on the front page of *El Nuevo Sol* featuring a full page close-up of Ana María Cruz sweaty, unkempt and blindfolded; a still picture from last night's broadcast. The San Juan Gazette featured two full-page pictures side by side: Ana María Cruz blindfolded, and Barbara Tonos. The headline read: A WOMAN FOR A WOMAN! A story on page four declared: WHITE HOUSE MUTE ON PUERTO RICO!

All morning, phone calls had flooded Channel Four's switchboard from reporters all over the island who wanted to interview Karen Pérez about her meeting with Rigonaldo Pastrana and the First Lady. Karen declined all interviews, including the ones from the U.S. networks.

Tonio called in sick and didn't report for work.

In Fortaleza, Cruz was in his residence with Almeda. The Governor had been shaken by last night's broadcast and by the photo of his wife, in apparent pain, plastered all over the day's newspapers. He felt encouraged, however, by the information Montana had shared with him yesterday.

Montana had not yet arrived at Fortaleza. He was still at FBI headquarters personally directing Operation First Family. He began by sending a troop of agents grouped in pairs and disguised as food vendors, to be stationed at key positions along the street on Road 89 in Cagüey. The agents had been given photos of suspected members of September Twenty-third, even though the Bureau knew they didn't have pictures of the members of Rigonaldo's inner circle. Most of the pictures distributed were of former members of the Puerto Rican Revolutionary Army who were now believed to be working for September Twenty-third.

Another troop of agents were sent on "road tests" to attempt to establish the possible location of Rigonaldo's hideout based on the road description provided by Tonio, and on the length of time it took to reach a location from the site of the shooting of the federal agents yesterday. All road tests were being conducted in a fleet of Japanese vehicles, which could not be easily identified as property of the FBI.

The FBI was also studying maps of Cagüey and its surroundings, including the Guarite Forest. A surveillance of the area by helicopter – favored by Cruz – had been dismissed by Montana. He worried that if they flew over Rigonaldo's hiding place it would send him a message that the police and the FBI knew where he was.

Operation First Family also included the assignment of two federal agents to the home of Senator Orlando Tonos, disguised as detectives from the Puerto Rican police. Police Superintendent Calero had grudgingly agreed to this

In Fortaleza, Cruz had been conducting most of his business by phone. Secretary of State, Arias, was still representing him in all public activities. There was increased criticism on television shows and in the day's editorials, that in the face of such a crisis the Governor wasn't speaking publicly. Cruz ignored the criticism. He still thought that staying away from the public eye was the right thing to do at the current time. There was no need to challenge Rigonaldo Pastrana in public. The terrorist still held his wife.

Cruz listened intensely to and carefully read all of the information related to the kidnapping of Barbara Tonos. Wickedly, he found himself welcoming the actions of the terrorists that called themselves July 4th. If that led to the release of his wife, it was fine with him. Orlando Tonos had earned his hatred. Cruz, as well as Calero and Montana, had always thought that Tonos could lead the police to Rigonaldo Pastrana, but they had no solid information to prove it. Whoever was behind Barbara Tonos's kidnapping – cleverly calling themselves July 4th – was not in bad standing in Fortaleza. Senator Tonos had consistently introduced legislation in the senate calling for the cessation of celebrating the day of U.S. independence with a national holiday in Puerto Rico. Time after time his efforts had been defeated. Now a group by the name of "July 4th" had his wife, and two federal agents were on their way to Tonos's living room to help him get her back – in return for Ana María Cruz.

"What I want you to do, Sam," Cruz told Almeda in the residence's living room, "is to call Karen Pérez and see if she wants to come here and have a talk with me."

"Are you granting her an interview?" Almeda asked, making notes on a yellow pad.

"No," Cruz said pensively. "Tell her that I watched her report last night and thought that perhaps we should talk."

"So, you want to make this off the record," Almeda stated.

"You could phrase it like that," Cruz said. "Call her and see what she says."

Almeda stood up to make the call. Cruz gave a final suggestion. He said, "Actually, call her boss, Emilio Durcal. Have him send her here."

Almeda walked to his office and called Emilio Durcal's direct line. When he got the news director on the phone, he told him about the governor's interest in meeting with Karen Pérez. Durcal had several questions of his own, but by the end of the call he told Almeda that Karen would be there shortly.

Durcal went to Karen's office. She was seated behind her desk, speaking on the phone.

"I'll call you back," she said to her caller and hung up.

"Well," Durcal said, sitting down facing Karen's desk, "I just got off the phone with Mr. Samuel Almeda."

"Okay, what does he have to say?"

"Cruz wants to meet with you."

"He's finally giving me an interview?"

"Not exactly," Durcal said softly. "He just wants to have a chat with you . . . Off the record."

"Oh, come on Emilio, you just don't show up at the governor's mansion at a time like this to have tea with the governor as if he was Queen Elizabeth."

"Almeda said that the governor watched last night's broadcast with 'deep interest' – his words – and that he feels this is the most 'appropriate' time to meet with you."

"What did you tell him?"

"Oh, I told him you'd be there shortly."

"Emilio!"

"Karen," Durcal said with a smile, "I know you. You will come back here with something to report. Go and see what the man's state of mind is. Almeda said Cruz is interested to hear from you about the condition of his wife. Tell him about that and see what else you can squeeze out of him."

"If anything, he'll squeeze me."

"Can you handle it?"

"Of course."

"I know you can. That's why I told him you'd be there."

"When are they expecting me?"

Durcal got up. "Now," he said, and left Karen's office.

Karen was left there with words hanging in her mouth. But her next move had been set already. A meeting with Governor Elison Cruz: off the record. She knew that Cruz would want to know more than just how his wife was doing: like, how the hell she – Karen – got to find his wife when the whole world of law enforcement hadn't.

Oh shit! Karen rummaged in her purse and took out a beauty mirror, red lipstick and her powder pad. She touched up her makeup and then stared at herself in the tiny mirror.

"Ms. Karen Pérez," she said softly, "you are off to see the wizard."

In a matter of minutes she was driving to Old San Juan in her Saab. A funny thought came to her. What if they try to arrest me, right there in Fortaleza, as an accessory to the kidnapping of the First Lady? A phony arrest just to pressure me to say whatever I may know. Nonsense, she told herself quickly. I'm a fucking journalist. I do my job and I do it damn well. I really don't know how to find Ana María Cruz. I really don't know.

Chapter 46

Barbara Tonos was blindfolded, her hands and legs handcuffed to a bed, in a house at the foot of *El Yunque*. The room was large and bright with sunlight streaming through two huge windows. Outside, the forest was still and quiet. Only the singing of birds broke the silence.

Brenton entered the room carrying a tray of food.

"Mrs. Tonos," he said, placing the tray on a night table by the bed, "you are going to eat now. I hope you eat Chinese food."

He uncuffed Barbara's wrists and one leg and helped her straighten up on the bed. He placed the tray on her lap.

"I want to talk to my husband," she said softly.

"Eat first. We'll arrange something later."

When she finished her food, Brenton took the tray away and put the handcuffs back on. He went to his living room and lit an unfiltered Camel and scanned the day's newspapers for the third time that morning. Earlier, he had spoken on the phone with Montana and got instructions. When he finished his cigarette, he grabbed a cordless phone and dialed Senator Tonos's home number. Tonos answered.

"Tonos," the senator said with anxiety in his voice.

"Good morning, Senator," Brenton said in a sinister voice. "We speak again."

"I want to talk to Barbara," Tonos said quickly, recognizing the man's voice.

"Hold on."

Brenton walked quickly to Barbara's room and placed the receiver to her mouth.

"Say something to your husband," Brenton ordered. "He's on the phone."

"Orlando?" Barbara said.

"Barbara!" Tonos said quickly, knowing she wouldn't be allowed to talk much. "How are you?"

"I'm handcuffed to a bed."

"How are they treating you?"

"I want to go home!"

"How many are they?"

"Right now, I think there is just one of them here . . ."

Brenton pulled the phone from her. "Enough," he said and went back to the living room. "Okay," he told Tonos. "Now that you know that she's alive, I hope you are ready to work with us."

"What you are asking is out of my reach," Tonos said nervously. "I have no influence over Rigonaldo Pastrana, nor do I know where he is. You can't . . ."

"Listen, Tonos," Brenton cut him off, "cut the bullshit and listen to what I have to say. You cannot fool us. You have until noon this Friday to gain the release of Ana María Cruz. If you fail to do that, you can bid farewell to your dear wife. Do not underestimate us. We will harm her and you will never see her again."

"You have to give me more time than that!"

"No time, buddy. If you care about your wife, do what I've told you. Good bye, asshole."

Brenton cut the call.

Tonos replaced the receiver in its cradle as Eugenia and Tino waited for him to tell them what was happening. They were all in the living room waiting for the police to arrive. Tonos had turned down an offer to get the FBI involved.

"What did they say?" Eugenia asked, repressing tears. "Is Mom all right?"

"Your mother is fine," Tonos said simply.

"But dad, tell me what they said. I want to know. You've got to tell me."

"He just repeated the same thing," Tonos said, his thoughts racing. "They want to trade Barbara for Ana María Cruz."

"What do we have to do with that woman?" Eugenia asked angrily. "For Christ's sake."

"Gina, let me handle this. You have to trust me."

Eugenia began crying.

Tonos nodded to Tino, signaling him to follow him out to the patio. Once there, Tonos said, "Okay, call Rigonaldo again. Tell him that he has until noon Friday to release Ana María Cruz. And tell him to do it, damn it! And fill him in on what we spoke about earlier. Understood?"

"Yes," Tino said firmly.

"Okay. Now you walk out that door, make sure no one is following you and do not say a word to any of those reporters that are camping outside."

A horde of reporters were outside waiting for the senator to make a statement.

"I know what to do," Tino said.

"Tell Rigonaldo to come to his senses!" Tonos said angrily.

"I'll try," Tino said.

"Make sure he knows that I am fucking serious. Those bastards have my wife. Now go, go!"

Tino went through the front door, immediately feeling the click of cameras aimed at him. The reporters approached him with ferocity while he walked as fast as he could.

"What's going on in there?" a female reporter asked him, almost breaking his lip when she extended her microphone to his face. "What's Tonos doing?"

"I'm sorry, I have no comment," Tino said as he started jogging faster.

"Are you with the family?" a male reporter asked him.

"I work for the senator," Tino yelled, now running.

"Can he trade Barbara for the First Lady?" someone shouted.

Tino was gone. He reached Domenech Avenue and boarded a passing public bus. In a few minutes the bus turned onto Ponce de León Avenue where buses ran in a reserved lane going against traffic.

He waited a few minutes, rang the bell and got off. He kept looking behind his shoulder. He was sure no one was following him but got on another bus anyway, that took him farther. When he got off, he immediately went to the closest public phone. He dialed Rigonaldo's number.

"Hello," Luna said.

"It's Tino. Let me talk to Rigonaldo again."

"What is happening?"

"Luna, let me talk to Rigonaldo."

"Hold on."

In a about a minute Rigonaldo came to the phone.

"Yes, Tino, what do you want?"

"Listen, Tonos wants you to let her go. No later than noon, Friday."

Rigonaldo laughed.

"What?" Tino asked.

"That happens to be our deadline."

"What do you mean?"

"That's what I told Montana from the FBI, noon Friday, or the bitch is dead. And I don't know if you've noticed, but no one has reported on that yet."

"Rigonaldo," Tino said with frustration, "Tonos also thinks that this whole thing is suspicious but in the end it doesn't matter. They – whoever they are – have his wife and you have the First Lady. You let her go and Tonos gets his wife back."

"They won't do anything to his wife."

"Who's to know? Listen, Tonos thinks that if this wasn't orchestrated by the FBI or the Puerto Rican police, it was done by someone who is not necessarily their enemy."

Rigonaldo said, "I don't think the Puerto Rican police are capable of pulling this off. They are stupid. And if the FBI is behind this, the Puerto Rican police may not even know about it. That's how the feds operate. Tonos should know that."

"You may be right, but all I'm doing is what Tonos has asked me to do. He thinks this whole thing has gotten dangerous and out of hand."

"There is no danger."

"Rigonaldo, what do you want me to tell Tonos?"

"Tell him I never liked his wife, anyway. Too *bourgeois* for my taste."

Rigonaldo hung up.

"Shit!" Tino yelled. "Deep, deep shit!"

Chapter 47

Rigonaldo reached into a wooden box and pulled out a handgun.

"Luna," he ordered, "bring that bitch over here."

Shortly, Luna came back with Ana María. Rigonaldo was holding the phone. He placed the receiver to her mouth.

"Talk," he ordered.

Ana María knew who was on the other end. "Elison?"

"Honey," Cruz said, "I'm here. We are getting close to . . ."

Rigonaldo pulled the phone away from her and fired three shots at the front wall of the house.

Ana María screamed as Luna rushed her back to her room.

Cruz was frantically calling her name.

Rigonaldo talked into the phone. "Cruz?" The terrorist was calm.

"Did you hurt her?" Cruz yelled. "Did you hurt her?"

Rigonaldo said nothing.

"What the hell are you doing over there?" Cruz said, his voice trembling.

"Let me talk to the director," Rigonaldo said.

"Who?"

"The man from the FBI, Cruz."

Cruz glanced at Montana who had been listening to the exchange along with Almeda. "He wants to talk to you," Cruz told him. "I heard shots," Cruz said as Montana grabbed the receiver. Almeda just sat there saying nothing.

"This is William Montana."

"Hello, Mr. FBI," Rigonaldo said sarcastically. "I just want to let you know that you don't fool me."

"Is Mrs. Cruz all right?" Montana asked.

"She is fine," Rigonaldo said, annoyed. "You'll have to take my word for it."

"Mr. Pastrana," Montana said firmly, "we are taking your demand very seriously. No one is trying to fool you."

"I don't know what you expect from Senator Tonos's predicament," Rigonaldo said calmly, "but you should know that I won't fall into that trap."

"We are aware of the situation with Tonos, but you should know that he has refused our assistance."

"I see."

"I stress to you that we are taking you very seriously. This Friday at noon the governor will make an announcement that we know will be to your satisfaction."

"An announcement," Rigonaldo said softly. "I am thrilled."

"So, there is no need to lose calm, Mr. Pastrana. You will get what you want."

"You impress me greatly, Mr. FBI. I'll be looking forward to this Friday."

Rigonaldo hung up.

"What did he say to you?" Cruz asked nervously.

Montana glanced at Almeda, then at Cruz and said, "Could we speak in private, Mr. Governor?"

Cruz exchanged looks with Almeda. Almeda shrugged his shoulders.

"Sam," Cruz told him, "Could you . . . ?"

"Sure," Almeda said and left the room.

Once alone, Montana spoke.

"Pastrana thinks that we are behind the situation with Barbara Tonos."

"What do we know about that?"

"I'm sending López and Allende to Tonos's house," Montana said. "They've been trailing him. I want Tonos to make a public announcement requesting the release of your wife."

"He won't do it," Cruz said quickly.

"I think he will have no choice. He either gets in contact with Pastrana himself or he speaks to him publicly. You said you heard shots?"

"Yes, he put Ana María on the phone, then I heard shots and she was gone. But I heard her screaming in the background . . . I . . . don't think he . . . he shot at her."

"He's playing with us. That's his way of pressuring us."

Cruz collapsed onto the sofa. "Well, I am feeling the pressure."

Montana was about to speak when Damaris, Cruz's secretary, came in.

"Mr. Governor," she said, "Karen Pérez is here to see you."

Montana and Cruz exchanged glances. "I'll be in your office making phone calls," Montana told Cruz. "Do you want them out?" Montana said, referring to Special Agents Prat and García who had been operating the phone tracing equipment.

"Yes," Cruz said, "I want to talk to Pérez alone."

Montana left, along with both agents. When he walked out of the residence, Montana passed Karen. "Good morning, Ms. Pérez," he told her.

Karen looked up from her seat and returned the greeting. She watched him disappear down a hallway while the other two FBI clones stayed behind near the stairs just staring at her. Did their stares show curiosity? Contempt? She couldn't tell. And she probably didn't want to know.

Chapter 48

"Good morning, Ms. Pérez," Cruz said softly, extending his hand to her.

"Good morning, Mr. Governor," Karen said, shaking his hand.

"Please sit," Cruz said.

They sat facing each other; Cruz on a small couch, Karen at the end of a large sofa. And for a long minute neither of them said a word.

"I don't know where to begin," Cruz said softly, breaking the silence.

Karen smiled politely.

"A few minutes ago," Cruz said pausing, "I had to endure a very frightening experience . . ."

Karen waited for him to say more. When he didn't speak, she asked, "What happened?"

Cruz stared at her.

Karen cleared her throat.

Finally, Cruz said in a soft-spoken voice, "You see . . . that man . . . Pastrana . . . Rigonaldo Pastrana. He calls here. He puts Ana María on the phone for a few seconds and then . . . then he fires three shots. I heard those gunshots. They are still ringing in my ears. And after that, I had to assume that Ana María was fine because I heard her screaming in the background. But her screams were not those of someone who had been wounded by gunshots . . . Her screams were of . . . terror . . . panic . . . fear . . . desperation . . . Should I go on?"

Karen was at a loss for words.

"That devil has my wife . . . and he will harm her. I know he will. That's why we need to find him. Find him before he kills her."

"How close are you to finding him?" Karen asked. "How much do you know about his whereabouts?"

"Actually," Cruz said, looking Karen straight in the eye, "I was going to pose that question to you."

Karen shifted uncomfortably. She said, "I think you know about Cagüey, Mr. Governor."

"Oh, yes," Cruz said with an edge, "we know about Cagüey. And we also know that Pastrana may be hiding anywhere around there. That is a big area, Ms. Pérez. It includes the *Guarite* Forest, *el Cerro La Santa, la Sierra de Cayey*, the town of *Guayama* to the south, *San Lorenzo* to the north . . . Do you understand what I'm trying to say?"

"I think I do."

"Maybe you do not, Ms. Pérez," Cruz said flatly.

Karen swallowed.

"Would you like some coffee?" Cruz asked unexpectedly.

At first Karen didn't understand the simple question. Then she realized he had just offered her coffee.

"Yes," she said, "thank you."

Cruz called Damaris through the phone intercom and a few minutes later, the secretary came in carrying a tray with coffee, milk and sugar cubes. Cruz thanked her and she immediately left the room.

Karen helped herself. Cruz didn't take anything.

"How did you get to find my wife so easily, Ms. Pérez?" Cruz asked stone-faced.

Karen had expected this. The question ran through her head dozens of times as she was driving through the gates of Fortaleza a few minutes before.

"I don't think that is necessarily correct," she said.

"How is that?"

"I am the journalist they took there. And if you saw my report, which I know you did, you know how I got there. It's not like I just took a map and followed the lines, Mr. Governor."

"Yes, of course," Cruz said, now unable to hide his cynicism. "You were blindfolded, driven in a van . . ."

"A woman called me."

"I don't believe you, Ms. Pérez," Cruz said sharply and with penetrating eyes. "I think you know more than you are letting on."

Karen put her cup down. The Governor of Puerto Rico was calling her a liar straight to her face.

"How is it that you have met with that criminal twice? In his hideouts?" Cruz asked with contempt.

Karen knew the man was in pain. She was going to remain civil with him.

"Mr. Governor, I am a journalist," she said calmly. "All journalists have ties to the community, sources, confidants . . ."

"But if a journalist can solve a serious crime," Cruz said interrupting, "like a kidnapping, where a woman's life is in danger, my wife's, wouldn't you feel compelled to share with us what you know?"

"I do not know how to get to your wife," Karen said sharply.

"It must be difficult being a journalist," Cruz said. "Living with your conscience."

"Governors also make difficult decisions," Karen shot back in a soft voice. "Who gets what, when and how. Sometimes life and death decisions. Don't they?"

"There is no comparison here."

Karen was silent for a moment, thinking of what to say next. But she knew by the tension in the air and by the tone of the governor's voice that this man probably despised her.

She said, "Mr. Governor . . . I know how you must feel, even though you may think I do not. I am a journalist and all throughout my career I've always done my job and have done it well . . ."

"Who is your contact?" Cruz asked bluntly.

Karen got up. "I think I should leave now."

"Who are your contacts? Damn it!" Cruz yelled, slamming his fist against his bare hand.

"I will leave now, Mr. Governor," Karen said, visibly shaken. This is it, she thought. She was almost sure that right at this second the police or the FBI would barge into the room and arrest her.

Instead, Aida Colón, Ana María's angry sister, came rushing into the room trailed by Damaris.

"Mrs. Colón," Damaris was pleading, "you cannot interrupt. The governor is in a meeting."

Aida ignored her and immediately came close to Cruz and Karen.

"How appropriate to find the two of you together," Aida said sarcastically.

Cruz said nothing. Karen took a step back.

"Mr. Governor," Damaris said apologetically, "I am really sorry, but Mrs. Colón wouldn't listen to me."

"It's all right, Damaris," Cruz said. "Ms. Pérez and I were almost finished."

Damaris excused herself and left the room.

"I am sure you saw Ana María on TV last night," Aida said, sharply addressing Cruz. "And I know you saw today's papers."

"Aida," Cruz said, "how could I have missed that?"

"What are you going to do?"

"We are doing all we can," Cruz said calmly.

"You have to cancel the plebiscite," Aida demanded.

"We have other options," Cruz said. "I'm just not going to discuss them now." Cruz glanced at Karen.

"You are an insane bastard, Cruz," Aida told him. "If anything happens to my sister it will be your doing. You can't lose, can you?"

"Aida, this is not a matter of winning or . . ."

"Statehood is more important to you, isn't it?" Aida cut him off.

"That's not fair to say."

Aida looked at Karen and said, "And you, how did you get to see my sister?"

Karen was speechless.

"I already asked that question, Aida," Cruz said. "You won't get anything from her."

"You two are a poor excuse for human beings," Aida said angrily.

"I have to go," Karen said. "Excuse me."

Karen fled the room.

Aida looked at her as she walked out, then she addressed Cruz again.

"You aren't going to find Rigonaldo before he hurts Ana María," she declared.

"We are getting close to him and he doesn't know it."

"You are playing with fire, Cruz."

"I love Ana María."

"You love the *yanquis* more than her!"

"Bullshit!"

"It's true. Your whole life revolves around getting this country swallowed by the Americans."

"If you came to discuss my politics, you chose the worst time, Aida."

"I came to tell you that the family thinks you should give up on this plebiscite."

"Our family is divided."

"If anything happens to my sister, Cruz, I will use all of my power to see that your political life is dead."

"I think that's enough, Aida."

"Go to hell, Cruz, but don't take my sister with you!"

With that, Aida Colón turned around and left Cruz alone in his living room.

Cruz was shaken, even trembling. His shoulders contorted with pain. He went to the phone and buzzed Damaris through the intercom.

"Yes, Mr. Governor," Damaris said, worried.

Cruz said, "Get my son on the phone."

"Yes, Mr. Governor."

After this angry clash with his sister-in-law, Cruz pondered for one short moment as to whether – in the end – this whole thing was just a family affair.

Chapter 49

In Cruz's office, Montana was giving his final instructions to the agents who were to go to Senator Tonos's home.

"As I said," Montana was saying, "you will tell the senator that the Police Superintendent himself has sent you. And you will apologize for the time that it took you to get there. Explain to him that the situation with Ana María Cruz has occupied most of the resources of the police. Make him feel safe with your presence, if that is possible. And give him plenty of breathing space. Your main goal is to convince him to issue a public statement demanding the release of the First Lady. If we get lucky, you might even push him to go into one of his rat holes and call the terrorist himself."

"What do we know about Barbara Tonos's kidnappers?" Special Agent Melvin López asked.

"Not much at this moment," Montana said. "This is apparently a new group. But that is not our priority right now. Our priority is Ana María Cruz. I am convinced that when Pastrana releases the First Lady, Barbara Tonos will also be released unharmed. Make that clear to the senator. Any questions?"

"No," López said. He consulted with his partner, Esteban Allende, then said, "I think we are clear."

"Good," Montana said. "Call me later tonight."

Montana hung up and couldn't repress a mischievous smile at the thought of the whole scenario. He was sending the two agents who had trailed Tonos for the last days, to Tonos's own home. This, after the senator with suspected ties to the terrorists had requested police intervention to help him find his wife, who Montana himself was responsible for kidnapping. This sounded like a riddle, he thought, and had the potential to get messy. But the risk was necessary. He smiled to himself and dialed Brenton's number in *El Yunque*.

"Hello."

"Brent, it's Bill."

"What's up?" Brenton said casually.

"What did he say?"

"Oh, he tried to give me that bullshit that what we are asking is out of his reach. I told him he has until noon, Friday, to get the First Lady released."

"What did he say to that?"

"The usual, need more time. Told him no way, José. I called him an asshole and hung up."

Montana said, "I think we need to scare him a little."

"I agree. I think we've been far too nice."

"Okay. Think of something, but wait 'til later tonight to call him back. I just sent López and Allende there, posing as Puerto Rico police. He refused help from us. He despises the FBI, you know."

"No shit!" Brenton said with a laugh.

"I can't laugh right now, Brent."

"Relax, man. Stress is no good for you. It's worse than salt, sugar and cigarettes."

"I know. I'll call you later tonight."

Montana lit up a cigarette and felt the pressure of his own operation. This had to work until they could make a breakthrough somewhere else. And his instincts told him that one would soon come his way.

Chapter 50

Samuel Almeda was still in his office after having been politely thrown out of the governor's private residence by William Montana. He didn't know whether to feel mad or relieved that he was being left out of key conversations between the governor and the FBI. And he was also somewhat concerned about what he possibly could have said or done to raise the suspicions of the FBI. Because that's what he sensed. He knew William Montana didn't trust him.

And then there was the issue of guilt. Yes, in a way he felt some guilt by having fed so much information to that band of freaks, who had kidnapped the wife of his boss. But, oh, money, money, money. He had such a huge money problem that he couldn't resist the offer when it came. It was too late now. What was done was done. There was no going back now. But he was now determined to distance himself as far as he could from those "terrorists with buckets full of money."

He was so lost in thought, that when his phone rang he literally jumped at the sound of it. Shit! He answered. It was his secretary.

"Mr. Almeda," she said, "I have a call for you on line two."

"Who is it?"

"Well, I don't know. It is a man who refuses to give his name. He says it's personal."

"Reporter," Almeda said. "Take a message."

"All right, sir."

So, Almeda was thinking, what if I quit this job in Fortaleza and move to Miami to work for . . . His phone rang again. The secretary.

"What now?" Almeda said rudely.

"Sir," the secretary said, "the man says his name is Oso and that there's been a death in your family."

Almeda froze. He gasped and almost dropped the phone at the sound of that name. Jesus Christ!

"Put him on," he said quickly.

Line two blinked and the phone rang again. Almeda pushed the line.

"Almeda," he said nervously.

"Hi Sam, Oso here."

"How dare you call me here!" Almeda barked.

"You don't answer your home phone any more nowadays," Oso said calmly. "And don't tell me you've been out. We know when you are home."

"Listen," Almeda said angrily, "don't you ever call me here again! Do you understand?"

"My, my, my. I feel hostility from your end."

"Go to hell."

"We need to talk to you, my friend," Oso said matter-of-factly.

"Call me at home!" Almeda yelled and slammed down the receiver.

He placed his hands on his forehead. He was sweating. He took a handkerchief and wiped his face. He then realized that his secretary was standing across from his desk looking at him.

"Is everything all right, sir?" she asked.

"Yes . . . yes . . . everything is fine," he said, trying to appear calm.

"Did something happen?"

"No . . . nothing," he said. "It was a reporter. Those bastards are nothing but trouble."

"Oh, sir, I'm sorry. He said he was someone from your family and . . ."

"That's fine, Lourdes," he interrupted. "It's not your fault. It's my fault. I should have known."

"I'm really sorry, sir, I . . ."

"I said it's fine," Almeda said, annoyed. "Now leave me alone . . . please."

The secretary left.

Almeda took a deep breath. He knew he had been avoiding those people. But he never would have thought that they'd have the audacity to call him at Fortaleza. Why the fuck did I get into this? he thought. He left his office in a hurry.

Chapter 51

After the introductions were done, Senator Tonos, his daughter Eugenia and his assistant, Tino, were sitting face to face with Detective Edwin Rosario, a.k.a. Special Agent Melvin López and with Detective Aníbal González, a.k.a. Special Agent Esteban Allende.

The agents played their parts well, even bringing along phony ID's. After the phone tracing equipment was in place, Eugenia brought out coffee and sodas for the group.

After a half hour with the "detectives" in his home, Senator Tonos felt that perhaps calling them in wasn't a good idea after all. And it was ironic that they needed to install phone-tracing equipment in his home because he always thought that all his phones were tapped, anyway.

"Had you received any threats during the days prior to your wife's kidnapping, Senator?" Agent López asked.

"I always receive threats," Tonos said matter-of-factly.

"But did you get anything specific that could have predicted that your family was a target?"

"No."

"You've never heard of this so called group, 'July 4th-The Warriors, Keepers of Democracy'?"

"Very clever," Tonos said.

"Had you ever heard of them?" López asked again.

"No."

"How many contacts have they had with you so far?"

"They've called twice."

"What have they said?"

Tonos glanced at Tino and Eugenia. He said, "They think I can gain the release of the First Lady."

"They want you to obtain the release of Ana María Cruz," López pointed out.

"What do we have to do with that woman? For Christ's sake!" Eugenia blurted.

"Gina!" Tonos scolded.

"And," López continued, "if you gain the release of the First Lady, they will release your wife, isn't that so?"

"That's what they claim."

"They must have a reason to think that you have the power to do what they want," López said. "Otherwise, why target you?"

Agent Melvin López knew the answers to these questions. But he had been instructed to ask them anyway. He was amused by Tonos's response.

"Listen," Tonos said seriously, "I have been targeted by these people because of my ideas. I am the only independent voice in the entire Puerto Rican Senate. I do not respond to any political party. I respond to my conscience and to the people who have elected me time after time. And I have a right to my ideas. I am not going to apologize for what I do or say from my Senate seat . . ."

"Oh," López said, "don't misinterpret my question, Senator. I am not accusing you of any wrong doing. We live in a democratic country and you are certainly entitled to your point of view. We are here because we want to help you and we are just trying to better understand the motives of the individuals who took your wife."

"I'll do everything I can to find a solution to this mess. It's my wife we are talking about," Tonos said.

"And the First Lady," López pointed out.

"Of course."

"So," López said, "can you meet the demand of your wife's kidnappers?"

"You mean, can I get Rigonaldo Pastrana to release the First Lady by noon Friday?"

"Yes, Mr. Senator, that's my question."

Tonos pondered this.

Eugenia said, "That's impossible. My dad doesn't have any communication or influence with Rigonaldo Pastrana."

López was completely certain that neither Tonos's daughter nor his wife knew about some well-hidden skeletons that the senator had in his closet.

"What's your answer, Senator?" López pressed on.

"I don't know," Tonos said finally.

"Have you considered going public with this?" López asked.

"What do you mean?"

"It's not too complicated," López explained. "You call a press conference – or really, with all those noisy reporters camping outside your home, you wouldn't even need to call a press conference. You could just simply walk into your front yard and make a public plea to Mr. Pastrana to release Ana María Cruz."

"I hadn't thought about that."

"You hadn't?" López asked incredulously.

"I have just been too anxious over my own problem with Barbara."

"Your wife's problem is completely connected to the situation with Ana María Cruz. Even one of the headlines in the press said it very clearly, "*a woman for a woman*." That's the way things stand for you, Senator."

Tonos fell silent.

López glanced at his partner and allowed time to go by without saying a word.

After a full two minutes had passed, López said, "Well, what do you say, Senator?"

Tonos took a second to respond. He said, "I'll think about it. I'll consider it."

"We don't seem to have much time," López said.

"I'll think about it," Tonos repeated.

"Good," López said softly.

Tonos withdrew into deep thought. What can I possibly tell Rigonaldo on TV? he asked himself. And, will he listen to me? Based on what Tino had reported, Rigonaldo was not going to bend on this one, his biggest political hit. Tonos had not spoken personally to the fugitive in some time, but he knew that Rigonaldo was as stubborn as a mule, and that he didn't follow anyone's advice. He was a political time bomb that only detonated at his own will.

As they all sat quietly waiting for another round of conversation, the phone rang. Tonos exchanged glances with the agents and quickly answered it.

"Hello?"

"Senator Tonos?" a female voice said.

"Yes?"

"Karen Pérez." She was calling from her cell phone as she drove in her car from her meeting with Cruz in Fortaleza on her way back to the station.

"Karen," Tonos said, "good to hear from you."

"How are you making out?"

"Tense. Very tense. The kidnappers called again. They have Barbara handcuffed to a bed. And they gave me until noon, Friday, to get Ana María Cruz released."

"What are you going to do?"

"I don't know." He paused. "Calero finally sent two detectives, though."

"What do they say? Any leads?"

"They don't seem to have a clue."

"We've been asking around," Karen told him. "Nobody has ever heard of that group July 4th."

"I really don't care who they are anymore. I just want to communicate that what they are asking for is probably out of my reach."

"That's why I was calling. Do you want to go on tape and address them?"

"Not yet. I have some heavy thinking to do. The police have asked me to do something."

"What is that?"

"I don't want to talk about it now. But I promise you that as soon as I've made up my mind I will call you."

"Sounds fair."

"Bye now," Tonos said and hung up.

He turned toward the agents and took a second to light a cigarette. "That was Karen Pérez," he told López.

"Good," López said calmly. "I think she would be an ideal person to talk to on a one-on-one if you don't want to face a full press conference. She just spoke to Pastrana yesterday. And you know that Pastrana follows what Pérez does."

"How could I know?" Tonos said defensively.

"Listen, Senator," López said firmly, "I think at this time the ball is in your court. You have to talk to the press and address Rigonaldo directly. Unless, of course, you have his phone number and can just hit dial."

"I don't have his fucking phone number!" Tonos said angrily.

"It was an innocent joke, Mr. Tonos." López said seriously.

Tonos just stared at him, then at Tino.

"Let us know what you want to do, Mr. Senator," López told him.

Later in the day, López went to the patio and spoke to Montana on his cell phone. Montana was not pleased that Tonos was not responding quickly enough. The Assistant Director wanted a public statement from Tonos to Pastrana. And he wanted it now. The Senator would have to swallow his ego and do what was expected of him. That was the bottom line.

Chapter 52

The phone call came a little after 7 p.m. Tino had left. Eugenia was in her bedroom and Senator Tonos was with the "detectives" in the living room. Allende was almost falling asleep with a pair of headphones on that were connected to the phone intercept equipment. The ringing of the phone woke him up.

"Hello," Tonos said anxiously.

"Senator?" Brenton said in a deep voice. "This is your worst nightmare calling!"

"Who is this?"

"I have a name, you know," Brenton said. "But my friends call me 'George Washington' sometimes, you know, as in the first U.S. president."

"How can I help you?"

"Help?" Brenton said quickly and extending the receiver toward Burke, his accomplice, who was roughly twisting Barbara's arm behind her back. "I think your wife is the one who needs help here!"

Barbara screamed in pain as Burke twisted her arm and held a kitchen knife against her throat. "Jesus Christ! You are hurting me! You are hurting me!" she cried.

"That's the idea, ma'am," Burke said roughly.

"What are you doing over there?" Tonos asked frantically. "What the hell are you doing?"

"You know," Brenton said, taking the receiver back to his mouth, "I think my friend over here has lost his mind."

Barbara screamed louder.

"Barbara," Brenton said, "your husband is on the phone. Do you have something to say to him?"

Barbara yelled, "Orlando! Help me! Help me! These people are crazy!"

"Leave her alone, you son of a bitch!" Tonos screamed into the phone.

"It's all up to you, Senator," Brenton said.

Then, gunfire. Brenton fired four shots out a window and into the forest outside. Barbara screamed as Burke led her back to her room.

"What the fuck are you doing?" Tonos yelled.

"We are showing your wife a little Puerto Rican hospitality," Brenton said calmly. "That's all."

"You said I have until Friday!" Tonos said, sweat dripping down his face.

"Oh, it's not Friday already?" Brenton said, laughing. "My calendar must be messed up."

"Jesus Christ!" Tonos said. "We just spoke today." He could no longer hear Barbara in the background.

"Don't worry, Senator," Brenton went on. "I'll check my calendar again. Though my friend here is dangerously unpredictable."

"Let me talk to my wife. I want to make sure she is not hurt."

"No Senator," Brenton said softly. "She's fine. Just a little shaken, not stirred. As James Bond would say? Or is it the other way around?"

"Let me talk to my wife!" Tonos demanded.

"I said no, Senator," Brenton said firmly. "You'll talk to her on Friday when we have Ana María Cruz free and unharmed. I think it's time you call your buddy Rigonaldo and beg him to listen to you, or else you can say bye bye to your dear wife."

"Listen to me, I can't . . ."

"Bye, Senator," Brenton said and hung up.

"Don't hang up!" Tonos yelled. "Hello! Hello! Hello!"

"He's gone!" Allende said.

"Did you get anything?" Tonos asked him nervously.

"No," Allende said. "It seems they are blocking and rerouting the calls."

Tonos didn't believe him. They are Calero's people, he thought. Calero hates me. He wouldn't really help me.

"What in hell are those people doing?" Tonos asked out loud.

Allende said, "They are obviously making it clear to you that they are serious."

"I agree," López said. He had also listened to the call.

"I know they are serious, for Christ's sake!" Tonos barked.

López said, "I think it's time for you to call Karen Pérez, Mr. Senator."

Tonos stared at him and said nothing. He knew that that was what he needed to do, but it was extremely hard to do it. Was it a matter of his ego? Was it something like capitulation? Defeat?

Eugenia came into the room. "Is everything all right, Dad?"

Tonos didn't answer.

She looked at López and Allende. Both men said nothing.

"Dad?" she asked, worried.

Tonos moved closer to López. He said, "I'll call Pérez tomorrow." He paused. "First thing in the morning."

"Why not now, Mr. Senator?" López said.

"I said tomorrow, that's my answer," Tonos said flatly.

Eugenia looked on, not knowing what was happening.

Tonos dismissed his daughter, assuring her that everything was fine. He didn't tell her that the kidnappers had called again. His mind was a hundred miles away; in Rigonaldo Pastrana's territory. Tonos wanted to call Tino to make him reach Rigonaldo again, this time with a definite, razor-sharp message. But getting in contact with Tino would have to wait until tomorrow too. It was too risky to try him tonight.

Tomorrow.

Things needed to happen tomorrow.

Chapter 53

Samuel Almeda drove his brand new BMW into the driveway of his expensive home in Ocean Park, the rich neighborhood right next to the Condado tourist and hotel sector. It was another ocean-front neighborhood, with trees so thick and old lining the sidewalks that the glow from the street lights shone down onto the streets below with difficulty.

He got out of his car carrying a briefcase and a glossy folder with documents. He walked a few feet in near darkness until the motion sensor in his home turned on a small light pole near the front door. He unlocked his door, pushed it open and walked inside, closing the door behind him. His living room was cool from the air conditioner that had been on the whole day. He dropped the briefcase and folder on a soft leather couch and immediately walked over to his answering machine. A blinking light indicated that there were three stored messages. He pressed the play button on the machine and waited a few seconds for the tape to rewind. Then, there was a beep and no message. A second beep, and silence, no message. A third beep, and more silence, no message left.

He quickly figured that someone from that band of terrorist freaks was trying to reach him. Fuck them, he whispered. He took his shoes off. His feet felt good on the thick, white carpet. The suit jacket landed on a sofa and he loosened his red tie. In a mirror on the wall he looked at himself with his white, cotton shirt and the loosened tie. He couldn't look more yuppie if he tried.

He grabbed a beer from the refrigerator in the kitchen and walked back to the living room. He sat on a white leather sofa and used a remote control to turn on his huge widescreen TV at the lowest possible volume so that he wouldn't be disturbed, but would not be in total silence either.

Samuel Almeda, scheduling secretary to the governor of Puerto Rico, then bent forward a little, reached under the sofa, and pulled out a small mirror with a small pile of high quality cocaine, a razor to cut it with and a small straw to snort it. He wasn't planning to free base tonight. At least not yet.

He placed the mirror with the cocaine on an oak center table, used the razor to spread the drug into two thin but healthy lines and, with the tiny straw, he snorted both lines of the drug up his nose.

He closed his eyes and sighed in pleasure. He laid his head back for a while as the out-of-body sensation enveloped him. Then, he repeated the ritual two more times. Each time it felt as if his soul, if he had one, left his body to fly up to the ceiling.

But the ringing of his phone brought him right back to earth.

Shit!

He let the phone ring without answering it. After four rings his machine picked up: "Hi, this is Sam. I can't come to the phone right now. But if you leave your name and number, I'll get back to you as soon as I can." Beep.

There was a short silence. Then that dreadful voice again.

"Hello! Almeda! This is Oso. Pick up the phone." Silence. "Almeda! I know you are home. Pick up the phone!"

Oso had now interrupted Almeda's cocaine high. A capital offense by any addict's standards. Almeda bent forward and brusquely grabbed the receiver.

"What the fuck do you want?" Almeda said angrily and pressing a button on the machine to end the recording mode.

"Listen," Oso shot back, "we need to talk to you!"

"I said what the fuck do you want?" Almeda barked.

"We want to know what this bullshit with Tonos's wife is," Oso said firmly.

"I don't know anything about that!"

"You must have heard something."

"I haven't heard shit. I don't know shit. Now," Almeda was slurring his words, "leave me alone. Good bye . . ."

"Listen, motherfucker," Oso yelled, "don't you fucking hang up on me. You can't cut us off like that. You cost us a lot of money!"

"I don't want your fucking money anymore. You can have it back as far as I'm concerned," Almeda said.

"I might just come over there and take it back, you know," Oso said calmly.

"I don't give a shit! I just want you people to leave me alone. You are nothing but trouble. I don't think that's too hard to understand."

"Listen, my friend," Oso said without missing a beat, "I'm coming right over to pick up our cash. I'm so close to you I can smell your ass."

"Well, do it fast!" Almeda snapped, ignoring the remark. "I don't want any of you for more than a minute in my house."

"Wait for me," Oso said and hung up.

Almeda slammed the receiver in its cradle, got up and walked to the kitchen to pick up a large shopping bag from a cabinet. He then walked through a dark hallway and went straight to his master bedroom using a key to unlock the door. He switched the light on and walked hurriedly to a large walk-in closet. He opened the door, bent down on his knees and removed a large quilt spread out in a corner on the floor. There was money underneath. Lots of it.

He quickly grabbed several stacks of hundred-dollar bills bound together with rubber bands and filled up the shopping bag with them. When he was done, there was still more money on the floor than what he had put inside the bag. He replaced the quilt over the money that was left, closed the door to the closet and walked out of his master bedroom forgetting to lock the door behind him. He was too stoned on cocaine to know what he was doing. But he didn't forget to grab his .38. The one he had bought from a desperate crack addict at one of the projects. He shoved the gun into the waist of his pants and pulled out his shirt to conceal it.

He came back to the living room to wait for Oso, the freak. He sat on the sofa and snorted as much cocaine as he could. He was on a fast track right at this moment. He hoped that, once the money traded hands, those criminals with a penchant for prime time TV political statement-making would finally leave him alone. He'd really rather deal with drug dealers. They preferred privacy and anonymity. These thugs with political ideas were nothing but trouble.

The doorbell rang. Once. Twice. Almeda got up and looked out the window. It was him, Oso. The freak must have called him from a few blocks away. Before Almeda opened the door, he made sure that his gun was easy to reach.

On the third ring, Almeda opened the door. Oso stood on the porch. Almeda turned around and let him in. Oso closed the door behind him with his gloved hands.

"Why are you so agitated?" Oso asked calmly.

Almeda faced him and said rudely, "I told you. I want out of this bullshit."

"Do you have the money?"

"It's right here," Almeda said, flashing the shopping bag in his hand.

Oso nodded but said nothing about the money. "So, Sam," Oso said, "what can you tell us about the elegant Barbara Tonos?"

"I told you. I don't know anything about that. Montana has kept me out of anything significant. He doesn't trust me."

"Why is that? What have you told him?"

"I haven't told him shit."

"Well," Oso insisted, "there must be a reason why he doesn't trust you . . ."

"He's an asshole. That's the reason."

"Don't buy it," Oso dismissed him. "There must be a reason . . . unless, of course, you are lying to me."

"I'm not lying to you. Have I ever?"

"Well," Oso said with a bit of sarcasm, "first you talk like a parrot, then, all of a sudden you don't know anything useful. You go mute. You don't answer your phone, prompting me to call you at your fancy little office; only for you to get pissed off at me. Biting the hand that feeds your stomach and . . . your nose."

"Listen Oso, think whatever you want. The bottom line is that from now on I am out of this. Don't call me. Don't look for me. I don't know you. You don't know me. I should have never gotten involved with you people. You are too radical for my taste. I can get money other ways . . . and drugs too."

Oso remained silent as he studied the spacious living room while keeping an eye on Almeda's moves. The guy was a drug addict, a drug dealer, a compulsive collector of anything foreign and expensive, and a close aide to the governor of Puerto Rico. He made street lumpens look like CEO's.

"Okay," Oso said finally, "the money, please."

Avoiding eye contact, Almeda handed him the bag with the cash. Oso saw that their informant was now shaking. It could be the cocaine, or it could be that he knew what was probably coming next. Oso glanced into the bag. "How much we got here, Sam?"

"Fifty, sixty thousand, count it."

"Where the fuck is the rest?"

"I don't have it. You can check the whole house. I don't have it here."

"Really? And when are we supposed to get it back?"

Almeda hesitated. "I . . . uh . . . Sunday . . . I'll have the rest by Sunday." He lied.

"You put that dirty money in the bank? You are stupid, but not that stupid."

"Forget about where I put it . . . You'll see it Sunday."

Oso stared at him. And Almeda saw something in that stare that made him caress his waist to touch his gun.

But Oso was faster than him. In a second he was aiming a .357 Magnum with a silencer at this creepy and pathetic government worker standing in front of him.

Almeda froze.

"Keep your hands off your waist, Sam," Oso ordered.

"Jesus Christ!" Almeda cried. "What are you doing?" He didn't dare reach for his gun.

"I'm gonna take care of government waste, do some downsizing. It's a matter of principle."

"Put that gun away!"

"Almeda, you are a stinking liar, rat pig."

"Put that away!"

"No!" Oso said softly and pressed the trigger three times. Three clean shots to Almeda's chest and stomach.

"Oh, God, no!" Almeda cried as he fell backward; dead by the time he hit the floor.

Oso came closer to the body and fired a single shot at close range to Almeda's forehead. Blood splaterred onto Oso's face and onto the white carpet and furniture.

Oso used a handkerchief to wipe his face.

"Fucking banks are closed on Sundays," he said to the corpse as he searched him for his wallet. He took all the money and credit cards and threw the wallet on Almeda's bloody chest. The Puerto Rican police were so stupid, he thought, that they may believe the "it was a robbery" story.

Oso moved away from the body. "You don't want to talk to us," he said softly, "now you won't talk to anybody . . . Even better."

Oso hid his gun under his jacket and walked out of the house, closing the door behind him. He had parked a few doors down. He walked slowly to his car under the cover of the night, started the engine and calmly sped away. He was sure no one saw him. Rich snobs don't peek out through windows at this time of the night. They are too busy watching cable TV or having kinky sex with high-priced male escorts and street whores. This capitalist society *definitely* had to go.

Thursday, November 1

Chapter 54

Tino came early to pick up Tonos and drive him to his Senate office. On his way out of his home the senator ignored the reporters' questions thrown at him with a blunt "no comment." He couldn't believe the circus this whole thing had become.

Agents López and Allende had stayed in the house with Eugenia. Tonos had given them the excuse that he needed some documents from his office. But all he wanted was to give clear and final instructions to Tino to call Rigonaldo again.

"I want you to call Rigonaldo as soon as we get to the Capitol," he instructed. "Go to a payphone. Tell him I am dead serious. I want him to let the First Lady go. Tell him to drop her somewhere; *Ponce! Caguas!* I don't care. I don't know how he's going to do it. But tell him to fucking do it . . ."

"I don't know how he's going to respond," Tino said.

"He better respond the way I want him to. I am fucking serious."

"Has anything bad happened?"

"I got a call from those bastards yesterday. Barbara was screaming. Somebody was shooting. They were acting plain crazy. Who knows what they will finally do."

"From the little I know about Rigonaldo, I don't think he'll be impressed," Tino said.

"Listen," Tonos said angrily, "I am not going to risk my neck by calling him myself. *You* talk to him. What can he possibly say? Damn it! From what you told me, this whole thing was not even his plan. Oso did it. Oso started this bullshit. So you tell Rigonaldo to snap out of it.

To forget about it. He already made his point and there will be plenty of opportunities in the future to do other things. But this thing with my wife and Cruz's wife has to stop! This thing is out of control. Did I make myself clear?"

"Yes, sir."

"I couldn't sleep last night, you hear me?"

"I hear you, sir. I'll tell Rigonaldo."

"Good. Now drive fast. I want to be back at the house soon."

Tino sped faster.

Tonos glanced at a newspaper on the seat next to him. Today's press was reporting that Governor Cruz had met with Karen Pérez in Fortaleza. But there was no information about the meeting other than to say that it had been a tense conversation between the reporter and the governor. And the report came from third-party sources. Neither the governor nor Karen Pérez had said a word about what went on during their meeting.

Tonos pulled out a business card with Karen's numbers on it and grabbed his cell phone. He tried her at the station, but he was told she hadn't arrived yet. He called her at her home and got an answering machine. He ended the call leaving no message. He finally got her on her cell phone, stuck in traffic on *Ponce de León Avenue.*

"Karen," the senator said, "Orlando Tonos."

"Senator," Karen said quickly, "I was hoping you'd call."

"I think we should talk, Karen."

"I think so too. What do you want to do?"

"I want to send a message to Rigonaldo Pastrana on television. I think you are the best person to do it with."

"Great. When and where do you want to meet?"

"I'm on my way to the Capitol to pick up some papers, but I'm planning to go back home rather quickly. Can you be at my house in about one-and-a half, two hours?"

"Absolutely. I'll be there."

"Thank you, Karen."

"Thank you, Senator. I know this must be hard for you, but I think you are doing the right thing."

"Okay, Karen, we'll talk at home."

Tonos ended the call and looked out the tinted windows of his car. This was the first time in his life that he felt as trapped as a hunted fox. He lit up a cigarette and did not speak during the whole trip to the Senate. He just glanced at the cars in traffic, at the people crowding the streets, and at the tall, modern buildings that formed the landscape of metropolitan San Juan. He thought of Puerto Rico. For him, the island was a country that had suffered the tragedy and indignities of colonialism. And much worse, Puerto Ricans had been condemned to a fast and traumatic transition from an agricultural to an industrial economy. The sanctity of the family unit had been destroyed in the process, he believed.

Tonos despised what he called the vices of capitalist progress and development. For him it was nothing but neo-colonialism. He despised Governor Cruz and his American allies. The occupiers. But this crisis, which had started in the household of Elison Cruz, was now his own crisis too. It had now hit him at home. Now he was confused and extremely disturbed by the danger and the potentially tragic consequences of this political game that Rigonaldo Pastrana had started. This was not sound bite politics anymore. This was personal. And now he felt it in his gut. He had gone on television dismissing Elison Cruz's predicament as a mere political crisis. But no, now he understood how strictly personal this whole matter was. For him and for Cruz.

And he knew Rigonaldo's mind. He was a man fighting a war. And in a war there was always collateral damage. Could it be possible that Rigonaldo had already decided that Barbara would be a casualty of war? Tonos thought. A chill went down his spine. He feared he already knew the answer to that question.

Chapter 55

Tino left Senator Tonos at his office and took a cab to a payphone a few blocks down from the Capitol building. He made his phone call after assuring himself he hadn't been followed. Luna answered the phone.

"Luna," Tino said, anxiety in his voice, "let me talk to Rigonaldo."

Luna recognized the voice. She had been expecting the call. "I'm not sure he wants to talk to you, Tino."

"I have a message from Tonos. This is important, Luna," Tino said firmly.

"Tino, he's busy right now."

"Don't lead me around. What is he doing?"

"He's in the back. Feeding the pigs."

"Well, get him on the phone! Those damn animals can wait."

Luna hesitated for a second. "Hold on," she said. She put down the phone and went to the barn where Rigonaldo was busy and distracted, feeding his animals.

"Rigonaldo," she called.

He didn't answer.

"Excuse me, Rigo," she tried again.

Rigonaldo ignored her for a second. Then, "What is it, Luna?" He didn't face her. He kept at his task of feeding the pigs that ate voraciously.

"Tino is on the phone," Luna said. "He wants to talk to you."

Rigonaldo's silence made Luna uneasy. She was afraid Rigonaldo would explode at her. Instead, Rigonaldo spoke in a calm voice. "Tino is on the phone?" he asked. "What could that child possibly want?"

"He says he has a message for you. From Tonos."

Silence. Silence. Silence. Only the pigs seemed to respond to her.

"Rigonaldo," Luna said, "what do you want me to tell him?"

After a long pause, Rigonaldo said, "I'm busy feeding my animals. Tell Tino to send my regards to the senator. And tell him to call me tomorrow . . . after twelve noon."

Luna knew that that was it. She turned around, walked through the mud, came back to the phone and relayed the message to Tino.

"I can't wait until tomorrow to call him!" Tino snapped.

"Tino," Luna said, "I'm telling you what Rigonaldo told me. Don't jump on me now. That's the last thing I need."

"Luna, Tonos is frantic and in a viciously angry mood. He couldn't sleep last night over this whole thing."

"Well, don't tell that to Rigonaldo. He's going to tell you he's not a doctor."

"Fuck that!" Tino shot back.

Luna laughed.

"Don't laugh!" Tino said angrily. "This is not funny anymore."

"What can I tell you, Tino? I have to laugh at something."

"Is the First Lady still alive? Or did he bust her brains in already?"

"Oh no, the bitch is still alive, and if anything, Rigonaldo will saw her head off with a chainsaw, put it in a plastic bag and send it Federal Express to Fortaleza."

"You know, Luna," Tino said, "I think you are all a little off the wall."

"Oh, come on boy. Have a sense of humor. It will get you to your sixties."

"Listen," Tino said seriously, "I am going to call Rigonaldo again later today as soon as I speak to Tonos. And this time he'll have to come to the phone. I am in the very middle of this shit, and Tonos doesn't want to risk calling Rigonaldo himself. I'm feeling a lot of fucking pressure."

"Well, you try that, boy. Good luck."

Tino hung up. In less than twenty minutes he was in Tonos's office.

"I couldn't talk to Rigonaldo," he told the senator.

"He wasn't there?" Tonos asked incredulously. "Where the fuck could he possibly be?"

"He was there. He just didn't come to the phone. He said he was busy feeding his pigs."

"Feeding pigs? Did he know I asked you to call?"

"He knew. He said to call him tomorrow . . . after twelve noon."

"Has he lost his mind?" Tonos snapped as he placed documents in a briefcase. "Listen, you call that nutcase as soon as you drop me off at home. Do you understand?"

"Yes, sir."

"Now, let's get the hell out of here."

Chapter 56

When Tonos arrived at his house, he immediately asked Agent López if anyone had called. The answer was "no."

"Where's Tino?" Eugenia asked.

"He went to the pharmacy," Tonos lied. "He'll be right back."

Was Eugenia attracted to Tino? Tonos thought for a second. He brushed off the thought quickly; no time for that now.

Tonos said to López, "Karen Pérez will be here in less than an hour."

"Very good," López said.

"You are doing the right thing, Senator," Allende added.

Tonos excused himself and went into his studio to wait for Tino.

The phone rang longer than usual before Luna finally answered it. Tino insisted that she get Rigonaldo on the phone. This time, Tino said, he would keep calling until he got Rigonaldo to talk to him.

After a long wait, Rigonaldo finally came to the phone. "Tino, I thought I told you to call tomorrow after twelve noon," he said, irritated.

"Tonos can't wait until tomorrow, Rigonaldo. The people who have Barbara are acting real crazy. They called him and she was screaming, and they were shooting and just acting nuts. Tonos is afraid they will hurt her if you don't release the First Lady. He couldn't even sleep yesterday. He's angry and fed up with this. He says this whole thing is out of control and . . ."

"Hold it right there!" Rigonaldo snapped. "First of all, I can't do anything about Tonos's sleeping problems because I am not a doctor. Secondly, let those people shoot and act crazy because they won't do a thing to his wife. The FBI has her. I'll put my head under a guillotine like Marie Antoinette if that is not so . . . And thirdly, nothing here is out of control. *I am* in control and *I am* going to get what I want. That's all I have to say!"

"Rigonaldo, you don't understand. Tonos is raging mad about this. He's putting a lot of pressure on me because he says he won't risk his neck by calling you himself . . ."

"It wouldn't make a difference," Rigonaldo said firmly. "I will tell him the same thing I'm telling you. I will stick to my plan. The Cruz woman is dead if the plebiscite goes forward. And I expect Elison Cruz to announce tomorrow that there will be no vote on Saturday."

"Tonos says that you should remember that this thing was not even your plan in the first place. This was Oso's idea when we couldn't find Cruz at that house in Condado . . ."

"Oso is not in charge here!" Rigonaldo yelled. "How dare you? I am in charge! I set the rules! Oso did the right thing, and I approved of it. I could have shot that woman's brains out the minute she set foot in this house and dumped her body in the *Rio Grande*. Don't question my authority, young man."

"Rigonaldo," Tino said, regretting what he'd said, "I didn't mean to say that you are not in charge, I . . ."

"You know," Rigonaldo cut him off, "you have problems, Tino. Oso told me that you were questioning his judgment during the operation. That's not the behavior expected of a revolutionary. I thought you were on the same page with us."

"Rigonaldo, I'm only telling you what Tonos told me to tell you. You must understand, I'm caught in the middle here . . ."

"Well," Rigonaldo said, ready to hang up, "spare yourself the trouble and take a few days off. Go to Flamenco Beach in *Culebra* with a nice date or something. And do not call me again about this. My plan will go forward no matter who gets hurt in the middle. This is one of the biggest hits we've done. I won't let Tonos or anybody spoil it. I am not stupid, and Tonos is not stupid either. Tell him to get a grip on himself . . . Good bye, Tino"

Rigonaldo hung up.

Tino cursed, and for a few minutes he didn't move. He was stuck. He knew it. They were all stuck. This was a real shitty mess they were all in. He finally took a cab to Domenech Avenue and then walked to the house. The press vultures attacked him like wolves, but Tino held his ground and fled past them, not uttering a word. He walked into the house, greeted everyone inside and went straight into Tonos's studio.

The agents looked at him suspiciously.

The studio Tonos had built was tiny. Books in floor-to-ceiling bookshelves covered all the walls. A brand new computer sat on an oak desk. Tonos was seated behind his desk in an elegant, black leather reclining chair. Tino closed the door behind him. They spoke in whispers.

"What did he say?" Tonos asked quickly.

"He won't do it," Tino said bluntly.

"What do you mean?"

"Just what I said. He's not going to let the First Lady go. If Cruz doesn't cancel the plebiscite by tomorrow, Rigonaldo will kill the woman."

Tonos was listening intensely.

"And," Tino went on, "by the way he talks, it wouldn't surprise me if he'd kill her even if he gets Cruz to cancel the damn plebiscite."

"What else did he say?"

"He is convinced that Barbara's kidnapping is an inside job of the FBI."

"What if that's true? What difference does it make?"

"He thinks they won't hurt her."

"Bullshit!" Tonos said angrily. "Even if this thing was pulled off by the Feds they *will* hurt her. He should know that."

"Tonos, talking to Rigonaldo is like talking to a deaf person. He doesn't listen. He will do whatever it is he wants to do."

"Did you tell him that Oso started this whole thing?"

"Yes, and that really pissed him off. He screamed at me like a fucking hyena."

"I suppose there's no need to call him again."

"Waste of time. Oh, and by the way, he hung up on me."

Tonos let this sink in, then he said, "Shit, fucking shit! That stupid, stubborn idiot. After all the heat I've gotten because of him."

"Sorry I couldn't help," Tino said.

"Forget about it," Tonos said. "Stay here for a few minutes, and then join the others in the living room."

"Okay."

Tonos lit a cigarette. I should call the bastard myself, he thought, but dismissed the idea as too risky for himself. At this moment, the only thing he had left was a frank talk on television with Karen Pérez. Other than that, he couldn't really predict what was going to happen between today and tomorrow. Rigonaldo Pastrana, after all, was crazy. He had reached that conclusion today.

Chapter 57

Tonio drove Channel Four's news van right into the driveway of Senator Tonos's house. When Karen got out of the van she waved politely to her colleagues camping outside, but she went straight to the door and rang the doorbell.

The pack of reporters outside could not believe that Karen was in on this story too.

"Well, look at this one," said Ariana Peralta, a reporter from Channel Two who had been camping outside Tonos's house since the day before. "Who does she think she is? She spoke to Rigonaldo, she saw the First Lady, she spoke to Cruz, and now she just walks into Tonos's home like she's the Queen of England!"

"Hey!" another reporter yelled to Karen. "We need to eat in this town too!"

Too late. Karen and Tonio were led into the house by Eugenia amidst the loud protests of the reporters outside, who were kept at a distance from the entrance by a police officer posted there. The cop thought he was going to have a little riot here.

"Dad is in the studio," Eugenia told Karen. "I'll bring you in."

Karen and Tonio greeted Tino and the "detectives" in the living room and followed Eugenia to Tonos's studio.

When Karen came face to face with Senator Tonos she could tell the man was not his usual self. Seated behind his desk, Tonos looked even smaller than he was, and he was as pale as a ghost, except for the extremely apparent dark shadows beneath his eyes.

"Good morning, Senator," Karen said softly.

Tonos waved. Eugenia asked if he wanted anything. Coffee? Tea? Tonos said no, just leave me alone with Karen and her cameraman. Eugenia left and closed the door behind her.

Tonos was smoking another cigarette. Tonio followed. The small room was filled with so much smoke that it resembled a gas chamber. Karen ignored the smoke, but cleared her throat. She sat in a small chair across from Tonos's desk, while Tonio set up the camera and tripod.

For some reason, Karen didn't know how to start this interview. She was so struck by the Senator's appearance that she was at a loss for words. Here was a fighter who seemed to have lost his fighting edge. This scene reminded her of her meeting with Governor Cruz the day before. There, hidden behind anger, she saw another man of power humbled as never before. Vulnerable. Disarmed.

"Are you ready to begin?" Tonos asked softly.

Karen glanced at Tonio who nodded that he was ready. "I'm ready," Karen said.

There was a short silence. Then, Karen began her interview. "Senator," she said, "two days ago your wife, Barbara, was kidnapped by a group of people calling themselves 'July 4th-The Warriors, Keepers of Democracy.' They claim to have acted in retaliation for the kidnapping of First Lady Ana María Cruz . . . Do you think this is fair, what is happening to you?"

Tonos was pensive for a moment. Then, he said, "Of course I don't think that what they've done to me and Barbara is fair. But who cares at this point? What is happening is happening. And I am here to do my best to solve this matter in a way in which nobody is hurt. That is why I am talking to you."

"Have you been able to speak to your wife?"

A pause. "Briefly," Tonos said, almost inaudible. "She seems to be . . . unharmed. I hope she is not harmed. There is no reason why they should hurt her. Ever since this whole thing started, I have been cooperating with the people who are holding her. I have assured them that I will do everything I can to get what they want."

"They want you to gain the release of Ana María Cruz," Karen stated.

"Yes."

"Is that something that is possible for you to do, Senator?"

"I am doing everything in my power to make that possible."

"Have you had any contact with Rigonaldo Pastrana or any of his associates?"

"No," Tonos said quickly. "I have not had any contact with them. That's why I'm talking to you. I want to speak to Rigonaldo through you."

"Senator, what message do you want to send to Rigonaldo Pastrana and September Twenty-third?"

Silence. Tonos took off his glasses. Then, he said, "I am pleading with him to release the First Lady unharmed. I want him to listen to me closely and understand that, at this moment, letting her go is in the best interest of us all . . . I hope that Rigonaldo can see things the way I see them and realize that at this time I need his help . . . I need him to cooperate with me on this." He paused and looked straight at the camera. "Rigonaldo, I know you are watching this on television. I'm pleading with you. Let Ana María Cruz go now . . . Today . . . Unharmed . . . That is the patriotic thing to do. It will show the country that you are a man of great integrity and common sense. You are not a monster. You yourself know what family means. Let the First Lady go . . . for my family and her family."

Karen allowed a few moments for this to sink in. She knew that the audience *and* Rigonaldo needed a moment of silence after such a dramatic plea for common sense and mercy.

"Senator," Karen said softly, "do you predict any obstacles for Rigonaldo to do what you have asked him to do?"

Tonos pondered this. He said, "I only hope that Rigonaldo understands how serious this whole thing is and how serious I am in asking him to release Mrs. Cruz . . . And let me tell you this, because I know that the same thing must be going through his mind. I admit that I have my suspicions about what happened to Barbara . . . about who took her. I'm going to say this very carefully . . . The FBI may be behind this . . . or . . . someone close to them . . . or someone connected to the Puerto Rican police. But even if that is the case, it doesn't change anything as far as what I am asking Rigonaldo to do."

"Do you have any evidence that the FBI or the Puerto Rican police kidnapped your wife?"

"No, I do not. I am only relying on what I know them to be capable of."

"These are very serious accusations, Senator."

"Kidnapping is a very serious matter. It's evil. It's criminal."

"So, you do not approve of the kidnapping of Ana María Cruz," Karen stated.

Silence.

Tonos put his glasses back on. "No, I do not approve," he said flatly.

Tonio bit his tongue as he looked through the camera's lens. Mr. 'big mouth' Senator, he told himself, has taken a one-hundred-and-eighty-degree turn.

Karen went on. "So, you would agree that kidnapping as a way to advance a political cause is indeed wrong and extreme?"

Tonos was afraid that sweat would begin pouring down his forehead. He was hesitant. The radical fighter in him was against what he knew his answer needed to be. But this time it was different. He was trapped. He had hoped Karen wouldn't continue with this line of questioning, but he knew this was inevitable after the answers he had given her during last Sunday's interview.

He said, "I have to agree with that."

Karen knew what was going through Tonos's mind. She knew.

"Senator," she said, "what other options, then, do you give to Rigonaldo Pastrana with respect to his goal to abort the plebiscite of November third?"

"I have never been one to instruct or dictate anything to Rigonaldo Pastrana," Tonos said carefully. "I don't think I should be the one to say what course of action Rigonaldo or September Twenty-third should take. I think it is evident that Rigonaldo and his group have minds of their own."

"Senator, I am trying to put myself in their shoes – as impossible as that may be – to give you a chance to comment on probable actions that will make it possible for you to see your wife again, and for the

Governor to see his wife again, too. I am trying to find a way out. That is the purpose of my question, Senator."

Tonos pondered this for a second. He thought of lighting another cigarette but opted not to. "I think," he said slowly but firmly, "that Rigonaldo and September Twenty-third must join in the boycott of the plebiscite. That is a viable course of action, and it is also a significant political decision . . . It will stain the process, especially in the eyes of the international community."

"That is not a capitulation, in your opinion?"

"No, no. Absolutely not. It is a legitimate course of action."

"And, in that way, Ana María Cruz can return to her family and Barbara can return to you and your daughter, Eugenia," Karen pointed out.

"Yes, yes . . . that is my hope."

"How is Eugenia coping with what is happening?"

"She has cried a lot."

Karen was silent, expecting a longer answer.

"She misses her mother a lot," Tonos added. "This is obviously very difficult for her as well as for me. We are both badly shaken up and upset over what is happening to our family . . . I don't think I can properly describe our grief."

"So, Senator, your message today is very clear. You want Rigonaldo Pastrana to release the First Lady, quickly and unharmed."

"Yes. That is what I'm asking him to do."

"Do you fear for the life of your wife, Barbara?"

After a pause, Tonos said, "Yes . . . I don't know who has her. I don't know who is behind this. I don't know what type of people I am dealing with . . . I am, however, doing as they told me to do, to plead for the release of Ana María Cruz. I hope this will be proof to them that I am serious about my commitment to solve this crisis."

"Do you expect Rigonaldo to release the First Lady?"

"Yes, I do," Tonos said, attempting to sound confident. "I can't think of Rigonaldo not doing it, knowing that his actions will hurt my family. I think I have expressed my concerns very clearly to him. He must know this is the right thing to do."

"One last question, Senator."

He nodded.

Karen said, "Why do you think they chose you to retaliate against for what was done to Governor Cruz?"

"Someone asked me the same question yesterday," Tonos said. "And my answer is the same. I was targeted because of my ideas. No other reason."

"All right, Senator, thank you for sharing your thoughts with me and our audience."

"Thank you, Karen."

Camera off, Tonos lit up a cigarette. Tonio did the same.

"I hope this works, for God's sake," Tonos said quickly.

"I hope so, too," Karen said seriously. "Listen, I'll have the station run this as a special report as soon as I have it ready. We'll interrupt whatever is scheduled. And I will make sure it runs again at six and ten."

"You should run it tomorrow too," Tonos said worriedly.

"We'll do it," Karen promised.

Tonio grabbed his camera and tripod and followed Karen and the senator to the living room.

"Nice to meet you, gentlemen," Karen said to the "detectives."

"Thank you, Karen," Eugenia told her with teary eyes.

Karen hugged her warmly. "Don't worry, honey," Karen said. "Everything will be all right."

Tonos walked them to the door. For three short seconds he allowed himself to be seen and photographed by the reporters camping outside.

"What's going on in there?" someone shouted as Tonos shut the door again.

Karen and Tonio quickly got into their vehicle, avoiding eye contact with the rest of the press there.

"Well," Tonio said as he started the engine, "it seems that the senator had a change of heart."

"Let's go, Tonio," Karen told him. Then: "This hit home. What did you expect?"

Chapter 58

At 3 p.m., interrupting the regular broadcast, Channel Four ran Senator Tonos's interview. The whole country watched the dramatic performance. Except Rigonaldo, who didn't care to see any of it. He decided he'd watch the regular broadcast at six p.m. and amuse himself a little.

Governor Cruz sat through the broadcast with his telephone in conference mode so that Anthony, his son studying at Yale, could hear what was happening. Both father and son felt a shred of hope that Tonos's plea to the terrorists would in fact accomplish the release of Ana María.

FBI Assistant Director William Montana and Police Superintendent Roberto Calero immediately issued a rare joint statement sternly and strongly denying the accusations made by Senator Tonos. Neither the FBI nor the Puerto Rican police had any involvement whatsoever in the kidnapping of Barbara Tonos, they said. Both men also encouraged the senator to be more truthful and to do more to obtain the release of the First Lady.

Cruz, on his part, had also been in contact with the presidents of the Commonwealth and Independence parties. They had agreed to be with him at a scheduled press conference tomorrow at noon. Both men had been briefed that Friday at noon was the deadline Rigonaldo Pastrana had set for the governor to announce the cancellation of Saturday's plebiscite. Cruz had informed his political rivals that he and his aides had worded the statement in a fashion that could accomplish their aim: to stall in a non-threatening way to gain more time for the frantic search for Rigonaldo Pastrana and Ana María Cruz. The plebiscite, Cruz assured them, would still go forward.

At about 4 p.m. the phone rang in the residence at Fortaleza.

"Hello," Cruz answered.

"Governor, Calero here," the Police Superintendent said in a weary voice.

"What is it?"

"I'm sorry to break this news to you, but you should know that Almeda is dead," Calero said bluntly.

All morning Damaris had been calling Almeda's home trying to find out why he hadn't reported to Fortaleza. But this news came as a shock to Elison Cruz.

"Jesus Christ!" Cruz exclaimed. "What happened?"

"They just found him. In his house. He was shot four times. Apparently he's been dead since last night."

"I can't believe it!"

"I'm on my way there now. My officers are already there."

"Who found him?"

"A housekeeper. She said she came to pick up an envelope with her weekly pay and instead stumbled upon the body. She called the *Loíza* Street precinct. They went to the scene and she told them who Almeda was and they immediately called me."

"This is incredible, Roberto. Who would do something like this?"

"Let me get there and I'll have more information for you."

"Could he have been robbed? Did an intruder break into the house?"

"I'll call you when I talk to the officers there and assess the scene myself."

"Christ! Please, do call me."

"Governor," Calero said before hanging up, "please call Montana and let him know about this."

"Sure, I'll call him . . ." Cruz said. "You don't think that this is connected to Pastrana, do you?"

"Governor, I won't know what to think until I get there and assess the scene."

Cruz said, "Call me soon."

Chapter 59

Almeda's front yard was surrounded by yellow crime scene tape. There were three squad cars parked in the front, a couple of other official police vehicles and a handful of uniformed police officers walking through the premises and keeping the neighbors away from the crime scene.

Calero arrived in a matter of minutes and immediately walked into the house. Inside, he found four detectives, more uniformed police officers, the medical examiner and a police photographer who was taking pictures of Almeda's body.

Carmen Martínez, the twenty-something housekeeper who had found the body, was seated on the sofa in the living room, talking to a detective.

After a brief inspection of Almeda's body, Calero walked over to the senior officer in charge, Detective Ricardo Pacheco.

"How are you, sir?" Pacheco said to the chief.

"What do we got here?"

"Well," Pacheco began, "we've got a recording from his answering machine with the voice and name, or alias, of the possible murderer. And we found a closet in his master bedroom full of surprises: a hundred-and-fifty-thousand dollars in cash, and approximately half a kilo of powder cocaine. The guy was either dealing or he had an extremely serious nose habit. This was no robbery, I can assure you. You don't break into a house like this to steal from a guy's wallet. And here you have no forced entry and an intact house with lots of drugs and cash in it. Besides, we have a tape."

"Let me listen to it," Calero said.

Pacheco led Calero to the answering machine and quickly pressed the play button. Before the recording came on, Calero took a glance at the cocaine left on a mirror on the living room's center table.

There were three beeps signaling calls where the caller left no message. Then: "Hello! Almeda! This is Oso. Pick up the phone." A short silence. "Almeda! I know you are home. Pick up the phone." Then there was the sound of someone roughly picking up the receiver and saying, agitated, "What the fuck do you want?" Calero recognized the voice as that of Samuel Almeda. That was the end of the recording.

"He killed him," Calero said. "That Oso guy, whoever he is." He stared at the housekeeper, still answering questions from another detective. "Did she know about the drugs or the money in his room?"

"No," Pacheco said. "She wasn't allowed in his room. Almeda kept it locked at all times."

"She always got paid in cash?"

"Yes, and with all that money in the back it's not at all surprising."

"Let me take a look," Calero said.

Both men walked into the room. It was spacious, with mirrors on all of the walls and the ceiling. Probably to see himself in sexual acts, Calero thought.

The Superintendent went into the closet and stared at the huge pile of money on the floor. "Where did you find the cocaine?" he asked.

"On the top shelf. Inside a shoebox."

Calero was about to voice another question when his cell phone rang. He pulled it out of his jacket and answered it.

"Calero," he said.

"Superintendent? Bill Montana."

"Hi. Did you talk to Cruz?"

"Yes," Montana said, excitement in his voice. "What's happening over there?"

"He's dead as a fish out of water. Four shots. One straight into his forehead. There was no forced entry into the house. Apparently he knew the murderer. We've got a tape from his answering machine. Plus we found about half a kilo of powder cocaine and approximately a hundred-fifty-thousand dollars in cash in his love nest."

"I told you," Montana said, "the guy was dubious."

"As dubious as they come, I would say."

"Listen, I want to send two of my men over there. Do you have a problem with that?"

Calero hesitated for a moment. "Well . . . I . . . no . . . I don't see a problem with that. What are you looking for?"

"I'll have them fill you in once they get there. I'm sending Walker and Morales. You've met them before."

"Sure."

"Good," Montana said and hung up.

Calero put his cell phone back in his jacket. For all the camaraderie, politeness and cooperation between the state police and the FBI, there was still a slight sense of competition as to who knew how to conduct an investigation properly. But Calero knew that in everything dealing with Governor Cruz at this time he needed to let the FBI in. "The FBI is sending two agents here shortly," he told Pacheco. "They are free to act as they please. Just make sure you know what they are doing."

"Understood, sir."

Calero excused himself and went into the living room. Once again, he stooped over Almeda's body. The photographer took a break. Other officers were dusting doors, drawers, the telephone and furniture attempting to lift fingerprints. "Take pictures of the whole house," Calero told the photographer.

Almeda's eyes were open, staring at the ceiling and probably at the gates of hell as well, Calero thought.

The Superintendent lit up a cigarette, pulled out his cell phone and went outside to call Cruz.

The governor answered on the first ring.

"Cruz," he said.

"Governor, Calero here."

"Okay, what happened?"

"This was no robbery. His wallet was on top of his chest with no money or credit cards in it, but we found over a hundred-thousand dollars in cash in his bedroom and about half a kilo of cocaine. If the killer saw the cash or the drugs he didn't touch them."

"You can't be serious. Almeda? On drugs?"

"That's what it looks like."

"That much drugs? Do you think he was dealing?"

"We don't know that . . . Yet."

"Are you trying to tell me this was a drug hit?"

"We don't know. But I wouldn't rule it out."

"Good Lord!" Cruz exclaimed, visibly shocked. "I can't believe it. I just can't possibly believe it."

"Well, it really doesn't come as a surprise. Montana rang the warning bells, if you remember."

"Did he call you?"

"Yes. He's sending two of his boys here. Walker and Morales."

"What a fucking mess," Cruz said, almost talking to himself. "The press is going to have a field day with this."

"They are not here yet. But they'll be here soon. You know they have their people listening to our scanners 24/7."

"Calero, I have to make a few phone calls," the Governor said.

"Go ahead. I'll call you back when we have more here."

Cruz stood by the phone for a long while, trying to absorb what he had just been told about his close aide. His scheduling secretary, of all people. The idea that he was a cocaine user, probably an addict, and probably dealing, was just too frightening to entertain. He was going to need the best PR group on the island to cool down the avalanche of bad press that would certainly come his way.

But on top of all these political calculations, Cruz was saddened by the death of Samuel Almeda. This was just another schocking event in a week of roller coaster tragedy.

Chapter 60

Walker and Morales walked into Almeda's house and were immediately greeted by the Superintendent and Detective Pacheco. Calero filled them in on what they knew so far.

"We are really interested in seeing his address book," Walker said. "And his phone bills."

"We did find an address book," Pacheco told him.

"Can I take a look at it?" Walker asked him.

Pacheco looked at Calero, who nodded.

"Hey, Miro!" Pacheco called another detective. "Let me see that address book you've got."

Detective Ramiro Miranda quickly moved towards his senior officer and handed him Almeda's address book. He looked at the FBI agents with suspicion. Pacheco handed the book to Agent Walker.

Walker gave the book to Morales. "See if you find anything useful," Walker told him.

Walker glanced at the young woman seated on the sofa. "That's the housekeeper?" he asked.

"Yes," Pacheco said.

"Excuse me," Walker told him. He walked toward her, leaving the Superintendent and Pacheco whispering to each other.

"Excuse me, ma'am," Walker told the woman.

She looked up at him. She immediately thought he was very young and attractive. Tall, beautiful light brown hair and eyebrows, brown eyes, slim body, hairless face, probably a hairless chest as well. This young man standing before her was the most attractive police officer, or detective, or whatever, that she had seen so far in the house.

"I'm with the FBI," Walker said. "I know you must be tired and that you have answered lots of questions today . . ."

"I'm fine," the woman said quickly. "You said FBI?"

"Yes, ma'am."

She smiled for a moment. Then she remembered there was a dead body in the house. How could she be thinking of handsome men at a time like this? She lost her smile. But she wasn't feeling too much guilt. Samuel Almeda wasn't the kindest employer she had. Nor was he the best paying. She cleaned many homes in Condado and Ocean Park and she got much better cash from all of them, and had even made friends with some of the residents. Not Almeda. He was cheap, cold, distant and shady. He would bark orders: don't go in here, don't go in there, this or that isn't cleaned enough, and blah, blah, blah. I could have killed him myself, she thought.

"Would you know where Mr. Almeda kept his phone bills?" Walker said.

"I'm sorry?" she asked, back from her own thoughts.

"His phone bills," Walker repeated, "where did he keep them?"

"Sometimes," she said, "I think I've seen them in the kitchen. In the top drawer next to the refrigerator. But I think he kept all *that* in *his* room."

The last sentence carried the weight of contempt, Walker thought. He said, "Did you ever meet any of Mr. Almeda's friends?"

"No," she said firmly. "This one . . . I mean . . . Mr. Almeda never had me come in when he was entertaining. That was off-limits. Like his master bedroom. Locked with a key. Off-limits. I always kept to myself here. Clean up, take my cash and go."

Walker nodded. "Thank you, ma'am," he said.

"You're welcome, sir."

Walker turned around, walked a few steps and got a pair of Latex gloves from one of the officers in the house. He immediately went to the kitchen. He went through every drawer there but found nothing. With the curious glances of the police officers on him, he moved to the master bedroom and continued his search there.

Calero came into the room. "What are you looking for exactly?" he asked.

"His phone bills."

"Well, you already said that," Calero told him. "What exactly?"

Walker really didn't want to get too specific. He said, "We just want to know who he's been talking to."

"Okay," Calero said and left the room.

After a few minutes, Walker found a Horizon Communications envelope with phone records. He scanned through it carefully. It was a two-month-old bill. The cover sheet indicated that it was twenty pages long, divided into three parts. Part one, pages one to five, included the standard fees and fees for other features. Part two, pages six to twelve, listed international long distance calls and calls made to the continental United States. Part three, pages thirteen to twenty, recorded long distance calls within the island.

Part one was intact. Part two was missing two pages. And part three was missing altogether.

Morales came into the bedroom, "Did you find the phone bills?" he asked.

"Only one," Walker told him. "And it's missing pages, especially the island-wide long distance calls. What about you? Find anything useful in the address book?"

"Not a single address or phone number in the area of Cagüey. I'm taking it with me anyway."

"Me too," Walker said. "Let me call the boss."

"And I need a cigarette," Morales told him.

Both men walked out of the house, avoiding contact with the local police. Pacheco and Calero observed the men with interest, but did not ask them where they were going, or to return any material they may have taken from the house. This was not a time for petty rivalries between law enforcement agencies. This was a time to cooperate with each other and to get the hell out of each other's way.

Chapter 61

"**S**o," Walker told Montana, speaking from his cell phone in front of Almeda's house, "we haven't found anything yet that links him to Cagüey or that area."

"You said all the Horizon records of island-wide long distance were missing?" Montana wanted to confirm.

"Yes, sir."

After a short silence, Montana said, "Okay. I think you are about done over there. Get back here to headquarters, both of you. I have a better idea. Drive fast."

Montana hung up.

His desk at his spacious office at the FBI headquarters in *Hato Rey* was crowded with papers, files, documents of all sorts, and a brand new HP computer.

He moved towards his keyboard and monitor and went online to use Google, the search engine. He typed Horizon Communications Puerto Rico and the name Anabel Rivera and in less than a second got more than five dozen listings. He clicked on the first one, the home page of Horizon Communications in Puerto Rico. Once he was on the site he clicked on Corporate Headquarters and got the number for Mrs. Anabel Rivera, General Manager of Horizon Communications in Puerto Rico.

He looked at his watch. It was a little after 5 p.m. He was sure they were already closed, but he was certain that the administrators worked until much later.

He grabbed the receiver of his desk phone and dialed the number for Anabel Rivera. To his surprise he got a recording: "Hello. You have reached the offices of Anabel Rivera, General Manager of Horizon Communications Puerto Rico, with headquarters at 1700 Roosevelt Avenue in Guaynabo. We are unable to answer your call at this time. Please leave your name, number and a short message and we will return your call within the next business day. Thank you for calling Horizon. We are proud to serve you." Beep!

Montana hung up without leaving a message. He kept the receiver in his right hand, and with his left hand he browsed through a thick Rolodex on his desk. He pulled out a card for Anabel Rivera that she had given to him years ago during a reception at Fortaleza on the day of Governor Cruz's second inauguration. On the card, Mrs. Rivera had written her home phone number.

He dialed the number and after three rings a man answered.

"Hello," the man said.

"Good afternoon," Montana said. "May I please speak with Mrs. Anabel Rivera."

"What number did you dial?" the man said testily.

Montana recited the number.

"Well, that's my number," the man said. "And I don't know why they gave me that woman's former number. They should have given me a brand new, never-used number. Those people at Horizon don't know their ass from their dicks and . . ."

"So," Montana cut him off, "Mrs. Rivera doesn't have this number anymore?"

"No. And I know who she is. She is the big honcho at the phone company. She should never have allowed her number to be given to another person. That's stupid and plain . . ."

"Would you know her new number?"

"Oh, pleeeaaassseee! How the hell would I know? Call the damn operat . . ."

"Thank you, sir. Sorry to have bothered you." Montana hung up, leaving the man in mid sentence.

Shit! Time is running out, he thought.

Montana called the operator.

"Horizon," the female voice said, "good afternoon, what listing, please?"

"Anabel Rivera in Garden Hills, Guaynabo."

"One moment, please."

Montana heard the operator punching keys. Then she came back on with a quick response.

"Sir?"

"Yes."

"That number is listed as private."

Montana had anticipated this answer and he knew that if he pulled his *I am the Assistant Director in Charge of the FBI* line he might or he might not get the number from her. Too much time, which he didn't have.

"Thank you, operator," he said.

"Thank you for calling Horizon," the operator said and cut the call.

To Montana she sounded like a computerized voice machine.

Time. Time. Time. It will be six o'clock soon.

Reluctantly, Montana dialed Governor Cruz. Anabel Rivera was a friend of the governor. He didn't want to waste time briefing the governor on other matters. He wanted to get Rivera on the phone to get to Almeda's phone records NOW!

"This is Cruz," the governor said with a worried voice.

"Bill Montana here."

"Glad you called. What's happened?"

"My agents were at the scene. They are on their way back here."

"So, what happened? Who killed Sam?"

"Governor, we'll find out. That's for sure. I'm calling you because I need Anabel Rivera's home and cell phone numbers. I called her at her office but got a machine. The home number I dialed for her is no longer hers and I never had her cell. Would you have her most recent numbers?"

"I do, hold on."

Montana heard the receiver fall flat on a hard surface. He was already frustrated that something so simple as finding a prominent executive on a business day afternoon was becoming so complicated.

After three eternal minutes, Cruz came back on the line.

"Montana?"

"I'm here."

Cruz gave him both the home and cell phone numbers.

"She lives at the Golden Towers in Garden Hills," Cruz added.

"Yes, I know."

Montana was ready to hang up and get on with his plan.

"What is this about? If you don't mind my asking," Cruz said.

Montana did mind, but opted to share his thoughts with the governor.

"Governor, I must be quick with you. What I'm doing may be a long shot, but at this time we are trying everything that presents a possibility."

"What are you doing?"

"I want to get Anabel Rivera to get us access into Almeda's phone records. I want to see if he, by any chance, was in communication with anybody in Cagüey or that area overall."

"In Cagüey?" Cruz exclaimed, knowing the implications.

"Yes. As I said, it may be a long shot, but I think it's worth trying."

Cruz said, "The thought of it is more frightening than what I already know about Almeda."

"I'm truly sorry, Mr. Governor, but I've been in this field long enough not to let anything like this surprise me anymore."

Cruz said nothing.

"I must go now," Montana said quickly. "I'll keep you posted." He hung up.

Quickly, Montana dialed Anabel Rivera's home number. Each ring felt like the sound of a smashing hammer against his ear. He rummaged around the top of his desk, looking for his porcelain coffee mug. He had several. This one read: *I am James Bond.*

After seven rings, a male voice answered, a youngster, Montana could tell.

"Rivera residence."

"Good evening," Montana said. "Anabel Rivera, please."

"Mom is not home right now," the teenager said, a TV set screaming in the background.

"Would you please tell me how I can get in contact with her? I need to speak to her immediately. This is very important."

"Who's calling, please?"

"My name is William Montana, son. I'm with the FBI."

"FBI!" the kid said excitedly. "Wow!"

Time. Time. Time.

"So," Montana said quickly, "how can I find her?"

"She's at Plaza right now," the youngster revealed.

Montana could not believe it.

"Plaza Las Américas?" Montana exclaimed incredulously.

Plaza Las Américas was the largest indoor shopping mall on the island, and probably in the whole Caribbean region. It was the temple of prayer of consumerist Puerto Rican society. The very center of the world.

"Are you sure that's where she is?" Montana asked, impatiently.

"Yes," the teenager said. "She called me a while ago. But I don't know when she'll be back. She's with Adelina, a friend of hers."

"Adelina Pedraza?"

"Oh, I don't know her last name."

It had to be Adelina Pedraza, the head of the Puerto Rico Planning Board, a governor appointee. It figured. Anabel Rivera, a very important business executive, and Adelina Pedraza, a high-level government official, leaving work early to go to Plaza Las Américas on a shopping spree. Only in Puerto Rico.

This was beginning to look like a tragicomedy.

One of these officials, Anabel Rivera, could hold the last key to break the most pressing and important criminal case on the island. And right at this very moment she was probably picking, choosing and discarding shoes at the mall. If Cruz knew about this, he would probably ask for the heads of both women.

"Is your mother carrying her cell phone?" Montana asked, now beginning to sweat.

"You can try her," the kid said. "But she sometimes leaves it in the car."

"Listen, I'm going to call her cell phone. But first, do something for me please."

"What's that?"

"Get a pen and a piece of paper. I'm going to give you three phone numbers where she can reach me if I happen not to find her on her cell."

"Hold on," the kid said, and went away.

He came back on the phone after two minutes. Montana was about to have a heart attack.

"I got a pen and paper, sir," the teenager said.

Montana gave him his office, cell, and even his home number. He made the kid read it back. He got them right.

"If your mother calls you, you tell her to call me immediately. This is urgent. You tell her to call William Montana. You got my name?"

"Yes, sir."

"What's your name, kid?"

"Martin Xavier."

"And how old are you?"

"Sixteen. I'll be seventeen in March."

The kid was old enough to relay a message. "Bye, son." Montana hung up.

If he didn't get a call from Anabel Rivera within the next thirty minutes, or didn't get her on her cell phone, Montana decided that he would have a battery of agents call every single store in Plaza Las Américas to page the woman through their loud-speaker systems.

Six o'clock. Eighteen hours until noon tomorrow. Fortaleza had already issued a statement announcing that the governor would break his silence tomorrow at a press conference at noon. But Montana knew that nothing that Cruz could say at that time would stop Rigonaldo from hurting, or killing, the First Lady if there was not an announcement that the plebiscite had been cancelled.

Montana lit up his umpteenth cigarette and made half a dozen more phone calls. He requested a list that had been compiled earlier of every single household on the outskirts of Cagüey. The list had over three hundred entries, and they didn't have a resident's name for a third of them. The surveillance teams on Road 89 had found out nothing useful. Could the terrorists be using other routes to move around? The Parks and Forests Department had provided the bureau with aerial pictures of the *Guarite* Forest, *El Cerro La Santa, Guavate, Charco Azul,* and of the whole area of the *Sierra de Cayey.*

The terrorists were somewhere in one of those areas. Montana had eighteen hours to find them.

Chapter 62

Rigonaldo and his pack watched Channel Four's six o'clock newscast in its entirety.

"He chickened out on us," Rigonaldo said of Tonos.

"I think you should give him the pink slip," Oso said, with a grin on his face.

"He's stupid," Teco added.

Luna said, "What if some wackos really did take his wife?"

"Montana is a wacko," Rigonaldo said. "His people have her. Or it wouldn't surprise me if he himself has her stuck in his bedroom closet. They won't do a thing to her. They break the law all the time, but I doubt they will go as far as killing that woman. They kill *independentistas*, but Barbara Tonos is different. She is a pure-bred *burgesa*. She's almost one of them."

Rigonaldo ordered the pack to get their whole cache of weapons and to oil and clean them. He was already planning his next big hit. And his mind was racing with possibilities. A shooting within the Puerto Rican Legislature. Or a bombing at the Hyatt Regency *Cerromar* Hotel in *Dorado*, during the next conference of Southern U.S. Governors to be held there. Or how about a Manson-like killing spree in Garden Hills in *Guaynabo*, or at *Isleta Marina* off the coast of *Fajardo*? And they could set fire to all the boats at the marina. Rigonaldo knew that American targets and their Puerto Rican collaborators were where the money was. All he had to do to hurt the American colonial establishment in Puerto Rico was to follow the money.

The possibilities and expectations for the future were so great and inspiring that Rigonaldo decided to go out to walk in the woods to put his thoughts together. He had already fed the pigs. His other 'inspiration' technique was to walk in the woods.

The sun had already set. The woods were dark but for the shining of the stars and the moon above. He moved slowly through the heavy foliage and underbrush smoking a cigar that had come from that paradise of justice and democracy a couple of hundred miles away – right there in the Caribbean: communist Cuba.

Rigonaldo always thought fondly of Fidel Castro and of all of his accomplishments in Cuba. He liked to think that when he died, he, Rigonaldo Darío Pastrana Montañez, would go into the annals of history as one of the great revolutionaries, like Fidel Castro and Che Guevara. He knew his legacy would be as rich as theirs. Probably even greater because he had fought the great American empire in their last old colonial bastion. Fidel never had to deal with a full-blown American military occupation. Puerto Rico was infected with American military bases. All Fidel had to fight against was a bunch of third-rate *mafiosos* running a couple of casinos in Havana. But Rigonaldo would never tell that to Fidel or to any historian recording his and September Twenty-third's legacy. Let history speak for itself.

Tomorrow, Rigonaldo told himself, he would put a bullet in Ana María Cruz's head right after her husband-governor announced that there would be no plebiscite on Saturday – or never – and therefore no damn statehood victory. To dump her body he wanted something *'poetic'.* He would dump her into *El Río Grande de Loíza*, of course. From them on, that river would be known for more than just that poem by Julia de Burgos.

You see? Rigonaldo was headed right straight into the history books.

Chapter 63

Montana was unable to reach Anabel Rivera on her cell phone. He left her five messages on the cell's voicemail. Calls were made to the administration of Plaza Las Américas, Sears, J.C. Penney, Macy's and to two-thirds of the smaller stores in the mall. Anabel Rivera was paged several times. The call for Assistant Director Montana didn't come until 8:10 p.m., when Walker and Morales were in his office, seated across his desk, scarfing down the last slices of a large pie of Domino's pizza.

"Director Montana?" Mrs. Rivera said in her most official tone. "I've just been made aware that you've been trying to reach me. How can I help you?"

Where the hell have you been? Montana wanted to scream at her, but decided not to.

"Jesus!" Montana exclaimed. "I'm glad you called."

"I apologize. I couldn't call sooner. I was on official business."

Bullshit! Montana said to himself.

"No problem," Montana told her. "What matters is that we are talking now."

"How can I help you?"

"I am personally supervising the investigation of the kidnapping of Ana María Cruz, as you probably know . . ."

"I know. We are all following that terrible situation."

"I need your help in a matter related to this case."

"How is that?"

"We need the phone records for the last few months of an individual who we think may have information about the case."

"Do you have a court order for this?"

"No, we don't. But this is urgent, Mrs. Rivera."

"And who is this person?"

"Samuel Almeda."

"The governor's aide?"

"Yes, ma'am."

"Why don't you ask him? Wouldn't he give them to you? I'm sure he'll . . ."

"Ma'am," Montana interrupted, "Almeda is dead. He was murdered yesterday and we found his body today."

"Oh my God!"

"That's why we need your help."

"Does the governor know about this?"

"That Almeda is dead?"

"No. Does he know that you want his phone records?"

"Absolutely. He is, in fact, awaiting my call to inform him about this matter."

There was a short silence. "Well," Mrs. Rivera said, "I infer that I should help you with this. But I want you to assure me that you will provide me with the necessary court papers as soon as possible. I don't want this to cause unnecessary problems for the company."

"Mrs. Rivera," Montana said quickly, "we will produce any papers you need. That's the least of our problems.

"When do you want to do this?"

"Mrs. Rivera, I have two of my agents here with me and they are awaiting your instructions. We need that information as we speak, meaning now."

Rivera considered this. "Okay," she said. "Let me get in contact with my assistant, and I'll authorize him to go to headquarters and produce the records you need. He's very knowledgeable of the system. It shouldn't take long. I assume you want the information faxed to your agents. What are their names?"

"Ma'am," Montana said firmly, "my agents would like to accompany your assistant to headquarters and be present as he produces the records. We are extremely, extremely pressed for time. I'm sure you understand."

Silence. Then she said, "Fine, I'll tell him to contact you there and coordinate this with you."

"That is perfect, ma'am. But we cannot afford another long wait for a phone call."

"I'm confident he is home right now. Let me call him and he'll call you as soon as I hang up with him."

"Okay. I'm counting on you. What is his name?"

"Luis Alvarez."

"We'll be here."

Rivera hung up.

Montana replaced the receiver in its cradle. "I'll give him fifteen minutes," he told his agents and immediately lit up a cigarette. He leaned back against his chair and yawned. "This may be a long shot," Montana said, nervously glancing at his wrist watch, "but I expect almost anything from that Almeda guy. I even think that he was gay, you know. Young. Living alone. And in Ocean Park! That's where all the queers live!"

Walker raised his eyebrows, shifted uncomfortably in his chair and exchanged a firm glance with Morales. What does being gay have to do with anything here? Walker asked himself. I am gay, he thought of saying, and I don't live in Ocean Park. He kept silent.

"I hear that at night," Montana went on, "there is this huge caravan of cars driving around with men cruising each other from car to car, and men getting blowjobs on the beach. And that goes on around two and three o'clock in the morning, seven days a week. Especially Fridays and Saturdays when the clubs start to empty out. It's hilarious!" He laughed hysterically, visibly amused by his own words.

"Ocean Park is a very good neighborhood, Mr. Montana," Walker said seriously, not a sign of amusement on his face. "And, by the way, the residents there managed to gate a large part of the area."

Walker knew about the cruising in Ocean Park. He himself had done the rounds once or twice. Conservative, right-wing Puerto Rico provided so few outlets for gays to find occasional sex, that any place that had spontaneously surfaced as a cruising spot merited an obligatory visit.

"Oh," Montana said, realizing that his comments had touched a nerve, "I don't mean to say that Ocean Park is not a good neighborhood. I'm just repeating what I've heard."

Walker didn't let go this time. He said, "If Puerto Rico would provide more outlets for people, gay people, to meet safely, there probably wouldn't be a need for such a risky gay cruising area like Ocean Park. A lot of criminals and gay bashers gather on that beach at night to harass, beat and rob the gays that go there. If anything, the local police should provide protection and make the area safe. Or if they want to do the right thing, they should take a trip to the Netherlands and learn how to run a country. And you should also know that I've heard that in every neighborhood where gays become a majority, the quality of life actually improves."

Montana was now somewhat embarrassed by his comments. As a black man who knew racism from personal experience, the last thing he wanted was to be labeled a homophobic bigot. "I'm sorry," he said. "I didn't mean to gay bash. You are right about the quality of life thing in gay neighborhoods. I've read about it."

A short silence fell in the room. Walker and Montana studied each other. Both men were thinking the same thing: we are both members of a minority community; let's show some sensitivity here.

As for agent Morales, he wanted to say – but didn't – Mr. Assistant Director, don't mess with my partner, he's one of the best field agents you've got. Morales knew that Walker was gay, and once in a while Walker had felt free and confident enough to even tell Morales when he found another man attractive. Just like the straight agents did with attractive women.

"The only bad thing about Ocean Park," Montana said to break the silence, "is that when a hurricane hits, the area gets flooded."

Walker said, "I may have to deal with fish swimming in my living room once in a while, but I've sometimes considered buying a house in Ocean Park. I really do like the area." Walker knew the issue was settled.

"Good," Montana said, ready to change subjects. He moved to a small table with a coffee pot on it and poured some coffee into his *I am*

James Bond coffee mug. He sat back behind his desk and said, "This is going to be a long, sleepless night, boys. Get ready."

"We might get lucky tonight," Walker said.

"Lucky is not the word," Montana said seriously. "If we get something from this Almeda guy's records tonight, I'm going to make sure we get *evil*."

The phone rang. The three men glanced at each other. They didn't know why, but something in the air said that this phone call was the case-breaker they had all been waiting for. The mystics probably had a word for the feeling they were experiencing.

"Bill Montana," the director said into the receiver.

"Hello, sir," the male voice said. "This is Luis Alvarez. My boss, Anabel Rivera, told me to call you. She says you need some records from headquarters?"

"Mr. Alvarez," Montana said quickly, "speak to Special Agent Walker. He and Special Agent Morales will be working with you."

Montana handed the phone to Walker.

"Mr. Alvarez?" Walker said.

"Yes."

"Special Agent Walker. Where can we meet you?"

Alvarez didn't respond immediately. Perhaps he was a little intimidated about meeting with the FBI, Walker thought. And that simple 'yes' had revealed the voice of a young man. Twenty-five, twenty-six maybe. This is going to be fun, Walker told himself. I'm thirty-three, single *and looking*.

"Uhhh . . ." Alvarez said shyly. "Just meet me in front of the Horizon building. Do you know where it is?"

"Sure do," Walker said. "1700 Roosevelt Avenue."

"That's it . . . sir."

"How soon can you be there?" Walker asked.

"Thirty minutes? Is that okay?"

"That's close to perfect, Mr. Alvarez."

Walker thought of asking the young man what he was going to be wearing, but giggled at the idea of sounding like one did when setting up a blind date off the internet with a guy that hadn't sent an online picture.

"I'll be wearing a white polo shirt and khaki trousers," Alvarez volunteered. "My car is a white Honda Civic sedan."

Was the fact that he said what he was wearing a sign of something? Walker thought. There was something about this guy that Walker already liked.

"Good," Walker said. "We'll all be there at a little after nine. I don't think we'll have trouble finding each other." In fact, Walker told himself, that area and that building especially are fairly deserted at this time of night.

"Okay," Alvarez said. "See you in thirty minutes."

Walker hung up. He and Morales quickly got up to leave.

Montana said, "You call me as soon as you got something."

"We'll do," Walker said, realizing that the Assistant Director didn't say 'if' you got something.

"Got it," Walker said.

Morales nodded.

As the agents went to the door Montana said, "Make me happy."

With that, Walker and Morales were gone.

The longest night of their lives had just started.

Chapter 64

At 9 p.m., all the major TV networks on the island went on live with special programming dealing with Saturday's plebiscite, and with the kidnappings of Barbara Tonos and Ana María Cruz. Every TV station broadcasted the highlights of several massive rallies held earlier by the Statehood, Commonwealth and Independence parties. These massive rallies, attracting hundreds of thousands of people, had been organized in every major city in the north, south, east and west parts of the island. Political tensions were at the highest level ever. Many incidents between rivaling supporters of the three parties had been reported to the police. Several arrests had been made in the most violent confrontations. Angry mobs of opposing parties had thrown rocks at each other and had used their flags as weapons against anyone standing in their way: women, children and even party loyalist grandmothers.

On Channel Four, Karen Pérez was the host of *"Countdown to the Vote."* The show would last until after midnight and it would feature all previous reports about the kidnappings, live chats with calls from the audience, and experts' analyses of the latest polls on voters' inclinations.

Since the kidnappings had grabbed the headlines, support for statehood had plummeted. The sentiment on the street was that a statehood victory in the plebiscite would bring an unending bloodbath of political violence from left-wing extremists.

The Statehood party was getting a persistent beating in the press and over the airwaves. Both the Independence and Commonweatlh parties were exploiting the people's fears about what was to come if the country opted for statehood in the plebiscite.

Karen's show included an expectedly heated debate between three of the most articulate 'spinners' of the three rival parties. But the bulk of her show was mostly about the most sensational and dramatic developments in the kidnappings of Barbara Tonos and Ana María Cruz.

The country was frantic. That gave endless opportunities for drama and good television.

Chapter 65

Walker and Morales greeted Luis Alvarez in front of the Horizon Communications building. Walker was not disappointed by the young man's looks. He was young, no more than twenty-six. His skin looked soft and light. His hair was black, cut short and combed to the back, with a little gel to keep it perfectly in place. A tall, slender body with a few hairs on his arms promised a hairless chest and buttocks, Walker thought. He wore thin prescription glasses that for Walker added to the man's sensual appeal.

After Morales introduced himself, Walker shook Alvarez's hand for a little longer than needed and said, "I'm Agent Walker, but you can call me John."

"And I guess you guys can call me Luis," Alvarez said in return.

"Okay, Luis," Walker said. "Let's do this."

"Follow me," Luis told them.

The agents followed the young man through a set of glass, sliding doors and entered a large lobby where a very alert security guard asked for their ID's. Luis Alvarez flashed his company-issued ID and said, pointing to the agents, "They are with me."

"And who are they?" the guard asked properly.

Walker and Morales pulled out their ID's and put them close to the man's face. "We are with the FBI," Walker said. "Mrs. Anabel Rivera has authorized this visit."

The guard was visibly impressed. He carefully inspected the identifications and said, "Oh, as long as you are with Alvarez, I don't need to hear from Mrs. Rivera." He produced a large notebook. "I just need the three of you to sign in here and you are clear to go up."

The three men signed the book and thanked the guard for his cooperation. They then moved to the elevators. Luis used a key to open the doors and another key to choose a floor that had restricted access. He pressed the button to the twelfth floor and glanced at both agents as the elevator made the trip up.

When the door opened on the twelfth floor the three men walked into a large and extremely elegant waiting area with an oak desk for a receptionist who, of course, at this time, almost 9:30 p.m., wasn't there. Walker thought about how nice it would be to have sex with Luis Alvarez alone on this floor.

Luis Alvarez led the men through a dimly lit corridor to their right and stopped at a door that had a bronze plaque that read: Luis Alvarez García-Executive Assistant. He used a plastic card similar to a credit card and inserted it into a slot next to a bronze door knob. A tiny green light went on and the door opened. Luis Alvarez entered his office and immediately went to his desk and turned on a green banker's desk lamp. He moved to another corner and turned on a second lamp.

The office was large and handsomely furnished. The walls were adorned with framed posters of several graphic arts exhibitions in San Juan and Hato Rey. And there were several well-positioned natural plants that gave the room a refreshing scent. His desk was wide, meticulously organized and impeccably clean, and shiny from a recent waxing. A Dell computer keyboard and monitor sat on the right edge. The printer was on top of another table farther away.

"You can have a seat," Luis said, pointing to two mahogany chairs across from his desk. He sat on a leather swivel chair behind his desk.

Neither Walker nor Morales sat down. Walker said, "Actually, Luis, if you don't mind, we'd like to sit behind you and watch you produce the records we need."

Luis said, "Fine, just let me get my computer going first. In here we are very cautious with our passwords and I don't think my boss would be easy on me if the FBI walks out of here with it." He smiled gently.

Beautiful smile, beautiful arms, beautiful neck, beautiful hazel eyes. That is what was on Walker's mind as he looked at this gentle and polite young professional. "Of course," Walker said.

Luis swiveled around to his keyboard and did what was needed to get the computer logged on. He kept looking at Walker . . . John . . . because he had noticed that this attractive special agent of the FBI was also looking at him closely. His friends would die, Luis thought, if he got to go on a date with a real-life FBI guy.

Welcome to Horizon Communications Puerto Rico, the computerized voice said through the speakers.

"We are ready, gentlemen," Luis said with a smile.

Walker and Morales moved the chairs and sat behind Luis.

"Okay, what do you need?" Luis asked.

"We want to see the call records for a guy named Samuel Almeda," Walker said. "We are mostly interested in his island-wide long distance."

"What's his phone number?" Luis asked.

Walker recited the number upon taking a quick glance at the phone bill he had found in Almeda's home.

Luis punched in the number, clicked some features with the mouse and waited a few seconds.

Almeda's page appeared on the screen. Walker noticed a "1-A" on the screen right beside Almeda's name.

"What does this '1-A' by his name mean?" Walker asked.

"It means that this is a VIP account," Luis explained. "The customer gets credit, plus special privileges on long distance and in billing. For which month do you want his long distance record?"

"Let's start with the most recent," Walker said. "But we'll eventually want at least six or seven months back."

Luis clicked the mouse, hit enter, and in a matter of seconds Almeda's island-wide long distance history was on the screen.

Both Walker and Morales almost jumped from their seats when they saw the calls. There were several calls to a 247-6001. Two-four-seven was the exchange for the Cagüey area. Some of the calls were as long as 25 minutes. Several were less than 60 seconds. On these calls there was a 'CH-1A' next to them.

"What does that mean?" Walker asked, pointing at the screen.

Luis said, "As I said, this is a VIP customer. The 'CH-1A' means he will not be charged for calls where he doesn't stay on longer than sixty seconds. A regular customer would get charged for the whole minute even if the call was less than sixty seconds."

Walker said, "Could you print that out for me?"

"Sure," Luis said immediately, and then clicked on the print icon.

Walker nodded to Morales to take care of the printouts.

The printer was fast and in a matter of seconds it produced all of the needed pages.

"Okay," Luis said, "what do you want now?"

I want you, Walker thought.

"Give me a printout of each of his phone bills, the whole record, for the last six months," Walker said. "Will that take long?"

"Not at all," Luis said casually. "You don't want to see them on the screen first?"

"No. I just want Steven here to start going through them while you and I do other things."

Luis used the mouse and punched some keys and soon the pages began flowing into the printer's tray. Morales moved to the printer and quickly began to pick up the pages and study them.

Walker studied Luis.

Luis studied Walker.

"How long have you been an FBI agent?" Luis asked him.

"About seven years."

"You look young."

"I am. How old are you?"

"Twenty-six."

"I'm thirty-three."

Luis was silent for a moment. Then he said, "You look . . . good."

"You too, Luis," Walker said softly. "Where do you live?"

"Close to here," Luis said. "Baldrich."

"Do you live alone?"

"Uhh . . . yes."

"Good," Walker said, smiling. "I live alone too."

"Where do you live?"

"Close to here. *San Patricio*. I have an apartment in the Bel Air condo."

"That's a nice area. And I've seen that building."

"Good. You can come and visit sometime."

Luis was suddenly shy. Walker thought maybe he had said it too bluntly.

"That would be . . . nice," Luis said. "Do you mind if I smoke?"

"Hell no," Walker said quickly. "This is your office."

"Just don't tell my boss," Luis said as he pulled out a pack of Newports from his trousers. "We are not supposed to smoke within the building."

"I don't even know your boss."

"Good."

Luis pulled out a clean ashtray from one of the drawers in his desk and began to smoke his cigarette.

Walker kept looking at Luis's face and neck. He imagined himself kissing him all over.

His imagination was brusquely shattered by Morales who said, "Hey, Casanova, this is finished."

Walker went back to work. "Okay, Luis," he said. "Now I want you to look into the records of another client. All I have is the phone number."

"That's fine," Luis said softly. "What's the number?"

"247-6001."

"That's a number on the record I just printed."

"Yes. Let's find out who is the customer."

Luis minimized the window with Almeda's records and typed in the new number. He pressed enter several times after punching in some keys on his keyboard. A page came on the screen: LUNA RAMIREZ TOLEDO///PO BOX 682, CAGÜEY, PUERTO RICO, 00675.

Walker glanced at the screen. Morales did the same.

"Ah-ha," Morales said.

"Do you know her?" Walker asked him.

"Sure," Morales said. "She's supposed to have been P.R.R.A. a long time ago; allegedly for a very short while. And she made a couple of trips to Cuba. That's how she got to be in our files. But I think they sent her to the inactives after a while."

"Why?" Walker asked impatiently.

"We'll have to find out."

"What's P.R.R.A.?" Luis asked.

The agents looked at him. Walker didn't want to tell him about the Puerto Rican Revolutionary Army. The less he knew about what they were doing the better.

"People's Radical Republic of Argentina," Walker said and laughed softly.

Luis got the message that perhaps he shouldn't be asking the questions.

"No, Luis," Walker said. "That's just a code we have for some people." He returned his attention to the computer's screen. "This client shows a PO Box as an address . . ."

"That is the billing address," Luis said quickly. "It happens a lot in the countryside."

"Is there a way to see the physical address of this customer?"

"Sure, but to do that I have to exit the billing records and go to another page. You don't want this printed?"

"Yes, I do."

"Okay. How far back do you want these records?"

"Give me six months," Walker said, knowing that eventually they would get all of the records for this account.

As the printer began to produce the pages, Luis minimized the window and looked for the page with the physical address for the client. As he typed, used the mouse and pressed enter several times, Walker and Morales came very close behind him, their eyes fixed on the computer screen. In a few seconds, they had an address:

LUNA RAMIREZ TOLEDO///ACCOUNT NUMBER: 247-6001///BILLING: PO BOX 682, CAGÜEY, P.R. 00675///UNIT: 105, 18.1 KILOMETER, ROAD 89, CAGÜEY, P.R., 00675///

"Unit is where the actual telephone is located," Luis explained.

"I see that," Walker said calmly. He was purposely containing his excitement so as not to bring particular attention to Luna's address in Cagüey. "Could you print that out for me?"

"Sure."

Luis sent the page to the printer. Luna's billing records were still flowing into the tray; Morales was now collecting them.

"You've been a great help, Luis," Walker told the young man.

"My pleasure," Luis said.

Walker didn't say much more. His thoughts were now set on the fact that they had a physical address in Cagüey. Could this be it? Could they possibly get this lucky? What if this Luna woman was just Almeda's contact person and Rigonaldo is at another address with the First Lady?

Morales called to him as he collected the last page of Luna's billing records. Walker came close to his partner, away from Luis.

Morales said, "Just a wild thought."

"What is it?" Walker asked.

"Besides the planets in our solar system, what is the closest thing to the *Luna* (the moon)?"

"I can't think of shit like that right now." Walker said.

"*Las estrellas!* (The stars)"

"Estrella. I see what you mean. This could be her, but I'll fill you in on what's on my mind when we get to the car."

Luna's page with the Cagüey address fell into Morales's hand. The agents were ready to go.

"Luis," Walker said, "close all of those files up. We are done for now."

Luis did as told. "Let me give you a folder for those," he told Morales, who was holding all the printed records.

Luis got a glossy green folder from his desk and gave it to Morales.

"Thank you," Morales said, placing the records inside the folder.

"I'll have to let you out," Luis said. "Just wait a second while I shut down my computer."

"Sure," Walker told him.

As Luis was shutting down his computer, Walker moved to a corner of the office and called Montana on his cell phone.

"Montana," the Assistant Director said.

"Boss, it's Walker. Listen, we've got a name and an address in Cagüey. Get everything we have on a subject named Luna Ramírez Toledo. She lives right on Road 89. Here is the exact address."

Walker recited Luna's address. Montana was pleased.

"You two get here as fast as you can," Montana said and hung up.

Luis finished up with his computer, turned off the lights in his office and escorted the two agents out of the building. Morales went to their car. Walker followed Luis to his Honda.

"Here, Luis," Walker said, pulling out a business card. "Here is my number at work. My home number is on the back."

Luis was excited and a bit surprised. "Wow, thank you."

"Give me a call in a couple of days," Walker told him. "Maybe we can go out for coffee or something."

"I'd love that," Luis said softly.

"Me too. Call me."

With that, Walker walked hurriedly to his car and sped away with no time to look back. After all this mess with the First Lady was solved, though, John Walker wanted to have some sense of normalcy in his life. This young man he'd just met could bring some of that to him.

Chapter 66

The only photo that the FBI had of Luna Ramírez Toledo was from a *Grito de Lares* celebration on September 23, 1988. She was nineteen years old at the time. Today she was forty-one. The last entry in her file was from September 1999. The agent in charge, Alan Smith, had closed the file on her because, for the previous five years, Luna had been working as a tutor in a poor rural school in Costa Rica with no ties to any leftist groups either there or in Puerto Rico. The activities that brought her under surveillance had been limited: attendance at several meetings of the clandestine Puerto Rican Revolutionary Army, and two trips to Cuba with a youth brigade. All of this between 1988 and 1993. Agent Smith lost track of her for a year until he got a report that Luna was in Costa Rica. The Costa Rican police cooperated with the bureau on keeping track of her activities there. Everything was legitimate and Luna did not keep any contact with left-wing individuals or organizations either there or in Puerto Rico. Agent Smith dismissed her as a "young idealist that flirted with politics" in her late teens and early twenties. There was no record of when Luna left Costa Rica, no record of where she went from there or when she returned to Puerto Rico. Since 1999, Luna Ramírez Toledo had not surfaced anywhere.

Until now.

"She is involved," Montana said to Walker and Morales who were back in his office. "More likely than not she is the mysterious 'Estrella.' More likely than not her house on Road 89 is their hideout. And, more likely than not that's where Rigonaldo is, and that is where the First Lady is being held."

"What if she was just Almeda's contact and they are all hiding somewhere else in the same area?" Walker said.

"That's why we are not storming into that house as we speak," Montana told him. "I have two teams working on the maps and putting together all of our information from the road tests we've done. I expect everything to fit into place. I think that that house is *our* house. Tonight we are doing a stakeout. Tomorrow morning they'll get the wake-up call from hell."

"Are we in this alone?" Morales asked.

"No," Montana responded. "Calero has committed five SWAT teams to surround the house tonight, together with our people. But we'll be the first ones in, once we decide to go inside. We are in charge of the operation. Calero is using his people from that area. They know the mountains, they know the forest, and they know the area better than our people. So we work with the locals to get what we want. Any more questions?"

Both Walker and Morales shook their heads no.

"Good," Montana said. "You two go and make sure our teams are on the same page. I have to call the governor. We'll all meet in the auditorium in ninety minutes."

"Yes, sir," both agents said in unison.

Friday, November 2

Chapter 67

A little after twelve midnight, William Montana presided over a packed auditorium in the basement of FBI headquarters.

A hundred fifty agents – all in bulletproof vests and weapons in hand – now stared at three huge digital monitors displaying maps of the Cagüey area, an exact sketch of the location of Luna's house, and a sketch of the inside and outside of the house as it had been described by Tonio the cameraman. The screens changed as the director recited instructions.

Special instructions were given to the "Group of 40", the elite unit who would actually undertake the assault on the house. Within the hour, these agents would leave headquarters to Cagüey in several nondescript vans with black-tinted windows. They were to meet Calero's SWAT teams on Highway 52 and drive to the outskirts of the Guarite Forest. Once there, they would split into two teams and make their way on foot from the north and from the south, across the woods and through the heavy underbrush with the help of night vision googles.

Their instructions were to wait until sunrise to get a clear profile of the structure and compare it to what they knew the house should look like. They were expected to spot the house's residents, especially Rigonaldo Pastrana, before going in. That was to be their unequivocal assurance that they were storming into the actual hideout of September Twenty-third. Montana had gotten a search warrant to go into the house from a very cooperative and alert judge from the Federal District Court of Puerto Rico.

The Group of 40 would communicate through high frequency radios. The unit leader was a middle-aged, twenty-year veteran of the bureau named Rolando Tavares. The first priority of the operation was to rescue the First Lady alive and unharmed. The second priority was to arrest, once and for all, Rigonaldo Pastrana and his gang of criminals.

William Montana would fly to the scene by helicopter a few minutes before the assault was to begin. He was conscious that the terrorists could have collaborators in the vicinity that could alert them of excessive police activity in the area. But Montana, along with a medical helicopter, would be in the air right above the terrorists' hideout during the assault operation.

By the time the assault was taking place, the rest of Montana's agents and Calero's officers were to ensure that the town of Cagüey, Road 89, and the Guarite Forest were areas under a state of siege.

And to ensure the success of the operation, Governor Cruz had committed a hundred reservists from the Puerto Rico National Guard to be on stand by in five military choppers from the Guard's Salinas Training Center.

To Rigonaldo Pastrana, this night would seem as if the very gates of hell had opened up on him.

Chapter 68

This was another night in the forest. Or was it?

A dog was furiously barking somewhere in the depths of the night. Another one was howling like a wolf.

Rigonaldo opened his eyes and glanced at the red numbers of a small digital alarm clock by his bed. It was 4:15 in the morning. Already Friday. His Friday of death . . . and victory.

An AK-47 was readily accessible by his side. He slept alone in the largest room of the house, in the company of his weapons. He switched on a small lamp that sat on top of a three-drawer dresser by his bed and searched for a cigar. He found it with no difficulty and lit it. He blew the smoke into the air as his eyes stared at the wooden ceiling. But on this night, his eyes were staring at the unending possibilities on his horizon. The ones he had created with damn hard work.

That woman was blindfolded and tied up in his darkest dungeon. But not for too long. Soon, when the light of day could be a witness, she would wash up in the waters of *El Rio Grande de Loíza*. It would shock the country. It would defeat Cruz. This day was his meeting with destiny, he thought. What a silly cliché for such an important man as himself. He smiled. Alone in his bedroom.

He had shaken and shattered this country of worms. He had defied the great American empire. Who had christened the United States "the Great Satan?" The Iranians? The Iraqis? The Libyans? He couldn't remember. And it didn't really matter.

Staring at the ceiling he began to recite "History Will Absolve Me," that timeless piece of revolutionary defiance that Fidel Castro Ruz had immortalized. Rigonaldo knew the speech word for word. And he knew that someday he would stand side by side with Fidel, saluting the troops of Puerto Rican revolutionaries marching through the streets of the *New San Juan* in communist Puerto Rico.

Havana. San Juan. Pyongyang. The last three bastions of true communism in the world. An axis of revolutionary resistance. September Twenty-third would become "*El Partido Nacional de los Heroes de Septiembre 23.*" (The National Party of the Heroes of September 23.) And September Twenty-third would rule the country with an iron fist.

Oh, the future. Such grandiosity. Such opportunities. Exporting revolutions to Port-au-Prince, Kingston, Santo Domingo, Grenada, Trinidad, Martinique. No end. The whole Caribbean: one great region of revolutionary pride and struggle. And Rigonaldo, like an old warrior suspended in time, holding on to the long gone Cold War, had once predicted that the day would come when the Russians would once again come to their senses and resuscitate the U.S.S.R.

Rigonaldo kept smoking his cigar, lying on his bed and staring at the ceiling.

That dog barking.

That dog howling like a wolf.

A knock on his door.

Oso.

"Rigonaldo," Oso said softly. "I'm going to take a look outside."

Rigonaldo didn't answer. His door was now ajar. He just stared at Oso's face in the dark hallway.

Oso closed the door again.

Chapter 69

"**O**kay, we have movement in the house. The light on the front porch just came on and a subject is coming out the door . . . It's a male."

Rolando Tavares's voice was heard by close to two hundred police and FBI agents that were now surrounding the house in a perfect circle at a distance of approximately one hundred feet.

Oso did not hear the clicking of the still cameras aimed at him, nor the hissing of the video cameras that were recording his entrance into the chill of the night. He lit a cigarette and stood still on the porch, listening to the dogs. They seemed to be far away and close at the same time.

"Somebody shut up those dogs!" Tavares ordered through the radio. "Shut up those dogs!"

"10-4," someone replied.

Oso smoked his cigarette, totally oblivious to the battery of law enforcement men and women whose eyes were set on him.

The Group of 40 had identified a wooden shack for animals at the back of the house. And next to the door that led to the rear, a set of plywood sheets obstructed what had been a window. According to the information they had, this was most likely the window of the room where the First Lady was being held.

The sky was clear tonight. The air was cold. Millions of stars shined above the forest. And the forest was still. Silent. A willing accomplice to the siege.

In the distance, the dog stopped barking. Then, the howling stopped also.

Oso smoked two more cigarettes and went back into the house. A few seconds later, the light on the front porch went off again. Once more the house merged with the darkness of the night, illuminated only by the light from the sky that filtered through the thick leaves of the trees around it.

But the house in the forest was no longer the thief hidden from all. Four hundred eyes had now discovered it.

Chapter 70

Oso went back into the room he shared with Teco. Teco was asleep and had not been disturbed by the dogs' barking and howling.

So was Luna, sleeping soundly in her room.

Oso fell asleep again as he caressed a Winchester rifle that rested on his chest.

Rigonaldo moved out of his room and walked through the house without turning on lights. He carefully crossed the living room and the hallway that led to his prisoner's room.

When he entered the dungeon he flicked a lighter. The woman's head was resting above her breasts. The blindfold was in place. The ropes that kept her tied to the chair were intact. And outside, dead silence had returned to the night.

Rigonaldo put out the lighter and came close to the woman. Very close. He extended his arm and caressed her breasts with his hand. They were wet. And she was asleep. Dead asleep. He moved his hand over her breasts until his erection softened. A sign of old age.

What would Cruz say if I fuck his wife? Rigonaldo asked himself.

He smiled at the possibility. Maybe later in the morning, he thought, before I put a bullet in her head.

Walking in the darkness, Rigonaldo went back to his room. He lit another cigar, laid down on his bed and closed his eyes. But he had no intention of sleeping again. His Friday of death and victory had already begun.

Chapter 71

Ana María Cruz was not asleep. She had faked it when she heard the door to her room open. She sensed the presence of the monster by the thick smell of cigar and of raw, old sweat. And he touched her. Again. She felt his rough hands all over her breasts. She resisted the impulse to bite off his hand; to rip off one of his fingers with her teeth. But if she did that, he would hit her. Just like he had done before. She let her head collapse and hoped that the monster would leave her soon. He did.

The dogs in the distance had stopped barking and howling. She wanted to scream. She was afraid to sleep. Each time she did, nightmares haunted her. And she had lost track of how many days she had been a prisoner. Neither could she remember the last time that she had seen the light of day. They had kept her blindfolded forever, it seemed. She was enduring a long, endless night. Always dark. No light. Only darkness. And she was hungry. They hadn't fed her for days. Why hadn't they? Were they trying to starve her to death? Oh God! Oh God!

Chapter 72

6:30 a.m.

The sun had come up.

Luna was in the kitchen making coffee and breakfast for the men. Oso sat in front of the television surfing channels. Rigonaldo came out of his room, shirtless and shoeless, wearing only long trousers with a cigar in his hand. He ordered Teco to go to Cagüey to buy the day's newspapers.

Teco grabbed the keys to a Toyota pickup and went out of the house. He walked through muddy soil, and with a single push, opened the metal door to the garage.

The FBI agents and the police SWAT teams hidden in the forest could now see several vehicles, including a white van riddled with bullet holes and a shattered glass window – certainly the vehicle used in the shooting of the federal agents on Road 89.

Unit leader Tavares relayed that information to William Montana who was now boarding a helicopter in the parking lot of the Cagüey police precinct. The information was also relayed to Superintendent Calero. He was stationed on Road 89, off the entrance to the dirt road that led to Luna's house, waiting there with one of his SWAT teams.

"What do we do with the subject?" someone asked through the radio.

"Let's wait," Tavares responded. "See what he does."

Teco boarded the pickup, backed out of the garage and drove onto the dirt road.

"Team one!" Tavares alerted. "Subject, male, going your way in red pickup."

"10-4," someone replied.

"Try to get him without firing a shot," Tavares warned.

Calero said, "We'll arrest him at the end of the road."

Rigonaldo went to the back door and pushed it open. He stood there in the open doorway, facing the rear yard, calmly puffing on his cigar and caressing his bare chest.

"Team alert! Team alert!" someone said over the radio. "We got Pastrana in the back of the house! Easy target."

"Don't shoot him!" Tavares ordered. "We want him alive!"

Montana heard the astonishing news, flying in his chopper. "We got them!" he said. "Team 40, you are clear to go in!"

Teco was now nearing the end of the dirt road, gravel dust flying into the air, when he ran into a full police blockade. "Fucking shit!" he exclaimed, shocked. He stomped on the brakes and put the car in reverse, just as an avalanche of police officers and FBI agents came out of the bushes on either side of him.

"Get out of the vehicle!" he was ordered, two dozens rifles aimed at him.

Teco attacked the accelerator, speeding in reverse, using one hand to control the wheel and the other to pull a Magnum .357 out from the dashboard. The car backed up at high speed, but he lost control of it and furiously fell into a ditch. He hit his head against the steering wheel, cursed, extended his arm out the window and began shooting.

In a second, the windshield exploded in his face, shattered by a round of sharp gunfire.

Rigonaldo turned away from the back door, quickly throwing his cigar into the mud. Luna dropped the egg pan on the floor, rapidly coming into the living room. "What was that?" she asked, her eyes wide open, a strong chill flowing through her body.

Rigonaldo and Oso were on their feet, running for their weapons.

Luna looked out the front door and froze. An avalanche of police were now running towards the house.

"Police!" she yelled. "Police outside!"

In a quick move, Rigonaldo threw a handgun at her. She caught it in her hands. "Kill the prisoner!" he ordered. "Shoot the woman! Shoot her! Shoot her! Quick!"

Luna ran towards Ana María's room, her gun ready, but she didn't make it in time. Police or FBI – or whoever – were now at the back door.

"Put the gun down!" someone shouted at her.

Luna fired at them and hid in another room in the hallway. The assault team returned fire. The scene was total mayhem with Luna shooting at the agents advancing through the back door, and Oso and Rigonaldo shooting at the agents coming through the front.

"I'm in here! I'm in here!" The frantic screams of Ana María Cruz could barely be heard amidst the sound of gunfire.

Montana's helicopter was now flying over the house as he, along with agents Walker and Morales, looked at the impressive display of police and federal agents engaged in a fierce gun battle down below.

A dozen police cruisers, led by Calero, were now driving up the dirt road towards the house. Teco had been shot in the head and now lay dead in his car.

A caravan of ambulances was rapidly moving up Road 89. The medical helicopter was now above the house, waiting for instructions as to when and where to pick up the First Lady.

Two agents had reached the door of the room from where they heard the First Lady's screams, and used a sledge hammer to break it open.

Through the radio, as if he had eyes inside the house, came the voice of William Montana: "Get the First Lady out of there! Get her out NOW!"

Montana's pilot glanced out into the distance and yelled, "We have a chopper coming our way!" He knew it couldn't be a National Guard chopper. They hadn't been called yet.

"What?" Montana yelled.

"A chopper is coming our way," the pilot repeated, as he used a pair of binoculars to get a clear, closer look.

"It's a fucking press chopper!" he yelled. "Channel Four!"

"Karen Pérez!" Walker yelled. "It has to be her!"

"How the fuck did she find out about this?" Montana cursed, but returned his attention to the siege on the ground.

Now Karen's chopper was also above the house with Tonio videotaping the whole scene.

"You are looking at live pictures of an assault on Rigonaldo Pastrana's hideout!" Karen yelled to her live audience.

"Should we order her to leave?" Montana's pilot asked.

"Forget about her!" Montana barked.

Ana María's rescuers took off her blindfold and used sharp hunting knives to cut the ropes on her arms, body and legs.

"We are getting you out of here, Mrs. Cruz," an agent told her. "Can you run?"

Ana María was suddenly struck with a rush of strength and adrenaline. The agents helped her to her feet and the three of them ran out of the dungeon. On their way out, they were covered by half a dozen agents now inside the house shooting at Luna who was now firing rounds with a powerful automatic rifle. Within a minute, the rescuers and the First Lady stormed out of the house and into the mud in the rear yard.

"First Lady is outside!" someone yelled over the radio. "First Lady is outside!"

"Yes!" Montana exclaimed, a sense of relief overpowering him. "Get her out of here! Put her in the chopper!"

The paramedics in the medical helicopter lowered a cable with a seat on the end of it, and the agents helped secure the First Lady into it. A mechanical wheel slowly began to bring her up.

"Ladies and gentlemen," Karen yelled into her microphone as Tonio taped the episode, "the First Lady is being brought up into a medical helicopter! She seems to be alert. These are dramatic pictures that we are bringing to you live, exclusively here on Channel Four. Down below a fierce gun battle continues . . . We have yet to see Rigonaldo Pastrana or any of his people emerge from the house. All is happening at once. As you can see, SWAT teams and FBI agents have completely surrounded the house, some of them are inside and the fighting continues . . ."

Ana María reached the chopper's cabin and was immediately brought in. The helicopter fled the scene at high speed.

"Tavares," Montana yelled over the radio, "get our men out of there. Hit the house with tear gas from all sides." The director wanted to avoid casualties on their crew.

"Team 40," Tavares ordered, "exit the house now. We are hitting them with tear gas."

Shooting as they backed away, the agents that had entered the house moved back outside. Luna, Oso and Rigonaldo were temporarily confused. But in a matter of seconds they understood. The glass windows on all sides of the house shattered as tear gas canisters began to flow inside. The house was quickly enveloped in thick white smoke.

Luna was the first to come out, coughing furiously, her eyes red and drowned in tears.

"Get on the ground!" she was ordered. "Get on the fucking ground!"

She collapsed in the dirt, coughing, choking.

Oso was next. His eyes were red and teary and he felt like vomiting. He came out of the house with his hands raised and yelled, "Don't shoot me!"

Over three dozen rifles were aimed at him.

"Get on the fucking ground, you scumbag piece of shit!" someone yelled at him. "And put your hands over your head."

Oso dropped to the ground and did as he was told.

A full minute passed and yet there was no sign of Rigonaldo Pastrana.

Superintendent Calero, his cruiser now parked a few feet from the house, grabbed his car's megaphone and spoke firmly.

"Pastrana, get out of the house!" Calero said, his voice reverberating through the forest. "You are completely surrounded. There is no way to escape. Get out of the house now with your hands above your head."

Rigonaldo responded with a round of machine gunfire as he pressed a batch of wet towels against his nose and mouth.

Calero and the others hid behind their vehicles and shot a few more canisters of tear gas into the house.

Rigonaldo stopped shooting.

Calero once again ordered Rigonaldo to come out of the house, but this time there was no response.

As they waited, Montana's chopper landed in a clearing near the house. Walker and Morales followed him to Calero's cruiser.

"The motherfucker is holed up inside," Calero told Montana. "He can't go anywhere. The house is completely surrounded."

Montana was not going to wait for anything.

"We are going in," he said.

Montana spoke briefly with Tavares who quickly gathered a team to enter the house. The area had suddenly turned eerily silent, except for the noise of Karen's helicopter suspended above.

Tavares's team put on gas masks and carefully approached the house. Fifteen men and five women went in.

Montana waited. The fact that there was no sound coming from the house, no voices, no gunfire, nothing, made him nervous.

Calero waited. He was sure they were going to end up shooting Rigonaldo to death.

Karen Pérez waited. She wasn't sure what they were doing down below. Tonio kept shooting video of the scene, getting a good shot of the man and the woman sprawled on the ground with their hands over their heads.

Five nerve-racking minutes came and went. Tavares came out, a worried look on his face.

"He's not in there!" he yelled as he approached Montana and Calero. "The house is empty!"

"What?" Calero asked in disbelief.

Montana glanced at Walker and Morales.

"There is no way he's not in there," Walker said.

Montana wasn't so sure. He looked at the sky. "Get that press chopper out of here," he ordered.

Walker knew something was coming. He grabbed Calero's megaphone and said, "Hey! You in the chopper. This is the FBI. You are ordered to leave the area immediately. Leave the area immediately. This is police business."

Neither Karen nor Tonio clearly understood Walker's words. The pilot did.

"They are ordering us to leave the area," he said.

"I didn't hear that," Karen said.

A few shots came from below. The pilot looked down.

"They just shot overhead!" he screamed.

"That I heard," Karen said. "Let's get out of here."

The pilot fled the area.

Now that there were no witnesses in the sky, Montana walked to the man that lay on the ground with his hands over his head.

"You," Montana told him. "Turn around. Face me."

Oso did as he was told.

"Okay," Montana said, looking straight into his eyes. "Where is he?"

Oso gave him a bitter look and said nothing.

"I'm talking to you," Montana said, kicking him on his ribs. "Where is Pastrana?"

"I don't know!" Oso barked.

Montana pulled out a handgun from his chest belt. Oso looked at the gun, puzzled.

"Listen, asshole," Montana said calmly. "You are going to tell me where Pastrana is, or I will put a bullet in your leg that will leave you limping for years."

"Fuck you!" Oso snapped.

Montana aimed his gun and fired a single shot into Oso's right leg. Oso screamed like a wounded animal, his body contorting in pain.

As Oso moaned in pain, Montana asked the question again, "Tell me, where is Pastrana?"

"Oh, God," Oso screamed. "You shot me. You fucking shot me."

Montana said, "I'm going to shoot your other leg if you don't tell me where Pastrana is. And if you still don't tell me where he is, I'm going to blow your dick off. It won't be pretty."

Oso held his leg, trying to ease the intense pain. Montana put his foot over Oso's bullet wound and pressed hard against it. Oso screamed.

"Where is Pastrana?" Montana yelled back.

Oso saw in disbelief that Montana was now aiming his gun at his left leg.

Montana said, "One . . . Two . . ."

"A tunnel!" Oso yelled. "There is a tunnel."

"That's what I thought," Montana said, still aiming his gun at Oso's left leg. "Where is the entrance and where does it lead to?"

Oso coughed furiously. Then he said, "If . . . if . . . I . . . I tell you . . . can I cut a deal?"

Luna was dumbfounded at Oso's cowardice.

Montana, Calero and all the police and FBI agents surrounding Oso almost wanted to laugh.

Montana said, "Listen, piece of shit, you'll be lucky if I don't kill you right at this very moment." His eyes screamed that he meant what he had just said. "Where is the entrance to this tunnel and where does it lead to?"

Oso kept glancing at the gun aimed at him. He was sure that this man was crazy enough to shoot him again. He said, "The entrance is by the side of his bed in the largest room . . . where he sleeps . . . It . . . it leads to Squirrel's Creek."

Montana glanced at the local men that Calero had on his team.

"I know where it is," one of them said.

"Where in the creek?" Montana asked Oso.

Oso didn't speak immediately. He was tightly holding his wounded leg. Montana kicked him in the wound.

"Ahhhh!" Oso screamed. "God damn! There . . . there are three huge damn rocks. Three huge rocks . . . The exit is right there."

"I know the place," the local man said.

"Okay," Montana said, glancing at Oso and Luna, "get these two scumbags out of here."

A team of agents quickly handcuffed both of them and led them into an FBI van.

Squirrel's Creek, Montana learned, was ten minutes away on foot. He nervously calculated that probably enough time had elapsed for Rigonaldo to have reached the exit of his hidden tunnel.

There is no way, Montana told himself, that Pastrana will escape. It simply will not happen.

Chapter 73

Rigonaldo had crawled through mud, water and rats. Dozens of them. He reached the end of his escape tunnel and was not surprised to find no one there waiting for him. But he knew that he had to move fast. He knew that either Oso or Luna would give him away under the brutal questioning that his disappearing act would precipitate.

He pushed the dry leaves and bushes that had obscured the tunnel's exit ever since they finished excavating it a year ago and crawled out of it. He was literally fully covered in mud, shirtless and shoeless, but he was carrying a powerful twelve gauge rifle in a belt across his chest and shoulders. Now all he needed was to get to the mountain motorcycle that was awaiting him ten feet from the tunnel's exit. It would be underneath several sheets of linoleum and plastic, properly disguised with leaves, tree branches and dry bushes.

He moved fast and smiled when he saw that everything was going according to plan. The motorcycle was there and it only needed a few pushes from his bare feet to get it started.

He worried about the noise the engine made. But that was inevitable. He began his frantic escape, wildly riding over the forest's rugged terrain, just as he heard the familiar sound of helicopter blades approaching his way. He tried to think who gave him away. Oso or Luna? Those two cowards with goat's blood.

Montana's chopper made it to Squirrel's Creek in a matter of minutes. And five military helicopters from the Salinas Training Camp of the Puerto Rico National Guard were now on the way. Close to a hundred reservists, fully trained in military assault operations, would soon join the chase.

It was agent Walker who first saw Rigonaldo. Visibility was poor down below because of the trees and heavy foliage. But Walker saw him, and as Montana had predicted, the terrorist wasn't on foot. He was frantically going north, deeper into the forest, on a mountain motorcycle.

Montana relayed his position to the National Guardsmen in their choppers. They would arrive at the area in three more minutes.

Montana's pilot went as far down as the thick trees below allowed him and flew right above Rigonaldo. They followed him persistently until the Guard's helicopters appeared in the sky.

The military choppers immediately circled the area. Rigonaldo looked up, and for the first time in his life, he knew that he was trapped. In his attempt to flee from Montana's helicopter, he had made several wrong turns and he knew he was headed for the precipice of the Angel's Waterfall.

The voice from the sky reverberated in Rigonaldo's ears like a trumpet in a king's court: "There is no escape, Pastrana. Stop your bike! Throw away your rifle and give yourself up!" It was the unmistakable voice of that FBI man, Montana.

Rigonaldo Pastrana, the old warrior, looked up for the last time. He saw that three helicopters suspended in the sky above the precipice of the waterfall – Montana's and two military choppers – awaited him. And he saw countless bodies of military men and women now descending by ropes into the forest all around him from three more military choppers in the sky above.

Rigonaldo's only choice was to drive over the edge of the precipice, as fast as he could, hoping to fall into the water and swim for his life.

When Rigonaldo came closer and closer to the precipice, Montana and his agents knew what Rigonaldo had in mind. And, at that very moment, they knew without a doubt that Rigonaldo Pastrana was the most insane man they had ever encountered, or would ever encounter, in their careers.

Montana's voice boomed again from the sky: "Rigonaldo! The drop is over a thousand feet. You will certainly die! Stop the bike and give up. It's over!"

He had called him Rigonaldo, the terrorist noticed. Just as if his dead father was talking to him from heaven. But that was not the voice of his father. It was the voice of his enemy. The enemy of the Puerto Rican people.

Rigonaldo aimed his rifle overhead and shot at the sky. He shot at the voice from heaven. When his bullets ran out, he threw the rifle on the ground and pressed the motorcycle's accelerator to the highest speed. One hundred feet from the precipice. Seventy-five. Fifty. Twenty-five. Ten. Five . . . The end.

"POR LA PATRIA!!!" (For the motherland), he screamed.

Rigonaldo drove off the edge of the precipice, soon loosing his grip on the bike.

"Crazy son of a bitch!" Walker yelled, his eyes wide open.

In the eyes of the witnesses, the fall of the terrorist occurred as if in slow motion. Just like in that movie about the two women outlaws on the run. But this was no movie. This was happening in real life.

The motorcycle cracked into a million pieces as it hit the hard, huge rocks of the waterfall. Pastrana flew into the air, arms and legs jerking furiously, as if trying to grow wings that would allow him to fly. But he kept falling and falling, until he crashed onto a heavy rock at the very bottom of the precipice. All the bones in the body of Rigonaldo Pastrana were crushed at the point of impact, and his head almost separated from his torso. But even in death, his eyes remained open, staring, this time at the void of the other side.

"He yelled something!" Walker said, as he looked at the dead body below. "What did he say when he jumped?"

Morales had no words in his mouth.

Montana said, "I don't know what he yelled. And I don't care. Rigonaldo Pastrana is dead."

There was a moment of silence, but it wasn't out of deference to the dead. It was the silence of men shocked at the face of pure insanity.

The terrorist was dead, but Montana felt odd, sour. This last act of defiance from his nemesis, had it made him a martyr? Would this become the source of legends and fables that would inspire others to follow Rigonaldo's path? An unnerving thought kept invading Montana's mind.

Was this really the end of terror in Puerto Rico? Or was this just another beginning?

Montana's chopper landed on a clearing of rock at the foot of the falls. The Assistant Director walked to the dead man's body and stared at it. The other choppers landed elsewhere. There was now an eerie silence in the area. Even the birds in the forest had fallen silent. But the water flowed undisturbed.

Death was in the forest. It was the silence and the water's flow. And the forest, with its million eyes, stood there as a witness to the death of evil.

Montana was uneasy. He should be rejoicing at this moment, but he wasn't. In the end, Montana thought, Rigonaldo Pastrana had indeed escaped.

Chapter 74

Ana María Cruz was airlifted to the roof of the Ashford Presbyterian Hospital in Condado where she was met by a battery of doctors and by her husband.

Elison Cruz could hardly believe that he was once again reunited with his beloved wife. But as he embraced and kissed her, reality sank in. Ana María was back with him. She was alive and safe in his arms again.

"Elison!" she cried in his arms. "I can't believe what happened to me!"

"It's over Ana María," he said, crying. "The nightmare is over."

Sometime in the afternoon, Barbara Tonos showed up at the gates of the *Palmas Del Mar* Resort in Humacao and was quickly assisted by the staff there. She told them who she was. That she was in desperate need of help. She used a cell phone to speak to her daughter and to her husband, who immediately arranged for an ambulance to bring her to a hospital in the Metropolitan area.

At 4 p.m. Elison Cruz, flanked by Police Superintendent Calero and by FBI Assistant Director Montana, spoke to the press in Fortaleza. He officially informed the country of the success of the operation to rescue his wife and to disband the terrorist cell of Rigonaldo Pastrana. September Twenty-third, Governor Cruz announced, had finally been defeated.

The First Lady, he declared, was still at the Ashford Presbyterian Hospital for medical observation, but she was generally in good condition and in good spirits. Happy to be back with her loved ones.

Elison Cruz ended his press appearance, encouraging the country to move on and to vote their conscience in tomorrow's plebiscite.

When he moved away from the podium in the press room in Fortaleza, Elison Cruz was sure that a chapter in the history of Puerto Rico had been closed. It was now up to the millions of Puerto Ricans living on the island to write the next one.

Sunday, November 4
The Plebiscite and the Days After

Chapter 75

1,800,103 people cast their votes in the most controversial plebiscite in the history of Puerto Rico.

On Sunday night, every single network on the island bombarded the country with the commentaries of the most enthusiastic political talking heads. They made a living out of providing expert analysis of Puerto Rico's volatile political preferences. Some wondered if there was life after the plebiscite. And some others – who had been featured on the political talk shows of the U.S. networks – wondered if they should rush to hire managers and publicists to assess their chances of breaking permanently into the U.S. market of political commentary.

The final tally of the vote only added more chaos to the explosive issue of the political status of Puerto Rico:

The independence column received 300,103 votes. (16%)

Free association received 749,999 votes. (41.67%)

Statehood received 749,501 votes. (41.64%)

With a 498-vote lead, free association had "won" by a mere .03%. Or, did it?

In less time than the blink of an eye, officials from the Commonwealth and Statehood parties were making frantic airplane reservations to Washington, D.C. Some even booked flights on the cheapest airlines in an attempt to beat the others to the nation's capital.

The commonwealth officials wanted to ensure that the "victory" of free association in the plebiscite be recognized by the President and Congress.

The statehooders wanted to invalidate the plebiscite's results on the arguments that: 1) You couldn't declare victory with a lead of less than five hundred votes, and 2) simple high school math stated that when you added the three-hundred-thousand votes for independence with the seven-hundred-forty-nine-thousand votes for statehood, you had an overwhelming majority of the country rejecting free association.

Needless to say, free association advocates did the same fussy math in reverse.

In Washington, D.C. as the Puerto Ricans were booking their flights in San Juan, the President and the members of Congress who had promoted this "imbroglio" were also frantic, trying to find places to hide from this crowd of angry U.S. citizens who were coming their way, ready to wage World War Three.

There were 500 votes cast that were declared invalid by the Puerto Rico Electoral Commission: about 50 voters wrote on their ballots, "Restore the Spanish Monarchy, Long Live Mother Spain!" Some 50 more wrote "Let the Dutch Rule Here! Let Gays Get Married! Legalize Prostitution NOW!" A great number of ballots were just blank. Others were more colorful: Mickey Mouse got a vote. Ricky Martin got two. Austin Powers got two votes with the inscription, "Bring Some '*Mojo*' to this Island, PLEASE!!!!" And each of the four Puerto Rican women who at one time held the title of Miss Universe got a vote.

In a live broadcast, Karen Pérez encouraged Puerto Ricans to call in and say why they voted against statehood. Many people said they were afraid of political violence. Others were adamantly opposed to losing the National Olympic Team. Others said that under statehood, the Miss Puerto Rico contestants to the Miss Universe pageant would not be allowed to compete in the international competition, and would be relegated to trying to win the Miss USA pageant. They doubted that a Puerto Rican woman from the island would ever be allowed to win the "American" title. Many more callers were concerned with the Spanish language and the clash between two "separate cultural nations." Others emphatically declared that as long as there were "ultra-right-wing politicians" and Christian "coalitions" in the U.S., Puerto Rico had to stay away from "those people." Gay and lesbian voters said that they would rather become a state of the Netherlands, where "*we can marry*," than of the backward U.S.A., where "*we cannot*."

The calls went on, and on, and on, and on.

In the end, Karen thought, this whole thing would make a nice book. But as fiction. A novel with all of the surreal elements in it. When the lights went out in her TV studio, she had already booked a flight to Sydney, Australia – the only Puerto Rican who wasn't headed to Washington D.C., it seemed – and she had started to think about an appropriate title for her novel.

FBI Special Agent John Walker got his date with Luis Alvarez, the young man from the phone company. He was not disappointed with the way Luis kissed, and they were both willing to continue seeing each other to see "how things go."

William Montana began to furiously promote the death penalty for Oso and Luna, and for anyone else connected to those activities of September Twenty-third where people were killed. In his quest to "cut a deal" and save his neck, Oso gave Tino away as the other person directly involved in the First Lady's kidnapping. But when the FBI stormed into Tino's apartment near the University of Puerto Rico, they found it empty. Fellow students said Tino had hastily given away all of his possessions and had fled the country. Most likely to the pristine beaches of sunny Varadero in Cuba.

The Puerto Rican Senate, the U.S. and Puerto Rico Departments of Justice, the FBI, and the Puerto Rico Police Department initiated simultaneous investigations into the relationship of Senator Orlando Tonos with the now-fugitive Vincentino "Tino" Irrizary. Senator Tonos, without missing a beat, attacked the island's airwaves proclaiming, "I didn't know that young man was involved in any activities other than driving me around town, and trying to get good grades at the U.P.R. My wife was also kidnapped. I'm the victim here. Back off!" He dramatically announced that he would launch his own Senate inquiry into the kidnapping of his wife, Barbara.

Governor Elison Cruz – after risking his wife's life by not cancelling the plebiscite to gain her release from the kidnappers – was a little red-faced with the idea of now going to Washington to push to invalidate the plebiscite's results. But he strongly believed that had he been able to campaign publicly *and* furiously during the days prior to the plebiscite, statehood would have been the sure winner.

Supporters of free association, the 498-vote "winning" option, were vociferously saying to anyone who would listen that, "If former President George W. Bush won Florida in 2000 – and almost even Canada – in that messy election, and became U.S. President on a technicality, the President and the Congress today have no other option but to declare free association the final and sole winner in the plebiscite. And if we need to," they warned somberly and with a straight face, "we will go all the way to the U.S. Supreme Court to defend our victory. The highest U.S. court handed the 2000 election to Bush, the loser of the popular vote. They will have to hand this victory to us, the legitimate recipients of the most votes in the plebiscite."

Rumor had it that when the president of the Commonwealth Party relayed this diatribe via the phone to the U.S. President, the leader of the free world blurted out an obscenity and hung up on him.

The plebiscite's messy results had evidently added more fuel to the political fire of Puerto Rico. The explosive issue of the political status of the island would simply not go away. It was here to stay. Like a *santero's* curse.

With accusations of top-level conspiracies, fraud, unfair circumstances, dirty tricks, and even racism, Puerto Rico went back to business – with a vengeance. The only words of reconciliation and common sense came from First Lady Ana María Cruz who, in a brief television appearance, looked straight into the eyes of the viewers and said, "We in Puerto Rico must come together as a people of peace, and find a common ground that will lead us into a better future for all. And if we need to reexamine who we are, and what we believe in, we must do it with pride, integrity and humility."

Washington, D.C.
3:30 a.m.

Chapter 76

Donald M. Clarke, the President of the United States of America, had begun to have nightmares. Again. He was anxious to the point of needing medication. Klonopin today. Valium tomorrow. He just couldn't stop thinking of ways in which to secure Puerto Rico's oil deposits. Some of his "friends" in the oil business – who had somehow managed to decode Washington's best kept secret – were ready to blow the whistle and go to San Juan to deal directly with the Puerto Ricans, regardless of the political turmoil that that would create there.

President Clarke's plan to make Puerto Rico the fifty-first U.S. state had literally blown up in his face. The President decided he was going to push to invalidate the results of the plebiscite. There were hundreds of reasons for it: a 498-vote lead was not a definite mandate for change; the statehooders in Puerto Rico didn't get a fair shot at campaigning, with Governor Cruz holed up in Fortaleza awaiting word about his kidnapped wife. The poor woman! That was, by the way, an outrage. A vicious tactic by the left to prejudice and influence the plebiscite's outcome. The prospect of nationalist violence, the President affirmed, could only be described as a shameless attempt by the left to intimidate pro-U.S. voters; the Constitutional right to vote had been grossly violated.

Shame! Shame! Shame!

The list of reasons to have canceled the plebiscite in the first place was endless.

The President, very awake and alert in the Oval Office in the middle of this night, was now determined to hold another plebiscite on the island. But this time, he firmly declared, "Fuck that! There will absolutely *not* be the option of free association. Puerto Ricans will have to choose between statehood and independence. That's it! God damn! This time around," the President shouted, banging his fist against his impeccably clean oak desk, "we're gonna get away with it. You'll see."

Sitting across from the President, National Security Advisor Nathaniel Fisher trembled. "What do you want me to do now, sir?" he asked shyly.

"First," the President said, spitting out each word, "you'll draft me your best and most ingenious top secret memo on how to steal a God damn election . . . or plebiscite – whatever you call it – you know what the hell I mean. This time I will personally guarantee that statehood wins. If Bush got away with winning the 2000 election, I will *damn* get away with winning a vote in Puerto Rico."

"Mr. President," Fisher said carefully, "with all due respect, I don't think I would put something like that in . . . in writing . . . Sooner or later it could . . ."

"Shut up, you fuck!" the President ordered. "This mess is partly your doing. You brought up this shit of '*we'll give them a very*' . . . What did you call it? Oh, yes, a very '*inedible*' version of free association and blah, blah, blah. You see what you did? They are fucking us right up the ass! That's what. And as far as Grant Thompson is concerned . . ." The President paused. His eyes rolled. "I want to strangle that son of a bitch. I clearly told him that the CIA and FBI knew that statehood was going to lose. He basically told me to fuck them, and I stupidly listened to him." He pointed his finger at Fisher's face. "Just as I listened to *you*!"

Fisher swallowed hard. At a loss for words he said, "I . . . I think that . . ."

"Yes, *think* . . . for a change," the President advised. "But before you do that, do something for me."

"What is that, sir?"

"Get everyone in here!" the President yelled, the veins in his red neck protruding, both of his fists hitting his desk, papers and pens torpedoing every which way. "Right NOW!"

The top history-makers in Washington, D.C. would now debate the future of Puerto Rico.

Again.

Printed in the United States
53499LVS00002B/162